Book 1

Rand

by

Silvia Shaw

Rand

Cover design: M&J
Edited by Cath Walker
Contact: silviashaw@mail.com

This is a work of fiction. Any resemblance of characters to actual persons, living or dead, is purely coincidental.

Synopsis

An epic story of magic, heroism, love, and treachery, Rand is a magical world ruled by an imperial line of Queens.

Three hundred years ago, Rand's most powerful talisman, a medallion called the Circle of Sheda, was taken through the portal into Earth and lost. When Dr. Savannah Cole is on an archeology dig in Algeria, she takes shelter from a violent sandstorm and discovers the mysterious artifact under a Berber ruin. She soon learns unknown forces are at play, powerful secret forces beyond her control. Compelled to wear the medallion, she is swept through the portal into Rand. There she must forge a new life and embrace her role as the wielder of ancient magic.

Never before has someone from the 'other world' been chosen to bear the medallion, someone not a warrior. It's a puzzle Savannah must solve before it's too late. Why has she been chosen? As she battles demonic creatures and dark sorcery, she fights to take her place as the rightful bearer in the long line of warrior women.

But the question remains. What is coming that the lost medallion must resurface after so many years?

Table of Contents

For Mary

Chapter One

Algeria

Savannah found the Sahara a very harsh mistress.

She'd been on archeological digs in dry regions before, but this desert was the grandmother of them all. A super-arid desolate place, plagued with fierce winds, sizzling heat, and wide temperature swings. After four months, she'd lost six pounds, her arms were burnt brown, and the ends of her hair bleached to a dirty blond.

This morning, as she walked from the camp, she glanced around uneasily. Everything seemed off. The air was unnaturally heavy, the sky a leaden gray, and there were no signs of the little horned lizards scurrying amongst the rocks, or the brown-necked ravens that hunted in the stony outcrop above the dig. She looked over at the dunes in the distance that were the beginning of the deep desert. They were a ghostly white, as if all the color had been leached out of the sand.

Shrugging off her disquiet, Savannah climbed down into the trench. She was working alone this morning, her partner having been laid low with a stomach bug, a common hazard in foreign lands. With her favorite tool, a small flat-bladed trowel that had seen her through many digs, she knelt to continue the delicate excavation. And as usual, once she started, she completely forgot about time and the outside elements.

Three hours later, still totally focused on her work and with loud music pumping through her earbuds, she missed the first warning signs: the whistling wind that sent little dust swirls dancing angrily across the barren ground.

Nor did she hear the frantic voice echoing from the two-way radio.

Completely absorbed, she gently edged away the clay clinging to the ceramic bowl in the ground. When the last crumb was brushed away, she carefully lifted it free. She studied the ancient artifact in awe. It was a beautiful piece of pottery, featuring three blue doves painted on a white background, with gold leaf edges and a transparent glaze coat. Centuries-old, the bowl was completely intact, a perfectly preserved piece of Byzantine history.

A brilliant find.

After she'd placed it into a cocoon of bubble wrap in the wooden box, she removed her earbuds. The shriek of the emergency siren immediately filled the air.

Her boss's voice crackled from the hand-held two-way radio attached to her belt, "Where the hell are you, Savannah?"

She quickly shouted into the receiver, "I'm still in the dig, Wayne. Where are you?"

"Damnit. What are you still doing there? I thought you were nearly at the truck. *Get out now!* You…to….place…" The voice trailed off into static.

She climbed to her feet to look over the arid landscape.

Ohmygod! Ohmygod! Ohmygod!

Her stomach clenched as her heart drilled through her ribs.

Armageddon was coming.

A huge wall of roiling brown sand filled the eastern sky and was bearing down on the dig. She'd never seen anything so terrifying. The billowing dark cloud had engulfed the cluster of palm trees in the distance and was about to swamp the company truck parked across the flat at their camp. She swallowed back her shock, aware she'd acted like a rookie. If she'd followed protocol and checked in every half hour, she would have been safe in the vehicle with the rest of the crew. The state-of-the-art truck was designed to handle very high winds and had an air conditioning unit pressurized to manage sand and dust.

Fear replaced shock.

To curb her panic, she pressed her hands hard into the dirt. Five minutes max to get to shelter or she was screwed. The truck was no longer an option—it had disappeared into the ferocious haboob. Frantically, she scanned the line of hills to the west. The only structure in sight was the old abandoned Chaoui house built into the side of a slope. Once used as a Berber outpost, it was a rectangular flat-roofed brick building with a solid stone foundation. As was the customary style of these Algerian dwellings, it had only two rooms.

She'd looked through it earlier in her dig. Though she'd seen some gaps in the back room, the larger front one had seemed intact. If she hurried, she could make it. It was not as if she had any other choice in this desolate godforsaken place. Hastily stuffing her tools into her backpack, she shrugged it over her shoulders, pulled down her sunglasses and arranged the bandanna to mask her face. She scrambled up the three steps to the surface, tucked the box firmly under her arm and ran.

In headlong flight, she reached the narrow track leading up the hill. Somewhere in the thick swirling clouds behind, a camel bellowed in terror. Savannah took a fleeting moment to sympathize with the animal before concentrating again on her footing. The pathway was rough, uneven, and littered with stones. Though she stumbled occasionally, she managed to remain upright. The bulky box was making her progress difficult, but she had no intention of leaving it behind.

The sky glowed a dim orange, and then darkened until there was little difference between day and night.

For the last yards, adrenaline kept her going. Her breathing became labored. By the time she reached the house, the bandanna was clogged, her lungs on fire, and her eyes gritty with sand.

The old wooden door opened at the first push. But trying to close it against the wind was nearly impossible. The storm was roaring, sand stinging every part of her exposed body as the wind rose to tornedo-like velocity.

Nothing she'd ever experienced or read prepared her for this terrifying force of nature. Her brain screamed for her to hurry. If she didn't shut the door soon, she was going to die—she could barely stand upright in the gale. Desperation gave her the strength needed. With a superhuman effort, she shouldered her full weight against the wood. When it clicked shut, had there been any moisture left inside her, she would have wept with relief.

After a moment to get back her breath, Savannah dug in the front pocket of her cargo shorts for her small flashlight.

The room had just two wooden chairs and a table in front of the hearth. She sank onto a chair and wrestled with her dilemma. The only option was to sit quietly to wait out the storm—if the room was airtight, she should be fine. She learned soon enough it wasn't. Dust drifted down through holes in the roof when a few tiles flew off. The wind was howling louder, which dashed any hope of it abating in the near future. If it continued for much longer, she'd probably suffocate.

After adjusting the bandanna over her face, Savannah rested her head on the table to avoid sucking in the swirling sand. Her eyes closed, her thoughts wandered back.

✝

Though she loved the hands-on aspect of archeology, the dig had been mainly to collect material for her book on historical warrior women. A subject that had her enthralled. She'd been on two prior excavation sites for the project: Hampstead Heath, the supposed burial place of the Celtic Queen, Boadicea; and Themiscyra near the Black Sea, the home of the Amazons. Algeria was the last on the list. Numida, as it was called in the seventh century, was ruled by the legendary Berber Queen Dihya, a fierce military leader who united the Berber tribes to drive out the Islam invaders.

When Savannah heard there was a privately funded dig to find Dihya's burial place, she'd applied to join it immediately. Algeria had many archaeological sites, for human occupation in the country dated back to the Paleolithic and Neolithic eras, but it was a restricted and untouched area where they were going. Though she had a sound research track record and was well respected in her field, it had taken a personal reference from the Director of the British Museum to get her on the small elite team.

Before they'd left London for the dig, the bearded Algerian advisor had lectured them on the Sahara, "Where you're going is a hostile environment, so take care. Sandstorms, or haboobs as they're called out there, will periodically rip in from the desert. If you're caught in the open, you could die."

As he went on to describe the female dress code, the frowns he shot her way made it plain he thought the site was no place for her. He'd got her back up with his patronizing attitude. Just because she was young and feminine didn't mean she couldn't hold her own in what was predominantly a man's world. She'd made many sacrifices, monetary and personal, to get recognition in the profession, and she wasn't going to be intimidated by this condescending prig. She'd earned the right to be here. Her mother always said she was born stubborn, but she preferred to think she was resilient. And she'd learnt early in life that persistence paid off.

From fifty-eight applicants, seven had been chosen, two women and five men, and Savannah found them a good bunch of people. Dr. Wayne McLaren, a tall, thin Scotsman in his early forties, and a veteran of many digs, headed the working party.

The second-last leg of their journey from Heathrow Airport was Ghadaia, a city in the north-central region of the Sahara Desert. The excavation site being a day's journey east, they'd spent three days sightseeing through the city while they waited for the truck and equipment to arrive by road. It was to be their last taste of civilization for six months. A city of ninety thousand, Ghadaia still had its original well-preserved medieval architecture. A historian's dream, with its sandy golden buildings, narrow cobblestoned streets, and bazaars offering colorful silks, rugs, woven baskets, exotic spices, and vendors selling a myriad of dates. Savannah had even drunk water out of a dried goat carcass.

But on their last night in town, something downright spooky had occurred.

As they'd walked home from the Grand Market to their guest house, the city felt different. As if it were brooding. The shadows seemed darker, the streets narrower, and an odd spicy odor hung heavily in the air. Her companions didn't appear to notice, chatting and laughing on their way through the night streets.

As they passed by an old woman seated in a dim doorway, the hairs on the back of Savannah's neck twitched upright. When she turned to gaze directly at her, the air appeared to shudder and shift. It seemed charged with a hint of something not quite of this world. When Savannah looked around, the others were nowhere in sight.

Vaguely aware that time had somehow stopped, she turned back to the old lady in the dark alcove. Tiny necklaces of light smudged the edges of the recess and all was silent in the hollow stillness.

"Give me your hand, girl," the aged voice crackled from the gloom.

Savannah stepped closer to peer at her, taking in a big breath when she saw the completely white eyes. The old woman was blind. With no hesitation, she put out her hand. Later in the safety of her room, she wondered why she'd agreed so readily, but it had just felt the right thing to do at the time.

Claw-like fingers stroked her palm, crisscrossing back and forth, tracing every line. When her fingers ceased wandering, the old woman tilted her head and croaked, "What's your name, girl."

"Savannah."

"Ah… a strong name. You are the chosen one, Savannah."

Savannah stared at her. "What?"

"The link is here."

"Link?" Savannah echoed, bewildered.

"Go now. Remember, when all seems lost, the way is down."

Savannah felt a flush of annoyance. This was one crazy old woman. "I have no idea what you're talking about," she huffed out.

The voice became softer, more distant. "One day, you'll find the happiness you seek. Your love waits for you."

The air shimmered again and she was gone.

Savannah trembled as she briskly hurried to catch the others. What had just happened? Had someone slipped a magic mushroom into her fattoush?

Subdued, she trailed the crew into the guest house. She vowed to put it out of her mind. Fortune telling had no scientific basis and certainly didn't belong in her fact-finding world.

Savannah was brought back to her plight by her ever-increasing difficulty in breathing. The dust had sucked every bit of light out of the room, and outside, the wind howled even louder. Icy fingers ran down her spine, curdling her blood. It sounded like the wail of a Banshee heralding death. She took a desperate breath, trying to ignore it.

Her lips were so dry she had trouble separating them, and the heat oppressive. She dug out her water bottle and took a long swig. A wave of hopelessness enveloped her. If she didn't smother, she'd die of dehydration. The intense heat wouldn't take long to draw every drop of moisture from her body. Only a miracle would get her out of this one.

Suddenly, out of nowhere the old woman's voice jumped into her mind. *When all seems lost, the way is down.*

Savannah sat up straight. A long shot, but could there be a room under the building somewhere? A cellar? She shone her flashlight around. The large stone slabs on the floor would need more than one person to shift.

She turned her attention to the hearth.

She couldn't even hazard a guess when it had been used last. The ash and charcoal had been there so long they'd solidified. Cobwebs clung over the enclosure in grey veils. The iron rake hanging on a nail at the side was pocked with rust.

Savannah brushed away the webs and shone in the light. Gingerly, she used the rake to pull out the debris from the fireplace, careful to keep an eye out for any lurking scorpions. The Sahara Deathstalker was the most venomous in the world. Her luck would have definitely run out if she was bitten by one of those little horrors. She heaved a sigh of relief when she only unearthed a few scarab beetles and a cluster of ants.

Once she'd cleared the area, she studied the hearth floor through the dust. It too was made of stone, though the slabs were much smaller. She dropped to her knees to run her fingers over the surface. After a thorough examination, she choked back her disappointment. Nothing.

But as she continued to stare despondently, something bizarre happened. The air above the floor turned a hazy blue and a glint of metal winked into focus. When the mist cleared, she saw a bronze ring slotted into the middle slab.

After some fiddling, she managed to lift one end upright out of its groove. The other end was attached to the stone. She wrapped her fingers around it and yanked hard. When it didn't budge, she tried again. After four attempts, the stone budged and she slid the slab to the side. Gasping for breath now, she shone the light down to a vertical shaft the size of a manhole, with an iron ladder attached to a wall. With the little energy she had left, she backed down onto the ladder.

A four-meter descent led the shaft to a tunnel. Much to Savannah's immense relief, the air though stale, was dust-free and much cooler. Her first big gulps of air produced a coughing fit, but once the spasms subsided, she was able to get precious oxygen into her lungs. She wondered whether she should just wait out the storm where she was, but her scientific curiosity rebelled at the idea.

Whoever built this tunnel had made it wide enough for a person to walk through, so it must lead to something. After a brief rest, she continued on, swatting away cobwebs as she went. Judging how thick they were, she guessed the tunnel had been long forgotten by the Berbers. Some twenty meters further, the passageway widened into a cavern. It was a large room with a domed ceiling that curved up well out of hand reach. At the back wall was a small pool of water. The underground spring made it a perfect hiding place from invaders. Because it wasn't as stuffy as the tunnel, Savannah figured there must be an air vent to the outside somewhere. It made sense if this had been a refuge.

She sipped the water tentatively. It was cold—nectar on her chapped lips. Throwing caution aside, she drank greedily. Once revived, she wondered how the Berbers had lit the cavern. The light from her torch picked out oil lamps strategically placed on the walls. To conserve the flashlight batteries, Savannah used the lighter from her pocket and lit three wicks. She didn't dare risk anymore—oxygen was more important than light.

A soft glow spread over the cavern.

In one section, there were some wooden tables and long benches. Evidence of human habitation lay everywhere: skins, water carriers, bowls and cups, and a variety of weapons. From the condition of the objects, no one had been here for a very, very long time. She could barely contain her excitement. If this place could be traced back centuries, it was going to be an important archaeological find. She cut off a small piece of the dried hide and slipped it into her pocket for carbon dating later.

It was only when she walked past the pool, did she see the skeleton stretched out on a slab in a recess in the far corner of the cavern. From the breastplate, it was obvious the soldier was a woman. She was arranged in a warrior's death, in full battle regalia, her hands crossed over her chest and her sword in her arms. A shield lay at her feet.

Savannah's pulse pounded. Could this be the legendary Dihya?

She shone the torchlight over the skeleton.

This woman had been tall, seemingly well over six feet, which the queen was reported to have been. But the armor was all wrong for a seventh-century Berber. With the tip of her finger, Savannah rubbed a little dust off the shield. It gleamed in the beam of light. This soldier's armor was made of a shiny substance similar to titanium, and whatever metal or alloy it was, it hadn't eroded with time. Curiously, she lightly brushed the rest of the dust off the shield. There were markings on the surface, a script she didn't recognize. Certainly not Arabic or Libyco-Berber.

She flicked the flashlight back up to the sword. The same markings were on the handle. She was photographing the inscriptions when she noticed the medallion hanging around the neck of the warrior. When she reached over and gently cradled it in her palm to examine it, a warm tingle spread through her body. At that moment, Savannah just knew it was the link the old crone had mentioned. And though she couldn't explain why, she was also sure she was meant to put it on.

Despite knowing it was strange, she accepted it all—odd things had happened to her before. There had been some unexplained happenings in her childhood that had defied logic, things she'd pushed firmly from her mind. She didn't want to be different. But as much as she tried to ignore what was happening here, she knew in her heart that the stone slab had been under some sort of spell. When she'd first examined the floor of the hearth, there'd been no brass ring.

As outlandish as it seemed, she finally reached the conclusion she was meant to find this place. It had been waiting for her to arrive, otherwise someone would have found it long before this. Over time, being so close to a drinking well, many travelers would have camped inside the old house. It would have been well documented.

Savannah was aware that any artifacts she found weren't hers to keep, for the goal of an archeologist was simply to record history. Discoveries were the property of the country of their origin, their heritage. But she went ahead anyhow and ignored her ethics, powerless to defy the silent commands. She eased the chain up over the helmet and slipped it over her head. As soon as it nestled between her breasts, she knew what she had to do. The warrior was to remain undisturbed in her last resting place, and when Savannah went back up to the house, she was to slide the stone back and leave.

An hour later, she made her way up the tunnel, listening for sound of the wind before she climbed back up into the hearth. The storm had passed, though the room was heavily coated with dust. After she scraped the debris back over the fireplace floor, she made sure that all footprints around the hearth were cleaned away. Satisfied that no trace of her visit remained, she gathered up the box and opened the door to the outside.

At least she had the marvelous ceramic bowl to show the world.

Chapter Two

London. Four years later.

The fundraising venue at the prestigious hotel was packed.

As she waited to be introduced, Savannah gazed around the sea of faces. The room hummed with money. Stylishly dressed women filled the dining tables: wives of the city's most influential patrons, as well as many successful professionals in their own right. It was one of numerous such functions that she'd attended in the last eighteen months.

When the Director of the British Museum had offered her a position as a keynote speaker for their fundraising events and afterward to seek donations, she'd jumped at the chance. Not only because it was time to make a good living, but it was also a golden opportunity to discretely ask about the medallion. There were always a few academics in the audience who were interested in her research.

After she'd returned from Algeria, she'd taken three months off to investigate the origin of the mysterious object. She still wore it under her shirt, though had lengthened the chain to tuck it lower out of sight. Savannah knew it was ridiculous, but it had seemed to have claimed her. In the beginning, she would shudder as she visualized how a therapist would perceive the attachment, but in the end, she didn't care. It was what it was. The damn thing had some sort of hold over her and she had to accept it. It wasn't as though it was an uncomfortable feeling—far from it.

She had gotten nowhere in the archives. After poring over myriads of historical documents and drawings, she hadn't found anything remotely relating to it. Nor had she discovered the language of the writing on the shield.

When they'd arrived back in England, the team had been swamped by the press. After six months in the Sahara, their dig had proved to be an archeological treasure trove, the unearthed artifacts capturing the attention of the world. Because of its condition, the ceramic bowl that dated back to the 4th century AD, was one of the major finds. It had been embarrassing how many magazines she'd been featured in. Savannah had no illusions that her newly found celebrity status was the main reason she'd landed the lucrative fundraising job, rather than for her academic achievements. She didn't care. It suited her purpose.

When she'd compiled her photographs onto PowerPoint, she'd incorporated pictures of museum pieces similar to the medallion. She didn't put the picture of the real medallion out in the public eye, for there were strict penalties for keeping any artifact, particularly one deemed culturally significant. If the Algerian Government had even a sniff it came from the dig, she was in trouble. Once the scale of the discovery had been announced, they had immediately closed down the site to foreigners. Times had changed—countries had become very protective of their historical treasures.

She focused her attention back on the MC, a thin woman in a sleek fitted jacket and pencil skirt. After a spiel about the museum, she waved her forward and announced, "Please welcome archeologist, Dr. Savannah Cole, to the podium. Dr. Cole is going to talk about warrior women throughout ancient history. After lunch, you are invited on a tour to view the many artifacts in the museum relating to the subject."

Savannah gave a friendly wave to acknowledge the applause. Over the last year and a half, she'd honed her presentation until she'd become a very popular speaker. She'd spoken throughout the United Kingdom, Europe, and even a six-week tour of the US.

No matter what country, the audience was always the same. Mostly all women. She figured heroic military women were probably seen by men as a threat to their masculinity, but women were fascinated by them. Treadmills and Pilates were no substitute for down-to-earth gritty female strength. Xena be damned. These historical Amazons were the real deal.

And the wealthy ladies attended in droves.

Her first speech was nearly a disaster. No one wanted dry academic facts, they wanted to hear about women who kicked ass. It was only her images of women galloping into war in full battle dress that had saved the day. After that, she'd tailored her speech, cutting out the dry bits, throwing in a few amusing anecdotes, and putting in a lot more photos. She made the warrior women come to life.

When she began her speaking career, Savannah soon learned there was a certain standard expected. So she'd packed away her comfortable 'scholarly' outfits, and bought herself a new wardrobe. Since she loved clothes, with the extra money and incentive, she indulged herself at quite a few exclusive boutiques. Next was a trip to the hairdresser to learn how to arrange her hair into a modern braided style.

Then she began a strict exercise regime at the gym three times a week. If she was going to talk about warrior women, she wanted to look fit. She was pleased she had. Considering all the rich food and alcohol at these functions, it would have been easy to pack on a few extra pounds.

As always when she finished her presentation, she left some time for audience participation. "Has anyone any questions? Anything you would like me to elaborate on?" She took a sip of water.

An elegant elderly woman in the front row raised her hand. "Can they pinpoint when Queen Boadicea lived? It was such a long time ago."

"Good question," said Savannah. "Until recently, though they had a rough idea, when exactly she ruled was mostly supposition. But in 2020, a British bird watcher found a cache of thirteen hundred gold handmade coins in a field in Hampshire Heath. They appeared to be from the reign of Boadicea, around 61 AD. It was thought because of the war with the Romans, people hoarded their money."

Another raised hand. One of the roving aides carrying a mike immediately appeared beside her. "Is it true Amazons cut off a breast to use a bow in battle?"

Savannah chuckled. That question was always asked. "I believe it's a myth. There's no evidence that the practice of cutting or cauterizing off a breast ever happened. Of all the statues and art depicting women in battle, there're none with only one breast."

"Isn't there a kernel of truth in every legend?"

Savannah gave the woman a warm smile. "I imagine it was because Amazons were mainly always depicted with only one breast covered up. Believe me, I've done extensive searches and found nothing in historical records to substantiate the opinion. The belief has no substance."

"Why do you think they're always portrayed as scantily clad?" asked someone in the middle of the room.

"Because sex sells. It does today, and it did in the past. But as far as I'm concerned, it's a scam. Why would any sensible woman fight in close combat with one breast uncovered? She'd have to be mad not to protect the most vulnerable part of her body." She swept her gaze over the room. "It's only another instance of objectifying the female figure. It infers, even though they fought in battles, that these women were there for men to look at. Our own modern Wonder Woman fights for justice, but the focus remains on close-up butt shots of her in a short costume."

"How did they have babies?" a younger woman called out.

"I imagine the same way every female does," Savannah replied drolly. Titters echoed around the room.

"Um…what I meant was, how did they get pregnant without men?"

"Well, there wasn't any sperm bank in those days," Savannah answered smiling. Titters became laughter. "According to a Greek historian, the Scythian Amazons were neighbors to an all-male society and met annually for a mating ritual. The female children went to the Amazons and the boys to their fathers. The writings are considered authentic."

Then, completely out of the blue it happened.

After more lighthearted banter about mating habits, Savannah was about to wrap up the night when a voice with an odd accent came from the back. "Have you many medallions you've picked up in your travels?"

Savannah felt a sudden surge of excitement. She'd prayed someone would ask that question one day. She craned her head to see where it came from, but the back tables were in shadows. "Is there one you're particularly looking for?"

"There is one. Have you any you haven't included in your presentation tonight?"

Striving to sound nonchalant, Savannah replied, "A few. Not all are relevant to this subject. Maybe we might discuss it after lunch."

"I'd be very interested to talk to you."

"I'd be delighted to." Then with a warm smile, Savannah swept her eyes around the room. "If there are no more questions, I'll be available later if anyone would like to chat."

Now the formal program was over, she made her way quickly to the bar. Her mouth was dry as chips. After downing a glass of cold water, she ordered a Chardonnay and eased onto the barstool. She only took a sip because she was working. She hoped the mysterious woman would come straight over, for she'd have to start charming the patrons shortly.

Networking for funds was the most important part of the position. As the older women at these functions admired a successful younger woman, Savannah always made sure her age was included in the introduction. She had turned thirty-two in January this year.

She enjoyed the interaction with the guests, and over time, a few contact numbers had been pressed into her palm. She'd never been tempted. God knows, she should have, for she was lonely enough. And what was she saving herself for anyhow? An Amazon to sweep her off her feet?

But there was always something that held her back.

Since her mother passed away last year, she needed more than ever someone special in her life. Her only serious girlfriend had left her after eight months of dating, claiming Savannah cared more about the dead than the living. She'd met Heather while studying for her Ph.D. at Oxford. In hindsight, it hadn't been a good time for a relationship, for her dissertation required extensive fieldwork. And Savannah was guilty as charged. Even back then, she had been too wrapped up in her warrior women to give Heather the attention she deserved.

When she noticed a tall woman striding purposely toward the bar, her eyes widened. She pipped Savannah's interest immediately. It wasn't so much her height, over six feet, or her muscular body that looked like she worked out seriously. It was the way she carried herself. She had none of the hunched posture of someone who spent her life towering over everyone, which led Savannah to suppose she was used to being with tall people. And she walked lightly on the balls of her feet like a cat.

As this woman headed straight for her, Savannah schooled her expression to mild interest although her pulse was racing. It was exactly how she'd pictured an Amazon. As she neared, Savannah felt a touch of disappointment. She had to be in her late forties.

There was nothing delicate about her. She was a handsome woman, with a strong face, full lips, and a Roman nose. Her short dark hair was peppered grey, and maturity lines were etched into the sides of her mouth and eyes. She carried herself so well that her black pants and plain white top didn't look out of place amongst the designer labels in the room. Her only jewelry was a wide gold bracelet around her wrist. A small scar was visible on her cheek, which enhanced the look about her that said, "Don't mess with me."

"Hi," said Savannah brightly, trying not to appear intimidated. "Would you like a drink?"

"A Scotch and water, please," the woman called out to the bartender, then thrust out her hand. "Hello, Dr. Cole. My name is Tamasin Epona."

When Savannah slipped off the chair to shake her hand, she immediately felt dwarfed. A little above average height herself, she found it disconcerting to have to look up. "Please... call me Savannah."

"A pretty name. Mistress of the Meadowlands and Grasses where I come from."

"And were you called after Epona, Mistress of Horses?"

Surprise flashed across Tamasin's face, and then she chuckled. "I forgot who I was talking to. Not many people make the association."

Her mind racing, Savannah stroked her finger down the stem of her glass. This must be the woman who'd asked about the medallion. "No, I imagine they don't. You found my presentation interesting?"

"I've come from Japan to hear you speak."

"So far? I usually post a few thoughts online. Also photos. Not all at once—just one or two at a time for any history buffs interested in the subject. I have my followers, and it's a handy way to exchange information. I'm always willing to chat about my work."

"I came to speak to you personally to see if you had any other medallions you haven't posted. And if you have, I wanted to ask you if I might see them."

Savannah tilted her head to study her. "I have a few at home."

Tamasin tapped her fingers on the top of the bar. "May I see them, Doctor?"

Savannah took a sip of wine. "You're looking for a specific one?"

"Yes. I've searched just about every exhibit in every large and small museum in the world for it."

"Really? How long have you been looking?"

"For three years."

Savannah's eyes widened. "You've never even seen a photo of it anywhere?"

Tamasin shook her head, appearing frustrated. "No. I flew here hoping you may have it in your collection."

"I—" At the feel of a hand on her arm, Savannah quickly turned to find two expensively groomed women at her elbow and gave a silent groan. The mayor's wife wasn't someone to be ignored. "Hi, Mrs. Parkinson. It's a pleasure to see you," she murmured.

Estelle Parkinson's fingers tightened on Savannah's arm as she addressed Tamasin. "Now, now. Don't monopolize our lovely Dr. Cole."

A glint of anger flashed in Tamasin's eyes, but then her expression turned blank. "Of course not. I promised a friend I'd look Dr. Cole up when I was in London. Perhaps I could catch up with you when you're finished here, Savannah?"

"Come around at six thirty. My apartment's not far." Savannah reached in her pocket for a pen and scrawled the address on one of her business cards. "My number's on the card." Plastering on a smile, she turned to Estelle. "I'm all yours."

Estelle gave her a measuring look when Tamasin moved off. "Your friend seems interesting. Not the usual lady we get at our gatherings. Very…ah…large."

Savannah ignored the bitchy barb. Damned busybody. "Yes, she is. Now, I'm sure you ladies will have a few questions to ask me. I always value good debate."

As she listened with only half an ear to their rhetoric, she watched Tamasin disappear out the door. She wished she was going with her. It was going to be a long afternoon—she was impatient to talk to her.

She desperately hoped the medallion she wore was the one the woman sought. The puzzle needed to be solved.

Chapter Three

From the balcony of her third-floor apartment, Savannah looked down at the street.

With her size and easy stride, Tamasin wasn't hard to spot amongst the pedestrians on the footpath.

Savannah felt the hairs on her arms prickle, which had nothing to do with the chilly wind blowing in at nightfall. She was pleased she'd slipped the pepper spray into her pocket. She hadn't any idea what the imposing woman was likely to do if her medallion was the one she was looking for. Savannah couldn't take it off. After changing out of her dress clothes into jeans and a T-shirt when she'd returned home, she had desperately tried again to pull it over her head. But as always, she'd only gotten it so far before she'd hit an invisible wall. And no amount of tugging could make it go further.

Despite all her scientific beliefs, there was no doubt it was under some sort of spell. Something mystical. There was nothing else on God's earth to explain it. An idea struck when she heard the knock on the door. If Tamasin had some connection to the artifact, then maybe it'd come off for *her*.

"Come on in," Savannah said cheerily to hide her nervousness. When she saw Tamasin had also changed into casual clothes, she was pleased she had as well.

Tamasin handed her a bottle of wine and said stiffly. "Thank you for inviting me to your home, Dr. Cole."

Savannah eyed her thoughtfully. Reverting to her formal name suggested Tamasin was nervous too. And the wine meant she didn't intend to be shuffled out before her business was concluded. That could take a while—it was just as well she'd picked up enough take-away on the way home. "Hey, remember it's Savannah, Mistress of the Meadowlands. Come on into the lounge and I'll get us a drink. What'll you have? I've beer and Scotch as well as wine."

"A Scotch and water, thank you." Tamasin roamed her eyes around the room. "You have an interesting collection of antiques."

Savannah felt a flush of pleasure. The exotic pieces were her pride and joy, found over the years in out-of-the-way places of the world. Some were very rare and all legally obtained. "Thanks. I'm fascinated by the past." She chuckled. "I'm an archeologist—it comes with the territory. Have a close look at them while I get those drinks. I've Chinese takeaway if you'd like to stay for dinner."

"That's very kind of you. I would like that very much."

As she went into the kitchen, Savannah puzzled over the woman sitting in her lounge chair. Something was a bit off about her. Not in step with the modern world, as if she was carefully picking her words. Too formal. A stab of anxiety hit. She'd invited someone into her home who looked like she'd be able to snap her neck with her bare hands.

Pushing back the touch of panic, she looked at it logically. The big woman was hardly going to hurt her when the mayor's wife was present when Savannah had asked her to come over.

She handed the glass to her guest and took a seat opposite, feigning nonchalance as she crossed her legs. "Now tell me about the medallion you're looking for."

Tamasin leaned forward, her hands on her knees. "May I see your collection?"

"Well," Savannah said with a rueful smile. "I misled you a little. I have a mysterious medallion that I can't find anything about in any museum or archive. Maybe it's the one you're looking for."

Tamasin jerked up straighter in her chair. "You have it here?"

"Actually, I'm wearing it."

Tamasin slumped back in her chair. "Damn! For a moment I thought—" She threw up her hands. "I'm sorry for wasting your time, Doctor."

Savannah eyed her curiously. "Don't you want to look at it?"

"There's no point. There's no way someone like you could wear the Circle of Sheda."

"Someone like me?"

Tamasin shrugged. "You're not a warrior. You're a pretty little thing who talks for a living."

"Hey," said Savannah, affronted. "I'm not little. I'm five-eight and hardly thin. But can we backtrack a bit? What is the Circle of Sheda? I presume it's the medallion you're looking for, but I've never heard that name in all my research."

"It's a sacred object extremely important to my people."

"And where are you from?"

"Somewhere a long way from here. You wouldn't have heard of it," Tamasin muttered, shifting awkwardly in her seat.

Savannah dropped her eyes to the hands that moved restlessly on the knees. They were large but quite beautiful, well-proportioned, with long tapering fingers. The wide gold bracelet that glittered in the light was a thing of beauty too. She focused on the markings on the surface, and her heart thudded when she realized what they were. The letters were identical to those on the shield. This woman was from the same place as the warrior in the cavern.

She raised her head to look Tamasin in the eye and said without any more preamble, "I think you'd better look at the medallion." Before the big woman could reply, Savannah stood up and reefed her top over her head. She pulled it out of her bra and held it up. "Is this your Circle of Sheda?"

Tamasin's reaction to the revelation was unexpected and unsettling. She sizzled out a loud breath as the blood drained from her face. Moisture pooled in her eyes, a trickle escaping over her lids. She dropped to her knees. "It's been lost for centuries," she whispered hoarsely.

Savannah felt immense sympathy for the emotional woman kneeling at her feet. "And now it has been found," she said gently. "Tell me all about it."

Tamasin climbed back onto the chair, her eyes focused on the medallion. "I know you're curious, and you deserve an explanation,

Savannah. But unfortunately, I can't discuss it, so don't take it personally. But as I said, it is extremely important to us. I'll pay anything you ask for it. Just name your price."

For the first time, Savannah felt real anger at the medallion. Why didn't it pick this loyal woman who had searched relentlessly for it for three years? Not someone who didn't even believe in charms, or spells, or magic, or whatever the hell was going on with it. She reached over and touched Tamasin's arm lightly to convey her regret. "I'm sorry. I'd love to give it to you but I can't take it off."

Tamasin's eyes widened then narrowed. "That's impossible," she said.

"I'm not a liar," said Savannah warily. This was not a person to irritate. "If you can take it off, you can have it."

The anger faded from Tamasin's face. "I have no idea what will happen if I touch it? It's sacred. Only the Chosen One may wear it."

"Okay," Savannah replied, relaxing back in the chair. "Let's discuss this rationally and maybe we can work something out."

"When did you put it on?" asked Tamasin.

"Four years ago."

"That long!" exclaimed Tamasin. "And it's been around your neck ever since?"

Savannah grimaced. "Yep. And don't think that I haven't tried to remove it. I only get it to my neck and then I hit a wall." She eyed Tamasin closely. "Despite the fact that I don't believe I such things, or at least I didn't use to, I'm well aware there are magical forces at play here. Do you have a secret way to get it off?"

"No. It's only when a warrior can no longer fight does she relinquish it. Even then, it's entirely at her discretion."

"Hmm. In other words, she has to be a soldier and it's there for most of her life. And once she puts it on, she has control over it."

"A simplified version but yes, that's right."

"How on earth do they determine who to choose?"

"It's documented in the Book of the Two Moons. Putting it simply, it's the rule book we live by. A warrior has to win the right— not only the strongest but one with intelligence and empathy." She shrugged. "That contest hasn't been evoked for centuries, for the Circle was lost."

"Only women can wear it?"

Tamasin gave a ghost of a smile. "Yes. We are a matriarchal society."

Savannah's ears pricked at that. Where on earth would there be a society like that on this planet? She'd love to see a place like that. Even in the most liberal countries, women were still fighting for equality. She let it pass. If she wanted information, it wouldn't be wise to sound skeptical. "Why do you think it's turned up now?"

"What do you mean?" asked Tamasin with a frown. "Didn't you dig it up somewhere?"

"That's not quite how it went. And I had a bit of help." Savannah stopped, suddenly aware she was down to her bra. She blushed and hauled the top back on, arranging the medallion out of the shirt so it was visible. "Sorry about that. I forgot I was nearly naked."

"What do you mean you had help?"

When she opened her mouth to answer, the medallion gave a sharp tingle. "Ouch!" she exclaimed, then seeing the nonplussed expression on her guest, screwed up her nose. "Um…the medallion's telling me to keep that to myself."

"It speaks to you?" Tamasin asked, staring at her in amazement.

Savannah laughed, though there was no mirth in the sound. "No speech. It communicates with a zap. I can't explain it." She pushed up from the chair. "I'll get us another drink," and left her guest to digest the information.

As she filled the glasses, she thought over the events preceding the find. In retrospect, it had been far too easy to get on that dig. A lot of older, more experienced archeologists were passed over. Another thing that had puzzled her to distraction. How had the old blind woman known she was going to be caught in that sandstorm? Nobody could control nature—could they? The guys in the truck said it appeared out of nowhere. Savannah shook her head to clear away the disturbing thoughts. She was getting paranoid. Mystics and magic were unchartered territories, and the sooner she got rid of the thing the better. It was starting to blow her mind.

Back in the lounge, Tamasin was staring out the window. She turned to look at her. "Why haven't you put the picture of the medallion on your website, Savannah, when you wanted to know what it is. I would have seen it and come sooner."

Savannah cleared her throat. "Because when I found it, I didn't hand it in. Which means technically, I…um …stole it."

"Why are you sure I'm not from where you found it?"

Savannah fiddled with her glass, deciding, then came to the decision. There was no reason not to tell her. "The letters on your bracelet are in the same language as those on the warrior's shield and sword. She is your ancestor."

In three strides, Tamasin returned to her seat. "You found Elsbeth's remains and stole the Circle of Sheda from around her neck? Where is she?"

A tingle hit Savannah's chest. "Firstly, I didn't steal it. It's hard to explain, but I knew I had to put it on." She looked sympathetically at Tamasin. "Just as I'm certain her bones have to be left undisturbed. Your warrior is in a safe place and rests in peace."

Tamasin looked at her curiously. "You got another zap?"

"Yep. I can't tell you where she is."

"When you said you knew these things, did you hear voices in your head?"

Savannah breathed out a frustrated breath. "That sounds like I'm strange. Nothing remotely like this has ever happened to me before. There were no if or buts. No voices. I just *knew* what I had to do."

"Extraordinary. What is your bloodline, Savannah?"

Savannah nearly giggled. Who asked anyone that? "I guess you mean what is my nationality. I'm from New Zealand…my parents were both doctors and had a practice in Christchurch."

"Not archeologists?"

"No. They were Spanish and English descent."

"Any siblings?"

"Unfortunately, no. I was an only child of older parents. My father died in 2015, and my mother passed away last year."

"I'm sorry, Savannah." She looked around the room. "I take it you live alone?"

Savannah flinched. She sounded like a loser. "I do. What about you?"

Tamasin downed a huge gulp of her scotch. "I have a wife. But whether I still have her if I get back remains to be seen. I have been away for three years, and I didn't tell her I was going." She gave a half-hearted grin that looked more like a wince. "She has a temper."

"What do you mean *if?*"

"I may not be able to get back. Time might have run out. I have no idea if the portal can still be opened."

Savannah let 'portal' pass without commenting. It was getting weirder and weirder and she didn't want to know. "Why didn't you tell her you were going?"

"Ah… I couldn't. Like you, Savannah, I'm also a pawn in all of this. My name Epona means not only the Mistress of Horses but also of Dreams. I had a dream that I must come to this world to find the medallion. And I was to tell no one, not even Valeria."

"Your wife?"

"Yes."

A weight settled on Savannah. Enough was enough—she just wanted to hand over the medallion and get her old life back. Trying to forget the sandstorm had been nightmarish enough without having to cope with this otherworld bizarre stuff. She jumped to her feet. "C'mon. Let's adjourn to the dining table, and after dinner, you have my blessing to take the Circle of Sheda. I've figured out my role in all this. I was to find it and keep it safe until you came for it."

Relief flittered across Tamasin's face. "I believe you're right. As an archeologist, you were able to find it. Now my job is to bring it home."

They ate quietly, caught up in their thoughts. Savannah tried not to dwell on Algeria, but she felt she had missed something.

Something glaring she should have remembered. She pushed it to the back of her mind and as soon as the dishes were cleared away, led the way into the lounge room. "Shall we start?"

"Let's do it," Tamasin agreed.

Savannah hesitated as they faced each other. "Before we start. What if you can't get back?"

"I was thinking about that at dinner. Very strong magic is afoot. I was sent here to bring the sacred medallion back to my people. I have no doubt it will open the portal." Her eyes clouded. "But there'll be the question to be answered when I get back. Why has it resurfaced now after all these years?"

That was a topic Savannah had no intention of pursuing. Her part was over. She dropped her hands to her sides. "Okay. I'm ready. Let's get this over with. Take it off."

As soon as Tamasin's fingers reached for the medallion, Savannah knew she had miscalculated badly. The old lady's words popped into her head. *You are the Chosen One, Savannah.*

In the next heartbeat, it was too late. Tamasin's fingers curled around the metal disk. Immediately it began to tremble, gathering momentum until it was violently shaking. For one awful moment, Savannah thought it was going to explode. Then the room shuddered.

Suddenly, she felt a biting cold. So cold that her bones felt brittle and her skin ice. She fell into an abyss of nothingness. Vaguely aware of Tamasin beside her, she tumbled down through the vast and empty black vacuum.

Eternity expanded and then retracted.

Gradually, the emptiness receded. White mists appeared and she was floating like a dandelion on the wind.

The cold faded away and warmth seeped into her bones.

When the void shimmered, countryside appeared.

She was on a hill overlooking an emerald-green meadow, bounded by graceful tall trees. The sky was a vivid blue, and two shadowy purple moons hung above the horizon. A red road wandered through the grasses and wildflowers, to the valley beyond.

Savannah could only stand in mute appreciation of the colors of this world. Almost too bright. She was in no doubt she wasn't on the Earth she knew.

She heard someone move behind her and turned to see Tamasin stretching out her arms to embrace the landscape. "I'm home." Her eyes bright, she smiled at Savannah. "My world is called Rand."

A sudden fear tightened in Savannah's breast. She had been transported to a completely new world, with every possibility she'd never get home.

Tamasin's gaze softened. "I'm sorry, Savannah, I was completely wrong. I wasn't only sent for the Circle of Sheda. It was for you too."

Chapter Four

Rand

The bright light of the inn at the end of the street was a welcoming beacon.

"Keep quiet and I'll do the talking when we get there," said Tamasin.

"Okay," agreed Savannah. "All I want is a hot bath and a soft bed. I'm exhausted."

Tamasin looked amused. "They're called inns here. And it won't be the Carlton Ritz."

It had been broad daylight, the sun high in the sky when they had exited the portal. Her initial panic had subsided as they made the long journey down through the meadows to the town of Chesterton in the valley below. On the surface, though more colorful, this world seemed much like her own, with rolling hills, lush vegetation and a village nestled in a pretty valley. The travelers on the road seemed normal folk, though all were tall. They were in carts and on horseback. No cars in sight.

As they neared the town, it looked like she had stepped back into medieval England. But on closer inspection, while the buildings were wooden with the same architecture, the usual church spire and stone fortifications were missing. She was pragmatic enough to realize that she shouldn't be lulled into complacency. While everything looked familiar, it was still an alien place. This brought another wave of panic. Ruthlessly, she pushed it firmly away as she followed Tamasin down the street.

Now after sundown, darkness had swallowed the town square. The cobblestones glistened under the twin moons, and the night wind leaped in gusts, rattling the rooftops and banging the shutters. When they reached the front of the building, she could see a sign, *The Howling Wolf*, hanging at the entrance. She grimaced. Just dandy, the place had wolves. She wondered what other predatory animals lay waiting in the forest. She hoped they weren't too big or too vicious.

The door led them into a bright and cheery common room. At the sight, Savannah immediately felt much better. A roaring fire crackled in a large open hearth that was surrounded by wooden tables and bench seats. Across the other side of the room was a long bar, behind which rested three wooden barrels. Making his way toward them, a smile on his face, was a portly man wearing an apron.

When he reached them, his smile broadened. "Mistress Tamasin. As I live. It's been a long time. I'm very glad to see you."

Tamasin clapped him on the shoulder. "I've been away three years and you don't look a day older, you old rogue." She pulled Savannah forward. "Godfrey…this is my friend Savannah."

Smiling, the innkeeper nodded and guided them to the bar. "Your companion is as welcome as yourself. The best ale for my friends, barman."

Smiling, Tamasin accepted the tankard. "Thanks. This will go down well. I missed your brew. We'll require a room with two beds for the night." She glanced around the room. "What news in the valley?"

"Things haven't changed much since you went away. This year there have been stories of goblins and brigands troubling travelers. It's nothing new, but it seems to be going on more than usual. Wolves are reported to be thicker in the north country and bears have been sighted in the hills." He lowered his voice. "The new Mistress of Horses isn't popular. I'm pleased to see that you're home again."

"Who did the Queen appoint?"

"Mistress Bronwyn."

Tamasin let out a snort. "Then it is about time I came home. So, my old friend, can you rustle us up some food."

Godfrey gave a sly grin. "It might very well be your last supper, Tamasin. She'll probably run you through with her sword when she sees you."

"I'll be lucky if she only does that," groaned Tamasin. "She doesn't know I'm here."

"Best of luck then. You'll need it," he said, chuckling. "The serving girl will bring your meals to the booth at the back. You'll have privacy there. Take the bedchamber at the top of the stairs when you're finished." His face grew serious. "I'm glad you're home. Things haven't been the same without you. She needs you."

"I never meant to stay away for so long. It was unavoidable."

Savannah looked at her curiously when he hurried away. "He's a friend?"

"Yes. He's my eyes and ears in the valley." At the sound of boots stamping on the wooden landing outside, Tamasin pointed to the back. "C'mon. I prefer not to meet anyone from the castle until I get there."

The secluded booth was dark and cozy, ideal for a private chat. Once settled, Tamasin cleared her throat. "You prefer women to love?"

Savannah raised an eyebrow. "Oh. I thought you knew I do. Men do nothing for me at all. Is it a big deal in this world?"

"Not at all. That's why I asked," said Tamasin, faintly smiling. "You can be quite comfortable loving who you like in our world. We've more to do than worry about who anyone prefers as their pillow partner."

"That's a relief," said Savannah. "What kind of government do you have?"

"The Queen is the ruler, and she has a Council of ten to advise her. The thirty realms are governed by either sex, but being a matriarchal society, the Supreme Monarch is always female."

"Is it a peaceful world?"

"It has been for many years. Some skirmishes flare up from time to time, but nothing major. The warlike tribes to the west beyond the stony uplands are kept under control by our border patrols. But of course, there are the Crevlin."

"Who are the Crevlin?" asked Savannah.

Tamasin's voice dropped low and gruff. "They come from a place in your nightmares and magic. They feed off sin and rip off your skin."

"Really!" squeaked Savannah. "Have you ever seen one?"

Tamasin chuckled. "Relax. They're the bogeymen that mothers tell their children about, so they'll be good. It's an old wives' tale."

Savannah punched her arm lightly. "That wasn't nice." She drained her tankard. "I'll get you a drink. I better get some food into my stomach before I have any more alcohol. That ale was strong."

Tamasin pushed over some coins. "Thanks. I'd like another. Take these."

Savannah could see the inn had filled quickly. Workmen and women in rough-woven tunics and leather breeches, sat at the tables, laughing and lightly bantering as they drank their ales. The scene looked warm and friendly. She imagined they'd come for a couple of pints before going home. Godfrey was beaming, bustling through the tables as he greeted his customers.

At the bar, four tall women in dark blue uniforms were deep in conversation. Not wanting to catch their attention, Savannah skirted around them to the far end. They looked fierce. It wasn't only their magnificent physiques that were formidable. Both sides of their heads were shaved, the strip down the middle ending in a thick braid halfway down their backs. A bird of prey was tattooed around one eye.

The bartender cocked his head at her. "Same again?"

"Only one, please." She put the money on the table, hoping he'd just take what he was owed. He counted it out, pushed back a coin, and turned to fill the tankard.

When the air shifted beside her, she became aware someone was standing at her elbow. A voice murmured in her ear. "May I buy you a drink?"

She turned to see one of the soldiers smiling down at her. Some of Savannah's friends would have put her in the wow category, but she looked far too cocky. And by the way she was eyeing her, she was hoping to share more than a drink. "No thanks," she said brightly.

"C'mon, just one."

"Sorry. But I appreciate you asking," Savannah said, turning back to the bar.

"I could give you a good time tonight."

"Thanks, but I said no. Now if you'll excuse me," she said, picking up the tankard.

Someone laughed further down the bar. The soldier stood stiffly for a minute, then shrugged. "Your loss," she said gruffly and moved away.

One of the other women made a lewd remark and a rude gesture, which set the others laughing. Savannah glared over at them, hating being treated so demeaning.

As she turned, she caught the eye of a woman watching from a nearby table. From her uniform and hair, she was one of the soldiers, but this one was even more frightening. One whole side of her face was tattooed, her eyes were like flints and her mouth pressed into a hard line.

Still annoyed, Savannah frowned at her as she walked past the table. The next second, she stumbled, the tankard lurched, and ale splashed onto the table. When the woman snorted and half rose from her chair, Savannah called out, "Oops, sorry," and fled. By the time she reached Tamasin, she was shaking.

"What's the matter?" asked Tamasin, concerned.

"Nothing. Just a bunch of soldiers at the bar."

"What did they look like?"

"Dark blue uniforms, weird hairstyles, bird tattoos on their faces."

Tamasin stared at her. "Savannah…you can't mess with them. They're members of the Elite Guards. The best fighters in the country."

"Oh," Savannah said with a wince.

Tamasin shook her head. "Let's eat. We have a big day tomorrow and need our sleep." She covered Savannah's hand. "How are you holding up? It's a big thing to be taken away from your homeland." She smiled a little too brightly. "I'm fine…really. It's been a shock, but I kept telling myself all afternoon that as a historian, I'm living my dream."

But as she followed Tamasin upstairs to their bedroom, her circumstance really hit. And as she lay in the narrow wooden bed, she fingered the medallion around her neck to push back the anxiety. Who was going to pay her rent and collect the mail? Would the police start looking for her when she didn't turn up for work? When she didn't answer her texts, what would her friends do? The darkness pressed into her chest like cold hands. She felt like weeping. She missed her flat, the sounds of traffic in the street outside, the lights of the city through her window, the dings of the nightly incoming text messages on her phone beside her bed.

She missed her home.

It was a blessed release when she eventually drifted off to sleep.

†

Savannah opened an eye. Sunlight was streaming through the half-opened wooden shutters. For a moment she wondered where she was, and then it came flooding back. She was in an inn that belonged in the medieval era, though there were some differences. There was a communal bathroom with claw baths at the back of the building, and a privy box out in the yard. The maid had appeared with two buckets of hot water for her bath.

The panic of last night had receded with the good sleep, and she told herself to treat this like any dig in a foreign place. She had the medallion. If she wanted to, she could return.

The next bed was empty. It took some willpower to move from under the warm blankets when footsteps echoed in the corridor outside the door. The latch clicked and Tamasin stepped inside, carrying a tray. "We'll eat breakfast here. I'd like to be gone before the other guests come down."

Savannah ran her hands across her top to press out the creases. "I'll have to get some new clothes somewhere before we venture out amongst people. The lamps last night were dim enough, but these jeans will stick out a mile in daylight. You're lucky…your slacks don't seem out of place."

"I've already asked Godfrey to find you an outfit. His youngest daughter's fifteen. She's slightly taller than you, so her dress will be roomy enough to give space for your breasts," replied Tamasin. "Eat up and we'll get going."

As they were finishing, there was a discrete knock on the door. A girl, a bundle in her arms, entered the room,

Blushing, she nodded to Tamasin. "The clothes, Mistress."

Tamasin took coins out of her pocket and pressed them into the girl's palm. "Thank you, Anna."

She curtsied, then head down, hurried out the door.

Savannah immediately pulled the garments out of the parcel and held them up. There was a mid-length undergarment with a low neckline, plus a sleeveless woolen tunic with straps. She disappeared behind the screen, reappearing minutes later looking like a serving wench. Giggling, she twirled around. "What do you think?"

Tamasin grinned as she eyed her. "Very fetching."

"Isn't it delightful," she chortled. "Nobody would ever realize I'm the Chosen One."

"And make sure you keep it that way," said Tamasin sharply. "You don't want to have to defend that honor. Where we're going, there will be powerful women who will challenge for the right to bear the Circle of Sheda. Women whose birthrights demand it."

"Okay, I understand. Where are we going?"

Tamasin waved at the door. "Come on and I'll show you."

Chesterton's business area was lined with rows of brightly painted shops. Tamasin moved quickly along the main thoroughfare, and Savannah with her shorter legs had to hurry to keep up. At this time of the morning, the place was quiet, the only sound coming from the blacksmith hammering at his forge. Enticing freshly baked bread wafted from the bakery. Finally, after they left the last house on the outskirts, Tamasin walked another twenty minutes until she reached a small grassy area. It lay at the foothills of a mountain that towered over the southern side of the valley.

Savannah looked at her enquiringly. "Where are we going?"

Tamasin pointed into the air. "Up there."

Savannah blinked. The high mountain was shrouded in cloud. "Hey, come on," she moaned. "I'll never climb that in a fit."

"We won't be climbing." From her pocket, Tamasin drew out a three-inch-long metal cylinder. "Cover your ears," she ordered, then put it to her mouth and blew hard.

When a thin wailing shriek shattered the silence, Savannah jammed her fingers deeper into her ear canals. After more screeches, she realized there was a pattern in the sound. Some sort of code to whoever was up there listening. Though she couldn't imagine how anyone could hear it from so far up.

After another minute, Tamasin put the whistle back into her pocket. "Now we wait."

"For how long?"

"Ten…fifteen minutes."

Savannah gave an eye roll. "Yeah, right. If you say so."

Tamasin chuckled. "Ye of little faith."

"So, if by some miracle we get a lift, what's up there?"

"The Citadel City of Iona. It's the home to the Queen of Rand, ten thousand of her warrior women, plus staff and their families. All told, fifty thousand people live there. The top of the mountain is a plateau."

Tamasin's expression turned somber as she added. "Just keep a low profile, Savannah, until we know why the medallion has resurfaced. Don't make a target of yourself. I'm serious. I may not always be nearby to protect you."

"I promise to be as meek as a mouse. I've been meaning to ask the reason your language is the same as ours?"

"It's not. The medallion has given you the ability to understand and speak Rand."

Savannah gaped at her. "I had no idea…it just sounded like English. How did you manage when you went through the portal three years ago?"

"Because the portal has been used in the past, the palace Mistresses are taught the rudiments of English. However, it took me a year to speak it properly," Tamasin replied. She cocked her head. "Listen."

A faint sound like a long sigh began from somewhere up in the mountain. At first, Savannah thought it was the wind, but the sighing became humming, then fluttering, and soon became the sound of a million butterfly wings. A form appeared through the veil of clouds and swooping down the mountain was a huge flying horse. She blinked, gaping up at it, but the shock quickly vanished as she took in the sheer beauty of the animal. It was magnificent. A golden color, its unbelievably shiny coat was almost metallic in the sun. It was as handsome as the Arabian horses she'd seen stabled in Algeria, though larger and more barrel-chested. Long-spanned golden wings arched from its back and spread out across the sky.

She watched, awestruck, as it reached the bottom of the mountain, hovered over the glen, and glided down lightly onto the grass. The wings immediately folded into its body.

When Tamasin threw her arm around the muscular neck, the horse whinnied and nuzzled her hair. When she turned to Savannah, her eyes were bright with tears. "Meet Malkia. He's the chief stallion in our stable and my personal mount." She ruffled the horse's mane affectionally. "I've missed you, my friend. You have no idea how much. This is Savannah. You're going to give her a lift too."

Savannah leaned over to tentatively stroke Malkia's muzzle. She swallowed. He was enormous. "I hope I don't fall off."

"You won't. Sit in front of me and I'll hold you on."

"Don't let me go." She groaned. "I'm not so sure about this."

The horse nickered. If she didn't know better, she'd swear it was laughing.

Without another word, Tamasin grabbed her by the waist and heaved her up onto Malkia's back. Savannah squealed, clutching at the mane. With a bound, Tamasin swung up behind her, maneuvering her body until Savannah was cradled between her thighs. The horse pranced excitedly, its hooves thudding into the grass. Savannah squeezed her eyes shut as she felt the muscles bunch beneath her. The next moment he leaped into the air.

She heard the flap of wings, and the air rushed around them. When she opened her eyes, she let out another shriek. They were sailing straight up the mountain, the valley far below.

"*Relax and enjoy the ride. She's got you.*"

Savannah did as she was told, letting the tension seep out of her body. Tamasin's legs and arms held her like a vice.

It took her a full minute to realize that those words had been in her head. And it hadn't been Tamasin she'd heard. The place was getting weirder and weirder. Not only was there a flying horse, but it was also telepathic.

But then all those thoughts vanished when Malkia leveled out and the clouds parted. Before them, a majestic castle towered into the air. And she could only gape in wonder as they hovered over the front turret and began to slowly descend to the stables behind the massive courtyard.

Chapter Five

The Citadel City of Iona

Tamasin stroked Malkia's back affectionately. "Thank you, my friend."

The stallion whinnied, then dipped its head and trotted off down through the arched doorway into the stables.

Savannah dragged her eyes away from the magnificent horse as it clip-clopped over the cobblestones and raised an enquiring eyebrow at her companion. "Where to?"

"We go to the palace."

"Aren't you going to see your wife first?"

"She'll be there," Tamasin said quietly. "Now…I don't want to be recognized before we get there, so keep your head down. We'll act like kitchen hands and skirt around the outside of the courtyard."

"Why? I thought you'd be dying to see everyone?"

"I can't wait to see them," Tamasin said, smiling.

"Then why all the secrecy? Wouldn't you be welcomed with open arms?"

Tamasin's lips tightened. "The element of surprise is far more important than the ceremony. I want to see everyone's face when I turn up. Who seems unhappy for me to be back. Like any seat of government, there are power struggles and jockeying for favors. I've been away far too long and may not be able to reclaim my seat on the Council. Alliances shift. I have already been replaced as the Mistress of Horses."

"Is that an important position?"

"One of the highest. Even though there's a carriage pulley system for produce from below, people rely on horses for transportation. It's far quicker."

Savannah tugged her sleeve. "But you also said you were the Mistress of Dreams, Tamasin. That's more important. Who took over that role?"

"It can't be bestowed. I was born with the ability to *see* things in my dreams and interpret dreams of others." With a puzzled frown, she eyed Savannah. "Why did you say it was important?"

"When you mentioned it at my apartment, the medallion tingled. Are you the only one who has the gift?"

Tamasin shrugged. "I'm not aware of anyone else. Centuries ago, there was a society of dream seers, so I imagine there are others. But after so many years of peace, the group was eventually disbanded and never reformed."

"Yet you mentioned it to me."

"My dreams came back in earnest about six years ago. I've always dreamt, but these new ones were serious. Filled with warnings. Then I had one I couldn't ignore. It was much clearer than any I'd ever had—usually, they're cryptic, needing interpretation. I was instructed to go through the portal and find the Circle of Sheda. And to tell no one, not even Valeria. I don't understand why I had to be so secretive, but I shall endeavor to find out. I suspect one of the royal advisors may be a spy."

"For whom?"

Tamasin threw up her hands in frustration. "I have absolutely no idea."

"One thing that's puzzling me, Tamasin. How did you get through the portal when you had no hope of getting back until you found the medallion?"

"I had to be at a particular place at a certain time." She took Savannah's arm. "C'mon, enough questions for a while. I'm anxious to see my wife. Stay a few paces behind me."

As instructed, Savannah kept her head down, her gaze pinned to Tamasin's as she followed along behind her. Before her eyes, Tamasin morphed into a servant: her head bowed lower, her ramrod straight posture became slightly hunched, her stride no longer so self-assured. It was effective. Even though there were quite a few people in the courtyard, no one even glanced in their direction.

At the foot of a long white marble staircase, Tamasin stopped. "We'll go up there."

Savannah lifted her gaze. At the top was a huge carved oak doorway, the entrance to the palatial castle towering over the town. Two women guards armed with lances stood to attention beside the columns on either side of the door.

They began to climb, hugging the left. At the halfway point of the staircase, Tamasin detoured to a smaller flight of steps that veered off to the side of the building. Around the corner, they reached a service entrance. No soldiers guarded this door.

"It leads to the kitchens and servants' quarters," Tamasin muttered as they slipped through.

Once inside, they circled the kitchens that were hives of industry. Clattering pots and pans and aromas of roasting meats and baking bread. At the base of an inner set of wooden stairs, a maid appeared. Immediately, Tamasin bowed her head again, and pulling Savannah close, shuffled out of her way. The girl didn't give them a second glance as she hurried by. Quickly, they ran up the stairs that opened into a long corridor on the next floor. When Tamasin reached the third door on the right, she pushed it open.

Savannah gasped as she stepped into a spectacular room. The white marble walls were bedecked with rich tapestries and huge paintings that depicted heroic battles and long-dead warrior women. Rows of statues lined either side, so delicate that the sculpted cloth looked like it could move in a breeze. Up high, rows of shields hung from the carved quartz ceiling.

"It's the antechamber to the throne room," whispered Tamasin. "We did well...got here without being noticed."

But as they neared the far side, a white-haired woman carrying a bundle of books suddenly appeared from a side door.

When she saw them, her eyes went wide, her face paled. The books slipped out of her arms, and her hand went to her throat. "Tamasin. You're alive," she stuttered. "By all the Gods, we thought you must have died."

"Hello, Moira."

"What happened to you? Why didn't you send us a message? Valeria imagined the worst."

"Where I went, I had no way of contacting anyone." She reached out and touched the older woman's arm. "I had no choice, Moira. I was lucky to make it back."

"Was it one of your dreams?" she whispered.

Tamasin nodded. "But please, don't say anything to anyone. There's danger afoot. I fear an enemy is coming which we're not prepared to meet."

"I've become increasingly concerned as well." The older woman shook her head in frustration. "But there are many on the Council who won't listen. They call me too old and seek to retire me."

Tamasin pursed her lips. "Fools."

Moira turned to look at Savannah curiously. "Have you a servant?"

"No…no. A friend. This is Savannah."

Savannah gave the woman a shy smile. "Hi, Moira. Let me guess…Mistress of Destiny."

A look of surprise flittered across the aged face.

Tamasin chuckled. "She's an arc…um… a historian. You two will get on very well."

"And where are you from, young lady?"

"A fair way from here. At—" She darted a quick look at Tamasin.

"Ambrose Siding," said Tamasin smoothly.

"Oh…you *are* a long way from home. I'd be happy to show you our library one day."

"I'd love that," said Savannah.

"We must go," said Tamasin. "Is the Queen holding court?"

"Yes. With the Council in the throne room. I'm late as usual."

Tamasin regarded her, a gleam in her eye. "Shall we accompany you in?"

Moira shook her head quickly. "You go in. I will follow at a distance, thank you very much. You should have given her warning that you had returned."

"Coward," Tamasin said, grinning. "Let's go, Savannah. Stay at the back when we get inside." Squaring her shoulders, she pushed open the door.

Savannah exchanged glances with Moira who hadn't moved. Then the old lady winked. Wondering what was going to happen, Savannah followed Tamasin into the room.

Lagging discretely behind, Savannah watched her stride across the hall toward the council table. The earnest woman on her feet talking looked over and faltered mid-sentence. Her eyes widened, and she flopped down heavily into her chair. At once, the rest of the assembly turned to look.

The room fell into silence.

At the far end of the table, someone slowly rose to her feet. Savannah's breath caught. She was the most beautiful woman she had ever seen. Tall and regal, she had flawless alabaster skin, almond-shaped dark eyes, long curling lashes, and full lips. And a perfectly proportioned figure to match. Tamasin sank to her knees in front of her. "My Queen."

Savannah gaped. This woman was the Queen? She was flipping gorgeous.

Emotions flittered across the Queen's face: surprise, relief, hurt, and something else that Savannah couldn't quite name. "So Tamasin. You've decided to come back. Is it a fleeting visit, or do you intend to stay?"

"I couldn't avoid being away for so long. I need to talk to you in private."

The Queen's face hardened further. "You're not in the position to demand anything. You have been gone three years, and I haven't received one word in all that time. No letter, nothing to give me hope you were alive. If you have anything to say, then let everyone hear it or else hold your tongue."

Tamasin gave a tired sigh. "What I have to say is for your ears only. Please, Ma'am. It's important."

"Have you any idea what I've…we've been through. You are a disgrace to the position you hold…or did hold."

Tamasin narrowed her eyes. "I heard you promoted Bronwyn."

"Did you expect to take up where you left off?" She glowered at Tamasin. "You're lucky I don't throw you out of Iona."

Savannah was growing anxious as she listened. The Queen might look spectacular, but she had a fiery temper. Without thinking, she called out, "Hey, that's not fair. Give her a break."

The Queen froze. When she raised her eyes to gaze at her, Savannah felt like a worm under a microscope. "And who might you be?" she asked in a voice turned cold as the thin morning air.

Savannah gulped. "Um—"

"She's with me," said Tamasin, quickly rising to her feet. She threw her an urgent look. "Go to the other room, Savannah, and wait for me."

"Come, Tamasin, I'd like to meet your little friend….or whatever she is to you." The imperial voice was trailing icicles.

Tamasin's shoulders slumped in resignation. "This is Savannah Cole, Your Majesty."

Savannah quickly curtseyed, though this time had the presence of mind to be quiet.

The dark eyes bored into her, flashing sparks. She gestured to one of the younger Council members. "Get Ursula."

Tamasin looked shocked, then drew up to her full height. "Savannah is my guest."

"But also a stranger. She must be tested."

"I will vouch for her. She is not an enemy."

Savannah wondered what she had let herself in for, especially since Tamasin looked furious. They didn't have long to wait. At the sound of footsteps, she turned toward the door to see a thin, sour-faced woman dressed in a flowing gray robe. She carried a bundle in her hand.

Tamasin grasped Savannah by the arm and pulled her aside. "Don't fight it. Just relax as best you can," she whispered.

Savannah swallowed. "What's she going to do to me?"

"Ursula is a Silverthorne witch. Her cape is magic. It uses pain to seek out evil against the crown. The longer you can stand it, the less threatening you are. That's the theory. As far as I'm concerned, it's barbaric." She grasped Savannah's arm. "I'm sorry. I didn't think it would go this far. Don't make a martyr of yourself. As soon as the pain starts, throw off the cape."

"And let that bitchy Queen get the better of me. Not bloody likely."

Tamasin gave a little chuckle. "That's the spirit."

"Come here, girl," Ursula called out, "and sit on this chair."

Savannah sat down and said defiantly. "I'm hardly a girl, old woman."

"You won't be so smart-mouthed after this," snapped Ursula. As she flung the black cape over Savannah, silver thorns appeared in the middle of the witch's dilated pupils.

The drapes immediately shrunk in, molding the material to her body. Savannah was barely able to suppress a scream of terror as she fought to breathe. As soon as the light in the room extinguished, she felt herself drift away to another place, another dimension, and she was able to suck in air.

She looked around. It was bitingly cold, and the only thing she wore was a thin shift. She stood on a winding pathway flanked by tangled thorny bushes. Small spikes covered the path, and her feet were bare. It flashed through her mind that she could wait here without moving to do her time, but then a whip lashed across her bare shoulders. It bit into her skin, trying to force her forward. She yelped. Damn, that had hurt. She searched desperately for a way out as the lash fell again. Even if she could push through the thorny hedge, she could hear creatures growling behind it. Terrifying sounds, warning her that there were worse things than spikes in her feet.

As another lash whistled through the air above her, a tear leaked over her lid. She braced herself for the strike.

Suddenly, out of nowhere, a voice called out. "Close your eyes tight and rub the medallion. The black magic will go."

Without hesitation, she embraced the lifeline. When she opened her eyes, she was in an emerald-green meadow, and sitting under an apple tree was the old blind woman. Savannah gave a cry of delight.

The old woman cocked her head toward her. "Aye, it's me. I'm glad to see you have arrived, Savannah."

"Who are you?"

"I am an ancestral spirit of this land. A Guardian."

Savannah regarded her closely. In Algeria, she had thought her an old crone, but here in the sunlight, she looked like a kindly old woman. Feeling a wave of tenderness, Savannah reached out and gently clasped the frail hand. "May I call you Grandmother?"

Pleasure flittered across the lined face. "You surprise me, child, and that is rare for me. I would like it very much if you would. How have you been? You have had quite an adventure since we last met."

"I have. I'm finding this world fascinating."

"I knew you would. You have been good for Tamasin as well. She will be motivated now."

"She isn't the one you said was waiting for me, is she?" Savannah blushed. "I don't feel any vibes…from her or me."

The old lady chuckled. "No, my child. Tamasin is taken. No one can break that bond. She will be important to Rand in the dark times to come. The rock who will hold everyone together. But that is all I can say. You may ask two questions of me."

"Really?" Savannah said, pleased. "Okay. First question. Why has the Circle of Sheda come back to Rand?"

"It will be needed when they come. I can tell you no more than that, Savannah. The future must play out as it is meant to. I can only guide."

"Question two, then Grandmother. Why me? I can't believe it was merely because I was in a position to find the medallion. I think you somehow got me on that dig."

The sightless eyes stared straight at her, and she had the feeling that though blind, the old woman saw her very well. "Good, you've worked it out. You were chosen, Savannah, because your bloodline is of this world as well. In the times to come, we will need someone from both worlds."

Savannah stared at her. Flabbergasted, all she could manage was, "Oh!"

"That's enough. You will discover more in due time. Too much knowledge too soon can tear the threads of time. Sit by me for a while and tell me about your childhood."

"Won't they be expecting me back?"

The old woman looked amused. "Let them sweat. Only one person has lasted more than five minutes under that dreadful cape. Black magic at its worst. Ursula is a sadist, and Tamasin is right when she said it is barbaric."

"Can't they pull it off?"

"They wouldn't because it would defeat the purpose of the test. Ursula will be getting very nervous because she fears Tamasin's anger. The Queen may browbeat Tamasin, but even the Queen must be wary if she is really angry. Now come, tell me some tales to lighten my old heart."

So Savannah lay down beside her and related some of her personal history.

Finally, after what must have been over half an hour, the old woman stood up. "It is time I left, Savannah. I have enjoyed your company very much. When you go back, I want you to tell Valeria that it is time to prepare. She must gather the Dreamers. And the Hawks must be persuaded to fly."

Savannah lent over and softly kissed her cheek. "I will, Grandmother."

Then the old lady was gone.

With a heave, Savannah threw off the cloak. The world shimmered, and she was back on the seat in the throne room. There wasn't a sound from anyone in the room. They simply stared at her.

After a long slow stretch, she got up from the chair and cast a smile around the table. "That wasn't so bad."

Ursula looked sick. "Who are you? No one has lasted anywhere nearly that long under the cloak," she muttered.

Savannah forced a chuckle, though she would have preferred to kick the bitch. "I think that smelly old cape is past its use-by date, Mistress Ursula. Perhaps it would be better if you retired too."

Ursula's fingers began to glow orange, and Savannah felt an answering tingle at her breast. "Don't try to use your black magic on me, witch," Savannah said with more bravado than she felt.

Tamasin stepped in between them. "Enough, Ursula. Take your cape and get out."

"Go, Ursula. I'll talk to you later," the Queen ordered, then turned to study Savannah. "It seemed I underestimated you. You have won yourself a reprieve for the moment. Wait outside. The throne room's no place for a servant."

Savannah breathed a sigh of relief. She'd had enough of the lot of them. Then she remembered. "Before I go, I have a message for Valeria."

Silence fell again, and everyone looked horrified. Tamasin looked like she'd swallowed a lemon.

The Queen raised an eyebrow. "You have a message for me."

Savannah's stomach lurched. *Oh, crap!* The Queen was Valeria, Tamasin's wife. She should have twigged when they were arguing. It was a marital spat. She'd put her foot into it again. "Um...yes. I'm to tell you that it is time to prepare. You must gather the dreamers. And the hawks must be persuaded to fly."

The Queen's lip curled. "What exactly do you think that means?"

"I've no idea. I hope you do because it is important."

"If you say so. And where did you hear it?"

"I'm sorry, I'm not at liberty to say."

"Oh? Keeping things from your sovereign is an offense. But I have the perfect way for you to make amends. There is a position that I haven't been able to fill for years. By your clothes, you will be ideal for the job. I'm sending you to Falcon's Keep, to be Commander Pela's maid. I will arrange transport to take you there in two hours."

"Valeria," exclaimed Tamasin. "You can't do that to her."

"I can, and I will. And you, Tamasin, will be a groom in the Royal Stables. I believe there is a vacant bedroom above the stalls."

Tamasin's face turned to stone. She swept her eyes around the table, sizing up each woman as she passed, landing her angry gaze back on the Queen. "You are right, Valeria. My place is looking after those majestic animals. I will groom them and muck out their stalls willingly, for they are loyal and kind, playing neither the uncompromising distrustful lover nor the deceitful friend. But I'm warning you, if anything happens to Savannah, you will be brought to account."

Taking Savannah's arm, Tamasin strode to the door. On the threshold, she turned around and called out, "She will be waiting at the stables for her transport to Falcon's Keep."

Chapter Six

To Falcon's Keep

Tamasin made no further comment on the events in the throne room. Instead, after they exited the palace, she silently turned in the direction of the town.

"Shopping first," she announced after they walked out the courtyard. "We haven't much time, so we'd better hurry. We'll get you new clothes and personal essentials at the markets."

By the time they'd finished, Tamasin had regained some of her good humor, though underneath, Savannah could see she was hurting. Though her nerves still jangled, Savannah's spirits lifted when she was able to discard the serving girl's dress. She'd never been so pleased to see the back of anything. Her new outfit was far more practical: a brown laced short tunic over a white long-sleeved blouse, soft brown breeches, and black knee-high boots. Tamasin also insisted that she purchase a fur cape for the ride.

Once they arrived at the stables, there was little time to discuss the events in the throne room. Savannah told her how the medallion had counteracted the cloak's black magic but didn't offer to explain how she'd received the message for Valeria. Tamasin didn't ask but simply said, "Tell me the rest when you are able. Meanwhile, I shall work on the first part of the message. Moira will help me find out if there are more Dreamers in the land."

When the time to leave arrived, Savannah found it heart-wrenching to say goodbye. Not only was she leaving her only friend in this world, but she was going to be a servant to someone everyone thought the devil incarnate.

As Tamasin strapped her into the high pommeled seat behind the saddle, Savannah cleared her throat. "I do have a question I'd like answered."

"Go ahead."

Savannah couldn't stop the blush rising to her cheeks. "Does a personal maid mean just that, or am I expected to...um ...share the Commander's bed? If it does, it's not going to happen. I've no intention of being anyone's sex slave."

A frown creased Tamasin's forehead. "We are not barbarians, Savannah. We have strict laws about such things. Everyone has the right to say no, and there are very harsh penalties for breaking that law." She patted the pommel. "There...you're secure for the ride."

"C'mon, Tamasin, you've been ignoring the subject since we left the palace. Why is working for this Pela so dreadful? Everyone, including yourself, looked aghast when the Queen announced she was sending me there."

"Pela is a tough woman and a law unto herself," said Tamasin, avoiding her eye. "She is arrogant, stubborn, but the most brilliant military tactician the army's had in decades. Before I left, Valeria had been trying for at least two years to get her to accept domestic help. Things haven't changed."

"What happened to the other maids?" asked Savannah warily. She had a bad feeling about this.

"None lasted more than twenty-four hours."

"Oh my God. Did Pela hit them?"

"No. She just made it clear that she didn't want them. She's... um...intimidating to look at. And has an attitude to match."

Savannah groaned. "That's just dandy. I'm being sent to the boss from hell, and I have to stay."

"If anyone can handle the pressure, you can," Tamasin said in a reassuring voice. "The others were simple peasant girls, hardworking but nowhere near Pela's intellect. You're an educated successful professional woman. Pela will try to intimidate you, but don't be drawn into her game. And don't show any signs of weakness. She values strength and determination and despises meekness. And fools."

"Okay, I'm sure you're simplifying things, but I'll take it on as a challenge. I've worked with dominating assholes before today."

"Good," said Tamasin. "Just remember to keep out of trouble and don't talk back."

When her escort, a lieutenant in the Queen's Flying Brigade, cast her a look of sympathy before climbing into the saddle, Savannah flinched. Yeah, right. Easier said than done not to show any weakness. She was terrified already, and she hadn't even met the damned Commander.

†

As the afternoon sun hit the mountain, the sheer rock face turned the color of ripened wheat. Having no point of reference in this world, Savannah had no idea how far this was from the Citadel City. They were somewhere very high up in a rocky range, somewhere that looked like the most inhospitable place on the planet.

Their mount, a pretty bay mare with a sleek body and a set of impressive wings, gave a whinny as stone battlements came into view. *There it is*, she telepathed to Savannah, who craned her head over the horse's flank for a look at her new home. Stone buildings jutted up like extensions of the mountain, forming a semi-circle around a green common dotted with grazing horses. But it was the amphitheater that dominated Falcon's Keep. Having more arena space and less seating than a traditional Roman hippodrome, it took up one end of the compound. It didn't surprise her, for this was the training camp for the Elite Guards. Commander Pela was in charge of the facility that housed a thousand soldiers at a time.

As they glided down onto a well-used landing pad, Savannah wondered if the Commander knew she was coming. As if she guessed what she was thinking, the lieutenant said in a hushed tone. "Her

Majesty informed my captain that your appointment was a sudden decision, and Commander Pela was not to have forewarning of your appointment. I am to drop you off and come straight back."

"You're not coming with me?" squeaked Savannah.

The lieutenant's expression was apologetic but had a touch of relief as well. "Only as far as the guard room, ma'am. I have a letter of instruction from the Queen. They will escort you to Commander Pela's living quarters."

"Huh! That's like throwing me to the wolves," groaned Savannah.

The lieutenant looked uncomfortable. "Sorry. Orders." She pointed to the first building. "This way."

Her new valise tucked under her arm, Savannah pulled her fur cape around her body and followed the soldier to the building. The heavy door creaked as the flying officer pushed it open. The guard-room was austere: a bench seat set against the wall, a wooden desk, and a set of cupboards behind. The only adornment was a falcon emblem attached to the wall. Savannah tilted her head to study it, then gazed through the open door at the back. It was an armory filled with a variety of medieval weaponry.

The soldier behind the desk looked tough. Her hairstyle was the same as the soldiers from the inn, though she was older. A long scar puckered the side of her face, and with the tattoos, she looked like she belonged in a horror movie. Not someone to meet on a dark night, thought Savannah, shivering.

The flying officer saluted and handed over the letter. "From Queen Valeria, Captain."

With a skeptical stare, the soldier took the letter, broke the waxed seal, and flipped it open. When she raised her eyes, they had widened in disbelief. "The Queen has sent Pela a personal maid? By the Gods, has she gone mad? The Commander made it quite clear years ago that she wouldn't have one." She flicked a glance at Savannah. "You'd be well advised to go back where you came from."

"Begging your pardon, Captain, this is a direct order from the Queen," said the lieutenant stiffly.

The captain shrugged and jerked a thumb at Savannah. "It's her funeral. There's a room in the barracks you can have for the night, Lieutenant."

"I've been ordered to return immediately," the flight officer replied, then turned to Savannah. "Best of luck, ma'am." After hitting her fist against her chest in salute, she disappeared through the door.

The soldier turned to Savannah. "You will address me as Captain Killia. What is your name, wench?"

"Savannah."

The soldier studied her closely, then gestured with a finger. "Come with me. I'll take you to the Commander's house."

Without speaking, Killia strode through the stone-paved streets until they reached a cluster of cottages. The rest of the buildings appeared to be barracks, mess halls, and stables. The Commander's cottage had a bushy tree in the front yard, one of the few trees on the Keep.

"It'll be dark in an hour," Killia said as she pushed open the door. "I'll fix the lamps and light the fire. There's a latrine out the back."

Savannah watched as she produced two crystals from her pocket, rubbed them together, and a flame flickered into the air. Once the fire was roaring, she uncovered two large crystal globes attached to the wall, and immediately they began to glow. She was impressed— no electricity needed in this world.

"Commander Pela eats in the soldiers' mess before coming home. I'll get the cook to bring you over a meal," the soldier said before she vanished out the door.

Savannah surveyed the room. The dining cum living area was roomy but bleak. The serviceable furniture was well-worn, and the stone walls bare except for a stuffed head of an unusual creature that had horns and fangs. She walked around the rest of the house, finding a bedroom with one unmade bed, a walk-in cupboard, a bathroom consisting of a claw bath, a bench, a mirror and containers of water, a small kitchen, a sitting room, and a smaller room filled with papers and star charts.

The whole place was full of dust and needed a good scrub out. She rolled up her sleeves—no time like the present. Pela wasn't due for a couple of hours. By the time her meal arrived, the place was considerably cleaner. As she handed over the tray, the kitchen maid, a pretty young woman in her early twenties, gazed at her wide-eyed.

"Are you really the Commander's maid?"

"I am. I arrived this afternoon. My name's Savannah."

"I'm Lyn," said the girl, then giggled. "Nobody thinks you'll last a day."

Savannah pursed her lips. Gossipy hounds. "Does everyone know already? I've just got here."

"News spreads like wildfire in this place."

"What's Commander Pela like? I've never met her."

Lyn shuddered. "Very scary. I keep out of her way. I can't believe you took the job without meeting her."

"Unfortunately, I didn't have an option."

"Poor you. I'd better get back, but come over tomorrow to the kitchen if you want company."

"I'd like that," said Savannah, pleased to find a friendly face.

"See you tomorrow," said Lyn smiling.

The meal was simple but satisfying: a hearty meat stew, thick chunks of crusty bread, and a tankard of apple cider. She'd just washed up her dishes when she heard footsteps on the landing outside. Bracing herself, she watched as a figure stepped into the room. When she came into the glow of the lamplights, Savannah's breath caught in her throat.

Crap! She was well and truly screwed. Standing before her, staring at her, was the soldier from the inn. The fierce one with half her face tattooed, the one on whose table Savannah had spilled her beer. Surprisingly, up this close, she looked to be only in her mid-thirties. She had thought someone with her responsibilities would be a lot older.

The Commander broke the silence first. "What the hell are you doing in my house?"

Savannah winced. That'd be right—Killia hadn't told her she was here. No doubt the whole camp was waiting for the yelling to start. Probably laying bets how long she'd last. "I'm your new maid."

"Since when?"

"Since the Queen sent me."

Pela strode up and loomed over her. "Well, you go back to Her High-and-Mighty Majesty and tell her that I never asked for a maid and I threw you out."

Savannah forced herself to hold her ground. She schooled her expression and said quietly, "Sorry. I'm here to stay."

Pela peered into her face, her eyes narrowing to slits. "I recognize you. You're that upstart at the Howling Wolf who flicked off my friend as though she wasn't worth your time." She gave a wolfish grin and ran her finger down Savannah's face. "On second thoughts, I don't want a maid but a whore would be nice. What's your name?"

Savannah took a hasty step backward. No wonder the other maids bolted. No one would want to go to bed with this scary woman. But that ploy wasn't going to work with her. "Sorry, Commander. I've been told my rights. I'm simply here to look after your house. Nothing else. My name is Savannah, and the Queen has no intention of letting me leave," she replied. Then added in a reasoning tone, "I'm here to stay, so can't we make the best of it? I'll work very hard."

Interest flickered in Pela's eyes. "What did you do to deserve this?"

Savannah made a face. "It's a long story, but she was very annoyed when I came in with Tamasin."

"Tamasin is back?" Pela exclaimed.

"She is. I've had a big day and am very tired. Where do I sleep?"

Pela eyed her with dislike. "Blankets and pillows are in the wardrobe. Make a bed on the floor somewhere."

"No stretcher?" asked Savannah hopefully.

"There's no need to get too comfortable. You won't be staying."

"Yeah, right. I'll camp in the lounge near the fire."

Chapter Seven

Falcon's Keep

The Commander had gone when Savannah awoke.

She breathed a sigh of relief. Her reprieve, though, was short-lived. She had just finished a few stretches to get the kinks out of her back when there was a knock on the door. She opened it, expecting breakfast. Instead, regarding her with undisguised interest was one of the Elite Guards, a young woman barely past twenty-one.

"'Morning, Miss Savannah. Commander Pela sent me to escort you to the landing pad. There's a merchant from Chesterton flying out in an hour, and he's agreed to take you with him."

Savannah looked her up and down. The trainee might be young, but she was big and fit. "Really? And you are?"

"Justine of the Elite Guards," she said proudly, snapping her heels together.

"Well, Justine, go back to your Commander and tell her the Queen has ordered me to stay. I imagine the sovereign's order overrides hers."

The guard shuffled her feet. "I'm not to take no for an answer."

"Bad luck, then. I'm not going, which will mean she'll probably take her anger out on you. If you'll excuse me, I have work to do."

"She said you'd refuse to go. I'm sorry, but I've been ordered to use force if necessary. Please, be sensible. I don't want to hurt you. You're smaller than me."

Savannah dipped her hand in her pocket, leaned back against the wall, and spread her legs apart to brace herself. "I'm staying."

"Then you give me no option," Justine muttered and moved forward to grasp her arm.

As soon as the fingers touched her skin, Savannah whipped out the pepper spray from her pocket and shot a full blast into the guard's face. Giving an agonizing howl, Justine lurched back and clawed frantically at her eyes. When she began to gasp for breath, Savannah felt a stab of panic. *Oh crap!* She'd overdone it. The guard looked to be in trouble. She rushed to her side. "Okay, relax. Relax. Concentrate on breathing." She led her to a lounge chair and guided her down into it. "Sit down, and I'll get some water."

It took minutes of eye washing before the woman began to breathe normally. Savannah's anxiety receded. It would have been disastrous if the guard had choked.

"Sorry, Justine. It'll take a while before you'll be able to see again," Savannah said, squeezing her arm. "Stay here until you're better."

"I have to go," the guard exclaimed, attempting to rise. "The Commander will be furious."

Savannah pushed her firmly into the chair. "Ha. I imagine she will be. But you'll have to let your eyes settle down. Bright sunlight will make them much worse."

"I guess I haven't a choice. I'm blind. Tell the guard at the gate I'm here."

"No way," said Savannah. "She'll only try to get me on that ride. By the time you can see, the merchant will be long gone."

Justine's body language looked like she had a noose around her neck, waiting for the trapdoor to fall from under her. She fell silent.

"I have to get to work on the house. By the look of it, it hasn't had a good clean in years," Savannah said cheerily. Humming a Lady Gaga tune as she worked, she scrubbed the kitchen first, then proceeded through the rest of the house. Two hours later, it was much cleaner, and Justine had fallen asleep in the chair.

Wary the guard might still pounce on her, she shook her shoulder gently. "Rise and shine, Sunshine. See if you can open your eyes."

The swollen lids opened to narrow slits. "Oh dear, they're still not right. I'll bathe them again," Savannah said sympathetically. She disappeared into the bathroom, returning with a basin of water.

"Why are you helping me?" Justine asked.

"Hey. I'm not blaming you. You were just following orders. After this, you should be able to see enough to get home."

As Savannah gently sponged the swollen lids, she prodded for information. "What do you think of Commander Pela. Is she a fair leader?"

"She's the best. We are all lucky to be under her command. We're the best trained fighting force in the country. She's a perfectionist," Justine said, straightening her shoulders. "And I've let her down."

"What'll she do to you?"

The young guard gave a wry smile. "I expect she'll make me do extra hours of training. And I'll deserve what punishment she metes out. I let a housemaid defeat me."

Savannah chuckled. "Don't worry. It wasn't only you that I got the better of. Commander Pela still hasn't got rid of me. She underestimated me." She gave a last dab with the cloth. "Okay, that should do. Your eyes will be as good as new in a few hours. Off you go."

As soon as she bundled Justine out the door, Savannah hurried off to find the kitchens. She was starving. Following her nose, she found them on the lower level beneath the great mess hall. The service entrance was round the back. The ramp descended into the bakery, where three men in smocks stacked trays of risen dough into the big ovens. They barely glanced at her. Inside the huge kitchen, the staff were all women. Lyn was propped up at a table, sharing a meal with a group of scullery and kitchen maids. She guessed once the breakfasts in the mess hall were finished and the tables cleaned, the staff could eat.

"We're just finishing breakfast," called out Lyn when she spied her.

Judging from the curious stares from not only the maids but also the cooks, Savannah had been the main course on the gossip menu.

No doubt there would have been plenty of conjecture about whether she would be still here, so it gave her a deal of satisfaction to smile nonchalantly as she sat down.

"Hello, Lyn." She waved at everyone at the table. "I'm Savannah."

For the next half an hour while she ate, she was bombarded with questions about Pela. It didn't deter them that she couldn't answer any. It turned out none of them had been in her house or even spoken to her. The imposing Commander frightened them, especially the timid scullery maids.

"I'll pack you some bread, cheese and meat, and an apple pie for dinner," said Lyn as they rose from the table.

"Thanks, you're the best," said Savannah. "I'll see you again for breakfast tomorrow."

"If you're here," one of the cooks called out.

"I will be," Savannah called back, though with no real confidence. She hadn't any idea what Pela would do.

By mid-afternoon, she'd tidied all the cupboards and changed the bed sheets. Wondering what to do to fill in her time, she leafed through the books in Pela's study. They were bound parchment, written by hand, and beautifully illustrated. Most were military, but to her surprise, there was a volume on the flora and fauna of Rand. Excited to find such a treasure, she settled down to read. So engrossed in the book, she failed to hear the door open.

"By all the Gods, wench, what did you do to my warrior?" A roaring voice broke the quiet.

With a start, Savannah looked up. Her hands bunched into fists at her side, Pela glared down at her. She was livid, her face so pale with fury that the tattoo stood out sharply in stark contrast. All Savannah could see was the bird. And it looked like it was ready to attack.

Carefully putting the book down, she rose to her feet. "You're home early," she said, forcing herself to speak pleasantly.

"Answer me, or I'll wring it out of you."

"You did send her to man-handle me, so don't use that tone. I was only protecting myself." Savannah replied, backing behind the chair.

Pela took a step closer and bared her teeth. "Perhaps you might like to try to protect yourself against *me*. You'll not find me so easy to use your black magic on."

Remembering what Tamasin said about not showing any weakness, Savannah took a deep breath. The woman looked angry enough to kill her, so she may as well show some spirit. She wondered whether she should invoke the power of the medallion, but a sixth sense told her this wasn't the time. For some reason, she knew Pela wouldn't let her stay if she suspected any magic. It would be better to try to talk her way out of it and show some humility.

"For a start, Commander," she began in a soft tone. "It wasn't black magic. It was a simple spray, made up of common ingredients that burn the eyes. Mainly pepper. It's very effective against an attacker. There are other ways to fight rather than by force."

"You're telling me how to fight because you're familiar with herbs? Pah! You were lucky this time, but now you give me no choice. Tomorrow morning, I will personally carry you out in front of the whole camp and tie you to the horse. Killia will fly you out. She is not a callow youth to be taken in by your tricks."

Savannah stiffened. All thoughts of submitting vanished. How dare she threaten her with humiliation. And to be carted off by that ape Killia. "Is that how you solve everything, Commander? Brute force?" she snapped. "I told you I can't go back. What do you expect me to do? The Queen's worse than you. She made that witch Ursula put that dreadful cloak on me. So come on...hit me if that makes you feel better."

Pela stared at her. "If I hit you, you'd never get up."

Savannah put her hands on her hips. "I'm aware of that. But one way or the other, we're going to have this out. It's your choice. Hit me, keep me, but I can't go back. Not for a while anyhow. Not until Tamasin is in a position to help me."

"What happened to Tamasin?"

"She's been banished to work as a stable groom."

"Valeria tossed her out?" asked Pela incredulously.

"She did."

"What's your connection to Tamasin?"

Still fuming, Savannah took a deep breath to calm herself. "We're working together on a problem. But that's all I can say at the moment. I can't break her confidence."

"So… you're saying you're not the simple housemaid you're supposed to be." Pela flicked a look at the book on the stool beside the chair. "You can read?"

"Yes, I can."

"And write?"

Savannah nodded.

Pela appraised her closely, then waved to follow her. She led her into her study and pointed to the spines of the books. "Read the titles if you can."

When Savannah rattled them off, Pela opened one and handed it to her. It was a military book. Savannah surveyed the text and the detailed drawings on the page. It was a Roman-style catapult, but on a turnstile that indicated the enemy wasn't stationary like a castle. She guessed it was designed for aerial fighting.

Pela tapped the parchment. "Read."

Unused to the spidery handwriting, she began haltingly, but quickly adapted to the style. She was proficient at reading old documents—she'd pored over enough in her research. Soon she became hooked, finding it fascinating.

So engrossed, that when a voice grated out in her ear, "That's enough," she had to pull her eyes away from the page.

She turned to see Pela assessing her. There was a speculative, suspicious look in her eyes. "It seems I have grossly underestimated you. You are no more a simple housemaid than I am. You're educated, resourceful, and cunning as a sewer rat."

Savannah awarded her a long stare. "I never said I was a," she hooked two fingers in the air, "*simple* anything. You presumed because I was a servant, I was illiterate and a bird wit." She eyed Pela acerbically. "You should have asked yourself why, after so long, did Valeria send you a housemaid when she knew perfectly well that you would treat her like shit and frighten her off."

Momentarily, Pela looked disconcerted. Then her expression became wary. "You were sent here as a punishment?"

"To get rid of me. Think about it. Tamasin disappears for three years without any word and then turns up with me."

Pela's eyes widened as the words sank in. "You think Valeria was jealous of you?"

"Yep. And I…um…made the mistake of calling her Valeria."

"In due respect," said Pela sneering. "Why would it have crossed my mind? You may be considered reasonably comely in a tavern, but you're not in Valeria's league. Nowhere close."

Insulted, Savannah seethed. Who the hell was she to talk? With that ghastly haircut and tattoos, she was hardly an oil painting. She was about to respond with a cutting remark, when it struck her that she was deliberately being provoked. Pela was digging for information, so she changed tack. "I agree. Valeria's in a league of her own. She's the most beautiful woman I've ever seen. Yet she was upset when she saw Tamasin with me. Why do *you* think?"

Pela leaned close to her ear. "Tell me…how long did you last under Ursula's cape? I stayed ten minutes, and that record still stands."

Savannah stared at her. She couldn't imagine how anyone could last even half that time. A wave of compassion rushed through Savannah, stirring an irrepressible desire to comfort her. Without a thought, she reached over and grasped her arm. "Oh, Pela. I'm sorry you had to undergo that awful test. Enduring so much pain is the bravest thing I've ever heard."

When she felt Pela tense and look down at her hand, she carefully removed it. "Sorry. I didn't mean to touch you," she whispered.

Pela backed away, putting distance between them. "You may stay, but I have conditions. And they are non-negotiable."

Savannah did a silent fist pump—she had won. "Okay. I'll do whatever you want."

"Apart from your house chores, I want you to become my scribe. I'm recording my ideas for improving our military tactics. Are you agreeable?"

"I'd like that," Savannah said enthusiastically. "To be quite honest, it will make life less boring. Thank you, Commander."

Pela gave a wolfish grin. "Don't thank me yet. You will accompany me to all meals and serve me. You will eat with the servants later. You will not talk back to me in public."

Savannah glowered but nodded.

"Lastly, you will train with the squad two hours every morning. I cannot have my servant unfit. Oh, and you may have a mat to sleep on. Put it on the floor in the corner of my room so I know where you are. There will be no fraternizing at night." She looked at Savannah with a raised eyebrow. "Do you agree?"

"Have I a choice?" she replied tartly.

"No, you don't. You will start your new mess duties tomorrow at noon since I have an appointment elsewhere at breakfast. After that, you will be required for every meal."

In two minds, Savannah watched her go. The battle had been won but at the price of her self-respect.

She'd be virtually a slave.

Chapter Eight

The Citadel City of Iona

Tamasin woke abruptly, her head aching.

The dream had been a vivid nightmare, filled with menacing creatures that had yet to reveal themselves except as ghostly specters. And she had no trouble recalling the warning: the message still burned in her mind as she scrubbed the sweat out of her hair and nightclothes.

They are coming in eight turns of the moons. You must be ready.

Alarmed, though in part relieved that there was still time to prepare, she resolved to send a message to Moira to meet today. They could work out a strategy together. And she needed to talk to Valeria about her premonitions. As the Supreme Monarch, she had to be ready to mobilize the armies, and the call to arms has to embrace every kingdom, including those across the Sea of Sighs and beyond the Great Forest. The mystical creatures in the Forgotten Realms must be alerted. Though they kept to themselves, they were still part of the world.

Tamasin had no idea how she was going to get back into the palace. Their fight had been so bitter that there was little hope Valeria would give her an audience.

At the thought of what she had lost, Tamasin's shoulders slumped. The past hung in the air like flecks of dust lit up by the sharp rays of memory. It held the ghosts of her parents, both taken by the plague fifteen years ago; her sister, who'd left with her husband and two children to live far away across the wide Sea of Sighs; and

Valeria, who'd touched her soul, and the only woman she had ever loved, or ever would love.

All lost to her now.

She straightened her posture, forcing back the despair. This wasn't the time to wallow in self-pity. Her people needed her, and the Chosen One relied on her. Tamasin had been skeptical when she had first discovered Savannah had been appointed the bearer of the Circle of Sheda. It was an honor bestowed only on the absolute best of Rand's warriors. But since she had come to know the Earth woman, it was becoming clear why she had been chosen.

On paper, she was a most unlikely candidate. Though above-average height in her world, she was short here. And she wasn't built to fight. She had a curvy figure, a lively attractive face graced by bright blue eyes, and wavy brown hair that when loose, fell in soft waves to her shoulders. Not the typical alpha warrior woman. But Savannah had guts. She was intelligent, feisty, and brave. But for all those admirable traits, they weren't her greatest asset. She could talk persuasively. A talent that was probably going to be needed in the times to come. And whatever secret Savannah wasn't sharing yet had to be the most important key. She was getting help from somewhere other than from the medallion.

When Savannah had been sent to be Pela's housemaid, Tamasin had been furious. Without stopping to listen, Valeria was jeopardizing the safety of the world. Her wife's temper had never worried Tamasin in the past. It made her a strong Queen. Everyone knew, while fiery, she ruled fairly. But this time, she had been intolerant. In hindsight, Tamasin knew she had to take a lot of the blame. She should have gone quietly to their living quarters to see her, and not turned up at a Council meeting after three years of silence accompanied by a pretty woman. Where she was concerned, Valeria had a jealous streak.

As they had exited the palace, she had resolved to smuggle Savannah off Iona to a hideout Godfrey could arrange. But then it had come to Tamasin that Falcon's Keep would be the ideal place to hide and protect Savannah. There was nowhere safer on the whole of Rand. The training camp was strictly run by Pela, and she vetted every tradesperson and support staff that set foot in the Keep. Her Elite Guards were fiercely loyal to her, and it would be a brave man or woman who tried to sneak in unannounced. Pela had a nose for seeking out spies and dispatching them.

It had been the ultimate test for Savannah's abilities to persuade the feared Commander to allow her to stay. But after a week, she hadn't returned, which meant she'd won the initial battle. But finding the sheer endurance and willpower to stay would be the hardest trial.

Tamasin walked to the window and surveyed the yard. The rising sun had begun to stream shafts of light over the Royal Stables, and soon everyone would be stirring. After a week, she was yet to get used to the basic accommodation. It was a far cry from the opulent suite she'd shared with Valeria. The room above the stables was cramped, cold, and drafty. The roof slates slapped continuously like leathery wings in the wind, so unless she was dog tired, she woke constantly throughout the night. The fireplace was only big enough for one pot, and the privy was a long walk down past the stables.

Sighing, she sponged with cold water, then ate the simple breakfast of bread and cheese the cook had sent over. The stone floor was damp from the night fog, the windows rattling gently as she stepped into the corridor that led to where the pregnant mares were housed. After they were taken outside for exercise, as the lowest ranking groom she had to muck out their stalls. The first was already vacant, so she got to work sweeping out the old hay. She had just finished when she heard footsteps. She leaned on her broom, watching the two women approach.

The one in front had the hood of her fur mantle pulled up and drawn about her face, but Tamasin was well aware of her identity. She had been here two days ago for an early ride.

She sank to one knee when she drew level. "Your Majesty."

The Queen threw back the hood and said in an imperious voice, "Saddle Marigold, please. I wish to go for a ride."

Tamasin bowed. "Of course, Ma'am." She threw a glance at the woman behind her. At least it wasn't Bronwyn, feeling a stab of satisfaction. Valeria had another lady-in-waiting accompanying her today: Arwen, the wife of the Queen's cousin, and Tamasin's good friend.

Conscious of Valeria leaning against the rail in the saddling enclosure as she prepared the mare, Tamasin tried to ignore the tingling longing running riot over her skin. Her stomach was doing all sorts of somersaults as well. Once the girth strap was tight and the saddle secure, she schooled herself to look Valeria in the eye without flinching. "Your horse is ready, Ma'am."

The Queen's eyes gleamed. "Then you may help me up."

Tamasin nodded, though nearly rolled her eyes. Valeria had never had any trouble mounting—she was one of the best riders in the country. Without a word, she cupped her hands. Valeria put in her foot and lightly vaulted into the saddle. "Fix my boot, please."

Tamasin settled it into the iron stirrup, then slowly edged her fingers up the leg. The muscles quivered under her touch as she stroked the calf gently. She glanced up quickly to see Valeria staring down at her, her eyes hooded. She let her hand linger for a few more stolen moments, then dropped her arms and moved away. Without another word, the Queen dug in her heels. The mare moved a little distance away, unfurled her wings, and rose gracefully into the sky.

Tamasin watched it become a speck in the distance before she turned to the lady-in-waiting. "Hello, Arwen. It's nice to see you."

Arwen smiled, showing two little dimples. "Hey, Tamasin. It's good to see you back. We all missed you."

Tamasin grimaced, dropping her eyes in embarrassment. "Not the homecoming I envisaged. I missed you all too. You'll never know how much." She turned to stare over the nursery enclosure where mares frolicked with their foals. "How are things?"

"A little frayed at the edges. The Council seems to argue more lately. The Queen hasn't been happy since you…ah…left."

"Do you think I wanted to leave her even for one second? I was forced to. And quite frankly, I was lucky to make it home at all. And I'm fed up with everyone presuming I deserted my Queen and wife." Tamasin gave the yard post a frustrated smack. "I don't know how long I'll be able to take this exile in the stables. It's hard, knowing she's so close and that she's moved on without me. Valeria is a passionate woman and is meant to be loved. She must have had a lover in her bed by now."

"Do you think she had? C'mon Tamasin. How many times in the last three years do you think she's been riding for pleasure?"

Tamasin shrugged.

"None. Yet she's been twice this week. And avoids Bronwyn, her Mistress of Horses. That tell you anything?"

"I don't know what to think anymore. I can't see her without wanting to touch her. It's killing me."

Arwen gave a little snort. "You certainly gave her leg a lot of tender lovin' care. And she didn't pull away."

"If that's all I'm going to get, it's not enough. I've decided to move on. I have urgent things to do, but I can attend to them in more comfortable surroundings. It's not as though I'm not wealthy enough to set up a decent establishment."

Arwen looked shocked. "You can't go."

"She doesn't want me," she said bitterly. "Enough of my troubles. Will you ask Moira to come and see me? Tell her it's urgent. And please, Arwen, keep it to yourself."

"I will. You have many friends in the palace…you must remember that. I fear the Queen will be needing your counsel one day soon. My father sent word from home that there are reported sightings in the Misty Mountains of creatures not seen for years. And there's simmering unrest in the far-flung regions."

"I'm fully aware of the urgency," said Tamasin.

Arwen reached out and squeezed her hand. "I feel much better now you're home. And for the record, I never thought you deserted Valeria. We all did fear though, that you had met with some mishap."

†

A basket of food in her arms, Moira bustled into Tamasin's room at six in the evening. Without any preamble, she asked, "What's this I hear about you shifting to live downtown?"

"So what if I am?" said Tamasin a little truculently. She tossed her head. "Would you live here, Moira? Your old bones would be aching every night with the cold, and your belly would be shrinking with the food doled out."

Moira screwed up her nose. "It's dreadful. No wonder it was vacant."

"All the staff have houses downtown. I can't live here for much longer…I'm not getting much sleep and it's not even basically comfortable."

"It's going to make it difficult for us to get together if you're further away. I can hardly go off every day. I have my duties."

Tamasin ran her hand through her hair in frustration. "We'll just have to work it out. Let's get to the most pressing issue. How do we get the Dreamers together, that is presuming there are more?"

Moira handed her a meat pie, warm from the oven. "Here, eat this while we talk. I've done a great deal of research and can say categorically, that there will be many scattered all over the world."

"How do you know that?" asked Tamasin curiously.

"Because it is not learned but a heredity gift passed down through the ancestral female line. The last Dreamer Guild had many members."

Moira held her eye. "Your mother would have had the ability."

Tamasin nodded. "Thinking about it, I guess she did. She was never surprised when I used to tell her as a child about my dreams. I suppose it was considered just one family trait amongst many."

"Exactly," exclaimed Moira. "It was an ability always there but considered insignificant because it had little purpose. You said yourself that your dreams only became serious a few years ago."

"So, you're saying there are plenty of us out there, and way back in the past the Dreamers had a purpose."

"Yes. Firstly, we have to work out how to gather them together. And secondly, why was the Guild set up in the first place?"

Tamasin's expression darkened. "How in the name of the Gods, will it be possible in the time we have to find even a handful and train them?"

Moira threw up her hands. "The only thing I can think of is to send a message across Rand asking the women to come forward."

"That would require a royal decree. Valeria has to be convinced first and I doubt she'd believe either of us. It'd take too long as well, and women from peasant stock may not be able to read," announced Tamasin groaning. She wished she was back on Earth with their social media network. It'd only take two hours for everyone to find out. Then it struck her. Dreamers did have a kind of Facebook: in their dreams.

"Moira. In your studies, did you ever come across anyone that could walk in the dream dimension?"

Moira looked at her, puzzled. "What do you mean?"

"If there was someone, then they could relay the message through dreams. It'd only take one night."

"The only one who has that ability is the Goddess of Dreams." Moira stopped abruptly, her eyes wide. "Or the Mistress of Dreams. By Gad, Tamasin. That's you."

Tamasin blinked. Was it possible? Could she enter the Dream World? Tonight, she would find out.

Once Moira went back to the palace, Tamasin exercised to exhaust her body, ensuring she'd sleep well. Before she retired, she stuffed her ears with wax and tied a dark cloth over her eyes. Snug under the blankets, she soon drifted off.

The dreams began at midnight, faces flittering in and out of reach. In her dream, she was beckoning but something held them back. They came, then vanished into the fog. She was on a ship on the Sea of Mists, then floating on the wind to the Valley of Pipers, and then moving past the Vale of Storms. The images had no substance as they strained to connect and then faded. Faces, figures, they reached out, straining to touch. She screamed, "Come to me." But there were no answers. The images disappeared and she knew they wouldn't return to this sleep.

Suddenly, the scene changed. Darkened. A crow flew through the window at the end of the corridor outside the Queen's bedchamber. In the gloom, the bird began to change. The next minute, a hooded figure stood in its place, and in its hand was a long thin knife.

Gasping for breath, Tamasin woke with a start.

Instantly alert, she leaped out of bed. Not stopping to change, but only to haul on the boots with her knives, she bounded out the door and raced down the stairs.

Chapter Nine

At this hour, the courtyard was deserted. As Tamasin dashed across the paved surface, the cold breeze tugged at her loose nightshirt though she barely noticed it. When she reached the palace steps, fear gave her legs extra strength to take them two at a time. In less than a minute, she was on the portico in front of the door. The guards' eyes widened when she suddenly appeared before them. They stepped forward aggressively. With an impatient flick of her hand, she brushed away the spear leveled at her.

Keeping her voice low, but in a tone so urgent that they snapped to attention immediately, she addressed the larger guard. "To your post and don't let anyone out the door." She turned to the other. "Rouse the rest of the guards. Then to the Queen's chambers. Quickly," she ordered and then ran inside.

Her giant strides ate up the distance until halfway along the inner hallway, she reached the door of the Queen's chamber. Forcing herself to pause, she put her ear to the wood and listened. Nothing could be heard. No noise of a struggle. Very gently she reached for the knob, not surprised to find the door slightly ajar. Whoever, or whatever was inside, would want to get out quickly when the Queen was assassinated.

She eased both knives out of her boots, then taking a deep breath, crept into the room. With one sweep, she took in the scene. A shadowy figure had nearly reached the bed, the long knife she'd seen in her dreams, clutched in its right hand. Moonbeams fell softly onto the bed where Valeria lay asleep, her hair fanned out over the pillow. The knot in Tamasin's stomach eased and she let out the breath she was holding. She was in time.

The shrouded figure turned at the sound and Tamasin could see the shape of the body. It was a tall thin male, though, in the gloom, she couldn't make out the features of his face. Hissing, he launched himself at her, swinging the knife upwards. Tamasin yelled to wake Valeria as she pivoted sharply to the left to avoid the blow. The knife whistled past, slicing shirt but not flesh. The momentum of missing his target brought the assassin slightly forward. That was enough for Tamasin. With a quick stab, she sank the blade deep into his right side. When he staggered, she plunged the other into his throat. With a gurgling screech, he collapsed to the floor.

She stood over him and kicked the weapon out of his hand. Before she could examine the body, it disintegrated into swirling particles, until there were only a dead crow and the knife left on the floor. Tamasin spun around to find Valeria staring at her. After she sheathed her knives, she sank onto the edge of the bed. "Thank the Goddess I was in time. I saw him enter the palace in a dream," she said in a low voice, then turned to the direction of the door at the sound of boots thumping down the hall.

Three guards burst into the room with their weapons drawn. The most senior, a lieutenant's insignia on her shoulder pad, darted her eyes around the room before approaching the bed. "Are you all right, Your Majesty?"

Tamasin rose to her feet quickly. "She is now. She was very nearly assassinated. There's been magic here. We'll talk about it in the daylight. In the meantime, post guards outside the royal chambers until we understand what we're dealing with. In the morning, take that bird and knife to Mistress Moira, Lieutenant. If you'll excuse us, I'd like to talk to the Queen."

The soldier's expression tightened. "Who might you be to give me orders? I haven't seen you here before."

Valeria spoke for the first time, "You're new here, Lieutenant. She's the Mistress of Dreams and also my wife."

Red flushed across the guard's face. "I beg your pardon, Your Majesty." With a wave to a soldier, she pointed at the knife and the bird. "Collect those before we go."

When the door closed behind them, Valeria said, "I fear that assassination attempt was only the beginning of things to come. The world has grown restless this last year."

"I know. We have to talk."

"I've missed your counsel dreadfully." Valeria's eyes filled. "Why did you even bother saving me, Tam? I've treated you badly."

"Because I love you, Val, and always will. But if you don't want me, say so, and I will quietly disappear. I can't take this life I'm living anymore. Seeing you and not being able to touch you."

Valeria pulled her chemise over her head and threw back the bed covers. "Take off your clothes and join me. I'll just have to let you know how much I want you. I'll make you forget about that little wench you brought home."

Tamasin stripped off with a smile. "You can't seriously be jealous of Savannah?"

"Well… just a little."

"Really?" Tamasin took her in her arms and ghosted kisses down her neck. "Hmm… you smell so nice. Like home." She gently ran her hands down her back, then cupped a breast. When her lips were claimed urgently, it sent the blood singing through Tamasin's veins.

Valeria grasped her hair, pulling her head up to look at her face. "I don't want gentle, Tam. I want you to claim me, devour me. I have been waiting too long to be taken like a virtuous maiden."

Wordlessly, Tamasin pushed her onto her back and straddled her. The long years of forced abstinence fell away as she gazed into the dark eyes that were nearly black with passion. Desire shone in the depths like a beacon beckoning her home. Tamasin let herself go. With her lips and teeth, she began to rediscover all those special spots that she knew would send her lover wild. As Valeria thrashed and writhed beneath her, Tamasin pushed her relentlessly toward her climax.

When Valeria squirmed frantically and finally screamed out her name, a wave of exquisite pleasure rushed through Tamasin too.

Wanting her lover to realize how desperately she had missed her, Tamasin began again before the last contraction faded until she brought her yet again to a longer, fiercer height.

When her second orgasm hit, Valeria babbled incoherently as she rode it out. But after the waves ebbed away, she began to weep.

Anguish swept through Tamasin. The only time she'd ever seen the Queen cry was at her mother's funeral. Even in their most private times, she had never shed tears. Anger yes, but never tears. She cuddled her in her arms and kissed the top of her head. "Hey, love, don't. Please. I'm sorry."

"Why did you leave?" Valeria whispered.

"I was ordered to in a dream. And I was to tell no one, not even you, that I was going. Believe me, this dream I couldn't ignore." She pulled her tighter. "I missed you, Val, more than you'd ever know. Some days I'd ache so badly for you it was like my heart was being ripped out."

"Then why didn't you come home, even for a few days if you couldn't for longer? Or at least tell me you were alive," came the agonizing cry.

"Because I couldn't. I had no way of getting back through the portal until my quest was completed."

Abruptly, Valeria pulled out of her arms and sat up. "You went into the other world? No one's done that for three centuries. We lost the key to the portal when the Circle of Sheda disappeared." Wide-eyed, she stared at Tamasin. "You found it?"

Tamasin smiled. "I'm home, aren't I?"

"Where is it?"

"It's hidden away until we need it."

"We must find a Chosen One to wield it," exclaimed Valeria.

"Ah...about that. We have not interpreted the process properly. Everybody presumed that the noblest and the strongest warrior won the right to wear the medallion. I'm afraid that's not strictly true. Sure the process was followed, probably more for show, but it is the Circle of Sheda that chooses who wears it."

Valeria looked at her suspiciously. "You're not the Chosen One, are you?"

"No. I was sent to find it."

"Then it should be simple enough to gather our finest warriors together and it can pick one."

Tamasin cleared her throat. "Um...we had no say in the matter. The bearer has already been chosen."

"Really. That was quick. Can you—" Valeria stopped, her eyes narrowing. "Noooo...it's not possible. But that would explain why she wasn't affected by Ursula's cape."

"Yep. Savannah. And you sent her to Pela."

"Gad! Why didn't you speak up?"

Tamasin threw up her hands. "You wouldn't listen or have you conveniently forgotten? And all because you were jealous of a slip of a woman fifteen years my junior."

A spark flashed in Valeria's eyes. "Yes...about that. Any more talk of things outside this bed will have to wait. I have yet to show you that no woman who touches you, has any idea what real passion means."

Tamasin's pulse began to pound. Oh, Gods, she wanted this.

A blistering heat flooded through her as Valeria ghosted her lips down her neck. As she succumbed to the sensations, it brought to the surface all those lonely days of her unwanted celibacy. Her body that had craved so long for this woman's touch burst into flames. As her arousal soared, she nearly wept with the pleasure of it. When Valeria bent down to bring her to her climax, she came immediately, unable to stop the scream that erupted from her very soul.

Completely spent, she flopped back on the bed. She smiled up at Valeria, who gazed down at her smugly. "You've just killed me, my love," Tamasin murmured.

Her eyes sagged and she drifted into sleep.

✝

The dream came at dawn. This time there was no urgency as she floated languidly into another realm. As soon as she was there, she knew that this wasn't a seer's dream—she was actually in the Dream World. She gazed about. It was a topsy-turvy place, the sky an iridescent green, the grass a cornflower blue, the flowers all colors of the rainbow. She stood in the middle of the field, where glorious white horses circled above her in the sky. She laughed, calling to her Dreamer sisters to come. It was too beautiful to miss.

Before long they began to drift in. Slowly at first, then like an incoming tide. As they arrived, she greeted them and asked their names. Soon a thousand Dreamers surrounded her, their hands joined in fellowship.

She looked over the sea of faces, and stretching her arms wide, called out, "Dreamers, I am Tamasin Epona, the Mistress of Dreams, and Consort to the Supreme Monarch of Rand. I've come to tell you the Queen calls you, my friends. You are needed again. I am reforming the Guild. Who will answer the call?"

As one, a cry went up, "I will."

"Then be ready. For those able to leave their families, I ask you to come in two weeks to a training camp. I will tell you in a week where it will be. I will send my horses to take you there." She waved to them. "Farewell, until we meet again. Remember…it is the time for we Dreamers once again."

✝

Tamasin opened her eyes to see bright sunlight streaming through the open window. Contentedly, she looked over at Valeria half-sprawled over her. She was toying with the idea of waking her up for more loving when there was a tap on the door. Without waiting for an answer, a maid bustled in carrying a breakfast tray. With a desperate lunge, Tamasin grabbed the sheet and yanked it over them. By the shocked look on the young woman's face, she hadn't been quick enough.

Like a skittish deer, she edged inside, put the tray on the table beside the door, and turned to flee.

"Francine," Valeria called out.

The maid froze, her head bowed.

"Bring up another breakfast, please."

"Yes, Your Majesty," she squeaked, curtsied, then ran out.

Valeria chuckled. "In ten minutes the whole palace will be aware you're back in the marital bed."

"No doubt. I'd better get dressed before she comes back," Tamasin said, grinning. "I trust you haven't thrown out my clothes."

"They're all there, but I was tempted to when I banished you to the stables."

"Huh! You're going to have to make that up to me. The worst place I've ever had to sleep." She threw her legs over the side of the bed. "After we eat, could you come down with me to see Moira, Val? She's been working on the historical documents. I'll bring you up to date there about what's been happening."

Valeria's face took on a serious expression. "A few of the royal houses are reporting some unrest. I haven't been unduly worried, but after the attempt on my life, I had better take note."

"Something bad is coming. That is why the Circle of Sheda has reappeared. What it is exactly, we have no idea, but Moira thinks it's happened in the past. A long way back. And we must be ready."

Chapter Ten

Falcon's Keep

Savannah's legs felt as if they would give out any second.

On the way back from the amphitheater, she wondered how she was going to get through the next weeks. It was only her first training session and she was exhausted.

Pela had put her through the two-hour-long workout herself. Though the exercises were simple at first, they had become progressively more complicated. Savannah had drawn a lot of curious glances on arrival, quite a few of which were hostile, but once she'd started training, she'd ceased noticing or even caring. It had taken all her concentration just to keep up with Pela. She had been a hard taskmaster, making her learn every maneuver before moving on to the next. In the two hours, she'd only been allowed one brief break. By the time the session was over, Savannah had never hated anyone as much, and longed to wipe the smug look off her face.

As she turned to go home, Pela called out, "Lunch is at noon. Be there to serve me."

Scowling, Savannah dragged her aching bones back to the house.

Once inside, she flopped into the armchair, thankful she'd already thoroughly cleaned the house. Her arms were so tired, she doubted she could lift the broom, let alone sweep. After heating a big pot of water, she soaked in the bath, then spent the rest of the morning on her back. When the dinner gong reverberated over the camp, she gingerly climbed up off her mat.

The big mess hall was already full. She wondered where she was expected to collect Pela's meal, then saw it was a buffet. Two long wooden tables loaded with platters of meats, cheeses, fruits, and loaves of bread were lined up at the back of the hall. On the diners' tables were jugs of a brown liquid which she presumed was either apple cider or ale. In a place so isolated, these beverages would keep far better than milk.

She spied Pela sitting with five women at a smaller table away from the crowd. She surmised her companions were instructors rather than students—the Commander wasn't likely to fraternize with the rank and file. As she neared them, she recognized the four soldiers from the Howling Wolf. Killia also was eating at their table. They candidly appraised Savannah, though when Pela didn't introduce her, they remained silent.

Pela barely glanced at her. "You're late," she grunted.

"Sorry, you don't have a clock."

"What's a clock?" asked Killia.

Savannah squirmed. *Oops!* If she wasn't careful, Pela would become suspicious. She was nobody's fool. "Um...that's what my village used to call a...um...sundial," she said.

"Any fool should be able to tell the time by the moons," interrupted Pela. "Now...I'm waiting for my meal. The serving girl has it ready."

Savannah felt a niggle of annoyance. Really? It would have been far easier for the girl to just bring it over without all this hoo-ha.

"Of course, Commander."

When Savannah arrived back with the plate, Pela ordered, "Stand behind me. When our glasses are empty, you're to fill them."

"I would rather tip it over you," Savannah muttered under her breath. From the stiffening of Pela's shoulders, it was clear she'd caught the whispered words. Savannah vowed to be more careful in the future—the woman had eyes and ears like a hawk.

For the next half hour, she attended to their drinks while trying to ignore the curious stares from the diners. When the mess hall cleared, Pela swept off without a word, leaving Savannah to make her way to the kitchen for her lunch.

Lyn looked up at her sympathetically when she reached their table. "You must be dying to sit down."

"I am," said Savannah wearily. "Standing around in the mess was the last straw after the workout at the amphitheater this morning. I shall have to get fitter if I'm going to last the distance."

"Then you'd better make sure you eat properly," replied Lyn, handing her a plate.

"Thanks," said Savannah. But even though there was a good variety of bread, meat, and vegetables, she'd lost her appetite. She made her excuses to go as soon as she could, immensely grateful that Pela didn't come in until the night meal. Seeing her again so soon would have been the last straw. She had no idea how she was going to put up with her in the coming months.

Once out of the public eye, Savannah brushed away the tears that had escaped down her cheeks. Whatever way she looked at it, her situation seemed hopeless. Not only was she at Pela's beck and call, but she was also expected to be a crackerjack athlete like the other trainees. That she wasn't and never would be. And since Tamasin was in banishment, Savannah might never get off this awful place.

She kicked off her shoes, stretched out in an armchair, and forced herself to look at it logically. The old blind woman would hardly leave the Chosen One to rot here. If the old girl could arrange to get her onto the dig in Algeria, it would be no problem to fly her to safety away from Falcon's Keep when the time was right. Feeling much better after that reasoning, Savannah picked up her book and became emersed in *The Flora and Fauna of Rand*. She didn't skip a page, aware she would need the knowledge if she was going to survive in this world. God knows, there were plenty of weird things running around out there. And with the medallion around her neck, she would have plenty of enemies of the two-legged kind.

In the meantime, she'd have to be a lot smarter when it came to Pela. Tamasin had said not to show fear and she had been right. Savannah knew Pela's ploy was intimidation. She'd just have to beat her at her own game. After giving it some thought, she concluded that the best way to handle her was simply to 'turn the other cheek'. Let her bullying fall on deaf ears. One of them would break in the end, and she figured she could outlast her. One thing she understood about the Commander, her fuse was as short as the Queen's.

Savannah was waiting for Pela when she arrived at the mess for dinner. Brightly smiling, she filled her cup before going off to fetch her meal. When she arrived back with the overflowing plate, she arranged it carefully in front of her. "There you go, Commander," she said solicitously. "Enjoy."

Pela's expression didn't change, but it brought a smile from the handsome guard from the bar at the inn. "Hello there, Savannah. I'm Rhiannon. You look very fetching tonight."

Savannah flashed her a coy smile. "Why thank you, Rhiannon. That's very sweet of you. Would you like me to fetch your meal?" She congratulated herself— this was a perfect way to annoy Pela. "What about you other ladies?" she asked, though her smile didn't extend to Killia. The way that woman looked at her could only be described as predatory.

Pela glowered. "You will do only what *I* say, Savannah."

She bowed her head. "I'm sorry, Commander. I was only trying to be nice to your friends."

"Oh, lighten up, Pel," Rhiannon said. "Leave her alone. If you don't want her, I'd be only too happy for some home help."

Savannah inwardly groaned. *Yeah, right.* She knew the type of 'home-help' that woman wanted. She waited for Pela's reaction. It was her perfect opportunity to get rid of Savannah—the Queen would never hear she'd palmed her off to her friend. Strangely though, she suddenly realized she didn't want Pela to do that. And she had no idea why not.

"Aren't you forgetting the cardinal rule here, Rhi? No servants in the quarters. As much as I'd like her to go, I'm stuck with her. Queen's orders," replied Pela, shrugging.

"Since when have you taken notice of Valeria?" growled Killia.

"Never. That's all I'm going to say on the matter." She cast a look around the table. "There is an issue I want to discuss. Lately, there are reports of unrest in the provinces. Nothing major, but I want you all to be vigilant. Increase the night guards, please Killia."

Rhiannon paused cutting her meat to look at her. "You're worried?"

"Maybe. I have a gut feeling that I shouldn't be ignoring it."

Killia curled her lips. "There'd be no one stupid enough to attack Falcon's Keep. Our warning systems would pick them up long before they landed."

"Nevertheless, put three extra guards on," Pela ordered, an edge to her voice. "The Keep may seem invulnerable, but it pays to be sure."

Savannah listened with interest. If Pela was tightening her defenses, it probably meant she was working on more than a hunch. She wondered what she knew. There may be dispatches in her office. Savannah resolved to search tomorrow, and if she found anything, there should be a way of getting the information to Tamasin. Yesterday, a merchant from Chesterton was going to give her a ride out, which meant they came and went frequently. All she had to do was slip one of them a message for Godfrey to pass on.

She stifled a yawn. If they didn't hurry up she'd be asleep on her feet and she needed to eat. Missing lunch hadn't been such a good idea. It was time to go.

"May I fill your tankard, Rhiannon?" she said, leaning over her until her chest was only inches away from the soldier's shoulder.

Rhiannon's eyes gleamed. "Thanks."

"My pleasure," murmured Savannah. As she straightened, she caught Justine's eye in the crowd and waved. "There's Justine," she said enthusiastically.

"Get your dinner and go home," snapped Pela, then as Savannah turned to go, added, "And since you were so happy to see Justine, I shall pair you with her in a one-on-one combat session tomorrow morning. I suggest you get a good night's sleep."

"That sounds like super fun," Savannah replied calmly and hurried off to the kitchen.

†

With less bravado than last night, Savannah made her way to the amphitheater. Since she'd already had one reprieve this morning, she knew she wasn't going to get another. There had been no sign of Pela when she woke, only a note on the table that she wouldn't be required for breakfast. As she made her way down through the rows of stone seating, she watched the Elite Guard trainees going through their paces. They were all so big and fit. Even with their hands tied behind their backs, any of these warriors could knock her down. Perhaps it was easier just to give up and go home. But once she caught Pela signaling impatiently to join her, there was no going back.

She smiled timidly at Justine, who stood ramrod straight beside Pela. Her expression didn't waver, merely acknowledging Savannah with a small nod.

"You will be sparring together for the two-hour session," said Pela. "Justine… you will show this new recruit the basic maneuvers of self-defense, and you will not hold back."

Justine snapped her heels together. "Yes, Commander."

"Take your places," came the order.

Savannah copied the guard's stance, facing her and spreading her legs slightly apart.

"Begin."

With a smooth, well-rehearsed action, Justine moved swiftly at her. Flailing her arms desperately to defend herself, Savannah tried to wrestle. She didn't have a hope. Easily, Justine flipped her off her feet and laid her flat on her back.

"Again, and balance yourself as I taught you yesterday," ordered Pela.

Savannah got up, dusting herself down before facing Justine.

She hit the dirt again.

And again. Savannah groaned. That fall had hurt.

With her hands on her hips, Pela looked down at her sprawled on the ground. "By the Goddess, woman, you're hopeless. I'm going to give you a demonstration, so take note."

Savannah crawled to her feet, pleased to have a respite but dubious. No matter how many demonstrations, she knew she could never match any of them.

Pela indicated to Justine to take her position. They began to grapple, but this time, it was Justine who was outclassed. Savannah could only gaze in admiration at the sheer strength and precision that Pela exhibited to dispatch her opponent. She may be hard and uncompromising, but she was magnificent in action. Justine was on the ground in less than fifteen seconds.

"Take her through a few exercises and then start again," Pela ordered and moved off to supervise a pair further down.

Savannah gritted her teeth, pushing back the pain as she thrust and parried.

After the hour, they were allowed a five-minute break. Grasping the neck of the water skin, she drank deeply, only stopping when Justine pulled at her arm. "Go easy. You'll make yourself sick."

"I'm parched," she gasped out, but reluctantly put it down.

"It's only natural you're thirsty. But you won't be able to continue if you become bloated. The Commander will give you hell."

Savannah snorted. "What's it matter? You're too big for me. I haven't a hope."

"Then you'll have to learn to use your wiles. Look closely. There are ways to fight if you're smaller. Study at night. There're books in the camp library that teach techniques."

"Only if I get through today," groaned Savannah. "I'm aching, and my back's killing me."

Justine gave her a gentle nudge. "I'll go easy this session."

"Thanks," Savannah said gratefully.

Before she could say anything more, Pela's bark pierced the air. "To your places, recruits."

For the next thirty minutes, as they fought, Justine's blows slid off without really landing. When she occasionally threw Savannah to the ground, she made sure she fell without landing hard. But just when Savannah thought she'd make it unscathed through the session, Pela appeared beside them.

She glared at Justine. "Step aside. I'll deal with you later." She gestured to an older soldier behind them. "Take over."

"Yes, Commander."

This time there was no quarter given. After a brief tussle, Savannah was hurled face down into the ground. She lay there winded for a moment, then spat out the dirt and climbed to her feet. The next second, she was sliding across the ground on her bottom. When she got up this time, she rushed the soldier, slamming into her stomach. For her efforts, the woman roughly tossed her aside. Awkwardly bouncing onto her hip, she couldn't stifle a scream of agony. Her head spinning, she focused to see everyone had stopped to watch. Someone called out, "Stay down."

Savannah desperately wanted to. But a sixth sense told her that if she did, she would lose the respect of every warrior in the Keep. Slowly, Savannah struggled upright. She wiped the dirt away from her face with her arm, took a deep breath, and croaked. "Come on. Hit me again if it makes you happy, asshole."

Suddenly, the gong sounded across the training ground, signaling the end of the session. The recruits immediately ceased their maneuvers and walked over to sit down. Savannah knew if she sat she might never get up, so she summoned her strength for the walk home.

She had only taken one step when Pela appeared at her side. "You may be excused this lunch."

At the words, Savannah halted abruptly. Without turning to look at her, she replied in a voice laced with bitterness, "I never asked for any special favors, Commander, and I'm not starting now. I'll be there at noon."

Chapter Eleven

After three weeks, Savannah no longer dreaded the training sessions.

She found it had become progressively easier as her strength and confidence grew. Her newfound resilience she attributed not only to physical exercise but studying combat techniques as well. At night, she hid the book away, fearing Pela's ridicule at having to resort to written explanations and diagrams rather than catching on at the demonstrations. She'd never again been subjected to that harsh second lesson, though she knew the day would come again when she would have to face an opponent in real combat. But for the time being, Pela seemed content for her to just practice.

On the surface, her relationship with Pela had settled into a stalemate: Pela only spoke to her when she had to, and Savannah remained silent unless spoken to. But underneath, Savannah was becoming aware that something untoward was happening. At night, she would look up suddenly to find Pela studying her. Pela would look away quickly, clearly embarrassed at being caught. And as much as she tried not to, Savannah couldn't keep her eyes wandering to Pela in the training arena. She was as graceful as a big cat and just as lethal.

Yesterday, Savannah had even joined the crowd of recruits to watch the instructors dueling. They were all extraordinary fighters, but none were in Pela's class. From her studies in biology and human behavior, Savannah knew such a deadly grace was most likely inherited not taught. She resolved to find out her background—if anyone had the information, it would be Rhiannon. She doubted Pela would confide in many people.

She was aware, though, that she had to be careful with Rhiannon. The warrior was making it very plain she was interested in her, and she was used to getting what she wanted. While it would be an advantage to have a warrior protecting her in her Chosen One role, she didn't do anything for Savannah's libido, and she couldn't make herself even contemplate it. She had no idea why not—the woman was the very definition of charming and handsome.

Because the next two days were rest days on the Keep, Pela had asked her to scribe for her. It was the first time and she was looking forward to the activity. Not only because this work was more familiar territory, but she might learn a few things she could pass on to Tamasin. She imagined not many people would be privy to Pela's documents. During her house-cleaning duties, Savannah had poked around the office. Having found nothing of note, she figured the important documents were in the locked drawers.

Pela was already in her office when she arrived after breakfast. Charts, drawings, and scrolls were spread over the wooden desk. They weren't paper, but a parchment made from some sort of stretched animal skin. She smiled at the sight of quills and inkpots on the tabletop. A far cry from her laptop.

The cook had sent over lunch, enabling them to work through the day without interruption. Once Pela realized Savannah was a competent scribe and quick learner, she became an entirely different person. As well as answering Savannah's questions, she explained her military tactics in detail. The day was the first time she was treated as Pela's equal. She savored the moment, aware it wouldn't last into the next week.

When all the scrolls were packed away, to her surprise, Pela said, "I have a jug of mead in the cupboard. Would you like a glass?"

"I'd like that, thanks," Savannah answered, pleased.

"We'll go out on the porch…it's pleasant out there this time of evening."

When she returned with the glasses, Savannah took a sip, debating what to say. They'd never had a conversation the whole time she'd been there. What did one say to this taciturn woman? So she plunged right in and said, "I have no idea what to talk about with you, Commander."

To her surprise, Pela laughed. "I don't blame you. I've tried to scare you away for over three weeks, but you refuse to go. So I figure if we're going to live together, then it'd be better if we talked occasionally. And call me Pela while we're at home."

Savannah looked at her curiously. "If I may ask, why don't you want help in the house? It must make your life easier."

"I have my reasons. One I won't discuss, and the other…well, the only reason Valeria wants to send me someone is to keep an eye on me."

"You're right. I imagine she has spies everywhere. Tell me, Pela, why did she order Ursula to put the cape on you?"

"I was only eighteen when I came to Iona to apply to be an Elite Guard. I'd left my family, which didn't go down well with my father. He told me never to come back home. When I got there, I was an angry young woman. To cut a long story short, one of the palace guards made fun of my tattoos, so I beat her up. I suppose I was put under the cape and not in the brig because I had potential as a warrior. Ursula wanted me banished even when I lasted so long. But Tamasin defied the witch, persuading Valeria to let me enter the Elite Guards' training camp." Pela's composure barely flickered except for a tightening of her lips. "I've hated that Silverthorne Witch ever since."

"I don't blame you. And you became Commander in how long?" Savannah asked.

"Eight years."

Impressed, Savannah glanced across at her with a warm smile. "Your father would be proud of you," she murmured.

Pela looked at her curiously. "Not many people would look at it that way. You're not like anyone I've ever met, Savannah. Where are you from?"

"A long way from here. And that is all I can tell you at the moment." She smiled at Pela to soften the words. "Like you, I have secrets I must keep."

"Ah… I'm guessing Tamasin has asked you to be silent. I heard this week from a merchant that she's back in the Queen's bed."

Savannah jerked upright. "That's wonderful news."

"They say," said Pela, eyeing her closely over the rim of the glass, "that she saved Valeria from an assassin's knife."

"Oh my God. Really? Who was it? Tamasin said that—" She broke off and eyed Pela skeptically. "You're pumping me for information." She irritably waved at their mugs, "Was this just a way to get me to spill my secrets?"

"No. But I'm curious." When Savannah went to rise, she said quickly, "I've never had anyone in my home before. I'd like you to stay and talk to me. It's nice to have company."

"You've never even had a lover stay for a while?" The words just popped out of Savannah, and she regretted them immediately. Pela would have every right to be annoyed.

Instead, Pela shuffled in her seat and muttered. "Women don't find me attractive."

Surprised at the bald statement, Savannah tilted her head to look at her. "Hey, don't be so down on yourself. You have a great body." She peered closer, then added, "In fact, you're quite nice looking once you get past the hairdo and tattoos. Maybe all you need to do is smile a bit more. Or learn a few good moves."

When Pela just stared at her, Savannah realized what she had said and gulped her mead. "Sorry. Me and my big mouth. Just forget I said all that."

"I doubt I'll be able to," Pela said, chuckling. "Methinks there was a compliment under all of it."

Savannah broke into a laugh too. "Perhaps we can help each other out. You're teaching me to fight, so I'll teach you how to charm the ladies."

Pela looked disconcerted for a moment, then a gleam flashed in her eye. "It's a deal. Since this is a day off, the instructors leave the Keep, and the recruits usually party. No sit-down eating, only baskets of food. Would you like to see my special place while we eat?"

Savannah felt a flush of pleasure. "There'd be nothing I'd like better," she answered shyly.

"Then come on. We'll pick up a hamper on the way."

The *special* place turned out to be a seemingly impossible climb to the top of a rocky outcrop at the end of Falcon's Keep. Pela was like a mountain goat as she guided and cajoled her up the sheer face. Even carrying the picnic basket, it was no effort for her. Savannah doubted she could have managed if she hadn't given her a hand at the most difficult spots. When they reached the small recess on the top, Savannah was immediately reminded of an eagle's eerie and wondered if there'd been falcons here in the past. The place just seemed somewhere made for birds, not people.

She sat contentedly as she took in the spectacular view. There was a wildness about the place that stirred her blood. They were so high up that she could see across the rugged, desolate mountain range to the horizon beyond. As the sun sank, the twin moons became brighter, turning into rich purple globes in the sky, and pinks and reds spread over the faraway escapements.

"You like it?" whispered Pela in her ear. They were close together in the small space, but it didn't feel uncomfortable. It felt right.

"It's wonderful," she breathed back. So beautiful she was nearly speechless. "Up here on the roof of the world, it feels like a sanctuary. No wonder you love the place."

Pela chuckled. "Birds of prey fly up here, but you're more a little dove."

"Don't knock doves. They're cute," said Savannah with a smile. She pointed a finger toward the setting sun. "What's... out there?" She was going to say *west* but stopped in time. In this world, she had no idea if the sun set in the west. And even though the sun rose and set, the two moons remained visible in the sky, merely dimming in daylight.

"We are in the Iron Mountains. The earth is so desolate in the canyons between the peaks that only the hardiest vegetation can survive.

Creatures live down there you never want to meet. Things that prefer darkness and only roam at night."

Savannah shivered. "Do they come up here?"

"No. It's too far up."

"That's a relief. So what's past the range?" Savannah asked, then added, "I come from a tiny isolated village and have little knowledge of the world at large."

Pela glanced at her curiously but didn't ask her to elaborate. "The peaks you can see in the distance are called the Whispering Tips. The Moaning Pass takes you down into the Valley of the Pipers. It is the realm of King Gerard, cousin to Queen Valeria. And beyond his palace is the Windy Desert."

Savannah chuckled. "A lot of blowing going on."

Pela burst into laughter. "And Gerard is an old windbag." She passed over a slice of meat and a wedge of crusty bread. "In the East are the most fertile lands on Rand: Iona plus three Realms with Kings and seven with Queens. To the South, five Realms, and there are vast lands beyond the Wide Sea of Mists. North are fertile lands to the edges of the Great Forests. Past them are the Forgotten Realms."

"Why are they called Forgotten?"

"Because," Pela's voice took on a faraway note, "it is a land full of magical creatures who have chosen to live apart from the world of woman and man. They want people to forget about them. There're magicians here, but these creatures don't just practice it, they are the magic themselves."

"Have you been there?" whispered Savannah in awe. Somehow it seemed like a hallowed place.

"Yes. It's a special place."

"Is it beautiful? I would love to see it."

"You wouldn't be welcome, Savannah. You're not magical."

She felt a wave of disappointment. "Oh! That's a shame. I guess people must have hurt them in the past."

"They did," said Pela. "Eat up and tell me about yourself. How did you manage to learn to read in an isolated place?"

Savannah racked her brains for an answer, then figured she should stick to the truth as much as she could. "My parents were healers. My mother was from a wealthy family, and she met my father at a country fair. She taught me."

"Do you have any knowledge of apothecary?"

"Some," replied Savannah. "She taught me a lot of healing techniques. What about you? Where did you learn to write?"

"I taught myself."

"Really?" exclaimed Savannah, impressed. "You must be smart."

Pela looked at her slyly. "Smarter than you."

"Ha! Don't bet on it."

A smile glimmered in Pela's eyes. "Come on, eat up. We'll need some light to descend."

"Right," said Savannah, quickly swallowing the last of her cheese. "Okay," she announced. "I'm ready."

Pela laughed. "I won't let you fall."

The descent could have been scarier, but Pela held her hand tightly. As they walked back through the grazing commons, Savannah forgot to let it go. A pretty mare telepathed a saucy comment as they passed, and with a click of her tongue, Savannah waved her finger at her.

"Why are you waving at Sunflower?" asked Pela.

"Didn't you hear what she said? That mare is so cheeky."

Pela stopped dead in her tracks. "You can talk to the horses?"

"I sense how all the horses are feeling, but only Sunflower, Firefly, Shade, and a couple of others can talk to me. Can't you?"

"No."

"Oh!"

Pela stared at her. "I've never heard of anyone that could."

"Really? Hmm...that's odd."

"They're Malkia's progeny. Can you speak to him?" Pela asked, her eyes boring into hers.

"Oh, yes. He has a sense of humor. Is he different from the other horses?"

"He's from the line of the great Blue Fjord horses. When Tamasin was only eighteen, she went into the Forgotten Realms and brought him home to be the Queen's stallion."

"That's—" Savannah jammed her mouth shut when Killia came round the corner.

The captain stopped, a dark frown settling on her face when she dropped her eyes to their joined hands. Immediately, they both let go.

"You didn't go into Chesterton?" Pela asked, ignoring the displeasure on Killia's face.

Killia swept her gaze over Savannah. "No. I chose not to pick up a whore tonight."

The hairs on the back of Savannah's neck bristled. It was quite clear she was inferring she was Pela's whore.

Pela didn't react but merely said, "I'll see you at dinner tomorrow night."

But as they moved off, Pela didn't reach for her hand again.

Savannah knew she shouldn't be disappointed, but she was.

Chapter Twelve

Savannah's life in the Keep would have continued in the same vein if it hadn't been for the accident at practice two weeks later. The strict training regime that Pela enforced kept injuries down to a minimum, but there was always that odd time when someone was hurt. At the beginning of the second session, Justine, wrestling in a full body-lock, let out an agonizing scream.

When Rhiannon ran over to her, Savannah followed her closely. Justine, her face ashen, was sitting on the ground, clutching her arm. It only took one look to see the shoulder was dislocated.

Rhiannon squatted down beside the wounded recruit, and after a quick examination, yelled, "Quickly. Get Pela. It's her shoulder. She's back at the camp in the meeting house."

"I can help," Savannah said and knelt beside her.

Rhiannon looked at her in surprise. "You know how to fix her arm?"

"It's dislocated. I'm a healer. I've helped my mother with this injury." She hoped that sounded plausible. She could hardly tell them she had an advanced certificate in civilian medic training, a course her father had insisted she take to prepare her for isolated places.

Rhiannon glanced at Justine, who appeared ready to pass out. "Are you game?"

Justine gritted her teeth and nodded.

"Okay," said Savannah keeping her voice calm. "I want you to lie on your back and try to relax. Take deep breaths." When she judged her settled, she looked across at Rhiannon. "Hold her still." She smiled at Justine as she said soothingly, "This is going to hurt like hell, but that will be the end of it."

Slowly, she pulled the dislocated arm out to the side, dragged it over her head, rotated the hand down, and then pulled the arm across to the other shoulder. When the joint popped back into place, immediately Justine cried with relief.

Savannah silently gave one too. It had been a while since she'd done that maneuver. "We have to bind the arm to immobilize it."

"There's cloth here for bandages. I'll fetch the box," said Rhiannon.

When Pela ran in, Justine's arm was already in a sling and secured. She gave Savannah a nod of approval. "It seems we have a healer now in the camp."

"I'd like to help," Savannah said.

Pela called out to the women milling around. "The show's over… back to training." She turned to Rhiannon. "Savannah can stay on light exercises. Teach her how to use a sword and knife, but no combat. She's more valuable to us as a healer. We could run a clinic for an hour twice a week."

Rhiannon raised an eyebrow. "You're going to coddle her?"

"It only makes sense long term. We lose too many with injuries. I'll have to get back to work. I'll see you both at lunch."

When she disappeared, Rhiannon gave her a quizzical glance. "She's different around you."

"Since she can't get rid of me, she's decided it would be easier for us to live together if we were friendlier."

"Just expect not to get too close. Pela has always been a loner. I'm her best friend, but she's never shared much."

"Where's she from?"

"She hasn't talked about anything before joining the service. We were recruits together, so we were close as she'll let anyone get," Rhiannon told her.

"Has she had many lovers?" Savannah asked, trying to sound off-handed.

Rhiannon flashed her a knowing look. "Soooo… that's why I'm not getting anywhere with you. You like the Commander?"

"Oh, please. After how she's treated me? I'd have to be mad."

"It wouldn't do you any good even if you wanted her. She's never been interested in anyone. And believe me, when we were younger, many tried to get her attention."

"No one? That's hard to believe."

Rhiannon shrugged. "She told me once she was waiting for the one that was coming." She leaned close to Savannah. "But *I'm* available."

"C'mon, Rhiannon, just accept facts. I'm not interested in pursuing anything, no matter how charming you think yourself?"

Rhiannon eyed her in surprise. "You're into men? I didn't read that."

"No. I prefer women. But I'm just an ordinary person who wants to meet someone nice and caring, who likes the same things I do and is fun. Not some conceited goddess." Savannah winced at the words coming out of her mouth. If anything would turn Rhiannon off, that would. It sounded like a lame profile on an internet dating site. And nothing like what she secretly yearned. She'd always wanted an Amazon to sweep her off her feet. And here she was knocking her back.

"Well, that's a challenge. One I'm up for. Now, I'd better get back to work. You're excused for the rest of the session to escort our wounded soldier back to the barracks."

As Savannah watched her go, one sentence resounded in her mind: *She was waiting for the one that was coming.* She thought back to the old seer's words: *Your love waits for you.* Was it just a coincidence? She was beginning to like Pela, but love? Surely not. And apart from that, Pela had played her for a fool. If Rhiannon was to be believed, Pela's pathetic statement that she'd never had a lover because women didn't find her attractive was a big fat lie. Savannah pursed her lips. She wasn't going to be so gullible again, and she'd teach her a lesson.

At lunch, she was standing in her customary place behind Pela when she spied Cian, a pretty kitchen maid, bringing a jug to one of the tables. She signaled to her to come over, then reached for Pela's cup. She whispered in her ear as she straightened up. "Cian likes to have a good time. Smile at her."

"The Commander would like some ale, thanks, Cian," Savannah said when the maid reached them.

Pela looked around and bared her teeth, which sent Cian scurrying off as soon as she filled the cup.

Surprisingly, Killia helped her cause, though Savannah knew that she was motivated by dislike. "She'd be a nice little plaything for you, Pela."

Pela ignored her and kept eating.

"Why not," urged Rhiannon. "You deserve some relaxation."

"She's all yours," Pela said, not looking up from her plate.

"Oh, I've already sampled that one," Rhiannon replied smugly.

Savannah's anger rose. *Conceited ass!* How dare she treat the girl like that. Stepping forward, she leaned over to fill Rhiannon's cup, deliberately missed, and poured it into her lap.

Leaping to her feet, the guard snapped, "Watch what you're doing."

"Sorry, Lieutenant, but where I come from, we don't kiss and tell."

Killia pushed back her chair, her eyes flashing. "You're getting too big for your boots for a servant. She doesn't belong here, Pela. Get rid of her." She looked across to the other two instructors at the table for support. They ignored her and continued eating.

"Sit down, both of you," ordered Pela in a low, deadly voice. A shiver ghosted across Savannah's skin. The command was given in a tone nobody could ignore. For the first time, she came to realize just what control this woman had over her soldiers. She completely dominated them. "Get some dinner and go home, Savannah. I will deal with you later."

There was no argument from her. She fled.

She was on her mat pretending to be asleep when Pela came in three hours later. She heard her moving around in the bathroom, then the lights went out, and she heard shuffling.

Savannah snuck a look at her through lowered lids. Moonbeams filtered through the open window, bathing the room in a soft glow. Pela was stripping off her uniform. Savannah knew she should shut her eyes to give her privacy, but she couldn't stop watching her. When she was completely naked, Savannah sucked in a sharp breath. Pela's back was completely covered in intricate, delicate patterns that were candescent in the moonlight. She had never seen anything so unusual or stunning.

At the sound, Pela whirled round. Her torso was covered in ink as well. "I'm aware you're awake, Savannah."

Savannah opened her eyes and sat up. "Um…yes, I am."

Pela turned back to put on her nightshirt. "Now you know what I look like, go to sleep."

"They're so beautiful," Savannah whispered.

"I don't want to discuss it."

"Why? The design is spectacular." She rose to her feet. "Can I have a close look, Pela? Please, I'll never ask again. Just tonight and only in the moonlight. The ink is luminous in the glow."

"Recall I told you that all those years ago, when I first arrived, a guard in Iona said I was a freak," muttered Pela. She hesitated, then hauled off her nightshirt. "I don't want you to react in the same way. So, just this once."

"She had no idea what she was talking about," murmured Savannah, tracing the patterns lightly with her finger. She tilted her head to study the line of the tattoos as she stroked. "The ones on your face make more sense now I see the rest."

Pela began to quiver. "Stop touching me, Savannah, or you're going to have to finish it in my bed. And that can't happen."

Savannah moved back quickly. "Oh, sorry. Gosh…I shouldn't have…um…I'd better go to bed."

"Goodnight," Pela said gruffly. She pulled on her clothes and dove under the covers.

Savannah lay on her mattress, aware sleep was a long way off. Arousal hummed through her body.

A desire that Pela had made quite clear that would remain unrequited.

When she woke, the bed beside her was empty, and a note was on the kitchen table. She flipped it open. The handwriting was bold, the message bald. *I'll be gone for two days.* Savannah sighed, half in relief, half in disappointment. Last night's revelation had taught her two truths: Pela had dark secrets, and Savannah was getting too emotionally involved. She was out of her depth with such a woman. The Commander was a far cry from her only long-term lover, an uncomplicated academic.

On the surface, she and Heather had seemed well suited, their relationship built on good fellowship, scholarly discussions, and the same goals. All things that were important for a best friend, but not a lover. In hindsight, Savannah knew she had been stupid to have even started dating her, for they had no real passion together. Savannah had a wildness in her blood that someone like Heather could never satisfy. Two years after they split, Heather moved in with one of their mutual friends and was much happier. Savannah was pleased for her. She was a good woman who would make an excellent wife and partner. That someone just wasn't her.

Now Pela was gone, Savannah was able to whip through the housecleaning after breakfast. Before she made her way over for the morning's practice, she checked on Justine. Instead of chafing at her forced confinement, she was chatting with Lyn, who had brought her over breakfast. Biting back a smile, Savannah paused at the door. They looked like two starry-eyed lovers. Lyn guiltily rose off the side of the bed, and a pink blush crept over Justine's cheeks.

Savannah chuckled. "Don't mind me. I came to examine your shoulder. Pela has healing herbs stored in a cupboard if you need pain relief."

"No. It's only a little sore. When can I go back?"

"In a week, then only very light training. In the meantime, start gentle exercises but put the sling back on afterward."

Justine stared at her. "The Commander will expect me to go back tomorrow."

"Nonsense. Pela isn't a fool. Injuries like this take time, and she doesn't want to lose good soldiers for want of care. Give it time to heal, or it may dislocate again." She winked at Lyn. "I expect you to take good care of her."

Now in good humor, she walked through the amphitheater to her usual position among the newer recruits. Rhiannon was nowhere in sight.

"Where's our instructor?" she asked the girl next to her.

"Lieutenant Rhiannon and the Commander flew off base this morning."

"Who's supervising us today?"

The girl made a face. "We've got Killia."

Savannah froze. *Crap!* This was her worse nightmare. At the mercy of Killia without protection.

"To your places, recruits," came a roar seconds later.

They bounded into lines immediately, at attention while Killia moved through them. When she came to Savannah, she cast her eyes up and down her length, then yanked at her shirt. "Your uniform is sloppy. And stand up straight while I talk to you."

Savannah stiffened like a board, hoping she'd move on. She didn't. Instead, she bent down until her face was inches away and said vehemently, "It's time you were taught how a real warrior fights. And you will not lie down like a dog." She signaled to a burly soldier. "Come here, Xavia."

The woman snapped her heels together. "Yes, Captain?"

"You and Savannah will fight in hand-to-hand combat. Incorporate all techniques so I can explain them to the class. They will watch until the first gong."

Savannah gulped. It was the same woman who'd taken over from Justine in that first fight. She had to endure this for half an hour. When Killia yelled, "Take your places, recruits," she turned to face Xavia with a sinking heart. The warrior had limbs like tree trunks.

"Begin."

Suddenly, the medallion began to tingle, and images flashed into her mind. At each jab and lunge of her opponent, she knew what steps to take to avoid being hit. While Xavia was bigger with greater length in her arms, the woman relied more on brute strength than finesse. As Savannah danced, weaved, and ducked, Xavia became frustrated. Sensing her opponent's anxiety to finish her off, Savannah began hit-and-retreat tactics of her own. Steadily, she edged through her defenses, hitting her more vulnerable areas. Finally, after taking a hard kick to her knee, Xavia sprawled into the dirt.

"Get up," roared Killia as Xavia clutched at her leg.

Savannah stopped sucking in big gulps of air and wheezed out, "I hurt her kneecap. Let her alone."

The crowd that had gathered fell silent.

Her face a mask of hatred, Killia raised her eyes from the injured woman curled up on the ground. "You think you can order me about, serving wench. It is time to teach you a lesson. You'll not find me so easy to defeat. Take your position."

Savannah swallowed back the bile that rose to her throat. Even helped by the medallion, she wouldn't have any hope against this woman. She'd seen her in action. Killia was vicious, giving no quarter as she ruthlessly dispatched her opponents. She'd heard that only Pela had been able to best her in a fight. She wondered fleetingly, who gave her the scar, then there was no more time to think as she moved toward her. Her bulk was menacing, her eyes more so.

She swung a right swinging fist, which Savannah barely avoided. As she pivoted out of the way, the left fist glanced off her ribs. She grunted. *Damn!* That hurt. Sensing another attack, Savannah went into a crouch and drove her fist into her pubic bone. Doubling up, Killia howled in fury. When she straightened, Savannah knew that she meant to kill her. And then Killia came at her, using fists and boots kicking. More blows landed than Savannah could avoid. Then one connected under her breastbone, and a scream of hot pain lanced through her upper body. The next second, her face snapped back from a kick and she went down in a heap.

This time, when someone called out, "Stay down," Savannah had every intention of doing just that.

"Get up," snarled Killia, "or I'll kick you to death there."

Savannah had a struggle to rise but found the strength somehow. The second she was up, Killia had her hands around her throat.

She heard someone call out, "Get the other instructors." But no one moved when Killia said in a low, deadly voice. "Anyone that moves will be next."

As she began to squeeze, she whispered harshly in Savannah's ear, "Pela was under control until you came along, bitch. Now die."

Savannah kicked and struggled, but the hands held fast. As her head arched backward, Killia loomed over her in triumph. Their eyes locked. The pupils in the eyes staring down at her began to widen. Silver slivers appeared in their depths.

Savannah realized that she was being strangled by a Silverthorne witch.

The medallion began to vibrate violently. Power rose from the depths of her flesh and bones, spreading in a tidal wave through her body. It traveled down her arms until it bled out of her fingertips. With a cry, she plunged her fingers into Killia's neck. Immediately, the soldier went rigid, and her teeth clenched. Her hands loosened, then fell away as Savannah continued to press.

When she began to tremble, Savannah breathed out her ear, "When you come to, Captain, you had better leave Falcon's Keep. Pela will kill you. She has no love for Silverthorne witches."

Summoning more power, she pushed her fingers in harder. Killia convulsed, her eyes rolling back in her head as her limbs jerked erratically like a marionette. With a last violent spasm, she fell unconscious. After she toppled to the ground, Savannah raised her head to look at the watching recruits. They bowed their heads in acknowledgment, then silently parted to let her through. Without a word, she stepped over the body and walked away. She doubted any of them realized there had been magic involved. From where they stood, it would've looked like she knew as a healer what nerves to press to incapacitate an opponent. Nor would anyone feel sorry for Killia. They all hated her.

After a hot soak and a dose of medicinal herbs, she sat down at Pela's desk to write a letter to Tamasin. It was urgent to let her know that the Silverthorne witches were playing some dark game at Falcon's Keep. And to investigate Ursula. Once the letter was written and sealed, she went to see Justine. Since the young guard was under her care, she would be an ideal courier. She was also very loyal to Pela.

Justine was sitting up in bed when she entered and gasped when she saw Savannah's face. "You look a mess. I heard you fought Killia, and she beat you up. Was it true you dropped her?"

"I shoved my fingers into the nerve in her neck. I was lucky it worked."

"She's always been a real mongrel to the younger recruits," said Justine. "Lyn told me she's flown off the base."

"Good riddance," Savannah said. "I'm here to relay a message from the Commander. She wants you to carry out a secret mission."

The young recruit answered eagerly, "What do I have to do?"

"It won't be too taxing on your shoulder. Pela wants you to fly to Iona immediately with a letter for Mistress Tamasin. You must get it to her secretly. If you tuck it into your sling, no one will look there if you're searched. Stay the night and come back tomorrow afternoon. If anyone asks, I'll say I sent you to see a healer in Iona. Do you think you're up to it?"

Justine grinned. "I've had enough of sitting around. Who shall I ride?"

"I'll bring you Sunflower. Everyone's still at training, so you should be able to slip away unnoticed. I won't be long."

Justine looked at her in surprise. "Sunflower's on the common. There're other horses in the stalls.'

"No. I want her to go. Have a saddle ready," Savannah said and hurried outside.

Sunflower raised her head at her first whistle. When she waved, the mare galloped over. After she explained her task, she added, "Tell Malkia that the Circle of Sheda is back in Rand. When the time comes, the Chosen One will need his help."

Sunflower pranced excitedly. "*I will pass on the message to Father. The Blue Fjord horses have waited a long time to carry another Chosen One. It is our right. Where is she?*"

"She will reveal herself in good time," Savannah replied. Lovingly, she stroked her palm down the silky back. "You must fly like the wind, my beautiful friend."

Once the mare and Justine were only a speck in the sky, Savannah trudged back to the house. Her side hurt like hell and if she didn't rest soon, she'd fall.

As she rested, her mind drifted back to the old woman. She was beginning to have some understanding of why she had picked her to wear the Circle of Sheda. A warrior wasn't required this time; it was someone who could strategize what had to be done, with fresh eyes to view the whole picture with no preconceptions.

As an archeologist, Savannah understood the importance of thoroughly researching her subject and planning every minutest detail. But most of all, to have an infinite amount of patience.

And it was about time she started to do her job.

Chapter Thirteen

Savannah glanced out the window at the twin moons silhouetted in the sky.

There was so much she had to learn about this strange new world. Did it ever rain in these desolate Iron Mountains? She hadn't seen so much as a wisp of a cloud. Yet the common had green grass, and there were water barrels next to every building. She turned back to the desk and laid a blank sheet of parchment on the top. To make any sense of anything, she would have to start recording what she knew and then try to find connections. In all likelihood, some pattern would appear.

Savannah dipped the feathered quill into the inkpot, jotted down the major players, then studied the list. Where to start any project was always a problem. Her professor had advised them to begin with concrete facts, for suppositions wasted time. Conjecture wasn't the truth. The one thing she knew was true for sure: Killia's revelation that they had been controlling Pela. So she decided to start with the Silverthorne witches.

They had an agenda of their own. But what was it? Savannah couldn't guess how long the coven had been strengthening their position. Ursula had been putting that ghastly cloak on people for years—an ideal way to vet strangers coming into the palace. Anyone considered a threat would be closely monitored. The Commander must been one if they'd gone to the trouble to infiltrate Falcon's Keep. Pela had said Ursula had wanted her banished after she lasted so long under the cloak, but Tamasin had arranged a place for her in the academy. Could that mean she was dangerous to the Silverthorne Coven, not as Commander of the Elite Guard, but because of who she was or had done?

Savannah chewed the end of the quill. There was something the old blind woman had said when she was under the cape. Then it came to her. She said Ursula feared Tamasin's anger. Which could mean Tamasin had some power to counteract her witchcraft. Maybe she had some magic of her own—after all, she had persuaded Malkia to come out of the Forgotten Realms. And Pela had inferred that Savannah wouldn't be welcome there because she wasn't magical.

Grunting, she pushed away the parchment. She was overthinking things. She'd had enough shocks yesterday. It was bad enough to have the life nearly choked out of her by a witch, without finding she could turn into a human Taser. Best to leave it until she had more solid facts. In the meantime, she'd find out what she could. Pela had told her Falcon's Keep had a small library. It should have historical documents on Rand, as well as military books about past wars. Until she got back to Iona, she'd have to wait to talk to Moira for a more in-depth overview.

After donning her cloak, she left the study. She had been excused from practice, and since Pela wasn't due back until tomorrow, it was an opportunity to visit the library. As the Commander's servant, so far she hadn't spent much time anywhere except at the mess and training ground, so it took a while to find it. The librarian, an elderly woman with white hair and a military bearing, gave her a nod when she entered the building.

The small library was well-stocked with leather-bound books and rolls of parchments. Worn reading desks sat in rows under a wooden coffered ceiling. When Savannah asked if she might be allowed to read some of the books on past Rand conflicts, the woman pointed to an aisle. "They're down the back row. No one has looked at them for years." She eyed her curiously. "You're the Commander's maid, aren't you?"

"That's right. I'm Savannah."

"Hello. I'm Glenda." The old librarian laughed. "Everyone knows who you are, Savannah. You're the talk of the place. Killia left the Keep with her tail between her legs yesterday evening. Word has it, she won't be coming back. Good riddance, I say."

Savannah grinned. "I agree. She was a tyrant."

"The girls said you knocked her unconscious." She eyed her skeptically. "How did you manage that? You're only a slip of a thing."

"Oh," said Savannah, giving a vague wave of her hand. "I didn't actually hit her...just pressed her throat to cut off the air supply. I'm a healer."

"I'd say you were lucky. She has bad blood, that one."

"I thought she was going to kill me," Savannah replied, then changed the subject before the old woman prodded further. "Have you been here long, Glenda?"

"More turns of the moons than I can count. I became an instructor and never left. Falcon's Keep has been the only home I've known. The Commander gave me this position when I retired."

"Are you familiar with the histories of the wars?" Savannah asked, then added as a way of an explanation. "It's for my research."

"Aye, girl, I am. I've plenty of time in my old age to read," Glenda chuckled. "None of the Elite Guards could be described as bookish. It'll be nice to have some company."

Savannah gave her a shy smile. "I would like that too. If I want more information, I'll give you a call. Now I'd better get to work."

Armed with three big books and a load of scrolls from the war section, Savannah retired to a corner to read. Since Rand had had no major conflicts for centuries, the dated scrolls were frail. When she opened the first, she found once again she had no trouble reading the script. She should have because the ancient words wouldn't be the language used in Rand today. This time, she willingly embraced the gift the medallion had bestowed on her—it would have taken her weeks to decipher the pages.

She read all morning until her eyes needed a rest. Only some of the technical military terms were the same as those on Earth, and there were battles with creatures she hadn't heard of or knew what they looked like. She jotted down the names to look up in the flora and fauna book. After stacking the documents neatly in a pile, she made her way to the front desk.

"May I go with you to lunch, Glenda?" she asked.

The librarian pointed to a small room off to the side. "I usually eat here in the middle of the day. I've plenty if you would like to join me."

"That'll be super, thanks. I've things to ask you."

"Ye have a strange way of speaking, lass. Where are you from?"

"A long way from here," Savannah began, desperately trying to recall the place Tamasin had said she was from. The name didn't come, so she improvised. "Across the Wide Sea of Mists. My parents were healers in a small village."

That seemed to satisfy Glenda, who placed an assortment of meats, fruits, and cheeses on the table. Smiling, she passed over a plate and took a sip of her drink. "Did you learn much today?"

"I read about the Mystic War. When that one ended, the great magical clans retreated into the Forgotten Realms."

"Ah, yes," said Glenda. "That rift has never been mended."

"How long has Falcon's Keep been a military outpost?"

"It's been a training school for the Elite Guards for a hundred and fifty years. The Keep was left in ruins after the Prophecy Tower was destroyed three centuries ago."

"The Prophecy Tower? What was that?" queried Savannah.

Glenda lowered her voice as though the ghosts of the past might come through the walls. "There was a time when magic was everywhere in the land. Many clans of magical creatures lived in harmony with those not gifted. And then there were the witches, wizards, necromancers, and sorcerers, all magicians who practiced witchcraft."

"What caused the Mystic War?" prompted Savannah.

"It is said that the magicians envied the power of the magical beings. They persuaded the Imperial Queen to drive the magical clans into the Forgotten Realms. After that, Rand came under the indirect influence of the magicians. Prized as advisors to the crowns, they were a secretive lot, coveting power. The most powerful order was the Silverthorne witches who resided in the Prophecy Tower. The last head witch, Agatha, thought to depose Queen Jessica and take the crown. But Jessica's armies defeated the Silverthornes at the Battle of Briar Ridge. Some say that without the Chosen One wielding the Circle of Sheda, the Queen would have been defeated."

"So what happened to the magicians after that?"

"They were stripped of their lands and titles and forbidden to congregate. There is only one witch in any court on Rand, and that is Ursula, who is the Supreme Monarch's bondservant."

Savannah leaned over the table, eagerly asking the question she most wanted answering. "Who was Sheda?"

"Wouldn't we all like to know. That knowledge has been lost in the annals of time. I only know she lived well before the Mystic War. Historians have speculated, of course. A Goddess, an oracle, a warrior, a mage…but no one's sure. The common folk believe she is the soul of Rand."

Savannah carefully turned the information over in her mind. "Tell me, Glenda. If the Elite Guard has only been here for one hundred and fifty years, how do you have all these much older records?"

"Ah…beneath the site where the Prophecy Tower stood, are tunnels, storage rooms, and vaults. They were stored there. There is also an underground water reservoir which fills in the storm season. It's our water supply. Pela has the key to the vaults. They had been locked up for years before she arrived. Our previous Commander, Tamron, was head of the school for forty years and wasn't interested in history. Pela and I are the only ones who have been down there. We retrieved what we could." Glenda looked speculatively at her. "I'm guessing the Commander employed you to scribe for her. You're hardly a housemaid."

Savannah decided to go with that. "I'm her scribe and researcher as well as her housekeeper."

"Good. She needs both."

"You like her?"

"She is an excellent Commander," replied Glenda. "She governs the Keep with tight discipline but is very fair. I'm afraid Tamron had become very lax in the end, letting standards slip. But Pela is not a leader troubled by indecision or doubt. She has plans laid down if we ever have to go to war again."

Savannah glanced at her quickly. "She thinks there will be another war one day?"

"She's never confided that thought to me. But if an enemy does come, she'll be ready."

"I'd better get back to my studies," said Savannah rising from her chair. "Tell me, Glenda, are there any books or scrolls relating to a great war before the Mystic War?"

"Hmm… nobody has wanted to go that far back, but I've never seen anything. We found a small vault right at the bottom of the underground labyrinth, but when we opened it up, there were so many rats we closed it immediately. Any documents stored there would have been chewed up years ago."

"Could I have a look inside?"

Glenda peered at her dubiously. "The witches would have put all their important documents in the sealed vaults."

"I guess," said Savannah, letting it go for now. She had plenty to do for the time being but resolved to get the key at a later date. The witches were no fools. What better place to hide their most important documents than in a sealed container in a room full of rats?

By mid-afternoon, she had to call it a day. Since the medicinal bark had worn off, her head was pounding and her joints throbbing. As well, her black eye was puffing shut, and her throat felt on fire. Promising to come back tomorrow, Savannah made her way to the house. After a bath and medicine, she flopped down on the mattress. Sitting all day hadn't helped. As she drifted off to sleep, she thanked God for small mercies—she didn't have to serve Pela in the mess.

†

The next morning, Savannah woke stiff and sore. Groaning, she glanced out the window—by the position of the moons, it was mid-morning and too late for breakfast. After some limbering-up exercises, she found that the long rest had helped considerably. The soreness under her ribs was bearable without the painkiller, and her throat felt far less inflamed. The bruise on her cheek was a deep purple, finger marks were imprinted on her neck, and she sported a huge black eye. It hit home as she gazed at her reflection, what a close call she'd had.

In the afternoon, she was reading a history book when she heard thumping boots outside. Before she could react, the door crashed open. Pela, in full riding gear, swept into the room.

"What the hell happened?" she ground out. "I go away for two days, and the place disintegrates into chaos. I heard some cock-and-bull story that you and Killia fought and that you knocked her unconscious. And she's gone."

Savannah peeped round the door. If she thought she might get some sympathy, by the look of fury on Pela's face it wasn't going to happen. "It's quite true," she called out, keeping her distance.

"Don't be ridiculous. If you fought, you wouldn't have lasted ten seconds."

"Well, I did. I cut off her air supply."

"She would have been putting you through exercises. You'd be dead if she meant you harm. Come out here and face me."

Savannah pursed her lips and strode into the living room. "I should have known you wouldn't believe me. Well, here I am."

Pela stared at her face, wide-eyed. "She did *that* to you."

"Plus some solid blows under my ribs."

"Let me have a look," ordered Pela.

Suddenly remembering the medallion, Savannah hastily retreated a couple of steps. "I'm fine. It's just bruised. A lot of this is your fault, Pela," she said bitterly. "You knew she hated me, yet you took Rhiannon and left Killia in charge of the new recruits. What did you think was going to happen?"

Pela let her hands fall to her sides. "I can't be seen favoring you, Savannah. It's a hard life here, and you wanted to stay."

"I've never asked for any special treatment, but I did expect a level of protection. Killia is a cruel and vicious woman. All the recruits fear her." She turned away so Pela wouldn't see the tears gathering in her eyes. "But you're right. I did ask to stay, but I'll never be good enough for Falcon's Keep in your eyes. I'd appreciate it if you would send a letter to Tamasin with the first person to fly out to Iona. I'm going to ask her to come and get me."

Pela lowered her head. "You can ask her in person. She and the Queen will be coming for the graduation ceremony next week. Rhiannon and I went to Iona to prepare for the visit." she said and walked back out the door.

Chapter Fourteen

In the early hours of the morning, Savannah's eyes sprang open. She had no idea what woke her. Disorientated, she lay for a few moments to shed the last vestiges of the deep sleep, then strained to listen for any unfamiliar sounds in the night. All was quiet. A second later, she felt a tingle from the medallion. Alarmed, she swallowed to moisten her suddenly dry throat. Danger must be imminent.

Cautiously, she rose quietly and padded over to Pela's bed. It was empty. *Damn!* Just when she needed her, she was sleeping somewhere else. Savannah crept to the window and peered out into the gloom. Seeing nothing suspicious, she quickly shuttered it. When she received a harder tingle, she stealthily pulled on her boots, then took the knife she'd been given in training in one hand and the pepper spray in the other. In two minds about what to do, she decided to face it full-on. Better to be on the offensive rather than wait for trouble.

Carefully, she eased the front door ajar and slipped into the shadows outside. It was lit enough by the moonglow to see that the front yard was empty. She scanned all the buildings in view. Finding nothing unusual, she was about to go back inside when she noticed a black bird on the path. It looked like a carrion crow. With a hoarse caw, it hopped onto the landing and tilted its head to stare at her.

Something about those beady black eyes sent a wave of apprehension through Savannah. The bird appeared to be assessing her. Suddenly, it fluffed up its feathers and began to grow. Her eyes widened in alarm as it kept getting bigger until it morphed into a black shrouded figure, at least a head taller than herself. From the body shape, she knew her assailant was a man, though covered by the shadowy hood, she couldn't make out any facial features. Before she could dash back inside, he rushed toward her, his right arm raised. Only then did she see the long knife clutched in his hand. Reacting instinctively, she squirted the pepper spray into the hood. When he cried out, she had the immediate satisfaction of knowing he wasn't some sort of ghostly wraith. He hurt like the rest of them. But that was short-lived. As he sprang at her again, she realized the material must have saved his eyes from most of the spray. The sleeve fell to his shoulder as he arched the knife above his head. Just in time, she remembered the maneuver the instructor had drummed into her. She jerked sideways, bringing her knife up as she went. It caught him in the fleshy part of his upper arm, and he grunted. When she pulled her blade back, she saw the tip was red.

"So you can bleed, you bastard," she said, plunging the knife again. This time he easily avoided it.

"Who are you?" he snarled, lunging this time with his whole body. His thigh hit her hip, sending her sprawling onto the flat stones.

Desperately, she tried to summon the power of the medallion. It didn't come.

Then he was on her, raising the knife for the final blow. Frantically, she pushed the pepper spray straight into the hood and jammed her finger on the button. Giving an agonizing scream, he lurched backward. Summoning the last of her strength, she drove the knife right up to the hilt under his left rib bone. He doubled up, and with a clank, the knife slipped out of his fingers onto the stone floor. Blood began to bubble out of his mouth as he collapsed backward.

To her astonishment, he disintegrated before her eyes, dissolving into swirling spirals of particles until there was only a dead crow on the ground.

Stunned, Savannah sank to her knees. She was lucky to be alive, under no illusion that Pela's training regime had saved her.

But then she felt the air move, as chilling as an Arctic breeze as it rippled across her skin. Shivering, she was horrified to see two more crows materialize out of nowhere. They landed on the pavement, their dark eyes focused on her.

She knew this time she was going to die.

As she mentally prepared herself, out of nowhere came the sound of wings flapping. A dark shadow settled over the yard, blocking out the moons. She looked up to see a huge hawk in the sky. The crows turned to look as well. The hawk let out a piercing scream and banked in a tight gliding turn. The crows tried to flutter away, but they were no match for this enemy. The hawk dived at the first crow, grasping it in its talons. It settled on the ground and ripped it to pieces.

The other crow only managed to fly to the front gate before the hawk wheeled back into the air and snatched it mid-flight. With a snap of its beak, it bit off its head.

Savannah gaped in awe as the massive hawk descended, gracefully gliding to perch in front of the stone step. When it hunched down before her, she instinctively knew that it wouldn't hurt her. She scrutinized the magnificent bird, aware of a sense of familiarity. Then it all fell into place. The pattern of the tattoos.

It remained still, regarding her with intelligent eyes.

Certain now, Savannah simply said, "Hello, Pela."

The hawk began to shiver. A whirlwind of colors spun like a kaleidoscope around its body, and when the air cleared, Pela stood on the path. "Are you all right, Savannah?"

Savannah shook her head. "Not really. I thought I was going to die, and I've seen some really weird stuff tonight, which just tops off a pretty shitty week. I don't want to talk anymore. I've never killed anyone before." She turned and went inside.

A few minutes later, she heard Pela lock up the house and climb into bed.

As much as Savannah tried, sleep wouldn't come. Her nerves were shot, and she was so lonely that all she wanted to do was cry. Finally, she couldn't stand it any longer. She sniffled back the tears and called out, "Can I come into your bed, Pela? I don't want to be alone tonight."

The silence stretched to a minute before Pela spoke. "All right. Just for tonight."

Savannah ran over and crawled under the covers before she could change her mind. She sighed with the sheer pleasure of being in a comfortable bed. Pela had her back to her and grunted a goodnight.

"Do you think they'll be back?" Savannah whispered.

"No. Go to sleep."

She waited until she heard Pela's breathing become slow and regular, then gently snuggled into her back. To have human contact again felt wonderful. The thought came that Pela was hardly human, but she didn't care. She felt just fine.

Pela was still in the bed when Savannah opened her eyes. Not only there, but looking at Savannah, who was half-draped over her.

Savannah flashed her a lazy smile. "'Morning." Then realizing where she was, she hastily wriggled off. "Sorry. I…um…didn't mean to get so close."

"We'd better get up. It's too late for breakfast in the mess hall, so after you're dressed, go to the kitchen," Pela said, though she didn't make a move to rise.

Savannah propped herself on an elbow and said quietly, "Shouldn't we talk?"

For once, Pela looked indecisive, but with a resigned shrug, she nodded. "I guess we should. You realize, Savannah, that I should probably kill you for discovering my secret," she said in a half-joking, half-serious tone.

Savannah regarded her intently. "I know, but we are both aware it is time for some secrets to be shared. I have mine too."

"I understand that. You are an enigma I haven't figured out. There's no way you could have defeated Killia. And why did she just disappear like that? She was a trusted member of my command…she would never abandon her post."

"She's a Silverthorne witch, sent by the coven to keep you under control."

"*What!* Where did you get that preposterous idea? That's impossible?"

"Is it?" asked Savannah, aware that this might be her first real test as the bearer of the Circle of Sheda. If she couldn't persuade Pela, then she had just forfeited her life. The Commander was ruthless with those she considered enemies. "Think about it."

"Go on," said Pela quietly.

Savannah pushed back the thought, *she's watching me like a hawk.* It wasn't an analogy she wanted to dwell on after seeing the crows dispatched so efficiently. "For a start, I bet she turned up at Falcon's Keep soon after you arrived as a recruit? Probably as an instructor, or perhaps the head guard. She would have befriended you, taken you under her wing. Become a valued advisor. When Valeria wanted to send you housemaids, she would have been egging you on to get rid of them." Savannah gave a small smile. "Mind you, I don't think you would have taken much persuasion there. You dislike the Queen with a passion because she put you under that Silverthorne's cape, and Killia would have fueled that hatred."

Pela narrowed her eyes. "You could have found that out from anyone. I heard you were in the library all day. Glenda's tongue wags too much. I imagine you wouldn't have any trouble finding out the information. She likes company, especially someone who's willing to listen to her stories." She leaned over Savannah. "I think *you're* the witch. Tell me, how did you defeat Killia? You might have pulled the wool over the eyes of everyone else, but not me. What spell did you put on her to leave her post, witch?"

Savannah's temper rose. "I told her you would kill her once you found out she is a Silverthorne witch."

"And how were you so sure she is?"

"Because she damn well told me as she was choking the life out of me," Savannah snapped.

"Pah! If she is a witch, then how did you defeat her?" snarled Pela. "Tell me or I'll wring it out of you."

"You could try but you won't succeed," Savannah said with more bravado than she felt. If Pela lasted ten minutes under the cape, she'd need a lot of power to subdue her.

"I could snap you like a twig. You're so puny," Pela said, flexing her hands.

"You wouldn't be able to."

"Why."

"Because I wear the Circle of Sheda," she spat back.

Pela stared at her. "*You* are the Chosen One?"

Her anger gone, Savannah got out of bed and walked to the window. She pushed it open and stared out. "I am, but I never wanted it. The medallion chose me." She turned to regard Pela solemnly. "The scales are tipped against you, Pela. You must answer *my* questions."

"If I can see it, I will."

Savannah hesitated, then made up her mind. "Only if you promise not to divulge my secret until Tamasin says it's safe. We'll need surprise when the enemy comes. Do you swear?"

Pela stood and thumped her fist on her chest. "I do. I haven't a quarrel with the one who wields the Circle of Sheda. It is sacred to my people too."

Savannah pulled her nightshirt over her head and held the medallion up for her to see.

Pela moved closer to study it. Her face paled, then bowing her head, she knelt on one knee. "I am sorry, Savannah. I would never have treated you so badly if I had known."

"Oh, do get up, Pela. I can't have you kneeling to me. You're ten times the warrior I'll ever be. I've none of the attributes that the Chosen One is supposed to possess. I'm just an ordinary person," she grinned, "and as you say, puny."

"I think you do yourself a disservice. You persuaded me to let you stay and that's never happened."

"In a way," said Savannah. "Maybe that's one reason why I was picked. Who would believe I'm the Chosen One?"

"Why didn't you use your powers on the assassin?"

"Ah…I've been thinking about that. It woke me up, but I couldn't draw any power when he was fighting me. I'm guessing it didn't want those crow creatures to know it has been found."

"But they came to assassinate you," said Pela with a puzzled frown. Savannah shook her head. "No. He asked me who I was. I think they came to kill you, Pela."

"Me?"

"You must be a threat," said Savannah, then stopped as a thought hit. "Didn't you tell me Tamasin just saved Valeria from an assassin's knife? That's too much of a coincidence. We'll have to ask her when they get here if it was the same kind of killer."

"If it was, then it becomes clearer. It's easier to wage war if you eliminate the generals first. Basic military strategy." Pela pulled on her uniform. "I will tighten our defenses immediately. All crows to be killed on sight. You will keep out of trouble. Eat in the mess at my table."

"Hey," protested Savannah. "That'll look suspicious if I eat with you. And I have to go to the library. I'm in the middle of researching the old wars."

"All right, but no walking around at night. Run if you see a crow."

"Just one thing, Pela. Do you have the key to that lowest vault?"

"I have all the keys in my study. But there's nothing in there but rats, and trust me, you don't want to go near it. They're vicious." She gave her a salute. "I'll see you at lunch. Oh…and Savannah."

"Yes?"

"I will arrange for another bed to be brought in. You'll be more comfortable off the floor."

Savannah's smile of gratitude vanished when Pela continued with a gleam in her eye. "You'll exercise for three hours instead of two. The bearer of the medallion must be able to defend herself."

Chapter Fifteen

The Citadel City of Iona

The burly guard banged his truncheon against the prison bars. Tamasin strained to hear someone calling to her over the racket. She couldn't make out the words. The guard was looking beyond her... She jerked around. Someone stood on the other side of the bars...Valeria...she met her eyes...they were wide with anguish. Tamasin stretched out her hand... the image shimmered. It wasn't Valeria...it was Savannah.

Help me, Tamasin. The witches...

The sound of the truncheon came again. Banging...banging ... banging.

Tamasin jerked awake, her body a lather of sweat.

Valeria looked at her with concern. "It's only the breakfast maid at the door, love. What's wrong?"

"Another dream," said Tamasin. She lay quietly, waiting for her heart to stop pounding. Most of her dreams were unclear, needing interpretation, but not this one. She had no doubt it was going to happen. She sensed it wasn't immediately, though how far in the future, she had no idea.

The maid arranged the breakfast tray on the table, then curtsied. "Your Majesty," she said, flashing a shy smile at Tamasin before hurrying out the door.

"Thank you, Francine," Valeria called out after her, then chuckled. "After catching us that morning, she's been skittish as a foal."

Tamasin heaped the scrambled goose eggs onto her plate. "I don't blame her. Methinks catching the Queen naked should be made an offense." She grinned. "Because she's drop-dead gorgeous."

"You have acquired a few strange sayings from your time in the other world." Valeria eyed her speculatively. "I gather there were plenty of *drop-dead* gorgeous women beyond the portal."

Tamasin rubbed her chin. "Hmm... let me see. Ah...there were, my Queen, but none there to equal you."

"You are silver-tongued, Mistress of Dreams."

"I tell the truth. Now, enough of this. As much as I would like to stay all morning to convince you of my devotion, there's work to be done. The horses and riders have already left. The call for Dreamers was very successful, exceeding all my expectations. I had no idea there were so many or that they were waiting for me to gather them together. They should arrive at the Old Stone Mill by mid-afternoon. I'd better finish my meal and get on my way."

Valeria's light bantering smile vanished. "Be careful, Tam. We have no idea what this enemy will do next. You'll have little protection out there."

"Nonsense. I'll have five soldiers and the advantage of secrecy. Whoever these assassins are, they'll have to be aware of their targets' location. And you and I are the only ones with that information. None of the Dreamers have been told where they're going. Besides," Tamasin said, giving a reassuring smile, "that's why they're going there. To learn how to use their talents. Moira said in the past that Dreamers provided an advanced warning system."

"I can't help worrying."

"You'll be busy enough arranging the War Council," said Tamasin, as she pulled on her breeches. "Do you think they'll all come?"

"Since Queen Wren is sick, her eldest daughter Fern is coming in her place. The rest have said they'll be here."

"And the generals of the various armies?"

Valeria made a face. "All are coming, except I haven't asked Pela yet. She probably won't come since I sent her another unwanted housemaid."

Frowning, Tamasin stopped pulling on her boots to look at her. "Pela should be given the Supreme Command of the armies if there is a war. She's a brilliant tactician."

"I wish she wasn't so damned disagreeable."

"And who's fault is that? You ordered Ursula to put that nefarious cape on her, so don't complain to me."

"Savannah's still there after three weeks," said Valeria hopefully. "Pela might be thawing."

"Huh! I doubt it. We can only trust Savannah to continue to stay out of trouble," Tamasin said. At least she wasn't in the brig yet as she had dreamed. Only yesterday, Godfrey had sent a message to say that the courier delivering their monthly quotas of ale, had met her in the kitchen and she looked very fit.

"Would you go up there and talk to Pela?" Valeria asked with a tentative smile.

Tamasin snapped her fingers. "I have a better idea. Why don't we attend the graduation ceremony at Falcon's Keep? That way, you can view the defenses, and I'll talk to Pela. Whether you like it or not, she is the best military leader in Rand and we have to mend bridges."

†

The ride to the Old Stone Mill took the better part of an hour. Malkia was keen to get away from the stables, as was Tamasin who hadn't been out of the city since her arrival.

Once they passed over the town of Tuckburrow, Malkia began to descend a mile further on to the cluster of clay-brick cottages that surrounded a vine-covered dilapidated flour mill. Godfrey had organized the innkeeper at the Dirk'n'Dagger Tavern to send out bedding and supplies to last two weeks. He also arranged for the Fennel Bakery to deliver fresh bread every morning from Tuckburrow.

The campsite was ideal for her purpose—the mill had been replaced by a newer one in town, and the mill workers had moved on to seek work elsewhere. Nothing was left of the small village except abandoned cottages and the old mill. The waterwheel was still in working order, ensuring a supply of fresh water. It was ideal to house her Dreamers and there was plenty of pasture in the lush meadow for the horses.

No enemy should find them there.

As soon as Malkia touched down in the derelict village square, Tamasin jumped off his back, stripped the waterskin off her shoulder, and took a long draught. After removing the saddle and bridle, she ran a hand over Malkia's flank. "There you go, my friend. Get some water, and I'll inspect the state of the stable yards. Ten mounts will remain."

"I'll check out the meadow and return when the others arrive," Malkia telepathed back.

Tamasin affectionately looked at the Blue Fjord stallion as he ambled off to the millpond. He was indeed a magnificent, good-tempered animal. The magical Blue Fjords were long-living horses, their life-expectancy over a hundred years. Malkia was only thirty-nine, in his prime. She was proud to be his rider, but she was under no illusion that he chose her and not the other way around.

At the sound of whinnying, she looked skyward to see the five soldiers flying in. After they dismounted, the Captain snapped to attention. "Consort Tamasin, we are at your service."

"Captain Jocose. Welcome. The house on the far left is for the military. Settle in, and when the women arrive, picket a further five horses. The riders can take the rest home. Post two guards. I don't expect trouble, but we must be prepared. Crows are to be killed on sight."

Jocose snapped her heels together. "Yes, Consort."

"My title will be Mistress of Dreams here, Captain."

"Of course, Mistress," replied Jocose, then moved off accompanied by her guards.

By late afternoon, two hundred women had arrived. To have a thousand at once had seemed an impossible task to manage, so Tamasin had decided to stage the training. Out of this first bunch, she figured there would be a few capable of being instructors. With more pressing issues, she couldn't afford to stay past two weeks.

The Dreamers were of all ages, from eighteen to seventy, from all parts of the world, and all walks of life. But there was that unbreakable common thread, forged links of a linage that stretched back into the past. Their inherited gift was as much a part of Rand as the mountains and the land.

After personally greeting everyone, she told them, "You may choose your house companions. Has anyone had experience running a boarding house or inn?"

A well-groomed woman in her fifties put up her hand. "I'm steward of Middleway Castle."

Tamasin threw her a grateful smile. "Good. I'll leave the organization of the camp in your hands. You may pick your second-in-command." She cast her eyes around. "Everyone will be expected to help with chores. The old bakehouse ovens have been cleaned, ready for cooking. As it's a pleasant night, we'll eat around the campfire. I'll talk to you then."

As they sorted out their houses, she watched carefully who amongst them were the most assertive. She could see at once the steward was a gem, her organization skills admirable. By nightfall, there was a huge campfire burning brightly and cooked food on the tables.

Once they'd eaten, Tamasin began, "The time for the Dreamers has come, my friends. I'm sure like me, you took for granted the ability to foresee things in your dreams. But they began to change about four years ago for me. My dreams became more vivid, more focused. Menacing. Have any of you experienced this change?"

When every hand went up, Tamasin was shocked. She had imagined she'd have to persuade these women there was danger coming, but they already knew.

"We have been waiting for a long time for you to gather us together, Mistress," one of the older women called out. "Where have you been?"

"I've been three years in a place where I couldn't get home. But I am back, and we must learn how to use our gift immediately. We will be needed when they come."

"Who is coming, Mistress?"

Tamasin threw up her hands. "I have no idea. But our role will be twofold: to foretell the immediate future and interpret dreams that relate to the long-term. We must learn to differentiate between the two. It's imperative we learn how to control our dreams and use them to our advantage. Recently in a dream, I saw an assassin in the hall outside the Queen's bedchamber. I killed him before he reached her."

There was an audible gasp at this. "How did you discern it was happening immediately?" someone asked.

"I just knew. Perhaps we all have that inbuilt antenna." She stared into the fire. "Not all dreams are infallible. Some may only give a glimpse of the future that might or might not come to pass. Some will already have happened, and others may need to be interpreted." She added ruefully, "Unfortunately, I don't have many answers. But with your help, we shall learn together. Tomorrow morning, we will share our dreams of the night and those of the past. Some Dreamer lines may have passed down some invaluable information. Now, get to know each other. I'll check on the guard."

As Tamasin gave them a goodnight smile, her gaze fell on a stunning woman in her late thirties on the edge of the circle. She was one of the most attractive women she'd ever seen, rivaling even Valeria in looks, though they were on opposite ends of the spectrum. While the Queen had a regal fiery beauty, this woman was softer, more exotic, with velvet green eyes, ruby red lips, black glossy hair sweeping over her shoulders, and a lush, full figure. She sat cross-legged, looking at Tamasin as if she was thoroughly amused by it all.

Filing her face away for the morning, she made her way to the picketed horses. When they saw Tamasin coming, they whinnied and tossed their heads, hoping not to be left out. Each received a scratch behind the ear. Malkia was standing nearby, so she gave him a wave before moving on to the guard post.

Captain Jocose looked up as she approached, "Hey, Tamasin."

Tamasin sank beside her, pleased to be able to drop the formal titles now they were alone. "Hello, Jo. All quiet?"

"Not a murmur. How are the guests?"

"They're a good bunch. And judging by the meal tonight, there're good cooks amongst them. I'll leave you to it. Warn me immediately if you see anything suspicious. These women are going to be very important to us all in times to come."

An hour before sunrise, Tamasin dreamt about the assassin she had killed in Valeria's room. As he hovered at the foot of the bed, the moonlight glinting off the blade in his hand, she woke with a start. Even as she felt the dark lingering remnant of the nightmare, she dismissed it as immaterial. It was over.

As she waited for dawn to break, she was quite comfortable in the cloak of darkness. Years of living in the Dream World had taught her to slip unseen through shadows into private places. She knew all about secrets—she had one of her own. Not even Valeria knew that Tamasin's true bloodline had never been recorded in the Book of Births and Deaths. On her death bed, her mother had told her that she had been seduced by a handsome stranger from the Forgotten Realms. She couldn't tell Tamasin what manner of creature her father had been, only that he had been magical. Tamasin had buried the information with her.

An hour later, she heard the women stirring and rose from the bed to prepare for the day. She had no idea how it would develop, not at all confident about what she was doing or could achieve. But she knew it was crucial to find a way.

Straight after breakfast, she seated the Dreamers in rows and began. By late morning, they were getting nowhere fast. They had discussed their dreams, when they came, how often, in fact, every aspect they could think of, but nothing correlated. It all seemed so random. Tamasin's frustration was rising, made more so by the smug look on the beauty's face. At the start, when they had introduced themselves, the woman hadn't offered any information about herself except her name: Jezzine. Nor did she enter into any conversation.

In the end, Tamasin directly addressed her, "Care to share your thoughts, Jezzine?"

Jezzine laughed softly. Even that sounded like an invitation to hidden delights. When some of the women snickered, Tamasin suddenly realized where she'd heard the name. This was the famous Courtesan of Hesgate, sort after by both men and women of the royal houses. For one of the few times in her life, Tamasin was momentarily at a loss for words. Why would this woman come? Her loyalties would lie with those paying the highest price.

"Ah," said Jezzine. "I can see by your expression that you have just recognized my name, Tamasin, wayward consort of the delectable Valeria."

Ignoring the jibe, Tamasin eyed her thoughtfully. "And I see by your expression that you are very well aware how to manipulate dreams. And you're probably here under sufferance. Let's not beat around the bush. Tell us what you know. I have not the patience or the inclination to play your games, courtesan."

"You're quite right. I am a courtesan."

"Why did you come?" persisted Tamasin.

"Because I had no choice. I was told in a dream to come. An order I couldn't ignore," Jezzine said bitterly.

"I thought that might be the case," said Tamasin. "I understand how it feels. I was commanded in a dream to go on a quest and leave without telling my wife. I was three years in a place where there was no hope of contacting her. The delectable Valeria, as you so crudely labeled her, waited faithfully for those years, not even knowing if I was still alive."

Jezzine looked disconcerted. "My apologies. I had no idea." Tamasin wavered. Now was not the time for hostilities. "Let's put it behind us. We need your help. How can we control our dreams?" With a nod of acquiescence, Jezzine replied, "You're overthinking things. If you want to find out what's going to happen to someone within a few hours, make them your entire focus shortly before you go to bed. I imagine Valeria was in your thoughts when you saw the assassin in your dream."

"Quite likely."

"At first, your dream will be triggered by something unexpected about to happen to that person. Or your worst fears. But as you become more adept at focusing exclusively on that person, you can dream about them whenever you like. You can make a profile of the person if you're patient."

Tamasin smiled. No wonder she was such a good courtesan. She researched her subjects before engaging with them. She'd make a clever spy. "What about if they weren't people you knew but random assassins?"

"Ah…that requires being familiar with what they look like, but how they would be clothed would do. Have you anything specific?"

"If an enemy was an animal or a bird, could you see it in your dreams?" asked Tamasin, searching her face.

A furrow appeared in Jezzine's brow. "There would be a way if we knew what to look for and whom they would be targeting."

"The Queen's assassin appeared first as a crow, then turned into a man," Tamasin said in a low voice, then turned to the other women. "Are there any more amongst you that have learned to control your dreams? In any way? Please… I need to know. There will be no repercussions…the knowledge will never leave this camp."

She waited, then two hands crept into the air. The first was a spindly girl in her late teens, the other, one of the cooks. Tamasin addressed the girl first. "Tell me, Merna, how do you use the dreams."

The girl's lip quivered. "I am the property of the Grand Thief of Butcher's Bog. I find where rich merchants hide their money for my master."

Tamasin stared at her. "And how did you become his property, girl?"

"When I was ten, my father sold me to him for the price of a drink."

A collective gasp hissed into the air.

"Are there many young people like you in his service?"

Merna's head bobbed up and down. "He has a whole network of children working the streets, Mistress. Some are as young as five."

Tamasin's hands balled into fists, vowing as soon as she got back, to dispatch a platoon of the Elite Guards to clean out that viper's nest. "As the Queen's Representative, I free you, Merna. When you leave here, you may accompany me to Iona if you wish. As a Queen's Dreamer, you will be handsomely paid."

When Merna promptly burst into tears, one of the older women took her into her arms. "I am the wife of the Burgomaster of Greenhaven. I will look after the girl, Mistress. My home is lonely since my children have left."

Tamasin smiled her thanks, then turned to the third woman, an older brassy, plump woman sporting a mass of red corkscrew curls. "And what do you do…ah—? I'm sorry. I can't recall your name."

"I'm Esme, your Graciousness…um …Mistress. I'm…um…a fortuneteller."

"How do your dreams work there?" asked Tamasin, surveying her with interest.

"Oh," said Esme, loudly laughing. "One doesn't have to be asleep. A quick trance will do the trick. Easy enough if you train your mind. When the bit comes about findin' true love, you stare into the crystal ball and whip into a trance and see who they're daydreaming about. Fools 'em every time, Luv. Sorry, I mean Mistress."

Tamasin's mouth sagged open. Who would have thought a dream could be conjured up that way. She threw back her head and surveyed the rest of the women who were looking at her eagerly. "Well, there you go, ladies. We have three very able tutors who will start lessons after lunch. Each comes with a particular talent, so pay attention. We need all of us to be able to control our dreams, to manipulate them to be of greatest benefit. Jezzine will be the organizer and oversee the classes. Let's stretch our legs."

Tamasin hurried out of the camp before she burst into laughter. Whatever she had imagined was going to happen, it certainly wasn't finding a courtesan, a thief, and a fortuneteller as her experts.

Another burble of laugher erupted as she visualized Jezzine trying to control tawdry Esme.

Chapter Sixteen

After the fortnight, Tamasin was more than happy with the outcome. Since it had proven such a success, she could accelerate the program to take the rest in one block: all eight hundred and two of them. Time was marching on—her Dreamers had to be ready. Jezzine chose fifteen of the best pupils to stay as tutors under her supervision, plus Esme who was needed to teach her trance. Merna declined the offer to go to Iona, choosing to live safely with the Burgomaster's wife at Greenhaven, to get far away from Butcher's Bog and the clutches of the Grand Thief.

Jezzine had been an excellent coordinator and teacher, pushing them skillfully through the program until all had become proficient at conjuring up the dreams. Some had problems mastering the trance, but they promised to keep practicing at home. Before she left, Tamasin had to persuade the courtesan to stay to see the program through.

"Would you take a walk with me, Jezzine?" Tamasin said when they finished the afternoon practice. "I have a favor to ask you."

Jezzine fell in beside her. "I can guess what it is," she said, not breaking her stride.

"Would you stay on for the next two weeks? I am needed back at Iona. The Queen is mobilizing the country to be ready for war, and she wants me there when she meets Commander Pela."

Jezzine chuckled. "I don't blame her. Pela is very intimidating. All the Royal Houses are wary of her."

"She has a temper as volatile as Valeria's, so I shall be the meat in the sandwich," said Tamasin, wincing. "Would you oversee the rest

of the program? You're the only one I can trust to do it properly."
She flashed her a sly grin. "And the only one who can control Esme."

"I have already decided to stay. As for Esme…I shall persuade
her to go into a trance more often. That's the only way to shut her up."

"But you have to admit the cunning old fox is brilliant at manipulating Dreamtime. None of us would have ever thought of the
trance idea, and she's honed it to perfection," Tamasin said, chuckling. She stopped on the rise and sat on a flat rock overlooking the
meadow. "Let's sit for a while to enjoy the view. I love being out in
the countryside. You know, Jezzine, as a courtesan in the royal courts,
you would be invaluable to us."

Jezzine settled on the rock beside her, folded her legs, and
wrapped her arms around them tightly. Her chin on her knees, she
gazed for a long moment at the view before she answered, "No,
Tamasin. I'll never break the trust of my clients."

"I didn't think you would, but I had to ask. The dogs of war will
be baying at our heels in seven more turns of the moons, and I fear
we'll be ill-prepared to meet them."

"I can't be your spy, Mistress of Dreams, but I'll willingly follow
you into battle when the time comes."

"Thank you, my friend," said Tamasin. "I've misjudged you
badly."

"And I, you. I believed the gossipmongers when they condemned
you for deserting your wife. I realize now you would never do that.
You are one of the few genuinely honorable people I have met." She
snapped off a small yellow flower and spun it in her fingers. "I met
Valeria at a royal party while you were away."

The sudden surge of jealousy felt like a knife in Tamasin's gut.
She could never compete with this woman. Not only was she beautiful, but she was also likable, charming, and witty. She turned her
gaze away and could only manage to say, "Oh?"

"There's no need to look so sad," said Jezzine softly. "Even
though I could tell she was lonely, she didn't seek my favors. You

are lucky. For all that I am courted, I would give anything for such devotion. And for what it's worth, she's lucky too."

Tamasin turned to study her. "You have never met anyone for whom you would give it all up?"

"She disapproves of me."

Tamasin looked at her in surprise. She thought it would be Prince Delvin of Arcadia, Queen Wren's second son. He was said to be a particular favorite of the courtesan. "Then she's a fool. The heart doesn't judge."

"I don't blame her," said Jezzine sadly. "She's an honorable woman. If she was less so, I might have a chance."

"I'm not the one to be advising on the matters of the heart… I have only ever loved one woman. But I can say, love always seems to find a way." Tamasin rose to her feet and dusted her breeches. "We'd better get back. I have a few jugs of mead waiting for a farewell party."

†

Back in Iona, the stables were still quiet when Tamasin flew in an hour after daybreak. After letting Malkia out in the yard to water, she had just finished putting her saddlery away when out of the corner of an eye, she caught sight of a figure hidden in an empty stall. She immediately retreated into a shadow, easing out her short-bladed knife from the pouch on her belt as she positioned her back against the wall.

When the dark form came into the light, she recognized the distinctive hair and bird tattoo.

"Never creep up on me like that, guard. You're lucky I didn't gut you where you hid," Tamasin growled. Noting the shoulder sling, she slid the knife back into the pouch.

The young guard snapped to attention. "I'm sorry, Mistress. Savannah asked me to give you a letter without anyone seeing me. I'm Trainee Justine."

"You're from Falcon's Keep?"

"Yes, ma'am." She pulled a letter out of the sling. "I damaged my shoulder at practice."

Tamasin took the letter and slid it open. "Is Commander Pela aware you're here, Justine?"

The guard nodded. "Savanna said the Commander asked me to give it to you personally, then go straight back home."

"Stand down while I read it. It may require an answer." Tamasin eyed the letter curiously. Pela wouldn't have ordered her to come. She was in Iona and would have delivered it herself. She wondered what secretive game Savannah was playing.

She unfolded the letter.

Tamasin,

I'm sending this letter with Justine, a trusted friend, to warn you that the Silverthorne witches have their own hidden agenda for Rand. One of their witches, Captain Killia, has been working undercover here for years, making sure Pela and the Queen remain at odds. If they have managed to infiltrate Falcon's Keep, where else are they? With Ursula in the palace, no one is safe.

I am well.

Your friend Savannah.

Tamasin pursed her lips. Savannah's message was to the point, but she wished she'd elaborated. How did she find out Killia was a witch? Tamasin had met the soldier a few times over the years, finding her dour and unlikable. She recalled that she had transferred from Iona to the Keep when Pela started there. If Savannah was right in her assessment, then it was indeed a serious situation. Lord knows how long the witches had been fortifying their strategic positions. Maybe years. Ursula had been in the palace long before Valeria's mother died and privy to most of their secrets.

"Thank you, Justine. Tell Savannah I will see to the matter. There will be no reply. When are you flying back?"

"Immediately, Mistress."

"Then give Savannah my best wishes. Um...how is she getting on with the Commander?"

Justine gave a small smile. "Better than anyone expected. The Commander was tough on her for a start, but she's not so hard on her now."

"What happened with Captain Killia?" asked Tamasin.

"The Captain tried to choke Savannah at practice. Savannah poked her in the neck and dropped her."

Tamasin felt a moment of disquiet. By that news, Savannah had to have invoked the power of the medallion. Luckily, the onlookers thought she'd done a fancy maneuver. Whether Pela would believe that wasn't likely. Savannah wasn't a warrior, and Killia was a fighting machine. "Why did the recruits think she could do that?" she asked curiously.

"Because Savannah is our healer. She understands such things." Justine pointed at her arm. "My shoulder was pulled out, and she put it back."

"Killia wouldn't be happy losing face in front of the whole school. I hope she doesn't knife Savannah one dark night."

Justine grinned. "Nay. The Captain left the camp with her tail between her legs."

Tamasin smiled to herself—Savannah was proving a very resilient Chosen One. "Good. I have to get to the palace. Do you require a mount?"

"No, thank you, Mistress. Savannah arranged for Sunflower to take me here and back."

"Right then," said Tamasin. "You had better get going before the handlers arrive."

Tamasin watched Justine as she hurried off. It was a relief to see Savannah had made a friend in the Keep. But why did Savannah get Sunflower to come? Malkia's progenies were reserved for dignitaries, not mounts for the recruits. And how did Savannah, a housemaid, have access to the mare? Resolving to ask the stallion later, she hurried out the stables to the palace. There was much to do—the most pressing, the Silverthorne witch in their midst.

Valeria was finishing breakfast when Tamasin entered their bedchamber. As she approached, the Queen rose with a glad cry. "Tam, I didn't expect you for at least another hour."

Tamasin's face creased in a smile as she possessively encircled Valeria's waist. "I couldn't wait."

Valeria smiled back at her and leaned into her embrace. "I've missed you, my love."

"Me too," she said, kissing her soundly. She let her lips linger, then pulled away reluctantly. "But showing you how much will have to wait. We have a pressing problem to deal with."

Troubled, Valeria appraised her. "At the camp?"

"No. That was an unqualified success. I will tell you all about it later. It's this," Tamasin said, handing over the letter.

As Valeria scanned it, her face hardened. "Call the Council immediately into the throne room. I want to have witnesses when we interview Ursula." As Tamasin turned to leave, she added, "And Tam, get the captain on duty to post three guards outside the door. Once we start, no one will be allowed to leave. Neither Ursula nor any Council members. It might be that you weren't to tell me you were going through the portal because of Ursula, but we can't assume there isn't another traitor in our midst."

When Tamasin entered the throne room, the ten Council members were seated around the table while Valeria sat regally on her throne. They all watched her uneasily. Tamasin took a seat a little away from the proceedings, preferring not to take an active role. It was the Queen's domain.

A moment later, Ursula entered with the cape, approached the throne, and bowed. "You wanted me to test someone, Your Majesty."

"Sit down, Ursula. I have something to discuss," ordered Valeria, her expression uncompromising as she pointed to a chair away from the table.

Wary, Ursula sat and placed the folded cape on her knees.

"I accuse you, Ursula Nardrax, Silverthorne witch, of conspiring against your Queen. I deem you to be a spy, gathering information from citizens of the realm while subjecting them to your cape. You supplied these details to the Silverthorne Coven, who used them to act against the crown. What say you in your defense?"

Ursula went rigid. "That's nonsense. I've served you faithfully, Valeria, and your mother before you."

"You will address me by my title, witch," Valeria said imperiously. "Continue."

"What proof have my accusers, Your Majesty?"

"Your coven is under scrutiny. We're aware it has been controlling citizens important in the governance of the realm. People whose names you learned as my trusted advisor."

Tamasin studied Ursula's face carefully as she heard the accusation. Malevolence flitted across Ursula's face before her expression turned blank. So Savannah could be right.

Valeria stared down at her. "I want you gone from the palace by this afternoon, Ursula. You are no longer welcome in Iona."

Surprised, Tamasin glanced at her. She had expected her to ease in, be a little wary of Ursula, who was a powerful witch to be feared. But then Valeria had always been a strong queen, and while fair and compassionate, ruled with unyielding authority. She had thrown down the gauntlet, and Ursula could either argue or beg. But either way, knowing her wife, Valeria would never back down. She had given her royal command. From the hateful glare she threw at the Queen, Ursula knew it too.

She rose to her feet and tossed the cape on the floor. "Do you think, Valeria Argosa, that I have waited all these years to be dismissed like a servant? You stupid Queen. You have courted my power when you should have been dreading it. Now feel the full fury of my wrath." She slammed her foot down on the cape. "*Naeagus nage embollisa*. Come forth, demon. *Naeagus nage embollisa*."

While the women stared horrified at Ursula, Valeria rose from the throne. "Get out, witch, and take that cape with you."

A stench began to spiral out from the cape, acrid and foul like putrid flesh. Valeria didn't flinch. "Get out, or my guards will incarcerate you in the dungeons."

Ursula turned to nod at someone on the table while continuing her incantations in an even monotone. Bronwyn got up and hurried to the door. Tamasin was about to follow her, but an instinct held her back. Whatever was coming out of the cape was born magic, an enemy the guards had no hope of fighting. She would only be throwing away their lives by letting them in.

A long bang resounded as Bronwyn slammed the lever down into the slot. The room was now effectively sealed. The door was thick solid oak, harvested from the great forests of the west.

No one would be coming in.

Chapter Seventeen

Bronwyn ran to Ursula's side, who impatiently pushed her aside. Valeria began to descend the two stairs, then stopped abruptly when the cloak began to shake. With no further warning, it burst into flames. They roared fiercely, the inferno nearly reaching the vaulted ceiling. After burning ferociously for a full minute, the fire subsided as quickly as it began. When the smoke cleared, an enormous demonic creature stood on the marble floor. Tamasin stared at it in horror. Ye Gods, the son-of-a-bitch was ugly.

Red flames licked its scaled body as it bellowed out. "You dare summon me, witch?"

"I, Ursula Nardox, Silverthorne witch, do call on you, demon, to fulfill your bargain."

The demon stamped its cloven foot. "I have not reached the full height of my power. You have not fed me enough yet."

"How did she feed you, hideous creature?" Valeria called out.

The demon turned to look at her. Saliva slavered its fangs. "She has been bringing your people under the cape into my world for years, Queen. Fear and pain make me grow strong," it hissed. "Why didn't you wait for another twelve turns of the moons, witch."

Shooting a look of hatred at Valeria, Ursula replied. "I had no choice, my Lord. I had to summon you. She knows. You are strong enough to do it."

"I am only strong enough to change one of you, witch."

"No! You promised, Ursula," screamed Bronwyn. She pointed a finger at Tamasin. "I am to be turned into Tamasin. To rule by your side."

"Quiet, woman. My pact does not concern you," the demon snarled. Taking one step forward, it raked its talons across Bronwyn's neck. She gave a gurgling scream as a stream of blood gushed from the severed artery. It sank its fangs into her arm and ripped it off. Bronwyn was dead by the time her body hit the floor. Then the demon looked up at the Queen, its bloodied lips pulled back in a diabolical grin.

Valeria paled but stood her ground. Tamasin had never seen her quite this magnificent or regal as she stared down this ferocious enemy. "And who have you promised to Ursula?" she asked.

"I recognize you— you're Molvia. You are not invincible," a wavering voice interrupted from the table.

With a venomous glare, the demon turned its eyes on the old woman. "I will deal with you later, Mistress Moira. It was only because you had the ear of the Queen's mother, that I failed to reach my power long before this. You will not die so quickly. I will slowly rip the skin off your bones, eat your flesh and relish each mouthful."

"I asked you a question, demon," snarled Valeria.

It looked at her balefully. "It is not *who* I give her, but *what*. She will wear your crown."

"And what do you get out of it, pathetic creature?"

It strode forward to a foot in front of Valeria. "I get you, Queen. You will live with me, be mine to do with whatever I like. And make no mistake, you will scream and wish you were dead when I have you in my bed."

Tamasin swallowed, trying desperately to think of a way to defeat the demon. To rush it would be fruitless. She'd have to find an opening when it was off-guard.

"I am Valeria Argosa, of a long line of Imperial Queens. You will not take me so easily, spawn of hell. But, demon, if you let everyone in the room go unharmed, I'll accompany you into the darkness."

"No, don't," cried Moira. "Molvia's word means nothing."

"It is too late for bargaining, Valeria," shouted Ursula. "I call on you, Lord, to give me my reward."

The demon rose to its full height and spread its claws into the air. "Then let it begin. Stand still."

Valeria stiffened, the blood draining from her face. Tamasin could see her fighting whatever was happening to her. The demon hunched forward as if it too was having a struggle. Then slowly, Valeria sank to her knees. She was losing the battle. Next to her, Ursula's face began to change. At first, it wasn't apparent, but then Tamasin realized the witch was turning into Valeria.

Fury burst through Tamasin. *Damn you to hell. She'll never be yours.* Her body temperature plummeted until she felt so cold that it was as if her blood had frozen solid in her veins. She looked down to see her body had turned white, icicles trailing off her skin and ice crackling from her fingers. Only barely aware of the women around the table staring, she lurched toward the demon and yelled, "You can't have her, you son-of-Satan."

The beast whirled at the sound, its eyes widening in alarm. "Noooooo… what have you done, witch? You stupid fool. You summoned me when there was an Ice Elf in the room."

"I didn't know," Ursula screamed. Now the demon's attention was elsewhere, the Queen's features gradually faded from her face.

Valeria pulled herself upright and staggered to the crossed swords positioned above the throne.

Tamasin launched straight at the demon's body. It immediately burst into flames. Steam sizzled into the air as they fought. Jaws snapped and talons swiped. Though the demon was much larger, Tamasin had been well trained. Fueled by anger and vengeance, she gradually got the upper hand, and ice began to extinguish fire. The demon's scales turned blue, then white, and finally, glassy. Giving the last thrust, Tamasin plunged her hand into its heart. With a loud brittle crunch, the demon shattered into millions of shards of ice.

But as the ice scattered across the floor, she heard Moira shriek, "Watch out."

Tamasin swiveled quickly to see Ursula running at her with a knife. Even as Tamasin raised her arm to ward off the attack, she feared she was too late. The blade was already inches from her chest.

Desperately, she parried the blow, but weakened by her fight, she had little strength left. The witch was the stronger. As Ursula sliced again with the knife, she punched Tamasin in the face with her other fist. Tamasin fell backward, her upper body completely exposed.

"Die," Ursula screamed, raising the blade.

As Tamasin vainly tried to roll away, the witch suddenly stiffened and jerked. She began to stagger, losing her grip on the bone handle. The knife slipped from her fingers, and with an agonizing howl, she collapsed to the floor.

Valeria pulled the sword out of her back and drove it in again. "Just to be sure," she said vehemently.

Tamasin looked down at Ursula spreadeagled on the floor. Even in death, she looked malevolent.

She sank to her knees before Valeria. "My Queen."

Valeria placed her hand on her head and nodded silently.

One by one, each woman of the Council came to kneel at her feet. Some looked shocked, others ashamed, one in tears. After they had filed past, Valeria said, "Mistress of Music, please open the door for the guards."

The soldiers poured into the room. Tamasin could imagine their anguish hearing the screaming inside and not being able to get in. The whole garrison must have been waiting in the antechamber.

At the sight of the two bodies, the Commanding Officer hurried to the Queen's side. "Your Majesty. What happened? Are you hurt?"

"I survived, Captain, but I do need to rest. It has been a trying time for us all. Burn the bodies, please, and ask the staff to scrub the floor. Black magic has been here, and I want to remove its taint from the palace. I would appreciate it if your guards could escort the Council members back to their chambers. Mistress Moira will give a statement on my behalf. Now, if you'll excuse me." She turned to Tamasin. "Coming?"

Tamasin followed her through the corridors, uneasy at how deathly drawn she looked. As soon as they entered their chambers, Valeria fell onto the bed and silently curled up. Tamasin lay down beside her, though not sure if her embrace would be welcome. She tentatively put her arm around her. When Valeria shrunk away, Tamsin whispered, "Please, Val, don't pull away from me. I'm sorry I didn't tell you who I was. I didn't want to lose you."

"You think that's what this is all about? That I'm upset with you?" Valeria muttered. "Sometimes, Tam, you don't understand me at all. You and your sense of honor. You should hate me, not I, you. I should be getting down on my hands and knees, begging for your forgiveness. And every poor person I ordered to be put under that cape. In my stupidity, I didn't protect my subjects, instead, I allowed Ursula to send them into that demon's perverted world."

"Your mother started it. Don't forget that. You inherited Ursula and the cape."

"I continued the sadistic practice even though you kept telling me not to," said Valeria bitterly. "I made a royal mess of everything."

"You weren't to know what she was up to. And none of the Council saw it either. We're all guilty." Tamasin rubbed her shoulders soothingly. "How are you feeling?"

"I'm so tired." Valeria turned on her back and stared into space. "I have never been so revolted by anything. As I fought to prevent the transformation, the demon showed me his dark place, a cave, where there was only pain and anguish. There were people and creatures, half human, half animals in cages…some wept and screamed, while others looked at me with deadened eyes. Unmentionable things slithered and crawled, unholy beings born in the darkness. Hideous shrieking…"

Tamasin held her close, whispering words of love to ease the pain. And assurance that it all could be overcome together. Finally, Valeria relaxed against her, welcoming her kisses.

Tamasin drew back to look at her. "It seems I am an Ice Elf. You don't mind I'm half magic," she asked.

Valeria let out a chuckle. "Do I mind you turned into this magnificent creature who flew to my defense? Really, Tam? I can't believe you even asked that."

"My mother told me she only knew my father for a night. I hadn't a clue what kind of magical being he was."

"There are probably lots of mixed-breed offspring in Rand who keep their identities hidden," remarked Valeria. "I think it is time to try to mend the rift between our cultures."

"I agree," said Tamasin. Then to her annoyance, a knock sounded on the door. "What?" she called out testily.

"Commander Pela is waiting in the antechamber, Ma'am."

"Tell her we're coming," Tamasin replied, then screwed up her nose. Not a good time to have to talk to Pela.

"Oh, dear. We'll have to see her," groaned Valeria.

"I'll do it. I think you've had enough for the day."

"Would you?" said Valeria, a relieved look on her face. "She's probably heard about Ursula and will be insufferable."

"No doubt," replied Tamasin. In quick strides, she headed for the door. The sooner she had the interview, the sooner she could come back.

Pela and her second-in-command, Rhiannon, stood by a tapestry depicting a sweeping battle scene. With their formidable hair, tattoos, and military uniforms, the two looked like they'd just jumped out of the picture.

Pela's face twisted into a frown when Tamasin approached. She saluted. "Mistress Tamasin. Is the Queen indisposed?"

"It has been a taxing morning. She needs to rest."

"We heard from the Captain of the Guard there was trouble," said Pela. "And Ursula was killed in the throne room."

"Word travels fast," murmured Tamasin.

"The news would be welcomed by many. 'Tis a pity it was such a long time coming," Pela said. "What happened?"

"Just let's say she was using the cape for a despicable purpose. Not for the good of the crown."

"I could have told the Queen that if she'd listened."

Tamasin ignored the reproof. "We had better get on to the business at hand. I do have to get back. Is everything organized for the royal visit to Falcon's Keep?"

"Yes. Accommodation will be as comfortable as we can manage," Pela answered stiffly. "But it is not luxurious."

"We don't expect it to be. What's on the agenda?"

"Considering this is the first time for years that the Queen has attended our graduation, we will be having three days of games to allow our graduates to show their fighting skills. The palace soldiers are invited to pit their talents against our Elite Guard squad. Say, your best fifty against ours," said Pela, a gleam in her eye.

"I'm sure they would welcome the challenge," Tamasin replied, with an answering gleam. "The Queen has many seasoned warriors who would also like to prove their mettle."

Pela gave a predatory smile. "Then it's game on."

Tamasin was under no illusion that it would develop into an all-out contest between Valeria and Pela. Both were as pigheaded and proud as the other. "Good. Then I'll see you at Falcon's Keep. Who will be your liaison officer?"

"Captain Killia."

"Oh? I heard she left the Keep."

Pela stiffened. "Pardon?"

"She disappeared from the base after Savannah defeated her in a fight," said Tamasin. Even though she knew it was petty, she felt enormous satisfaction telling her. Pela would hate that she was the last to hear what was going on in her domain.

A dark frown settled on Pela's brow. "We'd better get back," she growled. "Till next week, Mistress."

Chapter Eighteen

Falcon's Keep

The morning of the Queen's arrival was clear and fresh, the crispness a constant reminder the training fortress was high in the mountains.

The Keep had been scrubbed clean for the royal visit, the stonework now a gleaming burnished grey. The blue and red banner of the Elite Guard, depicting a falcon in flight, fluttered proudly from atop the stone parapet behind the landing pad. A thousand trainees stood to attention in rows designating their seniority. Savannah was at the back with the newest recruits. The entire garrison was in the blue uniform of the Elite Guard except for Pela.

In black breeches, black boots, and a black tunic embroidered with the falcon emblem, she stood alone on top of the battlement. Her oiled braid was dark as midnight, and the tattoos on her face stood out sharply against the backdrop of the sky. A long double-edged sword hung at her side. Savannah had watched her sharpen the blade the night before, then polish it until it shone. It was the same light metal as Elsbeth's armor, which, according to Glenda, was called zenphin. It was rare, mined in the cold Bear Mountains of the North and forged by the blacksmiths of Bolderdore. Too precious for the common soldier, whose weapons were iron.

Pela turned from scanning the horizon and called out, "The Queen's entourage is in the distance. Remember, my warriors, the honor of the Elite Guard is on your shoulders. We have never been defeated in battle. Who stands with me?"

Fists rose in the air with cries of, "We do, Commander."

"Then, Guards, make me proud."

"For honor and glory. For you," they roared.

Caught up in the patriotic fervor, Savannah called out her allegiance with them. She wondered how she'd ever thought Pela unattractive. She looked magnificent, imperious, proud, a leader for whom every one of these tough warrior women would follow willingly into battle.

At the first hum of rushing wings, the soldiers snapped to attention. The advance squad flew into view in a wedge formation and circled the compound in a sweep before touching down onto the grassed area. Savannah was surprised to see there was a small contingent of male soldiers as well as female warriors from the Queen's Guards. After dismounting, the riders remained beside their horses.

"The men are from the Royal Garrison in Kasparian," the recruit beside Savannah whispered. "They're masters of the battleax."

Savannah studied them with some misgivings—they were no taller than the women but muscled like bulls. When a long trumpet blast sounded, she turned her attention back to the sky where two Blue Fjord horses flew over the battlements. They hovered in the air while the rearguard of twenty warriors circled past to join their compatriots. The visiting soldiers quickly formed into lines, standing proudly in a river of gold and silver. The flag bearer unfurled the golden banner emblazoned with the royal emblem: a crown above crossed swords.

Accompanied by another trumpet fanfare, Malkia and Marigold, the sleek golden mare bearing the Queen, glided gracefully onto the landing pad. Tamasin vaulted lightly from Malkia, then helped Valeria dismount. The Queen had discarded her regal robes for the visit and wore the armor of the palace battalion. A thin silver and gold crown was entwined in the braids of her hair.

A ragged roar went up when Valeria waved to acknowledge the Elite Warriors. Pela descended the battlement but didn't look happy when she bent her knee to the monarch.

With one in silver and the other in black, the Queen and Pela were opposite sides of a coin, yet they both had the stance of those born to command.

As soon as the greeting formalities had been completed, Pela led the Queen on an inspection of the trainees. Tamasin followed in their wake, frequently having a word with a recruit. When they reached Savannah in the rear row, Valeria stopped in surprise. "You're training your housemaid?"

Pela barely glanced at Savannah. "She was sent out here quite ill-equipped to defend herself."

"Oh?" said Valeria. "She was meant to help with menial duties, not to be a fighter."

"Be as it may," said Pela with a hard glitter in her eye. "If she works for me, she trains."

"Then I expect a demonstration of her abilities. Let it be a test of your coaching techniques. She hardly has the physique of a warrior," said Valeria.

Pela smiled coldly and bowed. "Of course, your Majesty. I'll organize a bout on the last day in the hand-to-hand combats. After lunch today, we'll start the proceedings with the archery and knife throwing competitions."

"Tourney weapons only," interrupted Tamasin. "We'll not have any open wounds when all able-bodied soldiers will be sorely needed in times to come."

When Pela turned to address Tamasin, her gaze softened. "I agree, Consort. It's a test of skill, not war." She called out to the troops. "Please salute your sovereign."

In accord, they stood to attention with their fists to their chests.

"Dismissed," Pela called out, then addressed Valeria. "Captain Rhiannon will show you to your quarters, Ma'am."

When they moved on Savannah let out the breath she was holding. She brought her gaze to Tamasin, who lingered in front of her.

"Bring us a jug of cider to our rooms please, recruit," said Tamasin.

"Yes, Mistress," Savannah replied and quickly escaped to the kitchen before Pela saw her. Judging from the barely controlled antagonism between her and the Queen, she doubted she would want Savannah talking to Valeria.

With an underlying urgency in the air, the main kitchen was frantically busy. Normally, the food served in the great mess was always plentiful but plain. For the Queen's visit, they had been instructed to serve menus fit for a royal table. Savannah gave the chief cook a wide berth, not wishing to be the target of her acerbic tongue. The portly woman ruled the kitchen strictly, and today she looked to be on the warpath, to be avoided at all costs. Thankfully, one of the scullery maids was getting a dressing down, which gave Savannah a chance to slip in and out of the pantry unnoticed.

Clutching the flagon to her chest, she made her way quickly to the royal quarters. At her first tap on the door, Tamasin urged her inside.

The Queen was sitting at the dining table, and Savannah glanced warily at her. She bowed deeply. "Your Majesty."

When Valeria smiled amicably and said, "Come, Savannah, sit down," she breathed a sigh of relief. The animosity outside must have been for Pela's benefit. Valeria's eyes fell to her chest. "May I see it?"

Tamasin took a seat next to her wife. "I've told the Queen, Savannah."

Savannah waited for a warning zap, but none came. "Of course," she murmured and pulled the medallion out.

Tears sprang to Valeria's eyes. "It's true. The Circle of Sheda is back." She studied Savannah curiously. "You can't take it off?"

"No, Ma'am." She smiled ruefully. "It seems to have claimed me."

"Why you, do you think?"

"Ah…I've been puzzling a lot about that. I've concluded that a historian is required, not a warrior."

Tamasin leaned forward. "I think that's only one of the reasons, Savannah."

"I'm aware there're probably more," said Savannah, "but at the moment, that's all I've got. I've no idea what mysterious forces are at play. I'm from a world where there's no such thing as magic."

"Extraordinary. That's hard to believe," murmured Valeria. "Who gave you that message for me?"

A sharp tingle bit into her palm. "Ouch!" exclaimed Savannah, dropping the medallion.

"You can't tell us," said Tamasin. It was a statement, not a question.

"No. Sorry."

Valeria reached a finger over to touch the dangling medallion. The metal began to glow until Savannah could feel the heat radiating into her breastbone. Valeria swallowed several times, then breathed out a hushed, choked whisper. Finally, she dropped her hand to the table, her face pale. "I have passed the test, though I felt my ancestors' ire at having trusted the Silverthorne witch." She looked sorrowfully at Tamasin. "I will do better in the future."

"You heeded my warning about the witches?" asked Savannah.

"Ursula is dead," said Tamasin. "I will tell you the story when there's more time."

"Good riddance," said Savannah. "But there's been a development since I sent that letter. Tell me…did the attempt on Your Majesty's life involve a crow?"

Tamasin's mouth became a hard line, her anger barely suppressed. "The assassin materialized from a crow. When I killed him, he dissolved back into the bird. Did one try to kill you?"

"Three actually, but they didn't recognize me. I'm sure it was Pela they were after." She continued urgently, "The Queen and Pela are two of the most powerful people on Rand. If someone planned an invasion, they'd surely endeavor to eliminate the most dangerous adversaries first."

"After this news, I shall order the Realms to be on assassin alert," said Valeria. "They are already gathering their armies. Since there have been centuries of peace, it will take a while to conscript soldiers into service."

"Um…have you worked out the meaning of the message?" Savannah asked quietly, recalling the old woman's words: gather the dreamers and persuade the hawks to fly.

"I've mobilized the Dreamers." Tamasin looked over at Savannah and added, "They can all see the threads of the future in their dreams. It's an inherited gift passed down through the female line. We've been learning to hone those skills. Though I've yet to understand where they'll be needed."

Valeria studied Savannah keenly. "Have you any idea?"

Savannah met her eyes. "I think they're meant to predict where the crows will appear. And don't forget the other part about persuading the hawks to fly."

"How are we supposed to talk to birds?" groaned Tamasin. "And what are the hawks supposed to do anyhow?"

"They'll kill the crows before they can turn into assassins," replied Savannah without hesitation.

Aware they were both staring at her, Savannah squirmed in her seat. She couldn't break Pela's confidence, so she stayed silent. The more she thought about it, the more convincing it sounded. Working together, the Hawks and the Dreamers could kill off the crows before they turned into men. But to confirm her supposition, she needed to find the historical documents relating to the war preceding the Mystic War.

Before they could debate her theory, she rose quickly to her feet. "I'd better go home before Pela discovers I'm missing."

Tamasin moved around to walk her to the door. "We'll talk again when we get a chance. You'll have to tell me how you managed to persuade Pela to let you stay."

"Oh, Savannah," the Queen called out. "I'm sorry I asked you to take a part in the competition. As you no doubt noticed, Commander Pela has a knack for annoying me."

Savannah bit back a smile. No one could miss the antagonism between the two of them. She didn't envy Tamasin in the middle trying to keep the peace. "I'll be honored to show you what I've learned, Your Majesty. Though I'm not up to the rest of the recruit's standard, I've mastered many moves in my time here."

"Perhaps it was ordained that you were sent to the Keep," whispered Tamasin as she showed her out. "The Chosen One does have to be able to defend herself."

"Perhaps," murmured Savannah back. She'd already worked out that whatever happened to her since meeting the old blind woman wasn't random. Somehow, the seer was manipulating events. It had become clear she was meant to come to Falcon's Keep. As well as learning self-defense, she'd discovered the riddle of the Hawks. And now also knew about the Dreamers.

Pela was waiting impatiently when she entered the house, the smell of hair oil and leather clinging to her like perfume. "You took your time," she growled.

"Sorry. I didn't realize I had to come straight back," Savannah replied warily, taking in Pela's sour look. Having to kowtow to the Queen had put her in a foul mood.

"Lunch will be ready shortly. We'll have to be there before the royal party," Pela said. She crossed to the wardrobe and pulled out the clothes Savannah had worn when she arrived at the Keep. "Take off the uniform and put these on. You'll be serving me...exclusively."

Savannah felt a twinge of hurt—Pela was using her to snub the Queen. She would be well aware that Valeria would have learned from Tamasin that Savannah wore the Circle of Sheda. And what better way to irritate her than to rub it in that the Chosen One was her servant? She pursed her lips. "You're making be dress as a serving maid? I've taken an oath to serve you at meals, Commander, but I thought I'd earned the right to wear the uniform for these games."

Pela looked down at her with a curl of her lips. "The Queen pointed out you were sent here for menial duties, so a serving wench you shall be."

Savannah tamped down her annoyance and without a word, took the clothes. If Pela wanted a lackey, then that's what she'd get.

As soon as she emerged from the bathroom, Pela strode to the door. "Let's go."

Savannah followed her silently down the path, determined not to let Pela's behavior get to her. At times like this, she had no idea why she was attracted to her—she was so infuriating. "Pride cometh before a fall," she murmured.

From the stiffening of her shoulders, Savannah realized she'd heard her. She'd forgotten Pela literally could hear as well as a hawk.

When they entered the dining hall, the military personnel were already in their places. The room had been rearranged, with the dignitaries up front, and long rows of tables for the soldiers. They stood to salute Pela as she strode through. The instructors were seated at the head table, and Pela took the chair next to one reserved for the Queen. A few minutes later, the Queen and her Consort entered the building, acknowledging the salutes as they made their way to the front. Valeria raised an eyebrow when she saw Savannah behind Pela's chair, though she didn't comment. Tamasin merely nodded to her as she took the chair on the other side of Pela.

Savannah was pleased to see the kitchen staff had produced out of the morning's chaos a feast fit for the Supreme Monarch. The tables were laden with exotic dishes, many types of meat and vegetables foreign to her. The center dish was a roasted animal that looked like a wild boar.

A maid appeared with a bowl of warm water and towel, offering them first to the Queen for the ceremonial cleaning of the hands. Once Valeria had wiped away the last drops, the maid presented the bowl to Pela. The ceremony over, another maid appeared with a plate to serve the Queen. Her first bite signaled the beginning of the meal. Pela waited until everyone at the table had laden their plates before she hooked a finger at Savannah. "I'll have everything except cheese."

Savannah took the plate without displaying any emotion. "Yes, Commander." She walked around to the front of the table and heaped the food onto the plate, aware everyone at the table was watching her. After she carefully placed it in front of Pela, she moved back behind her.

"I'll have wine, too," said Pela sharply.

Savannah didn't deign to answer, merely leaned over her shoulder to fill the cup.

Tamasin reached over and took the jug from her hand. "No need to pour mine, Savannah, I'm quite capable of doing it myself."

Pela's neck reddened at the inferred rebuke. "My servant always attends me at meals, Tamasin."

"Really? You must be getting soft," Tamasin said, her voice quietly censorious.

"I believe the Queen sent me a servant to wait on me."

Tamasin stabbed a piece of meat, then moved her head nearer to Pela's, so close that Savannah had to strain to hear her. "True. She did. But it takes a wise woman to differentiate between the common and the uncommon. Perhaps I've sadly overestimated you."

Pela's fingers twitched as if she was molding them to her sword. "I never wanted help," she said, keeping her voice low too.

"No, you didn't…you've made that abundantly clear. But the time for harboring old grudges is at an end. You either step up or step aside. The armies of Rand need a Supreme Commander who can take her place with honor among the ancestral lines of the great warriors. In seven more turns of the moons, we will be at war."

Pela stared at her. "You would give me that rank?"

"You are our finest tactician. It is not only the boldest or the strongest that win wars but also the cleverest. You inspire loyalty, and the soldiers will follow you." Tamasin's face became stern, her words direct. "If you accept, you *will* swear allegiance to the crown and mean it. We have to be united to face the enemy."

"I'm honored you think so highly of me. It will be a challenge that I will relish. I have to admit, though I enjoy my present position at Falcon's Keep, I need to get out onto a bigger arena and test my mettle." She gave a wry grin. "Though I'll need help with diplomacy. Assure the Queen I will swear allegiance and be very proud to do so."

"Good," said Tamasin with an answering smile. "I'm sure she'll be pleased."

Pela studied Tamasin's face. "Now, who is this enemy that is coming?"

Tamasin threw up her hands. "I have no idea."

"We're already working on it," replied Pela. "Savannah is studying the old documents in our archives. She thinks this enemy attacked Rand in the war before the Mystic War."

"So," Tamasin said, looking disconcerted. "You're already aware of how valuable Savannah is? And all this serving business is for the Queen's benefit?"

Pela chuckled. "Yep. If I tell her Savannah is a real asset, she might take her back. And it doesn't hurt for Savannah to serve me… she can get too big for her boots sometimes."

Savannah vainly tried to stifle a little snort escaping at this. She knew Pela caught it when she called out, "You may go and join the other soldiers, Savannah."

Chapter Nineteen

"What were you and Pela whispering about at lunch?" asked Valeria as she changed out of her formal gown. "She was quite civil for the rest of the meal."

Tamasin leaned over and pecked her cheek. "I told her the feud with you had to end."

Valeria's eyebrows shot up. "And she agreed? That's hard to believe."

"I did mention you were thinking of promoting her to the Supreme Commander of Rand's armies, but that it came with a proviso that she swears allegiance to you without reservation. She wants the promotion."

Valeria smiled. "Very clever. I must admit I'm tired of being at odds with her. She's much more palatable when she's pleasant."

"In light of the assassination attempts, we'll need her more than ever to bring the armies together. It'll require a strong leader to wield all the cultures into a united fighting force. Every monarch is wary, maybe in awe of her, which will be to her advantage. With the limited time we have to prepare, she's the only one who could do it."

Valeria took her hand. "You could, Tam."

"I prefer to be in the background. I have a network of undercover agents to control and the Dreamers to lead. Pela will make an admirable fighting leader," Tamasin said and squeezed her hand. "You'll have to be more tolerant of her too, Val."

"I will," Valeria replied with a sigh. "Though it will be difficult. She brings out the worst in me. Will you be taking Savannah back with us to Iona?"

"Only if she wants to come. She's good for Pela."

"What! She treats her like a lowly servant."

Tamasin chuckled. "That was for your benefit. Believe it or not, she respects her."

"Who would have thought?" murmured Valeria.

"Who indeed? But I wish Pela would tell her. Savannah needs to be here a while longer to hide the medallion until we have everything in place. But it'll be her choice. If she's desperate to go, then I won't leave her here," replied Tamasin. She gestured toward the door. "We'd better go. They'll be waiting for us."

A pleasant breeze ruffled across the Keep as they entered the amphitheater arena. The archery contests were ready to start, and the rows of stone seats were packed.

"This arena is quite an impressive venue for a tournament," remarked Tamasin as they made their way to the canopied viewing platform at the far end.

After Pela showed them to their seats, she signaled for the archers to begin. Ten competitors to a side, the Queen's finest archers were to shoot against the strongest from the recruits. The targets were mannequins rather than stationary targets—life-size figures of men wearing hooded capes. An instructor hovered on a horse above, controlling the target like a marionette, making it dash and weave like a running man.

"Clever," murmured Tamasin. Pela had fashioned the targets to look like the mysterious assassins.

The first bowman, a dark woman in a blue Elite Guard uniform, took her place in the circle. Her back was to the target, a longbow in her hand, six arrows in the quiver. When the bow master called out, "Go," by the time she'd turned to face the target, she'd already had an arrow notched. Her arm strained against the string of the bow as she pulled it back for release. No sooner had she shot the arrow than she had another ready for flight. After the fifth arrow, she pulled the string to her cheek, aiming the last one at the head. The mannequin sped up, swiftly closing the distance between them. In the next instance, the razor-sharp tip of the arrow pierced the center of its head.

A cheer went up from the crowd.

"Impressive," said Valeria, giving the archer a nod of approval.

The competitors came and went, the bow master judging them by the speed and hits to the vital organs. The final came down to the first Elite Guard, against a veteran from the Iona Garrison, a hard woman with a stocky body and solid shoulders. Four targets dangled from the air, and each archer had ten arrows to be loosed within the allotted time. After the final tally, the Elite Guard was the victor. A roar went up through the blue ranks.

"First blood to Falcon's Keep," said Pela with a self-satisfied smile.

Tamasin stole a glance at Valeria. She didn't look happy. "What's next?" she asked.

"Knife throwing. I thought since we have two more days and it's getting late, we'd have a one-on-one demonstration. Captain Rhiannon will be representing Falcon's Keep."

Tamasin looked sharply at Pela. Rhiannon was supposed to be unbeatable in this particular skill. Pela was stacking the odds. Valeria knew it too by the way her lips pressed together in a hard line. But then she flashed Pela a smile. "A demonstration, you say?"

"Yes, Your Majesty. Rhiannon is an instructor, not a recruit. But naturally, we will be scoring."

Tamasin nearly rolled her eyes. An exhibition match or not, it still mattered which side won.

"Then I name Tamasin as our representative."

Pela looked disconcerted. "Tamasin? Um... I respect your choice, Ma'am, but perhaps someone younger might have better reflexes."

"No... no. Tamasin used to be very handy with knives."

"Of course," murmured Pela. "If you'll excuse me, I'll organize the competition."

"What do you think you're doing?" Tamasin whispered sternly.

"I'm taking that supercilious smug look off her face. Make me proud, my love."

"I'll try to," muttered Tamasin, flexing her fingers.

Tamasin and knives were old friends. Even as a child, she had an innate ability to land the blade to a hair's breadth at wherever she aimed. In hindsight, she should have realized as she grew older that the talent was too unusual for someone without magic. On her eighteenth birthday, she joined the Queen's Army Officer School and became a Master of Impalement Arms in just two years. The knife had remained her primary weapon of choice.

When Rhiannon strode out onto the arena, the blue brigade cheered her on. Tamasin had always found Pela's second-in-command a likable, capable woman who perfectly complemented her commander's forbidding personality. She was looking at Tamasin with an embarrassed air, as though she was wondering how she could beat her without Tamasin losing too much face.

The targets this time were stationary, set apart at progressive distances. Tamasin had to squint to see the furthest, which would need a mighty throw to even reach it. After wiping her hands on her breeches, she went to the table that was loaded with throwing knives. Normally, she favored a short sleek tactical blade that slipped comfortably into the sheath in her shoe, but not this time. Once she tested the weight in her palm, she chose a simple set of eight-inch, straight throwing knives made from an alloy of iron and zenphin. Iron for the weight, zenphin for the sharpness. Rhiannon raised an eyebrow at her choice as she arranged her longer, fancier knives on the bench beside her.

Having accepted the challenge, Tamasin felt alive with purpose. The world around her fell away as she concentrated on the targets. Her body began to tingle when she picked up the first knife and threw it. The point burrowed into the center bullseye. Her next two throws hit the inner circle as well. Rhiannon did the same. The target was pulled away and they were on their second. Then third—the fourth. The scores were even by the sixth. She broke her concentration for a second to cast a glance at Rhiannon. She was wiping sweat from her eyes and caught Tamasin's gaze. "You're the best I've ever been against," she muttered.

Tamasin merely nodded and reached for a knife. A long distance away, the second last target was in the shape of a man. Rhiannon threw first, her knife catching the side of his hip. A roar went up from the wave of blue. Tamasin didn't hesitate, this time swinging her arm higher before releasing the knife. It arched through the air and the tip sliced into the head.

Rhiannon turned to look at her. "Well done. I've been beaten by a master."

"We've still one target to go. It looks like a melon on a stick," Tamasin said.

"Nobody could hit that. Pela put it there as a joke."

Tamasin grinned. "Then I'll do it to prove to Pela not to underestimate the opposition. And not to infer I'm too old to fight. You want to have a try?"

"Nah. You go ahead. It's an impossible shot."

Tamasin picked up a knife and stared into the distance. Her body hummed with energy as she visualized the path and calculated the trajectory. Satisfied, she summoned her strength and launched it. All eyes tracked it as it spun through the air. For a moment, Tamasin thought she'd overdone it, but it dipped quickly at the end and lodged firmly into the melon.

A gasp echoed around the arena, followed by loud applause.

Valeria was beaming when she arrived back, patting Tamasin's thigh possessively after she sat down. "Well done."

Pela gazed at her with admiration tinged with awe. "Forgive me, Consort. I was stupid to dismiss you so casually. In all my years in the force, I have never seen such skill with a knife."

Tamasin nodded at the compliment but answered reprovingly. "Never presume the age of a warrior makes her, or him, less valuable than a younger fitter one, Pela. With age comes wisdom and experience. You've been a very able commander of this training camp, molding our young into the best fighting force in the country. But you have more to learn. Once you're the Supreme Commander of all the armies in Rand, your role will be different. You will be working with some generals who may question your authority. Keep an open mind and choose your trusted lieutenants well. You'll need them in the times to come."

Pela blinked at her, emotion flitting across her face. "You sound like my father, Tamasin. He was the last person to give me a lecture." She gave a rueful twitch of her lips. "Though he wasn't so eloquent with his words."

"Your father's alive? I thought you didn't have a family."

"That is in the past. I haven't seen them for years." She bowed her head at Tamasin. "I will take heed of what you've said, and I'd appreciate it if I may seek your advice in my future role."

"I'm looking forward to working with you."

Pela stood up and bowed to Valeria. "My guards will escort you to your quarters, Your Majesty. Tonight, we have a special dinner in your honor, with some live entertainment. I'll see you there."

"My word. You've tamed the beast." Valeria exclaimed as she watched Pela walk away.

"I haven't, though I've made inroads," Tamasin said. "She's a bright woman and realizes she needs my help. Since she's fallen out with just about every ruler in the land, she'll need a diplomat to ease her into society."

Valeria looked amused. "Then you'll be busy. She terrifies most of them."

"It'll be a challenge."

"Where does she come from do you think? There's never been any mention of a father."

"I always thought she was living on the streets before she turned up at the palace," Tamasin said, then added. "Did you notice she lost her composure when she mentioned her father? A rare thing for her.

There must be some old unresolved wounds there. I'd like to know her background."

"I would too. You could ask her, but I doubt if she'll give you the information."

"I'm not going to pry into her private life," replied Tamasin.

"She's entitled to her secrets," agreed Valeria. "Especially when it involves family."

Tamasin smiled at her. "You're not going soft on her, are you, Val?"

"Huh! She's still very annoying, but now I see how austere her life is here, she must be lonely. Arwen says she's never taken a lover."

Tamasin looked at her incredulously. "How the hell would Arwen know?"

"From Connell. He tells her and she keeps me updated about what's happening here."

Tamasin was silent. Arwen's husband, Connell, would be a good source of information for Valeria's spy network. His garrison town of Hyperion was the main supplier of arms in central Rand, so consequently visited Falcon's Keep quite often. Obviously, he was as much a gossip as his wife.

Valeria gave her a sly grin. "You've no idea how much I learn listening to my ladies-in-waiting chatting."

Tamasin shook her head dubiously. "Gossip is seldom completely right," she warned. "It's usually embellished to make a better story."

"There is some truth in every tale. And it keeps me up to date with my subjects. Intrigues in the bedroom tell me a lot about where loyalties lie."

Tamasin took Valeria's hand and ran her thumb over her palm. For all her stubborn intractability and fiery temper, her wife was by far the most desirable woman she had ever met. She'd never had any interest in any romantic liaisons outside of their marriage. "Come. I see our guard patiently waiting to escort us to our lodgings. I could do with an ale."

Chapter Twenty

After she slipped on her dress, Savannah went to the bathroom. The mirror on the wall was beautiful: oval-shaped, with a decorative gilded frame reminiscent of the Venetian style of the sixteenth century on Earth. She thought it odd that out of all the furnishings in the house, the only elegant piece was a mirror. Pela wore no other clothes but her uniforms, and she used no makeup. She did oil her braid, probably just to keep it in place. She was the least vain person that Savannah had ever met.

Savannah, on the other hand, loved clothes. Tonight, Pela had excused her from table duties for the gala dinner, telling her to sit with the recruits and enjoy herself. So she'd grabbed the chance to dress up for a night out. She missed that part of her old life. At the Iona markets when she had first arrived, she hadn't been able to resist buying a pretty stylish gown among her more serviceable purchases. Tamasin had merely raised an eyebrow as she handed over the money.

In a delicate shade of green, it was an ankle-length, slim-lined gown with a silver girdle around the hips and flowing three-quarter sleeves. The embroidered bodice was cut low to show some cleavage. After painting her lips from the little pot of red cream Lyn had given her, she took her brown hair out of the braid and let it fall loose to her shoulders. With one last look in the mirror, she slipped on her only pair of flat sandals before she exited the house.

Since Pela had left two hours before to organize the festivities, Savannah strolled across the grassed area to pat Sunflower on her way. The two of them had formed such a bond that she intended to ask Tamasin if she could be her mount when she returned to Iona.

With a whinny, the mare galloped over. *"You look pretty, Savannah."*

Savannah stroked her silky neck. "Thank you, my sweet. I came to show you my dress."

"The Commander will like it."

Savannah snorted. "She won't even notice."

A soft nicker was the only reply.

The hall was already full when she arrived. Apart from those serving for the night, the entire Keep had turned out for the occasion. She was pleased to see there were staff members in gowns—Lyn had told her the chief housemistress had allowed the younger women to attend the festivities. The soldiers looked splendid in their dress uniforms. The hall had been made into a ballroom, with the tables set further back to allow space for dancing, and bright buntings and banners stretched across the ceiling. The official table sat at the northern end of the room.

The terrace was open for the long tables covered with spiced meats, sweetbreads, bowls of fruits, and exotic vegetable dishes. Alcoholic drinks were on the tables, the wine and mead served in goblets, ale in tankards. On a small stage at the back, there was a three-piece band: a woodwind pipe, drums, and an instrument that resembled a mandolin.

Savannah made her way towards Lyn, sitting with Justine and four other recruits. Justine's eyes widened when she saw her. "Holy hell, Savannah. You look like a princess in that dress."

"Thanks," Savannah said, flashing everyone on the table a smile. She sat down on the other side of Lyn who was staring at her enviously. "Where did you get that dress? It's …well … a bit fancy for a maid."

"I found it in the Iona markets. Isn't it divine?"

Lyn reached for two goblets of wine and handed one to Savannah. "Here. You're going to need this. You'll be inundated with offers tonight. You've caught a big Kasparian guy's attention as soon as you came in."

"Huh! Not interested," said Savannah. "When is the Queen due to arrive?"

As to answer her question, a murmur of voices could be heard and the crowd at the entrance parted. Escorted by Pela, the Queen and her Consort appeared. Savannah caught her breath when she saw the royal couple. Valeria was stunning in a golden damask gown clinging subtly to her curves, and a necklace of red gems that flamed in the glow of the crystal lights. Tamasin looked a regal escort, dressed in a white silk shirt and dark burgundy trousers and jacket perfectly fitting her athletic frame. At her neck was a chain holding a silver replica of the Queen's emblem. Pela was again in black, though this outfit was of a fabric finer than her uniforms.

"The Queen looks smashing," came a voice from the other side of Savannah.

"She sure does, Haili," Savannah replied, smiling at her. The recruit was one of her favorites in the camp. In her late twenties, Haili was a fair, red-haired woman, unassuming and good-natured, with a wicked sense of humor. Once a champion wrestler in Queen Wren's army, she'd been accepted to train for the Elite Guards a year ago and was one of the recruits chosen to represent Falcon's Keep for the hand-to-hand combat bouts. Many times she had gone out of her way to give Savannah tips on how to handle a larger opponent.

"You look pretty tonight too," Haili murmured.

"Thank you," Savannah replied, flattered.

"Very regal."

"It's the dress."

Haili tilted her head to examine her. "No. You've got the bearing that goes with the clothes. I've often wondered why you came here as a servant. You're no more a maid than I am...you don't have to be told anything twice. And you've worked out how to handle the Commander, which very few people can do."

"I was sent here as a punishment."

"Figures," grunted Haili. "The Commander doesn't like anyone in her personal space." She grinned. "I'd love to know what you did, but I won't pry. Do you wanna get something to eat?"

"You bet. I'm starved." As she followed her to the buffets, Savannah made a mental note to tell Tamasin to keep an eye on Haili for future advancement. She had the makings of an excellent leader. During dinner, there was a variety of entertainment: acrobats, fire eaters, and a poet. When the band fired up after the meal, Haili seized her hand. "C'mon. Let's dance."

Savannah eyed her skeptically, hoping the dance moves weren't too complicated but followed her onto the floor anyhow. She loved to dance, so she'd just have to bumble along until she worked it out. She needn't have worried. The dance was simple enough: each couple making a few cross-over steps, then one partner was twirled around a few times and they began again. Soon she was bouncing enthusiastically with the rest of them.

After the bracket, a drumbeat sounded, and the dancefloor cleared. A hush fell over the room when the royal couple rose. The music began slowly, throbbing out the notes as they stepped onto the floor. When Valeria swayed into her arms, Tamasin tilted her backward before they launched gracefully into the dance. Savannah watched them dip and glide, executing the steps that looked like a version of the tango. The music swelled and flowed over them as they spun.

After some minutes, Pela came onto the floor, and when she touched Tamasin's shoulder, the crowd sent up a wild cheer. Even though it was choreographed, Savannah felt a sense of pride that when Pela had cut in, the Queen accepted her hand. As Savannah watched, her breath caught in her throat. Pela held her spellbound— she moved lightly and smoothly like a cat on the prowl. The medallion tingled at her breast as desire ran through Savannah. Her limbs became heavy, her skin hot. The room faded away.

She was on top of a hill, and a tapestry of color spread across the valley below. On a distant mountain, a waterfall sparkled in the sun. A woman riding a snow-white unicorn came out of a group of tall trees. Strange little creatures scurried out of the grasses as the rider urged her

*mount toward the ring of tall flat stones at the base of the hill. When
Savannah felt someone stir beside her, she turned to see Pela smiling down.
Pela lowered her head until their lips were a mere breath apart. "I
have been waiting for you for years, love. But you must find the Prophecy
Chart. Break the curse to breach the rift. Only then may we be together."
She reached up to stroke Pela's face, but the vision was fading. She
desperately tried to bring it back, but all she could hear was a harsh voice
calling somewhere in the dark mist that was creeping over the landscape.
"You can't have her. You can't…"*

Savannah's hand tightened around the handle of the cup, understanding the vision had been only one thread of the future. She had
no idea how she knew, but she just did.

The room began to spin as she watched Valeria twirling around
in Pela's arms. Envy clawed at her. She wanted to be the one Pela
held. The medallion started to shake as her emotions banked danger-
ously. The wine in the goblet began to sizzle.

When a hand touched her shoulder, her senses spun back
under control. Shaken, she looked up to see Rhiannon at her elbow.
Clamping her hands on her thighs to stop trembling, she forced herself to smile. "Hi, Rhiannon."

"Would you like to dance?"

"Um…I'm not familiar with that dance," she replied, still flus-
tered. It was the last thing she wanted to do.

"Don't worry," said Rhiannon confidently. "I am a master of the
tantario. I'll lead you."

Conscious everyone at the table was looking at her, and she
would appear boorish if she refused, Savannah reluctantly got to her
feet. "Then I'd love to," she murmured. At least she was familiar with
the tango, so she should be able to adapt.

As soon as Rhiannon took her in her arms, Savannah knew she
hadn't been exaggerating. She was so light on her feet she was a dream
to follow. Soon they were moving together, dancing with grace and
precision. Caught up in the excitement of the dance, the vision faded

from her mind. When the music finished, they received a round of applause, which Rhiannon acknowledged with a wave.

She drew her arm around Savannah's waist as they walked back to the table. "That was fun. Perhaps we might have another dance later?"

Smiling, Savannah extracted herself from Rhiannon's arms. "Okay. Let's get a drink." She took a large swallow of spicy mead, determined to enjoy herself and forget the unsettling glimpse into the future. She was sick of the medallion running her life.

As the night wore on, their group grew more boisterous as their numbers grew and the alcohol flowed. Savannah knew she was getting tipsy but kept going. At one stage, when she caught Pela's glare from the head table, she flashed her a rebellious grin.

She didn't lack dance partners —she never been anywhere where there were so many alpha women in one place. And it wasn't only women. One of the Kasparian men was particularly persistent in his attentions, which spurred Rhiannon to be more attentive.

Finally, it was Haili who broke up the party when she called out, "It's getting late. We won't be popular if we're too hungover to compete."

Savannah looked around—the band was packing up, and everyone was on the move.

"I'll walk you home, Savannah," Haili offered. "You're a bit wasted."

"I'll take her," said Rhiannon.

Savannah waggled her finger in the air, "Hang on, you two. I'll take myself."

Lyn laughed. "You'd better both take her. She might have to be carried."

"Nonsense. I'm perfectly mapable of falking," slurred Savannah.

"Let them take you home, Sav," said Justine with quiet authority. "You're in no condition to defend yourself."

"I suppose so," Savannah agreed grudgingly.

When she hit the fresh air, her stomach lurched, and she swallowed hard. *Damnit!* She couldn't remember when she had drunk so much. As much as she'd been adamant about no escort, she was glad she had strong arms to support her. By the time they'd reached her front door, she was feeling slightly less like losing her dinner. She stepped onto the landing, looked around the yard, then gave them both a kiss on the cheek. "Thanks. I've made a bit of a show of myself."

Haili grinned. "I guess you needed a blowout."

"I did, though I'll be sorry in the morning."

Rhiannon reached over and gently tucked a curl behind her ear. "You're cute when you let yourself go. I'll see you inside."

"I think I can manage," Savannah said in a playful tone to take the sting out of the rejection. "I'll see you both tomorrow."

"Sleep well," said Haili turning to go. Rhiannon hesitated for a second before she followed her out the gate.

After Savannah watched them disappear, she called out, "You can come down, Pela?"

The foliage above rustled and the large hawk dropped from the low-hanging branches to the ground. With a shimmer, Pela appeared. Looking furious, she strode up to Savannah. "What the hell were you thinking wearing that dress? You're supposed to be my servant, not parading around making a spectacle of yourself."

"There's nothing wrong with my dress. And even if there was, that doesn't give you the right to spy on me."

"I was making sure you got home safely. You've been drinking all night. Anyone could have taken advantage of you."

"You mean Rhiannon," snapped Savannah.

"And that big oaf from Kasparian."

"He was a perfect gentleman." She narrowed her eyes. "You know I'm not into men, so it's Rhiannon you're worried about. That's a turnaround. It wasn't so long ago that you snapped at me for brushing her off at the Howling Wolf."

"You're too naïve for her. She's only after a good time," growled Pela.

"Let me worry about that. You're my boss, not my keeper. Besides, I could do with a good time. It's hardly a laugh a minute here. Now I'm going to bed before I fall down." Savannah pushed open the door and headed to the bedroom. With a whoosh, she collapsed onto the bed.

As she lay there with her eyes closed, trying to ignore her spinning head, she heard Pela whisper from across the room, "You looked beautiful tonight."

Chapter Twenty-One

Savannah cracked open an eye. By the way the sunbeams slanted through the window, dawn had been hours ago. Pela was nowhere in sight. Not that she expected her to be, she would have left early to organize the day's events. Savannah pushed back the blanket, sat up suddenly, and then groaned as pain shot through her head. She pressed her knuckles to her temples—she'd forgotten how godawful a hangover felt. She cursed herself for drinking the potent mead and not sticking to the light wine.

With an effort, she got up, sluiced a few jugs of cold water over herself in the bath, and dragged on her uniform. After dosing herself with pain-killer bark, she made a cup of the herbal hot drink she drank to replace coffee. Self-recriminations set in when the ache subsided, and she felt half-human again. She'd made an idiot of herself drinking so much. Pela would never forgive her; she still could see the fury flashing in her eyes.

But then the memories of the vision flooded in, and everything else faded from her mind. She went over the scene again and again until her head was spinning. *You must find the Prophecy Chart. Break the curse to breach the rift.* What was the Prophecy Chart, and where would she find it? And what was the curse? Nobody had ever mentioned them. She was certain where she'd been—the unicorn was a magical creature mentioned in Pela's book of flora and fauna, and only found in the Forgotten Realms.

She finally concluded she wasn't going to get anywhere on her own. She needed help urgently. The only person she could trust was Tamasin, which meant she had to have a serious talk with her today. But gaining access to the royal couple might take some doing, considering they were well guarded. A lowly maid couldn't just rock up to their viewing area.

An idea came as she walked over to the amphitheater. Sunflower might be able to help. The mare raised her head and nickered when Savannah approached.

"Tell me, Sunflower. Can you talk to Tamasin?"

"*No. Only to you.*"

Savannah wondered why but pushed that puzzle aside for another day. It probably was the power of the medallion. "Blow! I wanted to get a message to her."

"*She hears Malkia. I can relay it.*"

"You smart girl," Savannah exclaimed. "Will she hear him if he goes to the entrance gate."

"*She should.*"

"Ask him to tell her I must talk to her. Request her to meet me in an hour at the back gate."

"*I will,*" she telepathed and galloped off to the stables.

The wood chopping was in progress when Savannah entered the arena. As she crept around the back seats, the sight of the large men and women with their battleaxes made her flinch. The blades were sharp enough to slice through the wooden poles with ease. It was her least favorite weapon, having seen pictures of soldiers with limbs hacked off on the battlefields. All competitors favored double-edged axes engraved with decorative patterns.

As she sat quietly at the end of the top seat watching the competitions, Savannah kept half an eye on Tamasin. As it neared the time for their appointment, she began to despair the message hadn't reached her. But when Tamasin spoke to Valeria and then stood up, Savannah gave a mental fist pump. Quickly, she circled the walls until she reached the back door. Tamasin joined her, and they walked through together.

Savannah pointed toward the battlement. "There's a storeroom under the steps that leads up that wall. We'll have privacy there."

Filled with broken weapons, discarded boots, and used saddlery parts, the inside smelt of musty leather and stale oil. After brushing down an old cobbler's bench to sit on, Tamasin asked, "You can talk to Malkia?"

"Yes."

Tamasin studied her keenly. "Not even Valeria can do that. I'm the only one who has that gift."

"Well, actually, I can talk to all the Blue Fjord horses here. I was going to ask you if Sunflower could be my special mount. We've become friends."

Tamasin's eyes widened. "All of them?"

"It must be the medallion. Look, we can talk about the horses later, I've more urgent things to discuss," Savannah said with a touch of panic. "I need help. I'm getting completely out of my depth. I had a vision last night, and it's freaking me out."

"Steady down," Tamasin said soothingly. "As the Mistress of Dreams, I'm familiar with glimpses of the future and able to interpret their meanings. Describe your dream."

Savannah shook her head irritably. "You don't understand. It wasn't a dream, it was a vision and it doesn't need interpretation. It was quite clear. One moment I was watching the dance, the next second I was on a hill overlooking a valley. A woman was riding a white unicorn."

"Go on," said Tamasin quietly.

"I wasn't alone on the hill. Pela was with me."

"Did you have any idea where you were?"

"The unicorns are only in the Forgotten Realms," replied Savannah. "Then Pela said I must find the Prophecy Chart and break the curse to breach the rift."

"You don't think it was the alcohol you put away?" asked Tamasin lightly, but underneath, her eyes probed.

Savannah sighed and shook her head. "I wish it were that simple. It happened when I hadn't had much to drink, just after the meal when Pela danced with the Queen. It was a vision of a future. But it need not necessarily happen. Don't ask me how I understand that, but I just do."

"What do you think?"

"It's the dominant future thread, or I wouldn't have had a glimpse," replied Savannah. "I've begun to think that there are many possible threads, and whatever force is manipulating me, it can't foretell how the real future will pan out. I have to work that out. I'd like to know who put the magic in this medallion." She eyed Tamasin enquiringly. "What is the Prophecy Chart? Glenda told me about the Prophecy Tower, which stood here where Falcon's Keep is now. But I've never come across any mention of the Prophecy Chart in the archives."

"Nor I." Tamasin ran her fingers through her hair. "I'll ask Moira to see if she can find any reference to it. Have you any idea where do we go from here? We've yet to find the hawks."

"They're in the Forgotten Realms."

"How do you know that?" exclaimed Tamasin.

"Don't ask…I just do. After these games, I was going there to persuade them to come out, but I learned we have to break the curse first. What's the curse?"

Tamasin shrugged in frustration. "Again, I'm in the dark."

"Have you ever wondered, Tamasin, why after Elsbeth went through the portal, she stayed on Earth? When was it…three hundred years ago?"

"Yes. Queen Jessica was on the throne. I'll ask Valeria to look up her records exactly when she went."

Savannah stared at her as an idea formed. "I've been doing a lot of research on the Silverthorne witches here. Glenda also told me the Prophecy Tower was the seat of power for the witches. They governed all those wielding magic; the mages, wizards, sorcerers, necromancers, etcetera. They took over when the magical creatures retreated from the rest of Rand. Then the mages wanted all the power, and

Queen Jessica defeated Agatha's armies, the witches, at the Battle of Briar Ridge, three centuries ago. Is that how it happened.?"

"That's a simplified version, but yes, it's right."

"Could it be that the Queen sent Elsbeth, the Chosen One out of Rand so the Circle of Sheda wouldn't fall into the wrong hands? It's too much of a coincidence. Otherwise, she would have come home, wouldn't she?"

"We always thought she went seeking adventure after Queen Jessica's triumph. And was killed over there, so the medallion was lost."

"How powerful is the medallion?"

"Very, according to history books. That's why the Chosen One must be of exemplary character." She scanned Savannah's face. "May I ask where you found her body?"

The medallion tingled at her breast, and this time she ignored it. She gave it a sharp tap—the thing would have to learn she had a brain of her own. "At a dig in Algeria. When I was finding shelter from a violent sandstorm, I somehow found an underground cavern where her skeleton was laid to rest."

Tamasin smiled. "You got a zap."

"Yes, but I'm not going to be manipulated if I think I'm doing the right thing."

"Good for you. The cavern was sealed for centuries?"

"It had to be closed. Elsbeth's body wasn't buried. The place was made into her tomb, although there was evidence that it had been a Berber hiding place," said Savannah. She looked at Tamasin as a thought came. "I carbon-dated a piece of animal hide I found there. If Valeria has the exact time she went, I can roughly work out how old she was when she died. She could have lived a full life on Earth."

The more she thought about it, the more Savannah was convinced she was right. Elsbeth would have had to plan her burial to ensure the medallion wasn't lost. And the old seer had said Savannah was of both worlds. Maybe Elsbeth had had a child, and she was a descendant. But that information she would keep to herself—she wasn't yet prepared to tell Tamasin about the old blind woman. Instead, she asked, "Who in your dreams sent you to find the medallion, Tamasin?"

"The Goddess of Dreams. I never saw her face, but the message was quite clear. I didn't have the power to refuse."

Savannah frowned. "Why you?"

Tamasin shook her head. "I presumed because I was considered the best candidate."

"Can anyone go through the portal?"

Tamasin threw her a puzzled glance. "What do you mean?"

"I was just wondering if you have to be born with some magic to go through without the medallion," said Savannah, with the faintest of smiles. "You must have some in you to have gone into the Forgotten Realms to get Malkia."

"By the Gods, woman, how did you work that out so easily?"

"Because I was told that I wouldn't be welcome there because I didn't have any magic."

Tamasin cocked her head to look at her. "You're proving to be a very capable Chosen One. Now, I must get back…I've been gone long enough, and they might come looking for me. Do you want to come back to Iona with us when we go? You've done your time here. You can work with Moira in our archives."

"I'd like to stay a little longer. I still haven't finished with the historical documents here. Get Moira to see what she can dig up about the curse and Mystic War."

"You like staying with Pela?" said Tamasin, her face registering disbelief.

"Oh," said Savannah, trying to sound off-hand. "She's not too bad. Mostly all bluster."

Tamasin just shook her head. "You're the only person on Rand that thinks that." She stood up. "I'll talk further with you tomorrow. We have a private dinner with the graduating recruits tonight."

Savannah waited until she had left, then got up to go back to the arena. She felt better after the discussion. Her problems seemed less daunting.

†

Pela appeared soon after she arrived home. "How are you feeling, Savannah?" she asked solicitously.

Savannah looked at her in surprise. She thought she'd still be annoyed after their harsh words last night. "I was a bit seedy, but I'm fine now. Do you want me to serve you tonight?"

"No, I'm hosting a private dinner in the small mess for the graduating recruits and the royals. And it won't be necessary for you to serve me at meals in the future."

Taken aback, Savannah blinked at her. "Thank you, Commander."

Pela's voice lowered, her tone silky. "I'm sorry about last night. Your dress was quite appropriate, and if you wanted to have a few drinks, it wasn't my business."

Savannah's mouth dropped open. Had a pod person replaced Pela? "Um…okay. I did have too much to drink, but I've learned my lesson. I'll be going to bed early tonight."

"It would be sensible since you fight tomorrow. Did you enjoy the competitions today?"

"I'm not a fan of the axe, but the flying games were spectacular," replied Savannah, not dropping her defenses. Pela was after something.

"I noticed you and Tamasin disappear together."

Savannah pursed her lips. So, that's why she was so sweet. She was fishing for information. "We did. If there's nothing else you want me to do, I'll have to change for dinner."

For the first time since she'd arrived in Falcon's Keep, Pela looked unsure of herself. When Savannah began to move off, she asked abruptly, "Are you going back to Iona with them?"

Savannah stopped, then slowly turned around and tilted her head to look at her. "Do you want me to stay?"

Pela cleared her throat. "I'm used to you being here."

"I thought you'd be pleased to get rid of me."

"It's nice to come home to a clean house."

"Any of the girls can clean your house, Pela."

"But they can't scribe for me."

Savannah held her gaze and moved a step closer. "You haven't answered my question, Pela. You have to tell me."

Pela flushed. "All right. Yes, I want you to stay."

"Why?" Savannah persisted.

"Because...because I'll be lonely without you. Are you satisfied?"

Savannah laughed softly. "I've already told Tamasin I wasn't going back yet."

Her eyes bright, Pela bent over and gently pressed her lips to Savannah's cheek. "Thank you. I'll see you tomorrow."

With a whistle, she vanished out the door.

Chapter Twenty-Two

The sound of Pela moving about the bedroom woke Savannah. She remained in bed until she heard the front door close, then dressed quickly to head for the library. It was half an hour before first light, but a prickle of urgency had disturbed her dreams all night. She needed to reread the report on when Falcon's Keep had started as a training camp. The Prophecy Tower stood here at one time. When she'd studied the military documents before, she'd sensed something should be investigated further but couldn't pinpoint what it was, so she'd moved on. But instinct told her to find it before Tamasin left.

Savannah had always had an uncanny knack for picking out an important fact in a seemingly dry, unremarkable document. It was one of her strengths in gaining recognition as a bright upcoming archeologist and historian. Putting it down to an acute sixth sense, she never considered her hunches to be anything other than that. But now she wasn't so sure. If part of her lineage was from this world as the old woman had claimed, maybe she had a little magic in her.

There had been nothing to suggest that either of her parents were anything but hardworking doctors. They were so conservative, she couldn't remember them doing anything out of the ordinary. They had married in London when they were both in their late thirties and put down roots in Christchurch, New Zealand when Savannah was three. They'd lived a quiet life, raising her in a happy, loving home. Hers was a carefree unremarkable coming-of-age story.

She couldn't help wondering if she'd been too protected—if her life had been too perfect. But there had been no extraordinary family secrets divulged, no death-bed confessions.

Even when Savannah had announced, after dating a boy for a month, that she preferred girls, they'd accepted her life choice without a qualm. As their ambition for her centered around a university education, they had been proud when she had become an archaeologist. But when she announced she'd won a scholarship to Oxford for her post-graduate studies, they'd tried fervently to persuade her not to go. Looking back, she now wondered whether their reluctance was something more mysterious than just not wanting to 'lose' their only child.

Savannah pushed aside the thoughts; her imagination was running away with her. And she didn't want to dwell on her mother. She still missed her dreadfully, and it was upsetting.

As she made her way through the empty gray streets of the Keep, she concentrated on the task at hand. For some inexplicable reason, she felt jumpy and couldn't help searching the roofs and alcoves for crows.

This early, the streets were deserted, but not far from the library, she heard scuffling somewhere behind. Nervously, she peered over her shoulder. She stopped for a few seconds, convinced she saw someone lurking in the gloom. When no one appeared, she decided it must have been a trick of the light, maybe a windowpane sending a flicker of a shadow across a wall. Nevertheless, she picked up her pace, hugging one side as she hurried along.

When she reached the library, she took a moment to study the street from the doorstep, listening for any sounds from behind. Satisfied there was no one, she took the iron key that Glenda had given her and pushed it into its slot. Once inside, she relaxed after she bolted the door. She sucked in a deep breath, chiding herself for being so paranoid.

Taking a light crystal from the box near the door, she proceeded to the shelf labeled *Falcon's Keep*. The old leather-bound book was in the third row amongst the other records of the Elite Guards' history at the Keep. Every year the commanding officer wrote up a log, then after ten years, these were bound into a volume. She carefully pulled the first volume out of the row and placed it into the cradle the library provided to protect its rare books. Taking parchment and pen to record the facts, she began a new file. It was her usual routine—one she'd done thousands of times. The only difference here, she'd be doing it with cursive writing, not a laptop.

Soon she became engrossed as she carefully studied what had been left after the demise of the witches' stronghold a hundred and fifty years before. When there was a knock on the door, she swore silently. Not the time to be disturbed—her instinct told her she was very close.

The knock sounded again, this time louder.

She got up and went to the door but left it bolted. "Who is it?"

A male voice answered, "Miss Savannah?"

"Yes."

"I'm one of the Queen's grooms. A soldier gave me a letter to deliver to you."

Savannah slipped off the bolt. A young man barely out of his teens stood on the landing outside. He pulled off his cap and handed over a letter.

She unfolded the page, noting Tamasin's signature at the bottom. It was short and to the point.

Savannah,

I have some urgent news and need to see you. Meet me on the battlement at the east end of the compound. We won't be seen there. Please hurry.

Yours, Tamasin.

She nodded to the groom. "Thank you. There'll be no reply."

As soon as he scampered off, she pocketed the letter and hurried inside to get her cape. Only stopping to close the book, she dashed out the door, pulling it shut behind her.

It was past the first blush of dawn, shafts of sunlight painting shades of orange and beige on the roof shingles. Though the streets were still empty, she knew the Keep would soon be stirring. The first sitting of breakfast was due to start shortly. She didn't slow down until she reached the last line of houses and the end of the eastern battlement came into view.

The most desolate end of Falcon's Keep, this section of the wall was naturally fortified, needing no guards. The balustrade spanned a sheer drop down the cliff face, while towering jagged rocks on either side created a wind tunnel that made aerial landings nearly impossible. It was not a place an enemy would ever contemplate for an invasion.

Considered very dangerous, it was off-limits to recruits.

As Savannah climbed the stairs, she regretted leaving the house in her light cape instead of her warm flying coat. The wind was cold and sharp, cutting through her clothes. Once on the top level, she could see Tamasin standing further down on the most exposed part of the wall, a hooded cape clinging to her body to ward off the cold. She was staring at the mountains in the distance.

Savannah jogged along, more to get her blood flowing than in urgency. She had no idea why Tamasin would choose such an inhospitable place to meet, though figured, by the way she was standing so absorbed, there must be an interesting view out there. And they'd certainly be private.

Intent on keeping her balance in the buffeting wind, Savannah didn't realize anything was amiss until she reached the woman. It was only when she called out, "Tamasin. I'm here," that the hooded figure turned.

Her breath caught painfully in her throat. It was Killia, not Tamasin.

With a swift movement, Killia grasped the front of her tunic and lifted her over the side of the wall through the crenel. The woman was so strong, Savannah might have been a feather.

Suspended in space in the battering winds, she desperately grasped the witch's arm while trying to summon the power of the medallion. Nothing came, though she sensed the power trying to claw its way to the surface. It was clear that Killia had prepared herself with witchcraft to face her this time. Savannah knew the old magic of the Circle of Sheda was stronger, and it was only a matter of time before it broke the spell. But that was immaterial now.

Fear shot through Savannah. She knew it was too late. Even if she was able to harness the power of the medallion again, it was useless. Killia's arm was outstretched, dangling Savannah over the abyss. Killia would just have to let her go and she would fall.

Desperate, she tried to think. She was going to fall one way or the other— there was only one option to survive. Summoning up every ounce of concentration, she projected a frantic plea, "*Sunflower. I need you. I'm going to be thrown over the east wall.*"

Killia shook her like a rag doll. "It won't do you any good to use your magic, changeling."

Savannah swallowed back the feeling of hopelessness. Her only chance was to keep her talking as long as possible to give Sunflower time to reach her. "Pela will kill you if you do this."

"Pah! Don't kid yourself. When I announce in front of the royal bitch and her consort this afternoon at the games, that I've disposed of the spy, Pela will be delighted. She hates the Queen with a passion."

"Why did you call me changeling?" asked Savannah and sent out another anguished message to Sunflower.

"That's our only explanation for your power. No one has heard of any mage order where you trained. You have to be from the Forgotten Realms. Faeries are a sneaky lot. They steal healthy children and replace them with their sickly ones. You're puny enough to be a changeling."

It flashed through Savannah's mind that this particular history of Rand was not so unlike Earth's. Changelings featured in European folklore. The legends all described odd children, those who didn't quite fit in or didn't look right. They were regarded as the defective children of fairies or demons, swapped by fairies in exchange for healthy children. Of course, Savannah had a more scientific explanation.

"Why are you so intent on controlling Pela," Savannah asked, trying to ignore the wave of panic as the grip loosened on her shirt.

"Because she will help us get back our power. The Elite Guards will follow her when the time comes to defeat Valeria."

"If you let me go, she will be more inclined to listen to you," reasoned Savannah.

"Don't be ridiculous. Pela was only using you as a whore."

Even through her fear, Savannah felt intense anger. How dare she presume she'd prostituted herself. So she spat back, "Well, you wouldn't get anyone with that scar. Where did you get it? Someone you pissed off?"

As soon as she said the words, Savannah knew she'd hit a sore point. Vivid anger morphed on Killia's face, and she could almost feel the fury flashing in the witch's eyes as she shook her violently. "By a Bramble Hawk. It shouldn't have been out of the Forgotten Realms. They're cursed. I'll strangle the demon spawn with my bare hands if I ever see it again."

Before she could answer, Savannah's body tensed as the magic of the medallion began to break free. Energy crackled along her nerve endings. Killia must have felt the shift because she gave a sharp cry and let go of the shirt. When Savannah clung to her arm, she drew back her other hand and punched her in the face. As Savannah's head snapped back, her grip weakened. Though it was an effort this time for the witch, Killia shook her until Savannah's fingers slipped off.

With an urgent projection, "*Sunflower! I'm falling,*" Savannah toppled into space.

Immediately, she was spun like a leaf in the wind tunnel, only by luck narrowly avoiding being smashed against the jutting sharp rocks on the downward spiral.

As she hurtled erratically through the air, the precious words she'd be wanting to hear popped into her head, *"I'm coming around the side, Savannah,"* and hope sprung in her chest.

Somewhere in the back of her mind, she remembered reading that a person reached terminal velocity in the first twelve seconds of freefall, but when she looked down, the irrelevant thought vanished as panic took hold. Twelve seconds was a long time. The wind had abated and the ground was coming up fast.

She closed her eyes and began to pray.

The next second, utter relief rushed through her when she felt large teeth clamp her breeches. As her body slowed in mid-air, the words came, *"I've got you."*

But they were very low, the ground not far away.

They flew lower…lower.

As Sunflower flapped her wings furiously to halt her downward trajectory, Savannah braced herself for impact.

The mare teetered precariously for heart-stopping moments, then managed to surge upward. Fighting for balance in the backdraft, they hovered erratically. Finally, she became stable enough to land. But as she descended, one of her wings caught on a rock protruding from the canyon wall. With an agonizing scream, Sunflower lurched, tried to right herself, and skidded off the rock face. As they tumbled down, she tossed Savannah to the side before she buried her nose into the canyon floor amid a cascade of gray dirt.

Savannah took a deep breath as the dust settled. She stretched her limbs tentatively. Though she felt sore and bruised, her limbs were in working order. She dragged herself upright and urgently looked over at Sunflower. The mare had managed to move herself to a half-sitting position, though was wheezing and huffing in pain. One wing was tucked into her side, but the other was stretched out awkwardly along the ground.

Savannah scrambled over, flopping onto her knees beside the horse. Gently, she ran her fingers lightly over the bones of the damaged wing. Though she couldn't feel an obvious break, it didn't mean there wasn't one. She'd seen her mother treat a bird's broken wing once and imagined the same principle would work with these flying creatures. The feathers and components appeared the same, except much larger. She'd have to assume that the structure was no different.

But she had to get the mare upright before she could immobilize the wing. The only thing she had to bind it with was her cape, so it would have to do.

"You have to get up, Sunflower," she said firmly. "You could die if you don't. It's much hotter down here, like a furnace, and you need to get into the shade."

"*I'll try,*" came the reedy reply.

After numerous attempts, Savannah knew it was hopeless. She wasn't strong enough to help and the mare could barely lift her head to try anymore. Her voice hoarse with exertion, Savannah collapsed beside her. "No more. It's not working. Lie still for a while and rest."

Savannah stroked the silky neck soothingly as she took stock of her surroundings. They were in a wide canyon surrounded by granite walls pocked with wind-carved holes and ridges. The only vegetation in sight was small, spindly bushes crisscrossed by cottony spider webs. The fact the floor was covered with dusty gray dirt as soft as talcum powder, was the only thing that had saved them from permanent damage. Though if they didn't find water and shelter, they were dead anyway. This was much hotter than anything she'd experienced in the Sahara. She wasn't going to leave Sunflower.

As she tried to devise a way to lift the horse, Savannah idly rubbed the medallion through her shirt. She could feel the tingle in her fingertips whenever she pressed it. She blinked. Maybe she could invoke the power at will. It had always been in a desperate situation that it had come, but she must have at least some control over it. Tentatively, she slipped in her hand, grasped it, and concentrated. A tingle spread up her arm.

Okay, that worked.

She tried again, only this time was more forceful with her command. Her whole body felt as if it were alive with electricity. She let go of the medallion, pointed to a small boulder near the canyon wall, and called forth the power. Sparks sizzled from her fingertips. She fought to keep on her feet when there was a loud hiss as the rock flew into the air. Tiny insects skittered away in a flurry, and two green lizards sunning on a nearby rock darted for cover.

Stunned, she tried again, this time tamping down the order. After ten minutes, she hoped she'd gained enough control to use it safely. Sunflower was running out of time—if she didn't get up, she may not survive.

Gently, she stroked the mare's muzzle. "You have to give it another go, sweetheart. Come on."

When Sunflower weakly heaved her body, Savannah put her hands under the belly and invoked the power. Strength rushed into every muscle in Savannah's body. Slowly, she lifted the large horse upright until she was standing on her four feet. Savannah held her until she had gained her balance, all the time murmuring words of encouragement.

Finally, the mare gave a whinny. *"Thank you, Savannah. I can stand by myself."*

She patted her silky mane. "Good. If you can put up with the pain, I'm going to bind your wing to your body with my cape."

When she'd finished, Savannah stood back to admire her handiwork. It wasn't pretty, but it would do the job for a while.

She turned from the horse to stare down the canyon. It was one of the bleakest places she'd ever seen, and she'd been to a lot of deadbeat locations in her archaeology trips. She hadn't a clue how they were going to survive, but she would have to find a way. On an impulse, she threaded the letter from her pocket onto a branch of a spindly bush. If they were eaten by a predator, it would be evidence that they had been here.

Her eyes searched the landscape, but the canyon was unnaturally still, devoid of life. She opened her mouth to swear, then shut it abruptly when she caught movement.

One moment there had been nothing, the next figures appeared from the canyon walls.

She blanched. They'd been there all the time, blending into the ochre and rust-colored cliffs like chameleons.

Chapter Twenty-Three

Kandelora

Savannah froze.

With no possibility of avoiding or withdrawing, she would just have to wait to see what they were going to do. They stood like statues, then a burst of powdery dust exploded at her feet. She glanced down to see the shaft of an arrow an inch from her big toe. When she looked up, she caught sight of a bowman on the first ledge. He had another arrow already notched. Though she knew she was proficient enough to call up the ancient magic, Savannah hesitated. She had yet to learn to manage it properly, and there was no reason to go to that extreme. Only a warning shot had been fired.

It went against her nature to wantonly kill another human being. She had yet to find out if they were friends or foes.

"The horse will make a fine meal tonight," a male voice called out.

Someone gave a raucous laugh and quipped, "It's fat enough."

Savannah bristled. She stalked around to stand in front of Sunflower. "This mare is not to be touched. She belongs to the sacred Blue Fjord bloodline."

One of the shrouded figures took two steps toward her. "What do we care? Your kind isn't welcome here."

Savannah knew they thought she was a witch—they had witnessed her magic fumbling.

When she felt Sunflower's breath of fear touch her mind, she projected assurance that it was going to be all right. "Then give us water, and we will wait in the shade until someone comes looking for us."

"Kill the witch and take the horse," another roared.

Savannah took her combat-mode stance. Flexing her fingers, she was preparing to summon her power when a woman's voice cut through the air, "That's enough, Eric."

The group immediately parted to allow her through. She stopped in front of Savannah, eyeing her up and down. "You speak our language with a perfect accent. Have you been here before?"

"No."

The woman regarded her suspiciously. "What is your name, and where were you flying? These mountains are not on any trade routes."

"My name is Savannah, and I'm from Falcon's Keep. May I ask your name, ma'am?" said Savannah, trying her best to smile. The way she was being studied was daunting. The woman had an aristocratic manner, as though she expected obedience. She looked to be in her late thirties, attractive, with pale skin and dark hair that was swept high from her forehead, emphasizing her sharp cheekbones, aquiline nose, and hazel eyes. Her arms were bare to the shoulders, her clothing made from leathery animal skin. But when her gaze reached the left arm, Savannah gave a start and quickly averted her eyes. From the elbow down, it resembled a monkey's.

Her embarrassment was not lost on the woman. "My name is Luna. And this," she waved her arm, "is a Silverthorne legacy." She poked her finger at Savannah. "Tell me the truth. We have no love for witches here, and we saw you practicing your craft. No one your size could lift a horse without help."

"I don't practice witchcraft. I'm not at liberty to discuss it, but my power is something else entirely. I fell from Falcon's Keep." She curled her lips wryly. "Thrown over actually."

"By whom?"

"By a Silverthorne witch. I hate them too."

"The horse saved you?"

"The Blue Fjord horses are not ordinary animals. They are highly intelligent. Please...she can't be killed for food. She's my friend."

The woman looked at her thoughtfully. "I have to admit I am intrigued. You're pushed from a high fortress, saved by a clever horse, and speak with no accent. You wield magic, yet you say you're not a witch. Why should I trust you? We survive here because no one has any idea we exist."

"I mean you no harm. I just want to get back up to Falcon's Keep. And my horse needs urgent attention. The wing may have to be set if she's to fly again. My friends will come looking, but maybe not until tomorrow, and I'm guessing we won't survive out here without your help."

"No, you won't. There's a far worse predator in the canyon than us," Luna said. "No one goes out after nightfall, only the hunters."

Savannah looked around nervously, remembering Pela had also said vile creatures were roaming here in the darkness. "You wouldn't leave us to die, would you?"

Luna's eyes reflected shadows of guilt as she said, "I have no choice. There are more lives at stake than mine." She signaled to Eric. "Give her your bow and the arrows."

He strode forward, and when he tossed off his cape to pull the quiver from his back, his face was exposed. It was covered in fine hair like a dog. Then one by one, the rest of the men and women removed their capes. Each had some bizarre deformity, which could only have been from genetic tampering, or surgical experimentation. Or perhaps simply witchcraft.

Savannah felt a wave of intense pity—whoever did this needed to be punished. She focused back on Luna. "Whatever happened to your people is atrocious, Luna. I can't even imagine the pain and anguish it has brought and at what cost. But have you lost your humanity too?"

"You dare to judge me?" Luna snapped. When the rest of her troop moved aggressively forward, knives unsheathed, she waved them impatiently back. "Stand down. If there's to be any killing, I will do it." She refocused on Savannah. "You think after our people were so badly mistreated that we care about the rest of the world? We were abandoned, left to rot."

"No, Luna, your mother was not abandoned. Arcadia never stopped looking for its lost princess."

Eyes wide, Luna backed two steps away from her. "What did you say?"

"I didn't say anything," said Savannah, "But I heard the words in my head too."

It was becoming clearer that the old woman knew the past but only some of the future, and was seeing the world through Savannah's eyes. Savannah was also learning that understanding the power took time and the medallion tailored itself to the Chosen One's personality. She had to learn to wield it properly. Very quickly.

"And now she is found," Savannah murmured.

Luna's eyes filled with tears. She brushed them away irritably. "Come with me. There's someone I'd like you to meet. She's a seeker of truth. We shall see if you are to be trusted."

At least it's not Ursula's cloak, thought Savannah wryly.

She felt Sunflower's nudge of panic in her mind. *"Take me with you. I have no wish to end up in a cooking pot."*

"Don't worry. I won't go anywhere without you." Savannah replied.

"She understood me?" Luna asked incredulously.

"Oh yes. Sunflower doesn't want to end up on your dining table."

"You can talk to her?"

Savannah shrugged. "I can. Can she come, please?"

"I wasn't going to leave her. I know you'll never forgive me if we hurt her, and I sense you're not as harmless as you appear."

Savannah waved for Sunflower to follow, then trailed after Luna. The rest of the odd clan fell in behind.

When Luna reached the cliff face, she pressed a small octagonal rock embedded in the wall and a door slid open. Once they filed through, the last person pulled a lever to close it.

Directly inside, the land formed a large basin where neat rows of crops surrounded a reservoir of water. Light crystals stretched across the walls. They walked along the pathway to one side, then down a ramp that opened up into a cavern that looked like any town square. Savannah gaped at the sight. It was an underground city.

"My God," gasped Savannah. "How many people live here?"

"This is Kandelora, the City of Outcasts. It is made up of subterranean spaces joined by a network of tunnels. We've six thousand living here. The living areas are in the smaller corridors off the tunnels." She pointed to a gated enclosure. "The animals are housed through there. I'll get the healer to have a look at your horse's wing."

A handler appeared almost immediately. When Savannah began to follow the mare in, Luna put a restraining hand on her arm. "She will be well looked after. I'll bring you back later."

"Okay," said Savannah reluctantly. After a reassuring pat on the mare's rump, she joined Luna to walk down a corridor. She could see the enormous advantage of living underground in these harsh mountains: the temperatures would be comfortable all year round, and it was a protected environment. She guessed it was no different from the rail systems and underground shopping malls that had become commonplace in many megacities back home.

"The woman you want me to see isn't old and blind, is she?" asked Savannah, feeling a glimmer of hope. Maybe this was where the old seer lived.

Luna chuckled. "See for yourself." At a red door, she knocked three times. "She's in here."

"Come in," a lilting voice called out.

The woman sitting in an armchair wasn't anything like Savannah expected. She imagined she'd be cross-examined by a wise old Maggie Smith lookalike, straight out of a Harry Potter movie. Instead, the woman in front of her was young and slender, with a fragile beauty that was breathtaking. Her silver hair floated in delicate ringlets around her heart-shaped face and she had beautiful bright blue eyes.

Luna bent down to kiss her cheek. "This is Savannah, Floris. Would you have a chat with her?"

"Welcome to my home, Savannah," Floris said, looking up at her with a smile. "I'm sorry I can't get up to greet you, but I've lost the use of my legs." She shot a glance at Luna. "Did you tell her I'm an Empath? I hate surprising people."

"She didn't, but that's fine, Floris," said Savannah. She smiled back, though it took an effort. As soon as she'd entered the room, she'd felt the pulsing electricity. Her skin was alive with it.

Floris turned to Luna, who hovered protectively at her shoulder. "Could you leave us alone while we talk, please. I'll be fine."

Luna looked undecided but moved toward the door, albeit reluctantly.

As soon as it closed behind her, Floris slumped back in the seat. "What manner of creature are you, Savannah. I've never felt such energy as this."

"Nor I. You're a magical being?"

"Yes. A Faerie and an Empath. Give me your hand."

Steeling herself, Savannah complied. But as soon as their fingers touched, a warm, incredible feeling of well-being enveloped her. Their emotions melded together in such love and harmony that it became almost too much to bear. She hung on until Floris was the one to pull away.

"You're an Empath too," Floris gasped. "I can sense other forces within you, an ancient power in perfect balance with nature. It feels like the beating heart of Rand. I've…I've never come across anything quite so wonderful."

Savannah didn't hesitate. Having touched her mind, she knew this woman was as innocent as she looked, totally without guile. "I wear the Circle of Sheda."

Floris's eyes flew wide. "It has been found?"

"It has. I found it in my world and came with it to Rand through the portal. It seems to have chosen me to wear it, though I'm not a warrior."

"You are kind, which is a far greater virtue. Such power cannot be used for those seeking to harm. It would destroy the soul of the world. May I see it?" Floris asked shyly.

"Of course. Though I have to ask you to keep quiet about it for a while until Tamasin gives me the okay. Have you heard of Tamasin?"

"Even in a place so far removed from society, there are Dreamers. She's the Mistress of Dreams and recently called us together. I couldn't go because I'm a cripple," she said bitterly.

"You're a Dreamer? That's wonderful. There are some in the Forgotten Realms?"

"Many."

"Tell me, Floris, what happened to your legs?" Savannah asked, then quickly added, "Only if you want to tell me."

"I'd like to tell you," Floris assured her. "To explain, we have to go back in history…to the aftermath of the Mystic War eight hundred years ago. No one can remember the precise reason for the bitter conflict, but aided by the mages, the Queen and her armies went to war against the magical beings. After years of fighting, my ancestors were driven past the Great Forests of the north into the wilderness beyond. Then the mages used witchcraft to seal the borders. And thus the Forgotten Realm was created."

"The magic barrier still stands after all these years?" asked Savannah. "That's a long time."

"They say that the Supreme Witch made a pact with a powerful demon to weave the spell," replied Floris.

"But magical folk do come out of the Forgotten Realms?"

Floris's expression saddened. "But only for a short time. If we stay away, we'll die. It is a wasting death; most die before forty. It's called The Curse. I don't think anyone has left for anything but a fleeting visit for hundreds of years." She pointed to her legs. "This is evidence the spell is real. My jailors took great delight in telling me the legend."

Savannah felt a rush of unease. Was Pela doomed to suffer the same fate? "How long have you been out of the Forgotten Realms and here in Kandelora?" she asked.

Silvia Shaw

"When I was fourteen, I strayed too close to the barrier and was captured by a Silverthorne witch. They wanted to see if their black magic would work on a magical being. I was taken to their stronghold and put to work as a maid for a few years until I was stronger. When they finally took me down to the dungeons, my magic reacted so badly to their black magic that the witch's arm burst into flames. The next day, I found the door unlocked and escaped down the mountain," Floris said. A tear spilled over a lid. "That was twelve years ago. I'm thirty-two, and I lost the use of my legs two years ago."

"What!" exclaimed Savannah. "Do you mean to tell me those atrocious black-magic experiments are still going on?"

"The witches were quiet for a time after the fall of the Prophecy Tower, but they began again later."

Savannah filed that information away for action when she got back to the Keep. "Has anyone any idea of the purpose of these experiments?" she asked.

"We believe the poor unfortunate souls were, and still are conduits to the demon world. To give the witches access to black magic."

Remembering Ursula's black cape, Savannah could quite believe that theory. She shuddered to think what that cape had been made of.

Now Floris had solved the riddle of The Curse, they would have to work out how to break it. She turned her attention back to the Faerie who was looking at her expectantly. With a quick twist, Savannah undid the two top buttons on her shirt and pulled out the medallion. To her surprise, when Floris leaned forward to study it, the metal sent a pleasurable warmth through her. That hadn't happened with Tamasin or Pela.

"Floris… would you be willing to let me try something? If The Curse is a spell, then the Circle of Sheda may be able to break it."

Floris looked at her dubiously. "The Curse has been there for eight hundred years. If it could have been destroyed by the Circle of Sheda, surely a Chosen One would have done it years ago?"

"There could have been a reason why they couldn't. Would you be game to try?"

Floris swallowed. "I'm going to die soon anyway."

Savannah felt a wave of apprehension. Tampering with witchcraft might be like pulling the pin from a grenade. And she hadn't a clue what she was doing. "Or when Tamasin comes to find me, she can fly you back to your faerie home. It should halt the sickness."

"No, Savannah. This is my home now and my people. I...I wouldn't leave Luna."

"Then you must follow your heart," Savannah said gently. "Though I'm sure your loved one would like you to live."

"I haven't told her how I feel. But I'd prefer to face the icy hand of death near her than live a lonely life without her."

Quashing down the sudden urge to cry for what had been done to this lovely innocent woman, Savannah smiled reassuringly. "Then let's start. We'll hold the medallion together. When our minds meet, I'm going to try to unravel the spell. I have no idea what will happen, so be prepared."

"I'm ready," Floris said, with her hands outstretched. She was trembling, though Savannah wasn't sure if it was from excitement or fear.

Savannah pushed back the anxiety at the enormity of what she was going to try to do and took Floris's hands. As soon as they touched the metal, the room shuddered out of focus, and time seemed to stop.

They entered a world within the world.

A place of magic.

Chapter Twenty-Four

When the haze cleared, Floris was no longer beside her.

Savannah stood in front of a wall that was a kaleidoscope of colors and shapes. As they whirled, a giant tapestry began to appear, which at first seemed to be random patterns. But the more she looked, the clearer they became. She made out figures, thousands of them caught up in the threads that now resembled spider webs rather than needlepoint.

Strange breezes blew across her face, while feathery things brushed against her. The air pulsed faintly, punctuated with odd sighing sounds. The place stank of black magic, a fetid odor of decay. A slimy slug slithered down her cheek, the pain of which made her flinch.

Ignoring her fear, she moved closer to search for Floris. It was impossible with so many figures in the weave.

The next moment the surface cleared, revealing a glorious garden in front of a snow-white palace. The sheer beauty of it took her breath away. A lilting siren song, seductive and enchanting, filled the air. The melody was so moving that it became too much for her senses. Too wonderful to bear. The agony of not being able to cross over tore at her heart.

She would have been lost in the whirlpool of emotion if it hadn't been for the sharp tingling at her breast. It only ceased when she dragged her eyes away. Crying replaced the singing. She turned to see Floris caught in the spidery threads, hands outstretched toward the palace garden. She was naked, weeping uncontrollably. The fine hairs on the back of Savannah's neck stood up as her sixth sense trumpeted a warning. She knew if she didn't get the Empath free quickly, she'd be permanently damaged from the emotional overload.

She rubbed the medallion frantically, calling forth its power. Rays of energy sizzled from her fingertips. Determinedly, she burnt through the threads binding Floris to the wall. She noticed as she lasered the strands, weak black ones were falling off the stronger ones as if part of the barrier was already breaking down. As soon as the last constraint was gone, a green glow pulsed from the severed ends, then faded away with a piercing wail. The air gave an ear-splitting crack like a clap of thunder.

Floris screamed and collapsed to the floor. Horrified, Savannah stared down at her. The Faerie looked ashen, dead. Placing a finger on her jugular vein, Savannah breathed a sigh of relief when she felt a faint pulse. Quickly, she scooped her into her arms.

As soon as they turned from the wall, they were back in Floris's living room. But the Faerie remained unconscious, her body cold. In a panic, Savannah carried her down the hallway until she found the bedroom. With one hand, she awkwardly pulled back the covers and shuffled her onto the bed. Even with extra blankets from the cupboard, Floris didn't improve. Her skin stayed icy, and her breathing labored.

"Please don't die," begged Savannah. At wit's end, she did the only thing she could think of doing. She stripped down, got into bed with Floris, and pulled her into her arms.

A moment later, she heard the scrape of the front door and the clatter of boots on the floor. "What's happening. I heard screaming," called out Luna. "Where are you, Floris?"

Before Savannah could reply, the door flung open, and Luna stood on the threshold. She stared at them and paled. A range of expressions flitted across her face: shock, anger, and finally devastation. With quivering lips, she averted her eyes. "I'm sorry. I shouldn't have burst in like that. Forgive me."

"For heaven's sake, Luna," said Savannah impatiently. "This isn't what it seems, and there's no time to waste. Take off your clothes and get under the covers on the other side of Floris. She needs warmth badly—she's in shock, and we have to get her temperature up."

The way she said the words must have alarmed Luna, for she stripped off immediately without argument. Once she was under the blankets with them, Savannah felt the extra heat seep in. As Floris began to warm, Savannah's emotions plummeted. She felt so drained that all she wanted to do was cry. It had been one of the stupidest things she'd ever done. She could have killed them both by tampering in witchcraft she knew nothing about.

"What the hell did you do to her?" muttered Luna.

Savannah sniffled back a sob. "I tried to help her." Then overwhelming fatigue overcame her, and her eyes drooped shut. "Please... let's talk about it later. I'm so tired. It was nearly too much for me too."

When Savannah opened her eyes, she had no idea how long she'd been asleep. Night and day had no meaning underground. The muted glow from the crystal lamps hadn't been turned up brighter, and the three of them were still in the bed. Floris had her back to Savannah and cradled in Luna's arms. Luna had left the bed at some time to put on a long leather glove to cover her strange arm.

When she raised her gaze from the hand, she found Luna watching her. "Is she much better?" Savannah whispered.

"She woke an hour ago but drifted off immediately. This time she's sleeping naturally," Luna murmured. "What happened to her?"

Savannah stretched over to touch her shoulder. "I'll tell you later. She still needs comfort. Needs to feel loved. Have you told her how you feel about her?"

"How did you..." She flushed. "Oh. It was obvious when I saw you two in bed together that I was jealous, wasn't it?"

Savannah laughed softly. "It was as clear as day. Why have you kept it from her? She loves you very much."

"I...I didn't think anyone so sweet could love someone deformed like me," Luna said, then her expression turned incredulous as the words sank in. "She does?"

"Very much. Floris refused to leave you even for the chance of stopping the sickness."

Tears pooled in Luna's eyes. "I didn't dare hope she would look at me that way," she said and clasped the Faerie closer.

Savannah carefully tucked the medallion into her bra. "I'm going outside to have a look around and leave you two alone. Tell her how you feel. She has to have a reason to live if she's going to recover fully."

When she began to slide from the bed, Floris stirred. She wriggled around to face her. "What happened, Savannah? And why are we all in bed together?"

"Because you were so cold, you nearly died. It was the only way to warm you up. Can you remember any of it?"

"Bits and pieces. I was caught in a web and heard the most beautiful song. It was calling to me, but I couldn't move. It nearly broke my heart. Then you did something, and there was a loud bang." She shuddered. "I must have passed out after the explosion."

Savannah swallowed back her guilt. "I thought I'd killed you. It was the worst moment of my life."

"Did it work?" whispered Floris.

For the first time since they'd arrived back, Savannah smiled. "Yes. You're free of The Curse. It'll take time for your legs to strengthen, so don't go jumping out of bed yet. But I'm sure you'll walk again."

Floris took her hand, her voice soft and gentle. "Thank you. I can feel how much it cost you to save me."

"To be quite honest, it knocked the stuffing out of me. I have a lot to learn about magic. There's an old saying where I come from, *Fools rush in where angels fear to tread.* I was a fool today. I'm going to dress and leave you two alone."

"Oh," exclaimed Floris blushing. She looked at Luna. "We're naked. I'll get dressed."

"Please, Floris, not yet. Would you let me hold you?" murmured Luna.

Without speaking, the Faerie turned and burrowed into her. Gently, Luna ghosted her lips over her eyes and down her cheeks, finally claiming her lips.

Savannah dressed hastily to leave the room. Sexual vibes radiated from the Empath like a beacon, which didn't help Savannah's state of mind. She felt terribly lonely. Right now, she'd give anything to have a carefree night out with her friends at home.

Quietly closing the front door behind her, she went in search of Sunflower. In the animal enclosure, she found her in one of the back stalls next to a pen holding six enormous animals that looked like a cross between a cow and hippopotamus. From their impressive udders, she guessed they were the city's milk supply. The horse whinnied at her approach, her ears pricked toward her. Savannah flashed her a big smile, which faded when she saw the restraints on the mare's legs. They were stretched so tightly around her fetlocks that the horse had to be in pain. Furious, she pointed a finger, and sizzling magic instantly shot out. With quick sweeps of her hand, she shattered the thick hide ropes.

A young man with enormous ears like a donkey appeared. "What the feck do you think you're doing?"

She glared at him. If she weren't so angry, she would have felt more compassion for his infliction. Instead, she felt like grabbing him by the big ears and giving him a shake. "What's the matter with you!" she snapped. "She doesn't need to be tied up."

"Without ropes, you can't control dumb beasts," he muttered.

"Nonsense. She's a quiet, intelligent animal. Don't you have horses here?"

He shrugged. "What use have we for horses? I've never even seen one that can fly."

"You've been here all your life?"

"I was born here as my father was before me." He regarded her uneasily. "Are you a sorceress? We don't like 'em here."

"No, I'm not."

"Then whatcha do to my ropes?"

"It's a magic trick I learned. Don't worry. I can't put a spell on you, so you've nothing to fear from me. How's Sunflower's wing?"

Though he still looked suspicious, he answered in a friendlier tone. "The healer said there's no break, only muscle strain. After a week, she should be able to fly again. Meanwhile, it's to stay bound up."

Savannah turned and scratched Sunflower's neck. "That's a relief. Promise me there'll be no more ropes."

"Okay. But only if she stays quiet."

"You hear that, Sunflower?"

"I'll be good, Savannah. Tell him to feed me some of those apples he has in the barrel."

Savannah ghosted her a wink and addressed the worker, "Apples keep her happy and docile."

"Right. I'll make sure she gets a few."

With a wave to the mare, she went off in the direction of the town square. Her stomach was rumbling—it had been a long while since she'd eaten. And the apples did look good!

After wandering through the shops, she entered a tavern called The Grotto. Half an hour later, Luna found her sitting on a stool in front of a trestle table, finishing off a plate of meat stew and beans. She slid onto the seat beside her and signaled to the serving girl. "I'll have an ale and one for my friend."

"Thanks," said Savannah, putting down her spoon. "I promised you'd fix them up for the meal. I was starving."

"I imagine you were." She laid her hand on her arm. "I'd like to thank you very much for what you did for Floris."

"How is she?"

Luna's face broke into a sunny smile. "Wonderful. She already has movement in her legs, and she feels much stronger in herself. She's…she's really happy at long last."

"And you are too?"

"I am," she agreed, then added quietly. "I've loved her for years, and it nearly broke my heart when I saw you together in bed."

"Sorry about that. I couldn't warn you."

Luna smiled. "No need to apologize. You got us together."

"Tell me about Kandelora," said Savannah. "I've been studying the history of Rand, and I've never come across any mention of this place."

"You won't. We have kept it a secret. To my knowledge, no one has ever left."

"Never?" exclaimed Savannah. "But it looks like it's been here for a long time."

"It has," replied Luna. "The first people came here after the fall of the Prophecy Tower three hundred years ago. The Silverthorne witches carried out all sorts of foul experiments with people and animals in the laboratories beneath their dungeons. We are the results of those experiments."

Savannah stared at her. "Do you mean to tell me that there're lot more levels under Falcon's Keep?"

"Of course. The mountain's filled with them. There is another entrance on the side of the mountain. Didn't you know?"

Savannah spun the spoon in her hand, then jabbed it into the table. "No. And there's been a damn Elite Guard training school sitting on top of the witches' stronghold for one hundred and fifty years. They've all been idiots." She drank a mouthful of ale and continued. "Floris said she escaped from their dungeons twelve years ago, and they're still experimenting?"

"They started up again about ten years after the Tower was destroyed."

"Good God! That long!" said Savannah, horrified.

"Aren't the witches back in power?"

"No. Nobody has a clue they're back under the Keep." She leaned forward. "How did your ancestors get to this place?"

Luna rubbed her fingers over her gloved hand as if reminding herself why it was there. "It is in our records that when the chief witch, Agatha, realized they were on the verge of losing the war, she cast a spell to seal off the lower areas of what is now Falcon's Keep, before the Prophecy Tower fell. The guards opened the cages before they left. All the food supplies were abandoned, so the prisoners carried them down with them through the honeycombed mountain."

"How *did* the people survive?" asked Savannah curiously.

"It was a nightmare navigating the ancient tunnels, but they found the way. When they came out into the canyon, they probably wouldn't have survived if they'd had to spend the night in the open. But just before dark, someone noticed a small animal come out of a slit in the wall at the base of the opposite mountain. They enlarged the hole and crawled through to find a pool of fresh water." A faint smile flitted over her face. "They planted the seeds saved from the food and bred the small animals from the cages and those they captured in the canyon. The light crystals are plentiful in these mountains. Then they voted to hide away from the rest of the world because of their deformities."

"Your mother was captured by the witches?"

"Yes. She escaped from their dungeons forty-five years ago. The witches don't bother giving chase if anyone gets free. No one can survive outside at night here. And they don't know we're here." Her expression saddened. "She died five years ago."

"What I can't understand, Luna, is why you have a disfigurement if it was your mother they experimented on?"

"We have no idea, but the deformities are getting less each generation. My mother had her whole arm replaced with an animal's. I only have it from the elbow down."

"And your father?"

Luna shrugged. "I didn't get his...affliction. He is dead as well."

Savannah was at a loss to explain any of it. It sounded like the witches knew how to tamper with genetics, but she hadn't seen any other evidence that this civilization was so advanced scientifically. The more plausible explanation was that witchcraft was involved, and the spell was getting weaker.

"So, the witches really aren't aware you're here?"

"No. And that's the problem, Savannah. We can't let you leave. We can't risk anyone finding us."

Savannah digested this statement, realizing she should have expected it. For three hundred years, the City of Outcasts had remained hidden. Every person had some abnormality they wouldn't want the rest of the world to see. They would be shunned and ridiculed. She had only one option—the time had come to announce she wore the Circle of Sheda. She wondered, though, where these people's alliances lay.

"Would you call a public meeting, Luna? As soon as you can. It can't wait. I've important information that will affect even this city hidden away in the mountains."

Luna stared at her. "You're serious, aren't you?"

"I am. I can't stay."

Chapter Twenty-Five

Falcon's Keep

Tamasin looked over the rows of spectators in the arena. She tried to shake off her growing unease, not having sighted Savannah all day. Her dreams last night had been disturbing, filled with a strange race of people: humans combined with animals. She had no idea what or where they were, but she felt they were involved with Savannah. In all her travels, she had never seen anything like such cross-breeding on Rand.

She leaned over and whispered to Valeria, who was absorbed in the wrestling match. "Who's fighting Savannah?"

Valeria cast her a side glance. "I can see your disapproving look. Captain Jocose has picked one of the smaller soldiers."

"Humph! The match doesn't matter. I've had a bad feeling all day that something is going to happen. Forfeit it."

"You know very well it does matter. The challenge was made, which makes it a point of honor. Besides, I'm interested to see what Pela has taught her." Valeria smiled at Tamasin sweetly. "You could try getting Pela to forfeit."

"Maybe I will." She signaled to Pela, who was restlessly prowling around the grounds.

She came over to the viewing tent immediately. "Yes, Consort?"

"I don't think it's necessary, or wise, for Savannah to fight. Would you call off the match, please?"

"The Queen is forfeiting?"

Valeria turned to scrutinize her. "I thought as a gesture of good-will that you could concede the bout."

"Unfortunately, Your Majesty, it would be in direct conflict with our motto, 'Never Surrender'," replied Pela, peeling back her lips into a grin.

Tamasin would have found their bickering amusing if she wasn't so anxious. She dropped the formalities and said abruptly, "Where is Savannah? I haven't seen her all day."

"I haven't either," Pela muttered. "She has to be here somewhere."

"Would she be at the library?"

"Glenda said she was there early this morning. She found the door unlocked after breakfast, and Savannah had the spare key," Pela said and added accusingly. "It's a pity she wasn't still serving me. At least I would have realized if she was missing."

Tamasin let the comment pass. She could see Pela was worried. "She's probably hiding somewhere to psych herself up for the match. When is it due?"

"She's up next."

"That soon?" said Tamasin, feeling tension gather in her stomach. "I'm sure she'll come when the master-at-arms calls her name."

They didn't have long to wait. As soon as the last two fighters saluted the Queen and the cheering died away, the drummer began the slow tattoo that heralded the beginning of the next match. The Palace warrior strode out to the center ring. When Savannah didn't appear, there were hoots of derision from the gold and silver ranks.

Suddenly, a familiar figure appeared at the entrance to the arena, and the jeering died away. When Pela went rigid beside her, Tamasin knew it wasn't Savannah. She sucked in a sharp breath as the woman in the Elite Guard uniform walked across the stadium. There was no mistaking that thickset body and the long scar puckering the side of her face.

Captain Killia had returned.

No one applauded her, instead, the recruits silently watched as she approached Pela.

Killia halted in front of her and saluted. "I will fight for the honor of Falcon's Keep, Commander. Your housemaid has left."

"To where?" asked Pela. The words, though said softly, held more menace than if she had shouted them.

"Somewhere she won't be coming back from. I made sure of that. She was the devil's spawn. Do you think anyone so puny could defeat me without black magic?"

"What did you do to her?" The words were spat out. There was no mistaking that Pela was furious.

Killia must have realized she'd miscalculated, for indecision flitted across her face. "You've never wanted a housemaid. You said yourself they were sent to spy on you."

"I won't ask again. Where is Savannah?"

"I threw her off the East wall," Killia said. "I did it for you, Commander."

Tamasin bolted to her feet. "You did what?" she exclaimed.

Killia turned to eye her with hatred. "Your little spy is dead, and the audience waits impatiently for a match. I challenge you to fight me, Consort."

Tamasin walked down off the platform and faced her. "I am not a raw recruit, soldier, nor do I need to fight for my honor. But I will bring you to account for what you have done to Savannah."

"Don't, Tamasin," exclaimed Valeria. She pushed off her chair, her eyes flashing. "Let Jocose take care of this."

"I have challenged her, Your Majesty," said Killia in triumph. "And she has accepted."

"Enough," Pela called out. Her face might have been carved from stone when she spoke again. "Go back to your seat, please, Consort. I will take care of this. What is your choice of weapon, Killia?"

"You're going to fight me, Pela? But I did this for you. I have always served you faithfully."

"No, you haven't. And you Silverthorne bitches still think to control me. But no more. For what you did to Savannah, you are going to die."

Killia swept her gaze around the tiered seating of the stadium, then settled it back on Pela. Her skin began to glow a faint orange as she took a knife out of her belt.

She's protecting herself with magic, thought Tamasin in alarm. As much as she wanted to intervene, she knew they were beyond that point.

This fight was to the death.

"Knives it is," grinned Killia, hefting the boned handle from hand to hand as she waited for Pela to arm herself.

Pela leaned down to pull a knife out of her shoe. When she straightened, her lips curled back over her teeth. "Take your place, soldier," she said, her voice deceptively soft.

They both dropped to a crouch, facing across six feet of space, knives ready, free hands to grab.

Killia unwound with a lunge, slashing with her blade. Sparks of light flickered off the weapon. Pela avoided the attack early and feinted to the right. She punched her fist into Killia's breastbone. Killia grunted, retreating for a second before again pressing the attack. Pela allowed her to get close enough, then dodged away with another punishing hit.

They continued grimly, circling, looking for openings. Thick and heavy-chested, Killia was more dangerous based on sheer muscle mass. Pela was rangier, having much more agility than brute strength.

Time after time, Killia plowed in, trying to turn her weight against the leaner, faster Pela. She did it once too often and lost traction. Pela countered quickly, ducked low, and slashed obliquely across her side. Killia howled in fury, kicking at Pela savagely while bringing up her knife. Pela swiveled to the side, then kneed her groin. Killia buckled with the pain, but not before she caught Pela a glancing slice on the hip.

Pela danced away, blood staining her breeches.

Killia retreated a few feet and grated out in a low voice, "Your little pet squealed like a hog when I tossed her over the side."

"And for that, I'm going to gut you, witch."

"You can try," replied Killia and muttered an incantation. The knife began to glow orange. She curled back her mouth and charged.

In swift movements, Pela parried the blow with her left hand and brought her right hand over. She plunged the knife into Killia's chest. Killia gasped, staring at Pela. "The spell didn't work. What the hell are you?"

Pela pulled out the knife and pushed it deep into Killia's belly. As the blade slipped from the witch's fingers, Pela rasped into her ear, "Who do you think gave you that scar, Captain? It seems my magic is greater than yours."

With a thin cry, Killia fell flat onto the ground, the force of the fall drove the bloody blade through to her back.

A silence fell around the arena, then the recruits began a slow clap. Pela held up her hand. "Enough. Whatever crimes she committed, she was still a soldier of our corp. Stand to attention for a fallen comrade." She signaled to Rhiannon, who jogged over immediately. "Remove the body. Tonight, organize a burial pyre and quietly burn her. She won't be honored with a warrior's send-off."

Pela paused to brush off the dust from her uniform, before she approached the royal box. Though she had won, she looked defeated. She bowed deeply to Valeria. "It's finished, Your Majesty. The Silverthorne witch played me for a fool for years, but no more. What is your wish now, ma'am? Shall we continue?"

Before Valeria could reply, Tamasin said quickly, "You two must remain to complete the games. There are still two matches and trophies to present. I'll take Jocose and two soldiers to retrieve...," she forced out the next words, "Savannah's body."

Guilt plagued her. She'd taken the woman from her world without warning or her consent and had failed to protect her.

Pela looked at her, clearly upset. "I know her secret."

"She told you?" asked Tamasin, surprised. Their relationship must have been closer than she realized.

"Yes. I want to go with you."

Valeria spoke before she could reply. "No, Commander, we must do our duty. The soldiers deserve a fitting end for their efforts," she said in a soft, almost apologetic tone. "Tamasin will retrieve Savannah and the Circle of Sheda."

Pela looked like she was going to argue, then nodded. "Of course, Ma'am." She called out to the drummer, "Signal the next bout in five minutes."

At the first drumroll, Tamasin was already out of the gate with Jocose and her soldiers at her side.

Malkia and three horses were waiting outside the stables. Wasting no time, they saddled their mounts. As she tightened the girth, Tamasin informed Malkia of the reason for the ride. The stallion snorted his rage and stamped his feet.

Tamasin stroked his neck soothingly. *"I know, old friend. We all liked her. Tell Sunflower to come with us. Savannah would have wanted the mare to take her on her last ride."*

"Sunflower has disappeared."

Tamasin dropped the stirrup iron and raked her gaze over the grazing paddock. *"Since when?"*

"Since this morning. I presumed someone took her out for an early ride."

A glimmer of hope sprung in Tamasin's breast. Savannah could mind-speak with the horses, and Sunflower was her favorite.

Maybe—just maybe—.

With renewed vigor, Tamasin vaulted into the saddle. "Let's go."

With precise movements, the horses unfurled their wings, lifted off the ground, and wheeled into formation as soon as they were airborne. Once they'd soared over the east battlement, they battled the howling winds that hit immediately, then once through, dived down the side of the mountain.

After two sweeps across the barren canyon, they found nothing. The heat was intolerable. Tamasin figured a person might be hard to see, but a horse wouldn't be. It was on the third run that she noticed something white caught on a thorny bush. Dismounting, she plucked it off the branch, elated. An animal wouldn't have been able to put the letter there, which meant Savannah had. The likelihood of someone else doing it was virtually zero—no one could live in this inhospitable environment.

Sunflower had to have helped her survive the fall, but where were they now?

She climbed back in the saddle and called out to Jocose. "She's been here. We'll each take a soldier and follow the canyon as far as we can before dark. You take that way, and I'll go the other." Worried, she looked up at the sky. "There's barely an hour of daylight left. If you haven't found them by sunset, fly straight back to Falcon's Keep. Pela says there's a big nasty predator down here that prowls at night."

"Will do," Jocose called out and wheeled to the north.

After Tamasin watched them go, she turned to her companion. "Let's go."

A few miles down, the canyon became a series of rocky gorges and plunging ravines. Tamasin wondered how anything could survive in this desolate wasteland. There was no sign of life, let alone a horse. Soon the rock walls turned red and orange, heralding the setting of the sun. Finally, and very reluctantly, she turned for home.

Pela was standing on the east battlement when Tamasin reached the top of the mountain. "Anything?" she called out.

"Nothing," Tamasin yelled back. "Go to our quarters. I'll meet you there as soon as I attend to Malkia."

Jocose was waiting when they touched down. From the look on her face, Tamasin knew she hadn't found anything either. "Nothing, Jo?"

"No, Tam. By the moons, it's the most dismal place I've ever seen."

"Did you let Pela know we found the note?"

"I did. She didn't say a word. Just walked out to the east wall and stood there in the wind."

"She's worried too," said Tamasin, turning to look at her on the battlement.

But Pela had disappeared.

Chapter Twenty-Six

Kandelora

The town square was packed.

Savannah stood quietly, facing the crowd. They appeared more curious than hostile, which heartened her. She didn't want this ending up as a lynch mob. Luna and Eric occupied chairs next to her but had made it plain that they would only listen and abide by the will of the people. As Savannah looked out over the sea of faces, she tried not to focus on their disfigurements and peculiarities. Instinctively, she understood that these people would resent her showing any pity. They held themselves proudly.

Taking a deep breath, she said evenly. "I'm here because you took me in, for which I'll be ever grateful. And you have given my horse a place to recuperate, and for that, I thank you from the bottom of my heart. But Luna has insisted that now I know your city exists, I can't leave."

Savannah paused and swept her eyes around the courtyard. "I don't blame you in the slightest. You've kept it a secret for generations, and to jeopardize that would be unacceptable. But I must leave. I have something vital for the survival of Rand."

A gnarled man in the front row got to his feet. Savannah tried not to flinch at his horns and hoofed feet. "What's going to happen that's so bad?" he asked.

"In another seven turns of the moons, the Mistress of Dreams has been warned Rand will be invaded. Already there have been two assassination attempts by an enemy appearing out of thin air.

Tamasin has gathered the Dreamers, and Queen Valeria will be marshaling all the armies of Rand in readiness for war."

"It's the witches," someone called out.

"Not this time. Tamasin thinks it's an enemy from another world or dimension. We suspect it's happened before, prior to the Mystic War."

"What has it to do with us," asked a woman with a baby on her lap. "We want nothing to do with the outside world."

"I know, and I understand," said Savannah patiently. "But I don't have that option. I must go back."

Eric got up from his chair, fixing her with a scowl. "What's so special about you? You're only a small woman."

Savannah glanced at him then turned to the crowd. They looked less friendly than when she had started. It was time to out herself. She only hoped these people had heard of Sheda. With no more hesitation, she reached into her shirt to pull out the medallion. After a little theatrical twirl, she held it out so everyone could see it. "Because I am the Chosen One. I wear the Circle of Sheda."

The effect of the declaration was beyond anything she'd expected. An audible gasp resonated from the room, and they sank to their knees. An arthritic old woman hobbled up to her and rasped out, "As it was foretold, the Chosen One has come at last. The Goddess has not forgotten us."

Startled, Savannah blinked at her. "It was prophesied I would come?"

"It is recorded in our seer's scrolls."

"Where is your seer now?" asked Savannah with a flash of hope. Maybe the old blind woman lived here.

"She passed on many moons ago. She was amongst the first to escape the Tower when it fell." The woman paused and bowed her head. "Her name was Chazona."

Savannah frowned. "A visionary. How dare the witches capture a soothsayer for their experiments. Damn them in their arrogance." She regarded the old lady kindly. "What else did she foretell?"

"That the Chosen One would lead us out of the darkness."
Savannah eyed her skeptically. "You have existed hidden here
for three hundred years. I'm sure it was extremely difficult for your
ancestors, but as far as I can see, you have a comfortable life. Do you
want to go out into the world?"

When a chorus of shouts echoed across the great market, "No!"
the old lady put up her hand. "Silence! Let Luna speak for us. She'll
know what we must do. We cannot ignore a seer's prediction of the
future."

Luna closed her eyes silently for a moment before she stood up.
"I, like you, want to stay where we are safe and loved. But the prophecy has been fulfilled. The Chosen One has arrived in Kandalora. It
was foretold that she will lead us out of the darkness. Look around
you…are we in darkness? Should we be bound by a myth? Those are
the questions we must ask ourselves."

"But also if you're denying your children a better future," said
Savannah firmly.

"They are *our* children," replied Luna sharply. "And if what you
are saying is true, Rand is going to be plunged into war. Why would
we follow you out now?"

"Because, like it or not, you *are* part of this world," said Savannah.
She wearily shook her head because though she argued, she knew
Luna was right to protect her people. And it would be wiser to stay
hidden. "But you're correct…you're safer here."

"We are the City of Outcasts," said Eric.

"But not the City of the Dead," said Savannah in frustration.
"Has anyone given thought to the possibility that *darkness* might
have an entirely different meaning?"

For the first time, Luna looked unsure. "What do you mean?"

"Dark times are coming, Luna. I feel it in my bones. The medallion has made me hyper-sensitive to what's happening around me,
like the very air we're breathing has permeated—" The words died in
Savannah's throat as her eyes swirled out of focus. There was the ringing

of steel and the pounding of blood in her ears. A vision flashed in front of her eyes. A battle raged on a wide-open plain, the screams of dying soldiers and horses filled the air. She saw a woman leaping to avoid the slash of a sword, and when she caught a glimpse of her face, it was her own. The melee dissolved, and she was back in the cavern. But instead of the crowd, a lone figure sat in front of her.

"Grandmother," cried out Savannah. "Where have you been?"

"Watching, my child, but I cannot tarry. Black magic is close. Leave the people of Kandelora hidden, for they have a part to play later. Persuade Luna and Floris to accompany you to Queen Wren in Arcadia, for the time will come when you'll need Floris. And Wren deserves to know what happened to her beloved sister before she dies." The old blind woman tilted her head and smiled. "Ask for Sanya and Pablo. They will help you get past the lowest vault."

Before Savannah could say anything more, she was gone.

When the world came back into focus, Savannah was on her hands and knees in front of a horrified crowd. Sheepishly, she rose to her feet and brushed back her hair. "Sorry about that. It was the second vision that I've had recently. They come out of nowhere."

"Do they affect you?" asked Luna with concern.

"No," Savannah reassured her. "I'm fine. I need your people to understand that even though I wield the Circle of Sheda, the spirit inside the medallion guides me occasionally onto the right path of the future. She has told me what advice I'm to give you."

"This could be a ploy to influence us. To make us let her go," someone in the back called out.

Savannah felt a sense of shame. These were simple folk who had lived their lives in peace until she'd entered their world.

To her surprise, it was Eric who came to her defense. "Enough. Let's hear her out. We can say we have the ideal life, but we all know that's not always true. We're safe, and the majority are happy. But for those who haven't found mates, it is a lonely existence."

She cast him a grateful smile. "I know the way forward. Your city is to remain hidden, but you may have a role to play in the future."

"What role?" he asked, clearly puzzled.

"I don't know," admitted Savannah. "We will meet that challenge if, or when it comes." She paused, trying to work out how to phrase this request. Luna and Floris could be approached privately, but she had to ask this while she had the crowd. "Um...I have a request. Would Sanya and Pablo be prepared to accompany me to Falcon's Keep? I'll need their help."

Luna raised her eyebrows. "How do you know the twins?"

"I don't."

"This is too fecking crazy," Eric growled. He tossed his head in the direction of the tavern. "They're over there. Ask 'em yourself."

At that, two figures lithely uncoiled themselves from the bench seat in front of the tavern. As Savannah watched them approach, it was quite obvious with what animal the brother and sister had been blended. Pablo and Sanya had the eyes and ears of a cat. Strangely though, the cross wasn't repugnant but quite cute. She noted that while they had hands and not paws, claws protruded from the end of their fingers. She chuckled softly—just the kind of help she needed with the rats.

"I'm Pablo," the male twin said, flashing her a smile. Two long canine teeth gleamed in the light. "You wanted us to help you?"

"If you would. When I get back to the Keep, we'll be cleaning out that coven of witches. I haven't discussed it with Tamasin, but since the rooms underneath are warded with spells, I shall have to go down first. The lower vault is full of rats, so I'll need help to get through."

Sanya hissed beside him, her ears twitching. "A room full of rats?"

"Big ones."

Reminding Savannah of *Alice in Wonderland's* Cheshire cat, both twins smiled and said in unison, "When do we go?"

Savannah glanced at Luna. "As soon as I'm allowed to leave."

Luna raised an eyebrow at Eric, who shrugged. "Do we have a choice? We can't keep the Chosen One here. And she intends to destroy the witches." He raised his voice to address the audience. "Anyone have any objection?"

When there was silence, he said to Savannah. "You're free to go. Pablo and Sanya may help you." He waved to the crowd. "The meeting is finished."

"Thank you. My friends will come looking for the medallion," said Savannah.

Eric took her by the arm and led her over to a seat in the corner. Luna sat down with them. "You'll have to wait for your horse to mend its wing. Four riders have already been here a while back. They left," he said.

"What!" exclaimed Savannah, unable to control her dismay. "Why didn't you tell me?"

Eric frowned at her unapologetically. "Gad, woman. You're lucky to be here. We weren't going to invite anyone else in, so don't push your luck," he snapped.

"Sorry. I do understand. Maybe they'll be back."

"Not today. Sunset was an hour ago."

"What does roam out there at night?" she asked curiously. They were full of frightening tales about things that lurked in the night, yet someone had to tell her what they were.

"You don't want to meet it. A black beast we call the Wind Howler. Arrows and spears are useless against it. We hunt small nocturnal animals, but when the Wind Howler comes we stay indoors for that night."

"So you have a place in the wall you can see outside?"

Eric nodded. "Of course. Many well-hidden viewing windows."

"How do the hunters know when the Wind Howler is coming?"

"When the wind springs up, dust billows in."

"Do you think the beast brings the wind?"

Luna interrupted. "Floris says it does when it comes up from its lair. She's sure it's a demon brought into this world by black magic. Being a magical being, she senses these things."

A theory began to form in Savannah's mind. Ursula's cape was a channel into the underworld, and the pain it caused was an offering to the demon, Molvia. And he fed off that suffering. Maybe the witches were in league with this Wind Howler. But what could they really offer it? "Does it come every night?" she asked.

"No. It will tonight because there has been activity in the canyon."

"What about when you find escapees from the witches' laboratories?"

"Always," replied Luna. "But there are plenty of other times as well."

"Have you ever wondered how people managed to escape? Surely their jailors wouldn't have been so lax not to lock the cells securely."

"What are you getting at?" growled Eric.

"Queen Valeria had a witch in the palace who put people under a 'truth' cape. Those unfortunates experienced dreadful pain, and were told the length of time they could endure it was a yardstick of their innocence. It was really a vile ruse to feed a demon their pain. Perhaps the people in the dungeons were deliberately let go to feed the Wind Howler. A price for his black magic. Many would have emerged from the mountain after dark because their eyes wouldn't be used to bright sunlight."

He stared at her. "Before Luna came, we were ignorant of magical folk and knew little of Queens or black magic. We are sheltered here. We know nothing about what goes on in the outside world. We only know what has been recorded by our ancestors."

"Just like me," mumbled Savannah.

Luna leaned closer to speak when a bowman appeared.

"Any sign of the Wind Howler?" asked Eric.

"No, but the Hawk flies tonight."

"Then no hunting," he ordered.

Savannah didn't catch the reply. She had already begun to sprint down the passageway leading to the water cavern and the entrance to the outside. Pounding boots echoed behind her as she reached the lever to open the door. She pushed it up, hearing Luna scream out behind her, "No, Savannah, don't go outside. We cannot protect you tonight."

Taking no notice, she stepped through the door and pushed it closed behind her. Pela was out there somewhere.

In the grey night, the dry gorge looked stark and forbidding, devoid of color like a black and white photograph.

A sudden gust of wind sprang up, and through it, she could hear the shriek of a Hawk.

Chapter Twenty-Seven

The wind increased to a gale.

It stank of an ancient evil so foul that bile rose into Savannah's throat. The ferocious windstorm shrieked along the canyon, sending blankets of dust into the air until the darkness became so thick it became a crushing weight around her.

As much as she strained, she could no longer hear the Hawk.

Suddenly, the wind spiraled downward like a giant corkscrew. A ragged tumbling surged like an earthquake. The earth ripped open into a jagged cleft, and something black sprang from deep within the chasm. The wind ceased as abruptly as it had begun, the silence now even more frightening. When the dust settled, she could finally see illuminated in the pale light of the twin moons, what had emerged from the underworld.

A huge demonic beast stood where the crater had been.

Aghast, Savannah stared at the monster. Without magic she'd have no chance. Resembling a bear, though larger than a full-grown grizzly, it had wide muscled shoulders and a thick body covered by black shaggy hair. Two prominent curved horns protruded from its head, and its long canine fangs dominated a mouth of yellow razor teeth. Needle-sharp claws jutted from its massive paws.

The Wind Howler.

Savannah froze, trying to blend into the wall. The beast sniffed the air, caught her scent, and shifted its head her way. Its red eyes flashed fire when they landed on her. With a blood-curdling roar, it lumbered straight at her. She forced herself to ignore the instinct to run and stood her ground as its mouth opened to strike. Fighting suffocating fear, she raised the medallion and let her mind envelop the power. Its foul breath coated her nostrils as electricity shot from her fingers. The demon pulled back at the last minute, its massive jaws snapping uselessly in the air.

After a series of angry bellows, it sank back on its haunches and projected a stream of vile images into her mind: maimed soldiers on a battlefield, dismembered limbs, clotted blood, and agonizing screams. Mustering the strength of the medallion, she fought, though it made her sick to her stomach. When she continued to douse the evil with scenes of beauty, harmony, and love, the Wind Howler finally abandoned the mind games.

It began to circle.

She retaliated by letting fly a series of sharp zaps. Though she knew by the way the demon flinched that they hurt, it continued to search for an opening. It lunged and pressed relentlessly. She began to tire, her whole body tingling with sharp pricks of pain as she continued to draw on the power. But after what seemed like an eternity, she eventually faltered. The magic became harder to muster. She took a frantic step backward, only to hit the hard cliff wall.

The beast darted forward. Up this close, she could see her reflection in its red eyes. She shuddered—it was only a heartbeat before she was consumed. As she prepared for the end, the screech of a Hawk pierced the air.

The demon swung around, then reared onto its hind legs as the bird's talons plunged into its muzzle. It howled, swinging its shaggy head to shake off the Hawk. The bird clung, ripping through to the nostril. Black blood spurted down the Howler's massive chest, and Savannah could smell its sickly odor. The Hawk loosened its grip then flew out of reach, waiting for another opening. The next moment, it swooped and wheeled, flying furiously at the demon. Time after time, it raked with its talons as the beast charged and swatted at it.

Savannah watched with heart-stopping dread. Though bigger than an ordinary hawk, it was small in comparison to the demon.

And it might be a magical being, but she doubted it could best this abomination from the underworld.

Then the Hawk miscalculated. It dived too close. A massive paw struck it in the chest, sending it somersaulting along the ground. When the bird lay there unmoving, the demon roared with triumph.

As it moved toward it, Savannah snapped. "You will not touch her, you ugly son-of-a-bitch," she screamed.

The demon stopped, its head swiveled in her direction.

Time stopped for Savannah. Her panic and terror evaporated, replaced by a wave of anger so intense that it consumed her.

All constraints vanished. Raising her arms, she called on the ancient power from the Circle of Sheda.

Demanded it come.

Light streamed from the medallion, enveloping every cell of her body. The air in the canyon crackled and sizzled. Heat built in Savannah's body until she could feel nothing but absolute power.

The Wind Howler looked at her in alarm.

She felt no compassion as she stared back. He was hers now.

She pointed both hands at the beast and unleashed the power.

A dazzling bolt of lightning shot through the air, followed by an enormous thunderclap.

The next second, the demon exploded.

Thousands of body fragments flew into the air. They burst into flames and disintegrated before they hit the ground until the only thing left of the beast was its black blood staining the earth.

The force of the blast sent shock waves spreading outward in a ring, driving the powdery dust before it. Rocks cascaded down the mountains.

When the earth stopped shaking, Savannah stared down at her hands. What had just happened? That power was entirely different from that which she had conjured up previously. So lethal that it had blown the beast apart.

Then remembering the Hawk, she pushed aside her swirling thoughts and ran over to it. The bird was standing up, silently watching her. Without hesitation, she threw her arms around its neck and hugged it. "Oh, Pela. I thought he'd killed you."

Pela gave a little squawk and wrapped her wings around her.

"Don't turn," whispered Savannah urgently. "We're being watched." When the intelligent brown eyes looked at her enquiringly, she continued, "I'll tell you about it when I get home. Sunflower and I have shelter for the night, so we'll be fine. Tell Tamasin to come alone in the morning to pick me up." She nuzzled into the feathers of Pela's neck and dropped a kiss onto it. "You'd better get going, Pel. They have arrows. I'll see you in the morning."

Pela dipped her head in agreement, then flapped her giant wings and soared into the air. Savannah waved and watched until the bird was out of sight.

Exhausted, Savannah sank to her knees. The fight left her feeling as if she'd been savagely beaten. She ached all over, but needed to get everything into perspective. Steadying herself with long deep breaths, she took a few minutes to mentally calm, then climbed to her feet.

The door in the mountain opened before she had a chance to press the button, and Luna, Eric, and four hunters silently watched as she stepped inside.

She smiled weakly at them. "You won't have to worry about the Wind Howler anymore."

"We saw," said Luna. "You were...very impressive."

"Scary, you mean," muttered Savannah.

"Was it a demon?" asked Eric, regarding her in awe.

"Yes, and a nasty one," replied Savannah. "You will be safe at night now."

He scratched his chin. "The Hawk fought it too. We've always been afraid of it."

"It saved my life," said Savannah. "Tell your hunters they've nothing to fear from it. It's a friend." She turned to Luna. "I need Floris's help."

Luna looked at her with concern. "Of course. Come with me."

No one acknowledged them as they made their way through the passageways. The news had spread. These were simple people, unused to magic, and would be wary of anyone capable of blowing anyone to pieces, let alone the Wind Howler. No doubt they would be relieved when she left, she thought sadly.

At the door to the Faerie's home, Luna touched Savannah's shoulder and said softly, "I can see you need peace. I'll come back in an hour."

She nodded gratefully. "Thanks."

Floris was sitting in the chair, looking healthier and happier than when she had last seen her. She greeted Savannah with a welcoming smile which faded as she looked at her closely. "What's the matter, my friend?"

Savannah sank in the chair opposite, unable to stop the tears trickling down her cheeks. "I don't know who I am anymore, Floris. I wear the most sacred magical talisman of your world, yet I come from a place without magic. Not only that, I've always been skeptical of anything not based on science and fact. Tonight, in a rage I summoned ancient magic that was capable of blowing a huge demonic creature to pieces."

"Give me your hand," ordered Floris.

Savannah complied, immediately feeling a calm spread over her.

"If you want to understand magic, Savannah, you have to embrace the force inside your own body. Every living entity has a magical life force, but except for the very gifted, or those born of magic, most only have it in a very mild form," she said, gently stroking Savannah's hands. "You have a strong force, but you won't be able to manage it properly until you learn how to project it outside your body. Magical creatures do it automatically, but their talents are limited to their species. Mages learn the craft through years of study."

"Am I merely a vessel and conduit for the ancient magic?" asked Savannah.

"Not at all. You're entirely different. There would be very few women capable of wielding the Circle of Sheda. They have to be perfectly in tune with their life force and the environment. I don't know anything about the past bearers or have any idea to what extent they could summon the magic. Perhaps few of them were capable of doing what you just did."

"I've never done anything special to warrant being chosen."

Floris's eyes focused on her. "Every night as you lie in bed in peace, you must put all thoughts aside and search within yourself. Concentrate on a single object, using it to bring your mind into focus. Eventually, you will find the answer within yourself. Can I ask you a question?"

"Of course."

"What made you so angry you were able to invoke such power?"

"Um…"

"This will go no further, Savannah."

"Okay, but it has to be our secret. The demon was going to kill Pela."

"Pela?"

"The Hawk."

"You know the Hawk and it has a name?" asked Floris incredulously.

"She's a Bramble Hawk, Floris."

"Oh, my. So one has come out of the Forgotten Realms. They are a fierce race. And you like her?"

"I do." Then added with a smile, "She is indeed very fiery."

Floris chuckled. "You will have your hands full with her. I'd be interested one day to hear how you managed to win her. They keep to themselves."

"Oh, she's not mine," Savannah replied, feeling a blush rise.

"She fought for you today," replied Floris gently. She rubbed her fingers before unclasping their hands. "I sense you're much calmer now. Tell me about yourself while we wait for Luna."

Savannah took a deep breath, as the happy memories filtered in. "As I told you before, I come from another world. I was the only child of older parents and I had an idyllic childhood in a lovely place. The only time I ever really saw my mother upset was when I told her

I was going halfway across the world to study. Looking back, they must have known I was different and tried to protect me."

"Where are they now?" asked Floris softly.

"My father died seven years ago and my mother last year. I miss her."

"Have you any ties in your world? It must have been such a wrench to be taken away so abruptly."

Savannah sighed. "It was. Though I think my life has much more purpose here, I miss my friends and my home. I had a great collection of valuable old treasures and only hope someone has put them away somewhere safe."

Flora rubbed her hand gently. "Tell me about them."

Savannah was still describing the artifacts when Luna arrived with a basket of food and a jug of cider.

She cast an eye over Savannah and smiled. "You look much more relaxed. After we eat, Floris has offered you her spare bedchamber."

"Thank you. I won't take much rocking tonight." Savannah put some meat and cheese on her plate, wondering how to phrase her next request. Better just to come out and ask, she decided. "Um… in my vision, Luna, I was to ask you and Floris to move to Arcadia. Queen Wren will be overjoyed to have you."

"Definitely not," said Luna firmly. "Floris is much safer here and I won't go without her."

"I know how you feel," said Savannah. "And she is much safer here. But apparently, Floris has an important role to play in the future."

Luna narrowed her eyes. "Leave her out of it. She's been through enough."

"What role?" asked Floris quietly.

Savannah looked at her miserably. "I don't know yet." She put down the slice of meat, her appetite gone. "Look…forget about it. I shouldn't have mentioned it. Whatever you were meant to do, I'm sure there are other alternatives." She got up stiffly from the table. "If you could show me the way, I'd like to go to bed."

Luna got up without a word, leaving Savannah to follow her. She could see Luna was upset, so silently took the towel she offered at the door.

As Savannah turned to go inside, Luna spoke, "You did an extraordinary thing for us today, Chosen One, and Kandalora thanks you very much. That monster has terrorized our people since the city was built. To our shame, we watched like cowards at the windows while you battled it with only the Hawk by your side." She made a wry face. "As much as I like to think you will go on your way and things will revert to normal, I know we've passed that point. Though we'll remain hidden, the people have at last come in contact with someone from the outside world. Someone heroic who has killed the beast for us."

"You needed magic to defeat it, Luna. Arrows and swords are useless against black magic," replied Savannah.

"I understand that, but we didn't even try to help. But we *will* redeem ourselves when the war comes. Whatever has to be done, we'll do. Or we'll not only be called the City of Outcasts, but we'll also be the City of Shame."

Savannah gave a single, firm nod. "Stay hidden for the time being. We don't know what manner of invaders are coming. Your city will be an ideal hiding place if it is needed. Your secret is safe with me. I'll tell Tamasin when the time comes when or if we need a sanctuary."

"Agreed. But how are you going to explain away the twins?"

"I'll come back the day after tomorrow and sneak them into the Keep. Time is now critical. Tell them to be ready at the first blush of dawn."

Luna looked puzzled. "Your friends have already been here. You'll have to wait for your horse to fly before you can leave."

"Tamasin will be here early in the morning to pick me up."

Luna raised an eyebrow. "Really? Well… If you say so."

"Trust me. She'll turn up." She held Luna's eye. "Would you come outside and meet her? She's coming alone."

"I'll think about it." Then comprehension flitted across Luna's face. "You can talk to the Hawk."

Savannah just shrugged.

"Extraordinary," Luna muttered as she turned to go. "I'd better let you get some sleep too. You look like you're ready to collapse."

Chapter Twenty-Eight

Falcon's Keep

Knocking woke Tamasin.

She raised on an elbow to peer through the window. The Keep was in darkness. The raps on the door sounded again, this time more insistent. When Valeria stirred beside her, she whispered, "Stay there. I'll see who it is."

After throwing on a robe and pulling on her boots, she hurried out of the bedchamber. If someone disturbed the Queen this time of night, it had to be extremely important. She was surprised to find Pela on the landing. Tamasin's pulse jumped at the sight of her disheveled state and the bloody gash on the side of her neck. "What's happened?" she asked, unable to keep the touch of panic out of her voice.

Unfazed, Pela flashed a wide smile. "I found her. She's alive."

Tamasin gripped her by the shirt and hauled her through the door. "Savannah's alive? Where is she?"

"At the bottom of the mountain. She wants you to pick her up tomorrow morning and to come alone."

Tamasin sat down heavily on a kitchen chair. "Take a seat. By the look of you, you've been in the wars. How did she survive the fall?"

"I'll let her tell you what happened. I arrived when she was in the middle of fighting a demon. I left straight after it died. She asked me to give you the message."

"Why didn't you bring her with you?"

"It's difficult to explain. She and Sunflower have shelter for the night, so there's no need to worry."

Tamasin drummed her fingers on the desk. "I'm not a fool, Commander. One moment you were on that east wall, the next you were gone. There wasn't a horse in sight. Who or what are you?"

Pela appeared disconcerted and, for a second, looked like she was going to walk out. Then she sank back down in the chair. "Okay, I'll bargain with you, Consort. A secret for a secret."

Tamasin narrowed her eyes. The woman was certainly a clever tactician. "Very well. My father was an Ice Elf."

Pela's eyes widened. "You're a half-breed?"

"I prefer to think I have the best of both worlds. And you?"

"I'm a Bramble Hawk."

Tamasin inhaled sharply as everything clicked into place. That's why Pela had never wanted a housemaid. Why no one could find out anything about her. The Bramble Hawks were the most withdrawn of all the magical beings and the unfriendliest. "You killed those crows, didn't you? That's how Savannah knew about the Hawks and the crows."

"Yes."

"Savannah keeps too many secrets. I've been wracking my brains about the message and what hawks we're supposed to persuade to fly, and she knew all the time."

Pela made a wry face. "We've all completely misunderstood Savannah. We presume what we see is what we get. Pleasant and smart, but too small to pose a threat."

Tamasin nodded. "She's likable and persuasive, but I think she was chosen to wear the medallion because she can accurately decipher the past."

"She's much more than that. I haven't yet told you what happened tonight," said Pela. "I was searching the canyon when a violent wind blew up. A sign the beast called the Wind Howler was coming. I often fly around the canyon at night. Usually, I go high when I see it and wait for it to go. Tonight I stayed, looking for Savannah, but I couldn't get close until the wind died down. By then, the monster was fighting Savannah. By the Gods, it was an ugly bastard. She was shooting rays of magic from her fingers at it, but eventually, it drove her against the wall. I joined the fight, ripping it with my talons. But it got me in the end and swatted me out of the sky. It was coming to finish me off when it happened."

"What?"

"Savannah screamed at it, and her body turned a dazzling white. Almost too bright to look at. A bolt of lightning shot out of her hands followed by a crash of thunder, and the demon exploded."

Tamasin stared at her. "Oh! She invoked the Death Vale. No Chosen One has been able to do that for a thousand years. Moira thinks it could be just a myth."

"I saw it with my own eyes."

They exchanged glances. "I wonder what her bloodline is," whispered Tamasin. "And what oracle is giving her information of the future. She's very close-lipped about that."

"Where is she from?" asked Pela. "She's completely absorbed in one of my books, *The Flora and Fauna of Rand*, and Glenda said she asked questions about the wars every child knows. It's as if she's new to our world." She frowned as if a thought struck and asked, "Where did you disappear to for three years? She came back with you."

"I went to find the Circle of Sheda."

"But I heard that Elsbeth took it to—" she blinked. "You brought Savannah through the portal."

"Now that is a secret you definitely must keep," said Tamasin. "But that's enough for the night. Valeria will be getting impatient. Savannah will have more to tell us tomorrow, and you need to get to bed."

"Please, Tamasin, don't tell the Queen what I am. The crown doesn't recognize anyone from the Forgotten Realms."

"I gave you my word, Pela," she reassured her. "And we're going to address the issue of the Forgotten Realms. All those people and creatures are as much a part of Rand as the rest of us. It is time to mend the rift."

†

Tamasin slipped quietly out of bed at soon as the sun was in the sky. Gathering up her clothes, she tiptoed out into the lounge to dress. After she had assured Valeria that the late-night caller wasn't anything to worry about, she had fallen back to sleep immediately. But knowing her wife, the questions would start as soon as she woke and Tamasin was impatient to be gone. Well aware that the royal temper would flare when she found her missing, she guiltily dashed over to the stables to saddle Malkia.

Having received Tamasin's mind-message, the stallion was already waiting eagerly in the stables. He pawed the ground when he saw her.

Wasting no time, she threw on the saddle. "I can see you're as keen to see her as much as I am."

"*Savannah is my friend too*," Malkia replied. As soon as Tamasin leaped onto his back, he soared straight into the sky, circled the turbulent winds on the eastern battlement, flew down the side of the mountain and then up the canyon until they reached the place where the letter had been on the bush.

When he glided to a stop, she looked around, finding the desolate gorge even bleaker than the day before. Dark morning shadows lingered at the base of the mountains, and the acrid smell of burnt hair and flesh hung in the air. Careful to keep her back to the horse, she dismounted. "Stay close," she whispered.

She was wondering how long she would have to wait when Savannah stepped from behind a boulder. With a glad cry of "Tamasin," she ran over and hugged her.

Tamasin picked her up and twirled her around. "Aren't you a sight for sore eyes? You've got more lives than a cat," she said, then laughed to hide the sudden welling of emotion.

"I'd be dead if it hadn't been for Sunflower. When Killia threw me over the wall, she managed to catch me." Savannah's expression sobered. "What happened to that rotten witch?"

"Pela killed her in combat at the games. A blood duel to the end."

"She got what she deserved. She was evil."

Tamasin swung around to study the terrain. "Where's Sunflower?"

"She hurt her wing but she should be good as new in a week," Savannah said, then added, "I can't explain it at the moment but she's somewhere safe. That's why I asked Pela to tell you to come alone."

Tamasin looked at her sternly. "Yes. About Pela. You and I will have to have a serious talk when I get you home. And now you've got even more secrets."

"I know," replied Savannah with a sigh. "But I can't break confidences—there are things I promised not to divulge."

"I appreciate that Savannah, but I can't plan anything until I have all the pieces. I need—" A flicker of movement near the mountain wall caught her eye and she turned to look. She was surprised to see a woman in a hooded cape coming toward them; she could have sworn there had been no one else in the canyon. Then she realized that the cape had the same color tones as the mountain wall. A clever camouflage.

As she neared, Tamasin eyed her in disbelief and burst out, "Fern. What are you doing here?"

At that, the woman threw back the hood of the cape. Tamasin blinked. It wasn't Fern but they were so alike they could have been sisters.

Catching her scrutiny, the woman began to back away.

Savannah jumped in quickly. "Hey, Luna. Meet Tamasin, and this handsome fellow is Malkia."

The stallion nickered.

"I'm very pleased to meet you, Luna," murmured Tamasin. "Sorry I was staring, but your likeness to a friend of mine is extraordinary."

Luna's eyes were wary as she asked, "Who is Fern?"

"Queen Wren's eldest daughter and heir to the Arcadia throne."

"Are…are you acquainted with Queen Wren?"

Tamasin nodded. "She's a good friend, as are her children. And where do you fit into that family? You're clearly related."

Luna's lips began to quiver. "My mother was called Zamara."

"The lost princess of Arcadia," gasped Tamasin, tears springing to her eyes. She was silent for a moment before she said gently, "You said *was*?"

"She passed away five years ago. I was born here."

"Wren has never stopped looking for her sister. A burden she's had to carry all her life. She'll be overjoyed to meet you and welcome you home. Any siblings?"

"No, and I prefer to stay here."

Tamasin studied her, noting her simple clothes and scuffed boots. "Queen Wren has only months to live, Luna. Would you deny her the news that her beloved sister had a daughter?"

Very upset, Luna stripped the leather glove from her left arm. "Looking like this," she said bitterly. "My mother had her whole arm changed."

Tamasin stared at it, horrified. "Who would dare do this to Arcadia's princess?"

"The Silverthorne witches have been experimenting on people and animals," said Savannah, "and still are."

Tamasin felt a rush of intense anger that curdled her stomach. "I will burn out their nest and execute every one of them," she grated out. She softened her voice. "Queen Wren looks after her own. You are a princess of Arcadia and will be welcomed as such."

"Who are you exactly to be making such promises?" asked Luna dubiously.

"She's the Mistress of Dreams and Consort to the Supreme Monarch," interrupted Savannah.

Tamasin held up her hand to silence her. "This is not about me. This is about your mother's family. They're honorable, loving people who will be overjoyed they've found you. Savannah says Sunflower needs a week to recuperate. Take the time to think about it and then decide."

Luna nodded. "I guess I will."

"And Luna. If you decide to share your secrets, they'll be safe with me. Now we must go. The Queen will be anxiously awaiting my return." She grinned at Savannah. "I didn't tell her I was going this morning."

Savannah nudged her with her elbow. "She'll be cranky."

Tamasin chuckled. "I know. We must go," she said. She heaved Savannah into the saddle.

Once she settled in front of Tamasin, Savannah looked down at Luna. "Give Floris a hug for me."

Luna blushed shyly.

Tamasin grasped the reins, gave Malkia a dig with her heels, and they sailed into the sky.

Chapter Twenty-Nine

Falcon's Keep

It was breakfast time when they landed.

The stables would soon become busy as the visiting soldiers prepared to wing their way back to their garrisons. While Savannah went to the washroom, Tamasin hoisted the saddle into its place on the railing before she led the stallion to his stall. As she finished filling his bag with oats, she heard the sound of running feet at the far end of the complex. It wouldn't be Valeria, she thought with amusement. The Queen expected her to do the chasing.

She poked her head around the corner to see Pela hurrying along the passageway, her boots clipping the cobblestones. As Tamasin opened her mouth to call out, Savannah appeared in the corridor. Pela's face broke into a delighted grin as Savannah launched into her arms. They hugged, but to Tamasin's surprise, they didn't break apart.

"Thank you, Pel," said Savannah, her voice a soft purr.

Tamasin's mouth sagged when Pela pressed a long kiss on Savannah's forehead, and her hands dropped to massage her lower back. Savannah wriggled closer to allow Pela to go even lower.

Her gaze transfixed on them, Tamasin stepped out of the stall door. "Have I been missing something?" she asked.

Pink tinged Pela's cheeks. She quickly snatched her hands off Savannah. "What do you mean?"

"Oh," said Savannah, not meeting Tamasin's eye. "I was just thanking Pela for her heroics in the canyon." She straightened Pela's collar. "Sorry. I was a bit enthusiastic."

Pela's jaw worked as her color rose even more. "I'm pleased to see you made it safely home," she said gruffly.

Savannah gave her another lingering smile before she turned to Tamasin. "Shall we adjourn somewhere to talk? I must discuss the Silverthorne witches with you and the Queen. And Pela too."

"Give me a half an hour to talk to Valeria and then come to our rooms."

Still stunned, Tamasin watched them vanish out the stable entrance. That Savannah had even managed to befriend the unsociable Commander had been a miracle, but that they had become more than friends was hard to comprehend. It was a coupling she wouldn't have imagined in her wildest dreams. She wondered if they knew themselves how much their emotions were entwined. By their greeting, they were both in deep whether they understood it or not.

As she recalled Pela's rage at Killia, Tamasin realized she'd missed all the signs. She should've had an inkling then that Savannah had meant a lot to Pela. When Killia had announced she'd murdered her, Pela hadn't hesitated, even though they had been comrades for years. Pela had slain her efficiently and without mercy. And from her description of the Wind Howler, she must have known she had little chance against the monster. Yet she was prepared to die to protect Savannah.

Tamasin chuckled as she made her way to their quarters. Valeria wasn't going to believe her.

The Queen was sitting in one of the lounge chairs, tapping her red nails impatiently on the armrest. She frowned darkly. "Where did you go off to so early? Or is it a state secret?"

"I've had a very fruitful morning," replied Tamasin. "Have we anything to eat in this place?"

Huffing, Valeria narrowed her eyes, "You look annoyingly smug. Out with it."

"As you command, Majesty," said Tamasin, smiling. She settled down in the chair opposite. "I went to pick up Savannah."

"You're smiling because you went to retrieve her body? What's got into you?"

"She's alive and well."

Relief washed across Valeria's face, loosening the scowl. "That's wonderful news. Apart from the fact that the Circle of Sheda is safe, we need her. Savannah's resourceful. How did she manage to survive if she fell off the cliff?"

"Sunflower caught her mid-air."

"That little mare out of Moon Sparks?"

"That's her. Savannah called her when Killia had her dangling over the edge."

Valeria raised an eyebrow. "You're not going to tell me she can talk to the horse?"

"She can," replied Tamasin. "Malkia too. I've never met anyone who can do that."

"Extraordinary."

Tamasin stood up. "I'd better have a quick breakfast. Since Savannah has requested an urgent discussion with us, I've invited her here. They'll be arriving shortly."

"They?"

"Pela is with her."

A groan escaped from Valeria. "Was it necessary to have her present?"

Tamasin chuckled. "You're not going to believe what I've just found out."

The red nails began to tap again. "I'm sure you can't wait to tell me."

"Savannah and Pela have become close."

"What do you mean close?"

"I thought you were an expert in the intrigues of the bedchamber?"

A look of disbelief flashed across the royal face. "Savannah and Pela? Impossible!"

Tamasin burst into laughter. "Your meddling in Pela's affairs has finally backfired on you. She has stolen the Chosen One from under your nose."

"Huh! There's no need to sound so pleased with yourself. You never notice these things, so I'll reserve my judgment until I see them together."

"Go ahead if you don't believe me. They'll be here shortly," said Tamasin, but then her smile faded as reality set in. She reached over to touch the Queen's hand. "I'm glad we had that bit of light-heartedness, Val. I'm afraid what Savannah is going to tell us will come as a shock."

Valeria's expression soured. "Whenever you think to warn me of what's coming, Tam, I know I'm not going to like it. Sometimes, I hate the responsibility I must shoulder."

"I know. But you're a capable and fair ruler, and Rand is going to need a strong monarch." She turned toward the door at the sound of a knock. When she opened it, one of the Queen's guards handed her a letter. "This came in for you, Consort."

She broke the seal and scanned the two pages.

"What is it?" called out Valeria.

"A letter from Jezzine. The Dreamers have done well and there are more women wanting to join the Guild. Apparently, she has a good recruit who's willing to continue with more workshops. She assigned those already trained to monitor strategic powerful people that are likely to be targeted first by the crow assassins, and plans to take up residence herself in the Arcadia Palace."

Another rap on the door. "They'll be Savannah and Pela."

As she rose to let them in, Tamasin reminded herself there were more important things to think about than these two women's personal lives. Besides, it was good for them—they were going to need someone to hold onto in the times ahead.

Savannah curtsied with a smile while Pela bowed stiffly.

"I'm delighted to see you look none the worse for your ordeal, Savannah," Valeria said warmly. "Take a seat and tell me all about it."

As Savannah related the drama on the battlement and Sunflower's injury, Tamasin noted she avoided all mention of the people who helped her. There was only one place they could be—in the mountain somewhere. She and Jocose hadn't found any signs of habitation in the dangerous canyons. Nor did Savannah mention that Sunflower was still down there. She left Valeria to presume Malkia had helped her back to the Keep.

She briefly recounted her fight with the Wind Howler. She described it as a ferocious large horned bear, omitting any reference to the Hawk. Tamasin presumed she glossed over the encounter to protect Pela's secret.

"Demons have to be summoned by magic to enter our world," Valeria said in a conciliatory voice. "The beast you killed would have been some predatory bear. There are plenty on Rand."

Tamasin pressed her lips together—Valeria was being patronizing. She had no idea what Savannah could do.

"What would a bear be doing in that barren place?" asked Savannah.

Valeria patted her hand. "I admit their normal habitats are the forests and bushlands, but they do appear in odd places. Believe me, it couldn't have been the Wind Howler. It's one of the oldest, most powerful demons in the underworld. It's already killed a Chosen One."

The Queen had Savanna's full attention now. "Oh? When was that?"

"In the Mystic War. It's recorded in the old scripts that the Queen's guards hid the body before the demon could take the medallion. After that, the Wind Howler disappeared back to the underworld."

"Has it been seen since?" Savannah asked. She cut Tamasin a sidelong glance with a tiny shake of her head. Tamasin closed her mouth, leaving Valeria to answer.

"Not according to the historical documents," Valeria replied.

"Is it written anywhere whose side it fought on in the war?"

Valeria absently rubbed the royal-crest ring on her finger. "Now that's an interesting question. It wouldn't have been with the magical creatures. They hate black magic."

"Yet it killed the Queen's champion. I imagine it murdered her to steal the Circle of Sheda." Savannah stared at the floor, deep in thought. Then she lifted her head and asked, "Do you know if a demon can wield the medallion, Your Majesty?"

"No, it can't. Demon magic is different from Sheda's. One dark, the other light. They repel each other, like putting two moonstones together."

Postponing a query about moonstones, Savannah continued, "Then he must have slain her for someone else, and there's only one group left that the demon could be in league with."

"The sorcerers?"

"Yes, and from what I've learned, specifically the Silverthorne witches."

Valeria's eyes widened as understanding dawned. "It really was the Wind Howler, wasn't it?"

"Oh, yes. It was that black bastard," replied Savannah.

"How did you kill it?" whispered Valeria.

Savannah gulped a breath of air. "I…I lost complete control of my temper. I demanded Sheda give me the power to destroy it. Then I unleashed a lightning bolt and blew it apart." She gave a mirthless smile. "Before I threw the bolt, I had the satisfaction of knowing the monster was afraid. I could see it in its eyes."

Valeria sat up abruptly. "You invoked the Death Vale?"

"Is that what you call it? At least it's got a name."

"You called up an ancient power that's the very soul of Rand." The Queen gazed at her in awe. "Who *are* you?"

"I have no idea. But I'm going to try to find out." She exchanged a look with each of them. "I do know I'm from both worlds, and that's one reason I was chosen. But how I learned this information is my secret."

"Of course," Valeria agreed. Her gaze sharpened, and she asked, "What have you learned about the Silverthorne witches?"

"The coven has reformed, and they're plotting again. For some time now, the witches have been experimenting with people and animals to create monstrous hybrids. Replacing limbs and body parts with those of an animal. From what you've told me, Ma'am, I believe they began as soon as they'd established the Prophecy Tower."

The Queen gaped at her. "What are you talking about? I've never heard anything so preposterous."

"Listen to her, Val," said Tamasin softly.

"Have you gone mad too? How could they have been doing such an inhumane thing for centuries and gone unnoticed? And what was the point of it? And what's happened to those...those hybrids?" Her face twisted into a frown as she glared at Tamasin, then narrowed her eyes at Savannah. "Go on."

"After the last head witch Agatha's armies were defeated and the Prophecy Tower razed to the ground, the practice ceased. The witches just waited and began their experimenting again when everything had died down."

Pela shot up from the chair. "Where?" she snapped.

"Beneath Falcon's Keep, Commander. Right under your nose."

When Tamasin took in Pela's expression, the thought flittered through her mind that this might well be a very short romance. Pela was livid. And in this mood, she was to be feared. Even Valeria sank back in her chair.

Savannah, though, seemed unconcerned. "There have to be more floors below that room with the rats if they're living there and carrying out experiments. And they'd have stables of course. There's no way out except by air."

"My guards would have noticed them."

"Not on the east wall. And don't forget Killia was in charge of your defenses. They will have an entrance somewhere down the mountain. The battlement walls are high enough to block any view from below. They'd fly in through the gorges, low enough not to be noticed. Probably after dark."

Pela put her hands on her hips and jutted out her jaw. "I've been here years, Savannah, and there's never been a hint of anything like that. Yet you come along, look up a few old books and work it out in no time at all. Pah! Why should I believe you?"

Savannah hooked a loose strand of hair back out of her eyes. "I didn't find it in the library. I discovered all this when I was in the canyon. I saw these people with my own eyes, and so did Tamasin."

"The hybrids? You saw them, Tam?" exclaimed Valeria.

"Only one met with me. A woman with a monkey's arm."

"By the Gods, then it's true."

Tamasin heaved a sigh and said miserably. "It gets worse. The woman I met is Zamara's daughter."

Valeria paled. "The witches took the princess? Wren and her family will be furious. They'll want her back immediately."

"Zamara died, Val. Her daughter's name is Luna. I'm hoping she'll decide to go to Arcadia, but she's ashamed of her disfigurement." She gave a wan smile. "She looks just like Fern."

Tears sparkled on Valeria's eyelashes. "Poor Wren. After all those years scouring Rand for her sister, she'll never see her again. How very sad." She straightened her shoulders and turned to Savannah. "Tell us all you know about the witches. They will be brought to account for their atrocities."

Chapter Thirty

After Savannah finished, she felt mentally exhausted.

It had been a tight-rope walk exposing the malevolent experiments while keeping the City of Outcasts a secret. She'd had to divulge that people were living down there but didn't hint at how many. Or that the self-sufficient city had been there for three centuries. She let them presume there was just a small community of survivors living in caves. When they went back to fetch Sunflower, hopefully Luna would show it all to Tamasin.

Since she would have to sneak away early in the morning to bring the twins back, Savannah wondered if she should take Tamasin into her confidence. She hated all this secrecy and subterfuge.

It had been interesting seeing each woman's reaction as they listened. Tamasin became quieter and more troubled, Pela paced around, fuming, but the Queen seemed most affected. At one stage when Savannah was describing a deformity, Valeria paled, then began to gag and quickly rubbed her stomach.

Afterward, they sat in silence while Tamasin fetched water. Once Valeria took a long swallow, she resumed a regal expression. "Do you think the Wind Howler was somehow connected to the witches, Savannah?" she asked.

"Most certainly, Ma'am. You said yourself that a demon has to be summoned."

"Why do you think they called it up?"

Pela stopped her restless pacing and spoke up, "The demon would make sure those who escaped from the witches' laboratories wouldn't live to tell the tale." She shook her head. "I can't understand how they got loose. No jailer would leave cells unlocked."

"If they wanted to get rid of the evidence," said Tamasin, "why summon a demon? Jocose and I flew through those gorges. No one could survive in them for more than a day. There's no water, and the terrain further down is impenetrable."

"The Wind Howler was so powerful they'd be playing with fire unless they had a good reason to call it," murmured Valeria. She turned to Savannah. "Do you have any ideas?"

"Maybe..." replied Savannah. "I don't know why the witches are conducting those gross experiments. It doesn't make sense. We'll have to find that out, but I do have a theory about their alliance with the demon."

"Go on," encouraged Valeria.

"My professor always said that the most obvious answer is usually the right one. I think this is all about magic. And it goes right back before the Mystic War. If all the sorcerers were in league with demons, then they would have had to be using black magic. They probably turned to the black arts when they craved more power. Or perhaps their magic wasn't strong enough," said Savannah. "Whatever the reason, it eventually caused a conundrum. As they relied more and more on black magic, they couldn't live with the magical beings. You said, Ma'am, that light magic can't coexist with the dark. They repel each other. So the sorcerers persuaded the Supreme Monarch of the time, Queen Lila, to wage war on the magical beings."

Tamasin eyed her curiously. "How do you know the magical beings are made of light magic?"

"Because the medallion isn't repelled by them."

"I'm only half magic. That's not a true test," replied Tamasin.

Savannah chuckled. "I'm not talking about you. When a Faerie Empath touched the medallion, it nearly purred."

Tamasin blinked. "We'll discuss that Faerie later. Why did the Howler kill the Chosen One to get the Circle of Sheda if the sorcerers couldn't wield it? They were all on the same side in the war?"

"I don't think he killed her for the witches, he did it for himself. He knew the old magic, which is distinct from both light and dark magic, was the one thing that could kill him. I imagine if he'd gotten his paws on the medallion, he would have hidden it well. Put it away so it couldn't harm him."

As Tamasin thought it over, her tone turned more speculative. "Your theory has merit, but there are a lot of gaps. What could the magicians offer the Wind Howler in exchange for access to its black magic? It was quid pro quo with Ursula."

Savannah chewed her bottom lip as she grappled with this natural part of Rand, magic, that was utterly foreign to her. She hadn't grown up around magic—it was all new. In some ways, though, that was a strength because she didn't have any preconceived notions about what was possible and what wasn't. To Savannah, all magic was unprecedented.

Out of the blue, the blind seer's voice popped into her thoughts. *Ask Valeria what Molvia had desired. To have waited so long, he would want more than a royal slave.*

Savannah swallowed as a sudden feeling of dread lurched through her. She was probably going to be the target of that fiery temper. But no matter how she tried to ignore the order, it persisted. Seeing no way out, she addressed Tamasin instead, "What did Ursula promise Molvia?"

Tamasin frowned. "What do you mean? He wanted Valeria."

"Yes, but why?"

Bewildered, Tamasin looked at her, then over at the Queen.

"Ask *me* if you wish to know, Savannah," said Valeria, her eyes narrowing.

"What did he covet, Ma'am? He'd hardly wait all those years and promise the royal throne to a witch if he wasn't getting something substantial in return."

Valeria's eyes flashed. "How dare you interrogate your Queen. You go too far."

Well, that got a reaction, thought Savannah wryly. Out of the corner of her eye, she caught Pela about to say something. She shook her head at her.

"I meant no disrespect, Your Majesty," she said, trying to sound humble. She'd have to do better than that if she wanted the answers. Valeria was glaring icicles. Then it dawned on her. Magic wasn't just light and dark, or old magic—the imperial line of Queens had yet another kind. "I'm just trying to understand."

It was Tamasin who saved the day. "Why are you angry at Savannah for asking a simple question, Val? Now I'm curious."

"Haven't you realized, Tamasin, that your little Chosen One never asks a *simple* question?"

"So answer it," said Tamasin calmly.

"It makes no difference now, and I won't be questioned like a servant," snapped Valeria.

"Of course, Ma'am," said Savannah, vainly trying to find a way to placate her. The Queen had the answers, but at this rate, she would never cooperate. "That's your business. Um...there is something I'd like to know, though, about magic. There are light and dark, and the old magic of Sheda. When you touched the medallion, it reacted differently. What sort of magic does the Imperial line carry?"

Valeria appraised her with surprise, her anger forgotten. "You felt it?"

"I felt a power surge but had no idea then what was happening. I'm more adept at reading the medallion now. You linked with your ancestors?"

"I did. The medallion guided me into the spirit realm of the Queens of Iona."

"Could you do it again?"

Valeria's hand on the armrest trembled. "I could. Though you must have a very good reason to ask me. It's a confronting experience."

"Forget about it, Val," interrupted Tamasin. "You don't have to do it."

Valeria ignored her. "What do you want to know, Savannah?"

"I'm trying to understand why that Queen sided with the magicians against the magical folk. And more importantly, why she allowed a demon to fight with her armies?" She added as a thought came. "If there was only one demon, which I doubt. I bet Molvia was there as well."

Valeria let out a tired sigh. "There's no need for me to meet with my ancestors. I know what happened. The cautionary tale is passed down through the royal line to make sure future Queens never make the same mistake." She looked over at Pela, hesitating.

Pela immediately rose and snapped her heels together. "If you'll excuse me, I must ready the Elite Guards for battle. Since the witches must soon be aware the Wind Howler has been destroyed, we must act quickly before they leave the Keep. I'll prepare a tactical force to go in tomorrow. The mounted guards will start patrolling the walls in case they fly out. I'll discuss it with you this afternoon." She smiled at Savannah before she departed.

Valeria waited for the front door to close before she continued. "Queen Lila sat on the throne at the time of the Mystic War. A weak, ineffectual monarch, she allowed her rule to be sabotaged by her advisors, a Silverthorne witch, and a Dark Hollow wizard. Both sorcerers were cold-blooded and dangerous, and heavily into the black arts."

"Did Lila dabble in black magic too?" asked Savannah.

Valeria's expression twisted into bitter regret. "Yes, to the dishonor of the Imperial Line. It tainted the throne for generations. After the magical creatures were driven to the Forgotten Realms, the royal houses embraced the sorcerers as advisors."

Tamasin, who had listened without comment, asked, "What happened to the demons?"

"They can't stay long in this dimension," Valeria replied. "They disappeared after Lila died, and her daughter, a stronger Queen, ascended to the throne and forbad the use of black magic. We know now the magicians continued their black arts, but they did it in secret."

Savannah fumbled for words, then came right out and asked, "Is the Imperial throne passed down from mother to daughter?"

"Yes, it's inherited," replied Valeria.

Savannah cleared her throat. "Who's next in line after you, Your Majesty?" she asked, shooting a glance at Tamasin.

"The Queen has two daughters, Savannah," said Tamasin, eyeing her with amusement.

"Oh, right," mumbled Savannah with a blush. She resolved to ask Pela about it later. There was no way she was going to ask Valeria who were the fathers. As the information wasn't offered, that subject was closed.

"I have a question for you, Chosen One," Valeria said, toying with her cup. "Do you think the witches have anything to do with the enemy who's coming?"

Savannah was surprised at the sudden change of topic. And the way the Queen wasn't meeting her eye. Suddenly, it all fell into place. "Molvia wanted an Imperial child," she blurted out.

Blood drained from Valeria's face.

"What the hell are you talking about?" growled Tamasin.

Savannah winced. Why did she have to go and verbalize her thoughts? She shuffled in her seat, bracing herself for the explosion to come. The Queen didn't say anything but looked angry. "Um…it was nothing…just a random thought," Savannah said lightly.

"What did she mean, Val?" Tamasin persisted.

Valeria's lips thinned. "What Savannah says is right. I was intended to be his royal breeder. He wanted his child on the throne of Rand."

Tamasin's face changed to intense anger in a heartbeat. She slammed her fist down on the table. It was the first time Savannah had seen her lose control; she was so furious it would make the strongest enemy quake. "I loathe those demon spawns and their vile magic. I will personally tear those Silverthorne bitches apart when I catch them."

Valeria grasped her arm quickly. "He didn't succeed, love. You stopped him. It's over."

Tamasin shrugged her off and fixed her angry gaze on Savannah. "You'd better start answering a few questions yourself, Savannah. I'm getting tired of your secrets."

"Like what?"

"Like who's helping you? I want to know."

Savannah looked away from her, not liking the suspicion reflected in her face. The medallion was stinging her chest. "I can't—"

"Yes, you can. Tell me," Tamasin shouted.

As Tamasin loomed over her, the metal circle at Savannah's breast began to shake violently, sending sharp currents into her tender flesh. She clawed at it wildly, fighting the increasing panic. Steeling herself, she gritted her teeth and fought the medallion with every ounce of willpower. It was impossible to halt the tears that ran down her face, only barely aware Valeria and Tamasin were staring at her, horrified. She fell to her knees, struggling to push away the pain and anguish. More than once it threatened to overwhelm her, but she battled on. Every time she tried to pull it off, the agony was intense.

"Stop it," she cried out at last. "I won't be controlled any longer. Listen to me! No longer, damn you."

The medallion immediately stilled. The pain stopped as quickly as it began, and she heard the old seer's voice in her head as clearly as if she was standing in front of her. *"Well done, Savannah. You've gone further than any other Chosen One. You may tell Tamasin and Valeria about me. But it's a secret they must keep."*

"That was a test?" Savannah mind-snapped back. *"You went too far, Grandmother."*

"You dare chastise me?"

"I do. It would have been far easier to discuss things rationally without all that crap."

A soft chuckle echoed. *"Until next time, my child."*

Her whole body throbbing, Savannah climbed to her feet and jerked her shirt back into place. She eyed Tamasin bitterly. "Happy now?"

Tamasin looked mortified. "I'm so sorry, Savannah."

"Yeah, well, I'm sorry too that you couldn't trust me. She said I could tell you, but you know what? I don't want to. I prefer to be amongst friends where I'm trusted. Whatever I do is never good enough for the two of you. I didn't choose any of this."

Without a backward glance, Savannah ran from the room.

Pela wasn't home when she hurried into their house, nor did she expect her to be. The Commander would be busy organizing her troops. Savannah searched the study for the keys to the vaults, finding them in the bottom drawer of the desk. After donning her flying jacket, she stuffed the keys, the pepper spray, and two combat knives into the pockets. She scribbled out a note to Pela, then headed off to find Sunflower's brother. With the visiting soldiers flying out, one more horse shouldn't be noticed.

As luck would have it, Shade was near the stables, which made it easy to slip him into a stall. *Can you carry three people, Shade?*

"Easily, Savannah. Where are we going?"

"To visit Sunflower. She'll be so happy to see us."

Shade pranced excitedly. *"Put on the big saddle."*

Savannah smiled. Horses were so uncomplicated and easily pleased.

Saddled ready to go, they waited patiently. When the platoon from Kasparian swung their mounts into the sky in a V formation, she nudged Shade in the ribs and they tagged onto one end. Once clear of Falcon's Keep, she ordered him to dive. Not far from the bottom, they leveled out and headed east until the familiar cliff face came into view. Her palms tingled as they flew over the black stain on the soil. The blood of the Wind Howler still held remnants of demonic magic. Perhaps it would always remain a cursed spot, a place to be avoided.

They had only landed for a few minutes before Luna and Eric emerged from the door in the mountain.

Luna eyed her in concern. "You didn't stay away long. Is anything the matter?"

"No. Since I was coming for the twins very early in the morning, I figured it was easier to spend the night here. You don't mind?"

"Floris will be delighted to see you." She smiled proudly. "She walked a few steps after you left."

Savannah regarded her fondly. "That's wonderful news." She pointed to Shade. "May my horse stay with Sunflower?"

Eric took the reins. He bit his lip as if he struggled with the next words. "I'm pleased to see you, Savannah. We owe you a great debt. It will be an honor to look after your horse. He's a fine animal."

Savannah felt like crying. These damaged people welcomed her without judgment or expectations, consideration she had not received anywhere else in Rand. "Thank you, Eric. I'd appreciate that."

"How many troops will be going in with you tomorrow?" asked Luna.

"After the twins get me through the bottom vault, I'm going in alone. The Silverthornes will be using witchcraft, something the Elite Guards for all their fighting prowess, have no defense against."

Luna stared at her. "Surely Tamasin will accompany you?"

"No. I made sure of that."

"How did you persuade her not to go? I can't imagine she'd let you go in alone."

"I threw a hissy fit and stalked off. It was the only thing I could think of doing. Otherwise, she would've insisted on accompanying me. Pela too." Savannah gave a rueful half-smile. "Mind you... Tamasin did annoy me, so it was easy."

Chapter Thirty-One

The Witches' Stronghold

A dry wind swept through the Keep.

Savannah led the twins through the narrow streets where the shadows were painted a deep purple, and hoots from the brown owls on the rafters rang through the darkness. Dawn was still an hour off when they reached the cordoned-off entrance to the Prophecy Tower vaults. At the first, she fitted the iron key into the lock of the wooden door. When she pushed it open, she felt the chill coming up from below. To her overactive imagination, it felt like the cold breath of doom. Pablo must've been spooked as well, for he hissed loudly in her ear.

She used a small light crystal to navigate through the passageway, the twins padding silently beside her on the balls of their feet. As quietly as they could, they worked their way through the vaults until they reached the last. This door was iron, rusted from long disuse, with strange markings carved into the surface. She guessed it was some sort of spell cast over the room inside. As she tried various keys, she ignored the feeling they were being watched.

When she clicked the lock, the twins came forward to stand by her. After an encouraging pat on their shoulders, she stood aside to let them push open the door. A putrid stench wafted out on the stagnant air. Gagging, she threw in another light crystal. The scene inside nearly made her bolt: the room was full of rats, some the size of small cats. At the burst of light, they raised their heads, whiskers twitching as they turned glowing red eyes in their direction. With high-pitched squeals, they bared razor teeth and en masse, swarmed toward them.

Pablo yelled, "Close the door behind us," and leaped into the room. Sanyo followed him in.

Terrified, Savannah slammed it shut. God, she hated rats. As she listened with her ear pressed to the door, cold shivers tingled down her spine. The seconds stretched into minutes, vicious snarls and squeals coming from inside. Though feeling guilty, she knew she couldn't help. To use the power of the medallion here would alert the witches—she needed to surprise them if she had any hope of success.

Finally, there came a knock on the door, and she nearly wept with relief when Sanyo called out, "You can come in now."

Her stomach heaved at the carnage that greeted her. Blood, fur, tissue, and pieces of the rodents littered the room. Every rat had been torn apart.

Revolted, Savannah turned from the sight to study the twins. "Are you hurt?"

Pablo grinned, looking self-satisfied. "A few scratches but nothing major. Sanyo copped a bite on the leg."

"Can you walk, Sanyo?" Savannah asked with concern.

"Yes, it's not deep."

"I can't thank you enough. We owe you a great debt." She smiled. "I'd liked to hug you, but not until you get cleaned up. You'd better get going. The sun will be rising shortly."

"Take care, Savannah," Pablo said, then hesitated. "We'd like to go with you."

"Definitely not," Savannah replied firmly. "I have to do the next part alone. Now, hurry. Shade is waiting. I'll see you next week."

She watched them run out the door, knowing that they'd be cutting it fine. She prayed the horse could get them home without being intercepted by the patrols. What to do with the saddle and bridle had been the weak link in her plan. Shade had to return without a rider, which meant there was no one to take them off. She decided the gear would have to stay at Kandelora until the fight was over. Hopefully, with all the activity in the Keep, it wouldn't be missed.

Ignoring the slaughter as best she could, she carefully picked her way through the blood bath until she reached the exit door at the far end. But the knob didn't budge. After a moment of panic, it occurred to her that she'd only used a few keys on the ring. Two more tries and the third slotted neatly into the keyhole to reveal a large circular room with seven passageways leading out of it. Some looked inviting, others dark and grim.

Savannah closed her eyes, calling on the magic to show her the way. There was only one corridor and the rest were an elaborate network of deadly traps. It was a killing field.

Not hesitating, she raced down the narrow passageway and climbed the short flight of stairs at the end. It led into a small room. As soon as she saw the circular staircase, the medallion tingled. Instinct told her she'd successfully crossed the spell and was now in the domain of the Silverthorne witches.

A waiting room with three comfortable chairs was at the bottom of the staircase. There was nothing else but a large door that reminded her of a bank security vault. She peered at it closely. It could very well be where the witches kept their most important valuables and spell books. No one could enter from the top without magic, guaranteeing a very secure location. It could be that the Prophecy Chart was locked inside. That is if it was a document.

She lightly touched the wall with her fingertips. It was so heavily shielded by witchcraft that she was knocked back a few feet. Praying she hadn't set off an alarm, she quickly exited the room and descended the flight of steps. She had just turned the corner at the bottom when she bumped into a woman carrying a box of bread loaves.

"Watch where you're going, slave," she snapped.

Recoiling, Savannah bowed her head. "Sorry."

By her apron, head covering, and floured hands, the woman worked in the bakery. "What quadrant are you from," she asked suspiciously.

Savannah pointed downward, which seemed to satisfy the woman. "Here," she said, pushing the box into Savannah's arms. "Make yourself useful. Take the bread to the kitchen. I'll get another load." She turned, walking back in the direction she'd come from.

Figuring it was a good place as any to start, Savannah followed the cooking aromas. On high alert, she darted her eyes around the cavernous kitchen. The tall woman directing the activities was the only one dressed in a flowing robe. Judging from their coarsely woven tunics, the rest of the women were peasants. All looked overworked, and some of the drudges had scarred limbs from the lash.

Making herself as inconspicuous as possible, Savannah dropped her shoulders and shuffled over the threshold. The box was instantly seized by an assistant cook, who then tossed her head in the direction of the sinks. "Wash 'em up," she grunted.

Seeing no way out, Savannah began to scrub the greasy pots. She darted her eyes around the room as she worked. There were no hybrid people here. She couldn't help comparing it to the cheery fellowship of Falcon's Keep's big kitchen. Here, no one even smiled. Under the piercing supervision of the dour witch, they just put their heads down and worked.

Savannah waited her chance as she bent industriously over the pots. It came when one of the oldest drudges who was scraping roots to be boiled, shrieked and held up a bloodied finger. A tirade of abuse sprouted from the witch as she rushed over to the woman. While everyone watched the drama, Savannah slipped along the far wall and out the back door.

She came out into a large courtyard, where small trees and flowers flourished under the artificial light, and bench seats were scattered about. An unexpected peaceful oasis. She sat down in the empty yard to think. There was no point in aimlessly wandering about, she needed to hurry to find the way down to the experimental dungeons. Finding the location of their landing pad was also a priority; that would be the only way the Elite Guards could safely enter this fortress. There were too many hidden hazards up the top levels, and God knows what other traps they'd activate if they were under attack. While the flight entrance would be well defended, it was less likely to be booby-trapped.

When Savannah reached an impressive columned portico, she realized the yard was a forecourt to a palatial building and the only way forward. Since she had no intention of going back to the kitchen, she had no option other than to go through the palace to find the way down. She wasn't going to be able to walk straight in. Two fierce black hellhounds squatted like brooding malignancies on either side of the door.

Suddenly, the sound of voices echoed from somewhere behind her. She had no sooner dashed behind a tree when two women came into view. When they disappeared through the main door, the dogs didn't move. Savannah sidled closer to study the hounds. Though extremely lifelike, they were statues. Holding her breath, she slipped between them to reach the door.

Inside, was an empty hallway. She passed through it, reaching an antechamber mirroring the one in the Iona Palace, with rows of statues, paintings, and artifacts. Tapestries as well, only the scenes were far darker, and many featured demons. She guessed, like that at Iona, the ornate door at the far end would lead to a throne room. The one place she had no intention of going—to be caught in a room with the whole coven would be a nightmare. As she was about to slip through a side door, a woman in a black robe appeared in front of her.

She showed no surprise at seeing Savannah, merely grasped her by the arm and dragged her toward the door. "Come along. We don't want to keep her waiting."

She was being led into an impressive room. As soon as she stepped inside, Savannah felt the power. Twelve Silverthorne witches were seated at a table, staring at her as she was pulled across the black obsidian floor. But it was the woman who sat on the elaborate throne under a heavily brocaded canopy, who radiated the most power. Much younger than Ursula, she had a dark beauty that was mesmerizing and terrifying. She was all angles, the only things soft about her were her full-red lips and lush black hair. Instead of the shapeless robes of the others, she was dressed in a dark red gown cut very low.

She stroked the riding crop on her lap as she cast predatory eyes slowly over Savannah. "What tasty little morsel have we here? Who caught this one?"

"She was wandering outside, Agatha," the witch replied.

The head witch hooked a long finger in the air. "Bring her closer." She swiveled the finger. "Turn around."

Savannah tried to plant her feet on the ground but was swung roughly in a circle. She pulled her arm free and said quietly, "I work in the kitchens, ma'am."

"Not any longer. I need a new bed companion. At least you look much stronger than the last," she said, slapping the crop against her leg. "Come here."

Savannah gave a convulsive swallow. God knows what this sadist did to the other poor unfortunate girls. Then it sank in that the other witch had called her Agatha. The name of the Silverthorne leader who was defeated three hundred years ago. Did head witches have the same names with different numbers? She looked around at the coven. There wasn't an old one amongst them—all were in their prime.

An outrageous theory began to form in her mind. The more she thought about it, the less absurd it seemed. Why the witches carried out these experiments had always been the greatest puzzle. It would be easier to conscript an army than make one. And when did they actually start up again after the fall of the Prophecy Tower? If she was right in her supposition, they had gone back as soon as everything had died down. She straightened—time to test the theory.

She took a step forward and raised her head to stare Agatha in the eye. "The Wind Howler has been destroyed, witch."

Agatha stood up abruptly, the muscles of her jaw flexing. "What did you say, slave?"

"Your demon is dead. How old are you, Agatha?" Savannah said, quashing her fear.

Agatha swept her eyes over the coven. "Whoever put her up to this will be brought to account," she growled, her eyes like beds of glowing coals. "It is *not* funny."

No one smiled.

"Death is never funny. Soon you'll feel its icy tentacles," said Savannah with satisfaction.

Agatha's face flamed red and she screamed, "Who are you that you dare to speak to me like that? I will skin you alive."

She strode down the two steps and grasped Savannah by the arm.

As soon as the witch touched her, there was an intense reaction from the medallion. Savannah had no control as it began to shake erratically. Bright sparks shot out of her fingertips. They ricocheted off the walls and ceiling and skipped along the floor sending out clouds of deadly fragments of stone.

Agatha counteracted with a ball of fire that knocked Savannah off her feet. She leaped up and lunged, spreading out her fingers to widen the arc. The bolts thudded harder into the stone, spewing sharp jagged shards streaking through the air. One of the witches to the side cried out, and blood splattered the wall.

Immediately, the women in the room began to hum. She felt Agatha's power increase as the coven projected their energy into her. Frantically, Savannah let loose a furious burst to bring down the ceiling. But they had formed a shield to block the blast. She drew on more power, but nothing happened. Summoning her strength, she dug her mind deeply into Sheda's magic. It was only a matter of time before the witchcraft shield collapsed; it was bending as she concentrated.

So absorbed, she took her eye off Agatha, and didn't see her next move coming. With lightning speed, the witch back-handed her. As her ears rang with the blow, she felt a cloth cover her face.

When she sucked in a breath, she smelt something foul. Her throat burned as if it were on fire and the room began to spin. Even as she fought vainly to fight the encroaching darkness, she knew it was too late.

"You are ours now," Agatha hissed.

Savannah finally lost consciousness.

Chapter Thirty-Two

When Savannah woke, her head throbbed and her stomach lurched with nausea. It was agony to have an intense urge to vomit without being able to throw up. She couldn't lift her head. She didn't know what poison she'd inhaled, but felt so ill she could quite willingly die. It would be a blessed relief. She carefully opened an eye, only to jam it shut again. Even the muted crystal light hurt.

Damn the witches!

Despite her nausea, Savannah gingerly tested the medallion with her mind. When nothing happened, tears sprang to her eyes at the sudden feeling of acute loss. She had no idea what the witches had done. Since there was no way the medallion would allow anyone wielding black magic to touch it, they would have had to get one of their servants to carry her. She slid her hand inside her shirt to make sure it was still there, relieved when she touched the metal.

Comforted, she drifted off to sleep.

When she awoke, she felt much better and sat up to take stock of her surroundings. It was a small cell, with a basic bunk with a sheet and blanket, and a drum for a toilet. There were no windows, and the top section of the door was made of bars. She put her face close, trying to see what was out there. The narrow corridor was dim, and since there were no sounds, she concluded this was the only cell in this section.

Savannah turned her attention back to the inside, trying to figure out why she couldn't tap into the medallion. Since it wouldn't allow itself to be controlled except by the Chosen One, whatever spell the witches had conjured up must be directed at her. But how could they do that without involving the medallion? As she wracked her brains to try to figure it out, she examined the cell. She'd read that for a spell to last any length of time, it had to be woven with something: fabric, letters, or objects. A short-term spell was simple, just conjured up by an incantation.

Then she noticed the walls. The surfaces weren't smooth because some of the stone bricks were slightly protruding. When she ran her hand over them, she found a pattern in the way they were laid. It registered that the cell itself was the spell, probably specifically designed to block the prisoner's ability to access any magic. She wondered what would happen if she could somehow change that sequence, even if by only one brick. Not that she had a hope of doing it—she didn't have any tool strong enough to break stone. She grimaced. She was unlikely to find something in here. Wishful thinking.

Then she remembered the knives in her coat. She dug her hands into the pockets, but they were gone. But when she searched through again, she felt the pepper spray caught in the lining. It was still half-full. She smiled. It wouldn't shift a brick, but it would disable a jailer.

She was despairing that maybe they were going to leave her in the cell indefinitely when she heard a whisper of footsteps on stone. A male guard appeared and banged his truncheon across the bars. "Stand back, slave."

The key clattered in the lock, and the bolt drew back with a reverberating clang. The door squealed in protest as it as swung open.

"Down on your knees," he ordered.

Before Savannah had time to obey, he slammed the truncheon across her shoulders. "I said kneel."

She quickly knelt, then nearly retched as her upset stomach rebelled at his body odor. Thankfully, there were no more blows—he merely grunted before departing. Almost immediately, Agatha appeared at the door. She'd changed out of the red gown into a skin-tight black leather outfit that left nothing to the imagination. Her hair was arranged in elaborate braids, and in her hand was a small whip with three-pronged ends. She looked incredibly sexy and very, very deadly.

"Stand up," she ordered.

Savannah silently climbed to her feet.

"What's your name, girl?" the witch asked, lightly stroking her hip with the lash.

Savannah pursed her lips. She was getting fed up with everyone thinking she was younger than she was. And she had no intention of giving this ghastly woman her name. "It's Liz."

Agatha ran a long fingernail down the side of her face, just enough to draw droplets of blood but not deep enough to scar. "Hmm. A name I haven't heard before. Which mistress brought you here, Liz?"

Savannah was about to say no one when it occurred to her that this might be an opportunity to glean some information. "My master sent me here for something."

"What?"

"He wants the Prophecy Chart."

"You expect me to believe this master, whoever he is, wants the spell?" Agatha struck her across the legs with the whip. "Why?"

"He didn't tell me."

"No wizard would want the magical folk loose," Agatha snapped and brought the lash down harder. "Tell me the truth, or I'll beat it out of you."

Savannah gritted her teeth. "Is that what you do to your poor unfortunate playthings?"

Agatha slammed a knee into Savannah's groin. "This is a taste if you're so anxious to find out."

Eyes watering with pain, Savannah rasped out, "Is that your solution to everything? I'm disappointed to be in the hands of a head witch who can't be more inventive than that." She sucked in a breath as a thought suddenly occurred to her. "You can't use your magic in here either, can you?"

"The cell is warded against all sorcery. But that won't help you. I am proficient in all forms of torture. I know how to hurt until you're screaming to be put out of your misery." She took Savannah's chin in her hand. "Who's your master? He taught you well, for you wield strong magic."

Savannah felt a touch of relief. At least the witch hadn't any idea she was the Chosen One. Though why should she? Only a select few knew the Circle of Sheda had returned to Rand. "I'm naturally gifted."

"That's nonsense, and we both know it." She pinched her fingers into her chin. "What do you know of the Wind Howler?"

Savannah jerked her head back. "He's that ugly demon that's been keeping you Silverthorne witches alive. What did you give him in return for eternal life, Agatha? Those poor tortured people you've been turning into animals? But that's all over. He's been destroyed."

Agatha hissed. "I don't believe you. Nothing on Rand can kill him."

"Don't take my word for it. When you start to age, you'll know."

The witch's expression turned to pure hatred. "You know nothing. You come into my domain, thinking to intimidate me." She drew back her fist and punched her in the stomach.

Unprepared for the blow, Savannah doubled up in pain. After a few desperate moments to draw a breath, she managed to spit out, "That hit a nerve, didn't it? He's dead. I killed the black shaggy son-of-a-bitch."

This time Agatha used the lash, bringing it down hard across Savannah's neck and shoulders. "How did you manage that? He is invulnerable to our magic."

Savannah forced back the scream of agony as the prongs raked her flesh. "Not mine," she said hoarsely. Her spirits sank. She couldn't take too much of this, and the witch looked like she was just getting started.

Agatha roughly grasped the front of her coat. "What sort of magic have you?" When she dragged her closer, Savannah felt a weak tingle from the medallion. Agatha must have felt it as well, for she quickly let the shirt go and grated out, "How can you summon magic here? It's impossible."

"I have something in my pocket. That's what you felt. It's nothing, only a child's toy."

"I'm not stupid. Show me." She whipped Savannah's legs. "If you make one wrong move, your face won't be so pretty anymore."

Savannah bit back the yelp as the lash struck. Gathering up her strength, she reached into her coat. She'd been given a lifeline, one chance, and she couldn't blow it. Grasping the pepper spray firmly and pressing her thumb on the top trigger, she slowly held it up. When Agatha leaned forward to look at it, Savannah squirted a full blast into her eyes.

Agatha shrieked, frantically clawing with one hand at her eyes while she swung the whip blindly with the other. Savannah just managed to dance out of the way as the prongs flashed through the air. As Agatha floundered wildly, flailing the whip, Savannah scooted around behind her. As hard as she could, she kicked her in the back of the knee. Agatha sprawled awkwardly, the momentum shooting her across the floor. Her head cracked into the wall, and she went still. Savannah kicked the knee again, this time from the side. It popped.

Frightened she'd would regain consciousness any minute, Savannah went to work quickly. She knew Agatha wouldn't balk at killing her, but she couldn't carry out a cold-blooded murder. She tore up the sheet, stuffed a gag in Agatha's mouth, and bound her tightly.

She had just finished the last knot when she heard footsteps. Hooking the whip through her belt, she lunged out the door into the corridor.

As soon as she appeared, the guard raised his truncheon and raced at her. But free of the room, her power was back. When she called it forth, sizzling magic immediately shot out in bright bursts from her fingertips. He stopped dead in his tracks as the currents engulfed his body. Screaming, he collapsed to his knees, the truncheon dropping from his hand. She kicked it savagely, sending it skittling down the corridor.

"What's your name?" she asked, glaring down at him.

"Leon," he said, then added surlily, "Mistress."

"How long have you been here, Leon?"

"I was bonded into service five years ago."

She let some magic leak from her fingers as she stood over him. "Where is the landing pad?" she demanded.

He stared at her hands and gasped out, "We have two. The main one is on the next level. When you reach the top of the stairs, a left turn will take you to the stables. It's at the end."

She gave him a small zap on the arm. "I'm going to lock the cell. Stay down. If you move, I'll fry you."

"I won't." He looked fearfully toward the cell. "What have you done to Mistress Agatha? If she gets loose, she'll kill you, and then me."

Savannah gave a harsh laugh. "She won't be doing anything for a while. When she wakes up, the bitch is going to learn what real pain feels like. Her kneecap's dislocated."

Though her breathing seemed normal, Agatha was still unconscious. Savannah hoped she'd stay that way until the troops arrived. With the door securely locked, she tucked the keys in her pocket and said to the guard, "Take me to the laboratories." When he looked at her blankly, she rephrased the request, "To the place where they're turning people into animals."

His face graying, he sank back on his heels. "We ain't allowed down there. I've only ever been below once and that was enough. You don't wanna go, Mistress. There are things there that'd turn your stomach. And when the beast comes," he shuddered, "you can hear the roars from up here." His voice dropped to a whisper. "They say she sucks the soul out of them."

Even though he had hit her with the baton, Savannah felt some compassion for the man. He looked terrified. But she had no option—she couldn't leave him here to alert the coven. "Come on. Introduce me as Mistress Liz, and give me one of your knives," she said gruffly and then added more kindly. "The beast won't be coming back."

He looked dubious but rose to his feet and handed over a short-bladed knife from his belt. After a dark glance toward the cell, he muttered, "Follow me."

The way down was through an uncomfortably narrow passage-way that tunneled into the bowels of the mountain. Leon used a light to show the way, but the roughly hewn stairs were so difficult to negotiate that she stumbled more than a few times. The bottom of the long descent emptied into a cavernous space filled with lines of prison cells. Savannah was hit with the sickening stench of animal waste.

She was wondering where the guard was, when someone appeared from a small room in a dim corner. The sight of him was enough to make her wary, not a man to take lightly. He was a giant, with a flat fleshy face, buttocks and biceps like balloons, and huge meaty hands. The ideal jailer to control animals.

After he slid an appraising gaze over Savannah, he turned to Leon. "Is this the only new one? Why are you bringing her? You know this place is off-limits to guards. Killia was supposed to bring a fresh one yesterday afternoon from the kitchens."

Savannah nearly shouted her outrage, but quickly schooled her expression to neutral. Not only were those poor people in servitude abused and beaten, but some ended up down here. It defied all sense of decency.

"This is Mistress Liz," said Leon stiffly. "Mistress Agatha wants you to show her around."

"I apologize," the guard said, dropping his head in respect. "It is not often we have visitors."

Savannah wrinkled her nose in distaste. *I bet you don't.* "Show me the cells first," she said haughtily.

"As you wish, Mistress."

The tour was harrowing. At the sound of their footsteps, hands clutched at the bars, while other prisoners scurried to the far recesses of their cells. Men and women howled like animals, begging for help. Hopeless sounds of incarceration.

Somewhere out the back, she could hear other cries that were not human. She presumed that was where they kept the animals for the experiments.

Fighting back tears, Savannah cleared her throat and manage to ask calmly, "How many people do you have at the moment?"

"Eighteen. Six are ready for her. I let four go last week."

"The four. They were no…" Savannah trailed off slowly.

"That's right… no good. They fought the change," the guard said. "The demon would have eaten them when they got to the bottom."

"Anyone here to help you?" asked Savannah.

"The wife. She's preparing the food."

He'd no sooner uttered the words when a slovenly woman appeared from a doorway. She carried a big pot, and Savannah eyed the green slop as she passed. Not stopping to talk, she hurried down the corridor. When they reached a room with an operating table and glass-fronted instrument cabinets, she'd had enough. Pela's soldiers could clean this mess up.

She ran her eye over the guard. There was no way anyone his size could make it through that passageway. "Where's your landing pad?" she asked.

He pointed to a door. "Out there. Follow me."

There was a small pad with a three-stall stable with no horses. "How do you activate the opening?"

He pointed to a lever. When he turned back, his eyes widened in alarm. Streams of light were dancing off Savannah's fingers, coiling into the air like serpents preparing to strike.

"Pull it," she ordered.

Chapter Thirty-Three

Falcon's Keep

The truncheon banged on the cell bars.

Clunk—clunk—clunk.

Savannah shrieked as the whip struck her across the shoulders. A woman in black leather came into focus, looked straight at Tamasin, and smiled triumphantly. *She's mine now.*

When Tamasin opened her mouth to scream, a hand grasped her shoulder and shook it firmly. The dream spiraled away into darkness.

"Tam love, wake up. You're having a nightmare."

Tamasin woke with a start, her body in a lather of sweat. She looked up to see Valeria gazing at her in concern. "She's being whipped," she cried out hoarsely.

"Who?"

Tamasin looked at her in horror. "Savannah. She's in trouble."

A frown creased Valeria's forehead. "It's only breakfast time. She should be still with Pela."

Irritably, Tamasin raked her hand through her wet strands of hair. "I saw her whipped by a woman. I've dreamt about that guard before. He was hitting the bars of the cell with his baton. I know it's going to happen in the next hour or so. It was too real."

"You don't think you had the recurring dream because of what happened yesterday? You're still upset."

"Of course I'm upset," Tamasin said bitterly. "I behaved badly. I should have trusted her instead of shouting at her."

Valeria gently caressed the back of her neck. "Stop admonishing yourself. It's as much my fault as yours. She was quite right when she said I didn't think she was good enough. I've never fully accepted her as the Chosen One. I thought the honor should go to an elite warrior of Rand. Not someone with little fighting prowess and from another world. She saw right through me and found me wanting."

Recalling how vivid the dream had been, Tamasin threw back the covers. "I'm going over to Pela," she said. "I hope I'm wrong, but I think Savannah might have already gone. If I'm right, then we must get into that underground fortress somehow."

"I'm going in with you."

"You should stay here," said Tamasin gruffly. "As the Queen, you have to protect the crown."

Valeria angled her head at her that meant "you must be joking," then she got out of bed and stretched to her full height. "I come from a long line of warrior queens. Even the Silverthorne witches must bow to the old magic of the Imperial Line. It is time I fulfilled my birthright." She waved her hands. "Go now. If Savannah is indeed gone, I'll be waiting."

Tamasin dressed quickly, gathering her knives before she exited the door. She understood it was one order she had to obey—Valeria would be coming with them.

When Tamasin knocked on the door, Pela was dressed, ready to depart for breakfast.

Her eyes narrowed at Tamasin. "What's happened?"

Trying to keep the alarm out of her voice, Tamasin replied, "Is Savannah here?"

"No, she didn't sleep here last night. She left a note saying she was going to stay with Lyn." When Tamasin raised an enquiring eyebrow, Pela added, "She's Savannah's friend who works in the kitchen."

"Does she occasionally stay with her?"

"Never. I just presumed because I'd be busy most of the night that she wanted company."

"Will this Lyn be at the kitchen now," asked Tamasin.

"She'll be getting the breakfasts. Why?"

Tamasin's heart sank. Even as Pela said those words, she knew she was too late. Her dream was happening as they spoke—Savannah was somewhere in the dungeons, being beaten by some sadistic woman in leather. They had no way of getting in there to save her. "I had a dream. Come, I'll fill you in on the way to the kitchen."

Pela must have caught her urgency, for she didn't argue. But she stopped at the door and said, "Wait a moment. I'll check if the keys to the vaults are in the drawer."

When she returned, her expression was grave. "They're gone."

"We've no time to waste," said Tamasin grimly.

When they approached Lyn, the news wasn't good. Savannah hadn't spent the night with her, and as yet, hadn't come in for breakfast. Which meant that, in all likelihood, she'd already gone into the vaults by herself.

"Surely, she wouldn't have gone in alone. She would have let you know what she was up to, wouldn't she?" asked Pela as if looking for a thread of hope.

Tamasin let out a heavy breath. "No. I did something to offend her. She won't forgive me in a hurry."

Pela bristled, anger reddening her cheeks. "What did you do?"

"It doesn't matter now. What's done is done. We haven't the luxury of an argument. Get your troops saddled and ready. Our only chance is to scour the sides of the mountain to find a way into the place."

"What about through the vaults?"

"Only at the last resort. Savannah's not stupid—she wouldn't have gone in alone if she didn't think it was necessary. And I agree with her. That route would be well protected with witchcraft. Your guards can't combat magic without help. It would be a blood bath."

†

"It's only logical the entrance has to be down the eastern side of the mountain," said Pela as she signaled the guards to mount. "But I'll send a squad of ten to each side. Follow me to the east wall, Consort." With a dip of her head, she urged her horse into the air. Her troop immediately swung into formation behind her.

Tamasin waited until they reached the battlement before she nudged Malkia upward. Looking regal in her silver armor, Valeria, riding Marigold, quickly joined her in the sky. Once past the wall, they entered the wind tunnel. Howling gusts buffeted Tamasin, pulling at her clothes, tearing at her hair. It took all her concentration to maintain her balance, and she could feel Malkia's muscles straining as he fought to stay level. Finally, the gale abated enough to allow her to safely turn her head to look at the cliffs, though the wind's constant wailing was aggravating because it masked any other sound.

When Pela pointed down, Tamasin nodded. If there were an entrance, it would have to be lower: no one could land in that maelstrom higher up. Halfway down the side of the mountain, part of the cliff face jutted out into a long ledge. As Pela headed in that direction, it struck Tamasin that she probably knew every nook and cranny on the way down. She would have flown around the area as a Hawk many times.

Once beneath the ridge, the wind dropped dramatically. With her troop wheeling behind her, Pela flew even lower and began to circle in a curious fashion. Eventually, she stopped, hovering in front of a particular spot in the mountain as though listening. As Tamasin watched, she realized that was exactly what she was doing—the Hawk was utilizing her acute sense of hearing. Pela stayed frozen in the sky for at least five minutes when the strangest thing happened. A rumble echoed from the mountain, and the cliff began to open.

In unison, three archers notched arrows and bent their bows. Pela held up her hand. With a grinding sound, the wall slowly split apart into two wings like a window opening. A gray landing pad came into view, and on it stood Savannah, shading her eyes from the bright sunlight. Two men with their hands on their heads knelt in front of her.

Tamasin had never seen a more welcome sight.

Pela signaled to three Elite Guards to fly in, and as soon as they'd secured the site, she followed. After a few words with Savannah, she dispatched the guards into the cavern behind the stables to check inside. After they disappeared into the gloom, she waved to Tamasin and Valeria, leaving the rest of the troop hovering outside to wait. As soon as Malkia glided onto the pad, Tamasin could hear the howling from inside the cavern. She tried to ignore it as she greeted Savannah, who stood with her hands on her hips, regarding her unsmilingly.

"Chosen One," said Tamasin, bowing her head.

"Consort," Savannah replied.

Tamasin grimaced. She wasn't going to make this easy for her. "I'm sorry, Savannah. I had no right to treat you like that. It was unforgivable."

"I accept your apology, Tamasin. Though in future, I want you to agree without argument any decisions I make when it comes to the medallion."

Tamasin nodded, eyeing her in surprise. Whatever had happened, Savannah had new-found confidence. The Chosen One was coming into her own. "Of course."

"Good," said Savannah with a tiny smile. "Now that we've got that out of the way, how did you know to come looking for me?"

"I had a dream. You were in a cell, being whipped by a woman in black leather. I realized that you'd gone down through the vaults."

"I'll tell you about it when I get a moment. But there's no time to spare. We have to move swiftly to take the top landing pad before the guards realize something is amiss. A large force will have to enter that way."

Tamasin cocked her head to listen. "Those howls and cries are coming from the incarcerated hybrid people?"

"Yes. The animal pens as well." Savannah looked over at Pela and Valeria, who were deep in conversation. She placed her hand on Tamasin's arm before she could move off. "Let Pela take the Queen in first."

"Why?" asked Tamasin, confused.

Savannah gazed at her earnestly. "A great wrong has been done to these poor people. She has to see them before she meets the Silverthorne coven, and she must be angry enough to invoke the Queen's Judgement. It is better this time if she doesn't have you to lean on."

"You had another vision?"

"Not a vision per se… a thought in my head. I have no idea what this judgement is," replied Savannah.

Tamasin cast Valeria a side-long glance before she focused back on Savannah. "Like your world, we have a justice system where an accused is given a trial. The Queen has the power to execute someone. That's the Queen's Judgement. She has only ordered the death penalty once, and that was for a horrendous crime against a child."

"I'll need the Queen's help when I face them. Collectively, the witches will be hard to defeat. Not only have they been using black magic, but they're saturated in it," said Savannah.

"I'll be going against them with you as well. My father was an Ice Elf… I have magic blood," Tamasin replied firmly. She looked round to see Valeria approaching with Pela.

Valeria nodded a little sheepishly to Savannah. "You've done very well, Savannah. I'm looking forward to hearing how you managed so well. But now, the Commander is anxious to inspect the cells. Shall we go?"

"Can you take the Queen, please, Pela. Savannah wants to get moving, and I'll organize bringing in the troops."

Valeria gave her a little puzzled frown. "You aren't coming?"

"Go with Pela," said Tamasin softly. "They're your people."

With a lingering smile at Savannah, Pela clicked her heels, and they disappeared down the dim passageway.

By the time they returned, all the Elite Guards, bar two, were in the mountain enclosure. Four horses were in the stables, the rest circling outside.

Pela came out first and looked ready to kill someone. She cast her eyes over the two men on their knees and snapped, "Execute them."

Savannah quickly grasped her arm. "Please, Commander, not Leon. He's sworn allegiance to the Crown. We'll need him to take us to the upper landing area."

Pela gave her a single curt nod before turning to the captain of the squad. "Dispatch the big one and throw the body over the side. The wild animals can eat it—he's been cruel enough to them. Take his wife back to the prison on Falcon's Keep. She will stand trial for aiding these atrocities."

"Yes, Commander," she said with a snap of her heels.

Valeria appeared, her face set hard in barely controlled fury. Tamasin was aware that in this mood, she was to be feared. Savannah quietly stepped back a few paces while Pela slipped off to supervise her squad, leaving her with a very angry Queen.

"They don't deserve to live," Valeria grated out. "These are appalling crimes. Those witches haven't a grain of decency or kindness. They're a blight and I shall bring them to account for what they've done to those poor souls." She gestured impatiently to Savannah, who looked wary in the face of her radiating anger. "Did you find out why they are doing this, Savannah?"

"I did, Your Majesty," Savannah said quietly. "The Wind Howler was extending their lives in exchange for the souls of the poor creatures they made. I think it's the only way to transfer the *life extending* magic to the witches. It seems to have to be transported through the life essence of a hybrid person." She didn't mention that she suspected the head witch was the same Agatha who was defeated three hundred years ago at the fall of the Prophecy Tower. She'd let the Queen get that out of her.

As the Queen stared at Savannah, Tamasin couldn't recall when she had seen her in such distress. "Do you mean to tell me that all this suffering is simply to keep a few privileged women alive?"

Savannah nodded mutely.

All signs of the royal temper disappeared, replaced by an iron control that was far more frightening. Valeria peeled back her lips and hissed, "Not even the darkest black magic can stand against the Queen's Judgement."

Chapter Thirty-Four

The Witches' Stronghold

"What do we do next, Savannah?" asked Tamasin. "Have the witches any idea you're down here."

"No, but eventually someone will realize the head witch is missing," replied Savannah. "I knocked her out and left her in a prison cell. She's tied up and gagged, so I'm hoping we have a bit of time. We need to get those poor people out before we go any further. The witches are sure to have something planned if this abominable place is discovered. They'll need to get rid of any evidence that it existed."

"My guards can take the poor souls to Falcon's Keep," replied Pela.

Savannah shook her head. "No, Commander. You saw how damaged they were. It would be too traumatic for them, and quite frankly, for your warriors as well. I have a place where they will be welcome." She turned to Tamasin. "Will you come with me, Consort. We must hurry."

Pela called out to the nearest guard. "Give Savannah your horse."

"Let's go," said Tamasin without argument. She trusted that Luna would look after them.

At the bottom of the mountain, she cautiously slipped off Malkia.

The canyon was deserted, but she was aware they were being watched. Unconcerned that they were exposed, Savannah jumped out of the saddle. To Tamasin, the territory was so hot and desolate that she couldn't believe anyone lived here.

At the sound of footsteps, she looked round to see two figures moving in their direction.

The woman in front hurried forward, threw back her hood, and hugged Savannah. "I'm so glad to see you, Savannah. We've been waiting anxiously for word after Pablo told us you went in there alone." She nodded to Tamasin. "You've come back earlier than planned, Consort?"

Savannah's face broke into a wide grin. "Hi, Luna. Eric, meet Tamasin."

Tamasin nodded, trying not to stare at the fur on his face. "Hello, Eric."

"It's a pleasure to meet you, Consort." His brow furrowed into worry lines. "What's happened?"

"I'll let Savannah tell you and explain why we're here."

As Savannah related the events, Tamasin watched their faces and realized what it must mean to these people to have someone champion their cause. They'd lived down here in complete isolation from the rest of the world. With their legacy of pain and grief, she wondered how anyone from those dungeons could ever begin again. She looked around, trying to figure out where these people lived.

She focused back on Savannah when she heard her ask, "There are eighteen in the dungeons. Will you give them a home?"

Eric bowed his head at her and spoke, "There's no need to ask. Of course, they can come here."

"After this is over, I'd like you to show Tamasin your home. She needs to know because she may require a sanctuary should war come. She will keep your secret."

Eric looked across at Luna. "What do you say?"

"I think Tamasin has earned the right. But I'll leave it up to you."

His teeth worried his bottom lip until he reached a decision, and then he spoke, "Come back when you are ready, Consort, and we will show you our city, Kandelora."

Tamasin's eyes widened at the mention of a city and when part of the cliff wall suddenly opened, her jaw dropped.

A slender woman with delicate blond curls came out.

"Floris… you can walk," exclaimed Savannah.

The woman threw her arms around her. "I can nearly run." She looked curiously at Tamasin. "You brought a friend?"

"This is Tamasin, the Queen's Consort and Mistress of Dreams."

Blushing, Floris said shyly. "It's a great honor, Mistress. I am a Dreamer."

"Then it is doubly my pleasure," said Tamasin taking her hand, then looked at her in surprise. As soon as she touched Floris, a pleasant feeling of well-being enveloped her.

"Oh," cried Floris, wide-eyed. "You're an Ice Elf."

Disconcerted, Tamasin stared at her. "You know that by just touching me? I knew my father was a magical being, but I didn't know what species until recently."

"Floris is a Faerie and an Empath," said Savannah. She eyed Floris thoughtfully. "You knew instinctively that Tamasin was magical and what species. Is that another talent?"

Floris suddenly looked shifty. "I don't know what you mean?"

Savannah reached over and took her hand. "Yes, you do, Floris? Perhaps we can talk later. There are a few things I'd like to know."

When the big blue eyes looked into hers, Savannah sucked in a breath and dropped her hand. She turned to Luna. "We must hurry. We'll be back shortly with the first ones."

"Eric and I will come with you. You'll need us."

Savannah took her hand. "You would do that, Luna?"

"They are our people now, Savannah."

"I'm coming too," announced Floris determinedly.

As soon as she touched down on the lower landing pad, Tamasin braced herself for the smell. She had taken both Luna and Eric with her on Malkia for the short trip, while Savannah doubled Floris. The warriors and Valeria on their horses had disappeared, presumably to rest their horses until they were needed. Pela and a squad of ten soldiers remained at the landing.

Pela looked curiously at the three visitors, then nodded and led them straight to the dungeons.

The two Elite Guards at the cells displayed heartfelt relief to be relieved of their post.

"Are the inmates able to walk?" Tamasin asked the oldest guard, a hard bulky woman who'd won a medal in the battleaxe competition. For all her size, Tamasin could see she was traumatized by this mission.

"Twelve will be able to make it out, Consort. Six are too far gone. They're..." She swallowed noisily. "they're animals ...not people anymore." She pointed to a corridor leading to a row of cells at the back. "They're in there."

Savannah smiled at the guard, recalling their hand-to-hand combat instigated by Killia. "Hi, Xavia. Glad to see your knee's better." Then she tugged at Tamasin's shirt and whispered, "They're the six who were ready for the demon."

"I'll see to them first," announced Floris.

Tamasin frowned. "You're not going in alone."

Floris turned her big eyes on her. "I'm an Empath, Mistress Tamasin. They'll need comfort."

"I'll go with you," said Savannah. "I may be able to do something about the black magic."

Luna had her lips pressed together in disapproval. "I'll go in first, or at least let me go with you."

Floris shook her head. "Savannah may come but no one else."

Xavia grasped Savannah's arm as she passed by and whispered. "You've got guts going in there."

When they disappeared down the corridor, Tamasin leaned forward with her hands on the cold stones of the wall. As she listened to the cries from within, her stomach churned with rage.

"Come on." She grimaced. "Let's get the others out of their cells and ready to travel."

As one-by-one they were led out, Tamasin's eyes filled with hot tears. She had never seen so much anguish and pain. She had fought criminals: thieves, brigands, and cold-blooded killers. She'd taken their lives, but she'd always made their deaths mercifully quick. This place reached another level of pain and inhumanity.

Seven males and five females remained, some no more than fourteen or fifteen. They were nude, covered in dirt, scratches, and excrement. When they hit the light, they shrieked in terror and tried to scamper away. Luna and Eric immediately went to work calming them down, even showing their disfigurements to allay their fears. Soon they had them settled, though they looked like at a moment's provocation they would try to flee.

Tamasin watched them closely, noting none were too far gone in their transformations. It was unmistakable with what animals they were blended. Some had fresh wounds, which confirmed that they had been operated on. She assumed they had been subjected to magic as well. It was becoming clear that these hybrids were the only way the witches could access the demon's black magic to extend their lives.

After talking with the prisoners, Luna took Tamasin aside and told her she suspected the experiments didn't work on everyone. Those strong enough to fight the change would be released to the Wind Howler eventually.

When Floris emerged from the back dungeons, she was openly weeping and shook her head. "We helped them pass peacefully," was all she said.

Savannah looked sick and simply said. "It would be better if their bodies were burnt."

There was no argument from Tamasin. She pulled the guards aside at once. "Torch the bodies after this is over. Destroy any sick animals and take the rest with you. They can be set free in the forests. We'll take these people away."

The soldier thumped her chest in salute. "Yes, Consort. Do you need help with transportation?"

"Thanks, but we'll manage."

After she watched the soldiers disappear into the back corridor, Tamasin turned to see Floris holding one of the younger girl's arms while Savannah ran her fingers over the cat's paw attached to it. Black strands sloughed off like a layer of dead skin. When she pulled away, the paw was still there, but the flesh around it was much pinker and healthier. The girl had a smile on her face as she exclaimed, "The pain's gone."

No longer cowering, the others lined up for the treatment. Savannah worked quickly through them and when the last was finished, she got up and stretched. "They're ready to go."

"I'll get them out of here while you go with Pela," said Tamasin. "I'll see you on the top landing pad. Be careful."

Chapter Thirty-Five

"Is that the only way up?" asked Pela as she peered into the dark tunnel.

Leon shuffled forward to join her. "Aye. It's rarely used because this place is off-limits to everyone topside. Prisoners and supplies are brought in here by air."

"How many soldiers in your garrison?"

"Thirty."

Pela looked at him in surprise. "That's not many."

He shrugged. "There's never been an attack on the fortress. If that ever happened, the witches would use sorcery to defend it. We mainly supervise the unloading of supplies and keep the bondservants in order."

"Where do the bondservants come from?" asked Pela.

"Some are bought from poor families, others are homeless folk on the streets. They ain't treated well. They're whipped to keep them in line." He lowered his voice. "Them witches are a freckin' nasty lot and hold grudges. There're tales they've taken important people too. I heard they kidnapped a princess because her Royal House helped defeat them in the war years before."

"What about you and the rest of the guards?" Pela persisted.

"I was a foot soldier in King Gerard's garrison. We mostly kept the Windy Desert tribes under control. Talk about a hot and thankless bastard of a job. Then Captain Killia turned up one day, all spick and span in her Elite Guard uniform, and offered five of us enough coin to join her service," he said, then added bitterly. "She didn't tell us we'd never be allowed to leave."

"The Silverthornes are overconfident," murmured Savannah. "They think they're invulnerable."

"Any soldiers guarding the top of this tunnel?" asked Pela.

"Nay. It comes out at the bottom dungeon which is hardly ever used."

Pela looked across at Savannah. "That's the cell where you were held?"

"Yes. A special one designed to hold those who wield magic."

"Then we should be able to slip in unnoticed," said Pela. "I'll lead the way. You two follow at the rear."

Savannah shook her head adamantly. "No, Pela. Leon must go first in the off chance there're more guards nearby when we exit the tunnel. I'll follow. The way is long and narrow, dark and rough. If there's someone at the top using magic, I'll have to be there to counteract the witchcraft, or you'll be trapped."

A frown creased Pela's forehead. Savannah thought she was going to argue, but she briefly nodded in agreement. Pela looked across at Leon. "Remember, we'll be right behind you."

With Pela and the squad of ten Elite Guards following, Savannah entered the tunnel.

She found the way up far more difficult than coming down, but it was comforting to feel Pela's warm touch on her back whenever she stumbled. Halfway up, even though she knew she wasn't alone in the darkness, claustrophobia began to stretch her nerves to screaming point. It was only once a glimmer of the light appeared in the distance that her tightly coiled body relaxed.

The corridor was empty when she slipped out of the tunnel. When Leon threw a fearful glance toward Agatha's cell, she touched his arm. "Have a quick check."

While the Elite Guards organized their weapons, he ran down to the cell. She could see by his face when he returned that the news wasn't good.

"She's gone," he whispered, casting a terrified glance around as if Agatha might step out of the walls.

"She wouldn't have expected us to have gone down that tunnel," Savannah replied reassuringly, then leaned over to Pela. "They know I've escaped and will be searching for me. Be careful."

Pela nodded, waved a hand at Leon to proceed, then pointed at three soldiers to follow him to the flight of steps. They ran up silently, signaling a moment later that all was clear. Once they were all at the top of the staircase, Pela raised an eyebrow at Leon.

"The entrance to the upper landing pad is at the end of the left passageway," he whispered.

Pela turned to her soldiers, quietly mouthing her orders, "You three go with Leon and disable any guards at the entrance. The rest fall into squad lines with flankers. Archers in front. Savannah, you stay at the back."

What followed seemed like an anticlimax to Savannah. The large cavern was empty, except for two guards and a few people attending to the horses. The guards were overpowered silently and efficiently, the ostlers tied and gagged in a stable stall. With most of her troops guarding the entrance, Pela and two archers entered the gatehouse that contained the pulley system to open the fortified window to the outside. Whirling and creaking echoed through the cavernous space, and the mountain slowly opened to reveal Rhiannon hovering outside on her horse, accompanied by a squadron of seventy Elite Guards.

By the time the royal couple landed, Pela with fifty of her warriors and Savannah had already run out the door. Systematically, they swept through the top levels, and though Savannah had warned them to avoid the palace and courtyard, they saw no witches anywhere. They had struck surprisingly little resistance from the workers or the witches' garrison. They were greeted as saviors.

But Savannah couldn't shake the feeling it had been too easy. She caught one of the kitchen drudges and asked, "Where's the witch from the kitchen?"

"She ran off just before you arrived, miss."

Savannah realized the rumble from the landing port had alerted the witches, and they were all entrenched in the palace. But the leading question was: why hadn't they defended their territory? And then it came to her—they didn't have to. They only had to do something to the landing pad, and with the horses destroyed, all they had to do was pick the invaders off with their magic.

Desperately, she tried to think. With luck, they'd have a few minutes' grace before they organized themselves, but by the time she ran back down, it could be too late. Pela was nowhere in sight, so it was up to her.

Then she remembered she had the perfect means of instant communication—telepathy. Concentrating, she projected her thoughts. *"Malkia. Do you hear me?"*

She nearly wept with relief when seconds later, he telepathed back. *"Yes, Savannah."*

She quickly relayed her message. *"Tell Tamasin to get everyone in the air at once, and the Queen has to come up here immediately. I think the witches are going to do something to the landing port. They may only have a few minutes to get away."*

After she heard, *"I'll tell her,"* Savannah breathed out the breath she was holding. Now all she could do was wait.

A little less than ten minutes later, she heard the sound she'd dreaded: a muffled blast two levels down. Even up here, she felt its effects. Whatever the witches had done, it had been mighty powerful. The lamps clattered in their brackets, and any loose furniture went sliding over the floor. After it died away, an acrid smell like burning rubber wafted up through the staircase. She had begun to despair that they hadn't been quick enough when she heard footsteps running up the steps. Tamasin and Valeria arrived, breathing hard.

"Thank God," exclaimed Savannah. "I thought I might have been too late. Did everyone get out?"

"Just," said Tamasin. "Good call. What made you think they were going to do something?"

"It was all too easy. We didn't see any witches. They were alerted by the noise at the pad, but they didn't defend their home. I figured they planned to cut off any escape, then pick the warriors off using sorcery."

"Was there much resistance from the other folk?"

"Very little, even from their garrison. By what Leon said, the witches ruled by fear, not loyalty," Savannah replied and added with a shiver, "He explained those poor people were simple folk plucked from the only life they knew and treated without mercy or compassion. They were slaves: bondservants, bought from their parents for a pittance, and homeless people. The witches used whips to subdue them."

Valeria's expression became even bleaker. "Where are the witches now?"

"Locked up in their palace."

"Then I must go there," said Valeria, stiffening her shoulders. She turned to Savannah. "Will you walk by my side, Chosen One?"

Savannah bowed her head. "I'd be honored, Your Majesty."

Valeria favored her with a warm smile. "It will be *my* honor. Now, we must find Pela and her warriors and hasten to the witches' palace before they learn we've escaped and conjure up more surprises for us."

Moments later, Pela appeared in a run. She hissed out a breath when she saw Valeria. "By the Gods, Ma'am. I heard the explosion and feared the worst."

"Savannah sent a message through to evacuate the landing port."

"And the rest of my warriors and horses?" Pela croaked out, fear for her troops etched into her face.

"All safe, Commander. Malkia sent a message to Tamasin that they managed to get out in the nick of time. They're waiting outside. Unfortunately, the Coven's ostlers were caught in the blast."

Pela visibly relaxed. "I've left guards to supervise all the staff. The rest of the squad will be here in a minute. What are your orders, Ma'am?"

"Savannah and I will be going inside the palace. I want you to guard the entrance in case anyone escapes."

"We'll cordon off the site," replied Pela. After a moment's hesitation, she pointed to a door nearby. "Could I have a quick word with you, Savannah, while we wait for my soldiers to arrive? That's an empty room."

Surprised, Savannah nodded. "Of course, Commander."

The small room was an abandoned cellar of some sort that smelt of sour wine, but Savannah didn't care, not with Pela looking at her as she was.

Once inside, Pela brushed her knuckles down Savannah's cheek. "You must be careful in there. No heroics."

"I will be," Savannah replied softly.

"When we get back to Falcon's Keep, we'll discuss what's happening between us."

Savannah sucked in a breath. Now wasn't the time, but she was finished waiting. She pulled Pela's head down and kissed her. "That's how I feel."

Pela claimed her lips again, pulling her closer with a barely contained urgency. Savannah moaned, trailing a finger down Pela's back. She itched to slide it more intimately under her shirt but resisted. For several heartbeats they stood pressed together, their tongues caressing.

Pela ghosted her warm lips down Savannah's neck before stepping out of the embrace. "We'd better get back, or they'll wonder what we're doing."

Her pulse drumming in her ears, Savannah nodded reluctantly. "I guess so," she said, aware that whatever happened in the future, her fate was now bound tightly with Pela's.

Valeria gave them a quizzical look when they returned but merely said, "Lead the way, Savannah."

Their footsteps echoed eerily through the empty kitchen as they made their way through to the green courtyard. Like everywhere else, the garden was deserted. When they reached the three marble steps leading into the Silverthorne palace, goosebumps shivered across Savannah's neck. Strange magic was heavy in the air, not witchcraft but something darker, more ominous. She halted, urgently waving the others back. Pela immediately joined her with twenty of her Elite Guards, who spread out forming a semi-circle in the forecourt. The archers silently notched their arrows while the others drew their swords.

The Queen raised her eyebrow at Savannah but didn't retreat.

Suddenly, to Savannah's horror, the two hellhound statues began to move. As they rose from their squatting position to their full height, she could see how large they actually were, and how utterly terrifying. Very slowly, they turned to look her straight in the eye. Mesmerized, she stared into their empty eye-sockets..

With teeth bared, they bounded down the steps. The medallion's power rushed into Savannah, bursting from her fingers, slamming into the beasts. They howled in anger, halting in their tracks. When she threw another stream, they simply stood there, embracing it. Her heart sank. Their leathery skins were absorbing the power.

The archers unleashed their arrows, only to see them slide off their hide harmlessly.

With a war cry and her sword raised, Pela charged straight at them and yelled, "To me, warriors."

At the sudden onslaught, the hounds bounded back to the portico, tails between their legs and claws sliding on the marble floor. The soldiers followed them up the steps, their swords swinging. They hacked and stabbed. The beasts twisted, striking with their long claws and snapping with their teeth. They battled on, but the warriors were doing little damage to the hounds.

Savannah was about to run up the stairs to help when Tamasin grasped her arm. "No, Savannah. Magic can't help here...they feed off it. It will only make them stronger. They're Helva Hounds, preternatural creatures that come from the Dream World. How the witches brought them into this world, I have no idea. The only thing that can kill them is the metal zenphin, so you have to leave this fight to our soldiers."

A cry came from a warrior, who collapsed in a splatter of blood. When another went down in the melee, Pela roared her anger. She brought her sword up with both hands and severed the Helva Hound's paw. The hound retreated to the corner, licking its wound.

"Kill it with arrows," she yelled. "Aim for its eyes."

The wounded hound screamed as the barrage of arrows pierced its eye sockets and nostrils.

The second beast swiveled quickly. Howling its fury, it rushed straight at Pela, its mouth wide. Just as it reached her, she leaped to the side, and with a graceful airborne pirouette, she brought her sword down on its neck. With one mighty cut, the head rolled off in a gush of green blood. The giant torso wobbled, but as it collapsed onto the floor, it slowly turned back into marble. When the captain of the squad decapitated the second beast, it too solidified.

Savannah hurried to Pela's side while she inspected the troops. One warrior was dead, her neck ripped open by a deadly claw. Four suffered severe gashes and bites to their limbs, another had a ragged cut through the metal of her breastplate. Three more had minor injuries.

Pela turned to Savannah, who was about to help with the wounded. Her eyes swirled with emotion: sadness as well as intense anger. "No, Savannah. My warriors will attend to them. We have to get inside before there are any more surprises."

Valeria nodded. "We must go, Savannah."

"I'm coming as well," announced Tamasin.

"You can't come. This is magic against magic," said Valeria firmly.

Tamasin gave a half-smile. "Have you forgotten I'm an Ice Elf? My place is by your side."

Valeria pursed her lips but agreed reluctantly, "All right, but be careful and don't get in the line of fire."

As they reached the door, Savannah was conscious that Pela was at her elbow. "You're not coming," she said brusquely. "They're too powerful."

Pela merely raised an eyebrow. "You'll need my help. Magic doesn't frighten me. I am magic."

"Yeah, well, it should," she muttered.

The Queen tapped her foot impatiently. "She's determined to come, so let her. If this door doesn't open, blast it with your magic."

Chapter Thirty-Six

Surprisingly, the door wasn't bolted.

Savannah guessed that the witches were aware even a reinforced iron lock wouldn't stop anyone wielding magic. They probably had something planned for them inside. Once past the empty sentry box in the lobby, they made their way cautiously down the hallway to the throne room antechamber. Though it too was deserted, Savannah could sense a malevolent presence somewhere in the room.

Valeria looked uneasily at the statues and tapestries. "There's something in here with us," she whispered. "Do you feel it?"

"I do," Savannah replied. "Get behind me. Whatever it is, it won't be a match for the medallion."

"Do you think you can conjure up the Death Vale if you had to?"

"I honestly don't know, Ma'am. I can't understand how I did it. It just happened when I became really angry."

"Hmm. It's something I know little about. Perhaps it can only be summoned against a demonic being. Moira would know." With a nod, Valeria pointed at the door. "Shall we?"

They had only walked another step when three beasts suddenly erupted from the floor like saplings springing from the ground. They were hideous: saber-toothed tigers, with serpent tails and large leathery batwings.

Alarmed, Savannah groped for the chain around her neck and hissed, "Get behind me."

When she clutched the medallion, it didn't react as violently as she thought it should. The beasts bellowed, their eyes pools of fire, saliva dripping from their fangs. As they bunched their muscles to leap, she heard the others hastily step backward but she held her ground. As she embraced the old magic, the tigers began to shimmer. She took a quick look at the floor in front of them. It wasn't wet, yet saliva oozed from their mouths.

"They're illusions," Savannah called out, walking straight at them. They bellowed and writhed, desperately trying to keep their forms as their claws passed harmlessly through her. The next moment, they vanished as quickly as they had appeared.

"Let's get that door open before we get any more surprises," said Valeria. "I swear they took ten years off my life."

"They were ugly bastards," muttered Pela.

Savannah flashed a relieved smile. "Those witches can frighten the wits out of an enemy. I wonder what other tricks they've got up their sleeves."

The smile quickly faded when her eye caught movement in the large tapestry hanging from the ceiling. It was a graphic war scene that depicted warriors fighting an army of demons. To Savannah's horror, the picture came alive. The room shuddered, floating away to leave them on the fringe of the bloody battle. When the medallion went berserk, Savannah turned icy cold as the truth hit. This wasn't an illusion—it was real.

"We have been transported to the Great War of Creation," exclaimed Valeria. "It is the battle for Rand between the Goddess Iona and the Demon Prince Dazorak."

"The warriors are being slaughtered," gasped Savannah.

"They eventually won the war," said Tamasin. "Prince Dazorak's forces were driven down to the underworld."

That news did nothing to allay Savannah's fears. This battle still raged and it looked like it would for some time yet. More troops from either side were pouring into the melee. The field stunk of blood and death and all she wanted to do was run away. But there was nowhere to go. The retreat was cut off by a host of demons coming over the rise behind them.

Valeria cast a frightened look at Savannah. "There's no way you can do anything with the medallion here, not with so many demons."

"Then we will go down fighting," Pela said resolutely.

Savannah thought frantically for a solution but nothing came. So she did the only thing she could think of, she called out to the old blind woman for help.

The reply came immediately. *Quickly join hands. Your combined magic will be enough to transport you back. But if any of you are touched by anything there, even a shield or a hand, the past will remain your reality. The spell is made from very powerful ancient magic.*

Savannah turned to find Pela and Tamasin readying for battle. She called out urgently. "*No!* Don't touch anything. Join hands now." Without waiting for a reply, she grasped Valeria's hand and Tamasin's with her other. "Do it now, Pela," she shouted over the screams of the dying.

At the sound of her voice, the nearest demon looked up from its kill. Pela wavered when it began to charge in their direction, but after Savannah yelled another, more forceful, "*Now!*" she obeyed the directive. As soon as the circle formed, the battle disappeared, and they were back in the room.

Her face a mask of fury, Valeria said curtly to them, "For that, there will be no mercy for anyone in the room. Stand at the back so no one escapes after I bring down my judgement." She turned to Savannah and commanded, "Smash it open."

Savannah complied with satisfaction, launching a ball of white energy at the thick wooden door. It exploded into thousands of fragments, leaving only the hinges swinging in the hole.

Without another word, Valeria marched into the witches' throne room, her tan riding coat sweeping around her legs. Savannah strode after her, Tamasin and Pela remaining at the rear. At least two hundred Silverthorne witches were perched on chairs like a flock of roosting blackbirds. Nine more stood under the canopy behind the throne. It was clear they hadn't expected the spells to be breached.

They looked rattled as they watched Valeria cross the floor to the three steps leading to the dais. Agatha, in black leather, hunched forward on her throne, her dark eyes flashing red sparks. But underneath her disdainful expression, there was a hint of wariness.

She made no move to rise when Valeria stopped in front of her.

"Kneel to your Queen, witch," Valeria ordered in an angry imperious voice.

Agatha stayed in the chair. "I don't acknowledge you as my sovereign, Valeria. I rule here."

"You think your coven is above the laws of Rand. What is your name?"

"I am Agatha Nardox, and you signed your death warrant when you entered my domain."

A frown wrinkled Valeria's brow as she searched the face of the woman in front of her. "You are a descendant of the Agatha whom Jessica defeated?"

The witch curled her lips. "I *am* that Agatha."

"No, it can't be. That would mean you're over three hundred years old."

"Four hundred to be exact."

"Are all the witches here that old?" Valeria whispered, her eyes wide with horror.

Agatha shrugged. "Ten of us from the old coven chose eternal life. The rest were too squeamish. We have been gathering new sisters for the last hundred years and soon we'll be strong enough to overthrow the Imperial Throne."

Valeria looked at her coldly. "As strong as the recently departed Ursula?"

Agatha flicked an angry glance at Tamasin. "For her death, I will personally whip every inch of skin off you, Consort." She sent Savannah a venomous glare. "As for you, my pretty little sorceress, by the time I'm finished with you, you'll wish you'd never been born." She stared broodingly at Pela. "We had such high hopes for you,

Commander Pela. I'll let Killia dispose of you. She's an expert with the hunting knife."

Valeria gave a mirthless smile. "For her crimes, Pela slew Killia yesterday in front of our entire garrison." There was a collective hiss from the room. Valeria ignored them and continued, "The Wind Howler has also been destroyed."

"He's a demon. Nothing here can kill him," shouted one of the witches.

"Molvia was also a demon and he was slain," Valeria replied, then refocused on Agatha. "Nothing or nobody is invincible."

"You lie," Agatha snapped.

Valeria didn't deign to answer but turned to the assembly of witches and raised her arms. "We found the poor unfortunate souls in your lower dungeons. For those horrendous crimes against my people, I, Valeria Argosa, Supreme Monarch of Rand, do invoke the Queen's Judgement on every Silverthorne witch who has used my people to extend her life."

Horrified screams burst from the witches and Agatha's head snapped up, her eyes wide. "Don't you dare invoke the Judgement," she cried. She lunged to her feet, magic beginning to stream from her fingers.

"Silence. It's too late," Valeria said coldly. "You have been judged."

To Savannah, what happened next was like the Sahara haboob but ten times worse. The tempest was harsh, vengeful, and unstoppable. Wind roared into the room like a freight train barreling up a tunnel. It began to spin, twisting wildly into a hellish tornado. The pressure inside her ears began to build, and the light turned an eerie gray. In the maelstrom, the tornado split into smaller twisters and plucked up the Silverthorne witches. They were smashed against the ceilings and walls. Though she wasn't touched by the spine-chilling twisters, Savannah still stood there petrified as the witches screeched and howled in the appalling wind as they died.

When it finally abated, the room looked like it had been bombed, with maimed bodies strewn over the entire floor. Not a stick of furniture remained intact, except for the throne, which for some reason hadn't been touched, though the plush canopy was gone. Most of the bodies were unrecognizable. Savannah silently vowed never to annoy the Queen again. Being able to unleash that much power was seriously terrifying.

Valeria stood with her head bowed, tears sliding down her cheeks. Tamasin hurried over to take her in her arms. "I've got you, love," she said quietly. "They deserved what they got. Come on, let's get out into the fresh air."

As Savannah watched them embrace, the medallion began to tingle the familiar warning that couldn't be ignored. Confused, she cast a look around the room, trying to determine where the danger lay. When her eyes landed on the throne, she caught flickers of movement. She turned around far enough until she could slip the knife from her belt without being seen from the raised dais. With the handle resting in her palm as she had been taught by Rhiannon, she pivoted quickly and launched the blade at the throne.

A sharp cry of pain came immediately. Agatha appeared out of thin air, followed by the nine witches behind the throne. Savannah guessed they were the original coven. She had the satisfaction of seeing her knife embedded in Agatha's arm.

As the witch pulled it free, she threw a look of hatred at Savannah. "You will live to regret that, girl." She cast a venomous glare at Valeria. "I will kill you for what you did here, Queen. Even the Imperial Line is not powerful enough to hurt the old coven. We have taken enough demon magic to live for centuries. Now prepare to die."

As Agatha stood up from the chair, something inside Savannah clawed out for freedom. She climbed the three steps to the throne dais and shouted, "You are an abomination, witch, and you will be brought to account for your sins."

When Agatha gathered a fireball into her hands, Savannah reached into herself to grasp the power that strained for release. As the missile flew from the witch's hand, she easily knocked it out of the air. Agatha reared back, her expression wary. She nodded to the nine women behind her and they began to inundate Savannah with magic fire as well. Time slowed for Savannah, and for the first time, she was completely in control and in perfect harmony with the power she wielded.

Though she effortlessly destroyed every missile, she knew she would have to break the deadlock somehow. If she could separate the others from Agatha, then she could concentrate on her. She sensed she had enough power to destroy the witch, but she couldn't deplete it before going in for the kill. She had to be careful—these witches had become more like demons than humans.

Suddenly, with knives drawn an Ice Elf appeared beside her. With a bloodcurdling cry, Tamasin leaped at the witch on the end.

A moment later, there was a rush of wings overhead and the huge Bramble Hawk swept down and raked its talons across the neck of another witch. Blood spurting from her artery, she collapsed onto the ground. Then with a shriek, Pela wheeled into the air, barely avoiding a burst of deadly magic.

Not sure if the witch could die even though it should be a mortal wound, Savannah twisted quickly and blazed out a jet of magic. The body burst into flames, burning to black charred bones.

Agatha looked at Savannah incredulously, the muscles of her jaw clamping as she gritted her teeth. "Who are you?"

"Your worst nightmare," she snapped, then zapped the witch Tamasin had just taken down with her knives.

"You won't take me so easily," said Agatha, calling out an incantation.

Within seconds, the air above the throne curled into a black haze that enveloped the Silverthorne witches in a shield. Tamasin ran back down to protect Valeria at the bottom of the steps.

Pela morphed back to her human form and grasped Savannah's arm. "Move back," she ordered urgently.

Savannah shook her head, suppressing the urge to run as the unholy shadow glided silently closer. "Get behind me, Pel. Your magic won't be able to handle whatever's coming," she muttered, watching nervously as a dark form began to take shape. Not knowing what to expect, she gaped in surprise when the cloud vanished, leaving an old woman standing on the marble floor.

Chapter Thirty-Seven

Savannah peered at the aged face.

The resemblance to her mysterious blind seer was obvious, though there were differences. The facial features were the same: the shape of the face, the high brow, the long thin nose, and the square jaw. But this woman's eyes were black and sharp, instead of opaquely blind, and her expression pinched and sour. For all that, they were plainly sisters. It went through Savannah's mind that perhaps Grandmother's sightless eyes could be interpreted as "justice was blind", while this old woman looked mean-tempered and judgmental. They were opposite sides of a coin.

The crone's eyes widened when she cast a look around the room. "What in the Goddess's name happened here, Agatha?"

"That banic Valeria invoked the Queen's Judgement," Agatha said bitterly.

At the indignant hiss behind her, Savannah guessed *banic* was an insulting word in Rand.

The pinched lips became even tighter. "Why didn't you stop her before it came to that?"

"Don't you think I tried?" Agatha replied, her eyes flashing hatred. "They were never supposed to return from the Great War of Creation. I have no idea how they managed to break that spell."

The old woman's voice faltered. "That's impossible. No one on Rand has that sort of power." She stopped to sniff the air. "There is ancient magic here. I smell it." Raising a boney finger, she pointed at Savannah. "It comes from her."

"She's killed two of us," Agatha cried with a touch of hysteria. "How could she do that? We're invulnerable to magic."

"I'll attend to her in a minute," the crone replied, then looked down at the three women at the base of the dais steps. "What is Commander Pela doing here with the Queen. I thought you had her under control. You need her army."

Pela snorted, and for a second Savannah thought she was going to turn into a Hawk again. When she frantically shook her head at her, Pela relaxed back, though her eyes were watchful.

"We made a mistake there. I trusted Killia to keep her restrained," snarled Agatha, "and now it turns out she's a Bramble Hawk."

"*What!* How didn't you know that?"

"Ursula had her under the cape and didn't realize either."

The crone's black eyes turned harder. "The magical beings must be kept locked up, especially the Bramble Hawks. They're dangerous. She can't be allowed to live."

That was enough for Savannah. The muscles of her jaw tightened as she gritted her teeth. "Shut up, old woman. Pela is my friend. If anyone touches her, I'll kill them."

The old face twisted into rage. If Savannah weren't so angry, she would have been justifiably terrified by the venom radiating from the woman. As it was, all she could think about was protecting Pela. She reached inside for the power. It sprang in a gush from her fingers in a burst of raw energy. The shield around the witches wavered but held. The old woman looked at her in surprise, then without warning, leaped at her. The thin hand glowed orange as her fingers clawed around her arm.

The touch sent a burning sensation through Savannah, though with very little effort, she shrugged off the alarming grasp. Immediately she was free, the crone's glowing fingers threw out a mass of gray tentacles that enveloped her like a cloak. They were uncomfortable at first but the feeling faded, becoming only mildly irritating as Savannah brushed the sticky strands from her body and clothes. As they flew into the air, they dissolved into little bursts of sparks.

The crone's eyes widened. "How can you remain unaffected. Nothing or nobody in the world has the power to resist my magic."

Suddenly, something clicked in Savannah's mind at the words, *nobody in the world*. Well, hello. She wasn't from this world, obviously another reason she had been chosen. Crafty old Grandmother had known this confrontation would happen and needed someone invulnerable to this woman's magic. Savannah pressed her lips together, tired of being a pawn. Was all this about a feud between two old sisters?

"For your information, I'm from another world."

"How?" exclaimed the old woman, then lowered her voice to a whisper. "What are you wearing?"

"You know perfectly well what is around my neck," Savannah snapped.

"It has been brought back? I thought Queen Jessica wanted nothing more to do with magic and sent Elsbeth through the portal to get rid of it." She cast a furious glare at Agatha. "Do you realize what you've done, you idiot? You've brought a viper into your midst."

Agatha stared at her in alarm. "This poxy weakling wears the Circle of Sheda? That's impossible."

As Savannah went to answer, something extraordinary happened. When she spoke, it wasn't her voice or her words that came out of her mouth. It was the old blind seer's. *"You were the stupid one, Hola,"* she crackled out. *"Jessica didn't send Elsbeth through the portal to hide the medallion, she was sent to protect her unborn child."*

While the others gaped at Savannah, Hola seemed to take the change without question. It was the revelation that caused her to falter. "Was...*he* the father?" she whispered.

"Of course. Elsbeth had a son and Savannah is their descendant. After three hundred years, it's obviously a large scattered family tree, but very few have been born with the pure blood. I have been searching many years for Savannah."

Hola's expression turned grim. "You knew what it would mean for us if she came to Rand, yet you brought her here."

"You're failing to see what's before your eyes, sister. The change cannot be stopped. It has already begun, and we must be content for the world to pass into a new era of magic. Our old ways will only hinder progress," said the blind seer, her voice filled with sadness.

Hola threw up her hands. "Why then have you brought the medallion back? It is old magic."

"Because we have one last battle to fight and there are many ancient spells to untangle. The old enemies are coming again shortly. Rand must be at peace and united or it will fall. You and I have to settle our differences and work in harmony. I fear the world is running out of time, for the sands are curling in the hourglass and the threads of the future are becoming increasingly difficult for me to interpret."

Hola's black eyes bored into Savannah. "How do you know they're coming? I've felt nothing."

"You're never in tune with nature. The signs are everywhere, yet you continue to play your petty intrigues."

Valeria's voice cut through the air, startling them all. "Who *are* you women?"

Hola warily circled Savannah and glided to the top of the stairs. "I salute you, Valeria. I can see you're a much stronger Queen than your mother and grandmother. They would never have had the backbone or strength of will to invoke the Judgement."

"I asked you a question."

Savannah's legs were propelled by an unseen force until she was standing next to Hola. *"I am a guardian of Rand, and Hola is my twin sister,"* the blind seer replied. She swiveled Savannah around to look Hola in the eye. *"Go now, sister. It is time to stop meddling. Let Valeria finish righting the wrongs that have been done to her people."*

Hola appeared as if she would argue, then nodded. "If they're indeed coming, then I'll stand with you, sister."

"Nooo," screamed Agatha. "You can't leave."

The old woman bared her teeth. "You failed to stop them, demon witch, now suffer the consequences."

With a twinkle, she vanished.

As Savannah shook herself free, she projected her anger. *Warn me before you do that again.*

A chuckle echoed in her mind. *You might have blocked me out. You're becoming very powerful.*

Am I here because of your feud with Hola?

No, Savannah. You're here for the Prophecy Chart, so don't forget it.

Before Savannah could reply, the old woman's spirit left her body. She looked round to see Agatha forming a ball of fire with her hands. Concentrating, Savannah reached for her magic clamoring to get out. A crackle sounded as the Ice Elf reached her side, accompanied by the sound of wings overhead.

Savannah motioned to the other witches with her hand. "Get them. I will handle the magic."

As before, time slowed, allowing her to destroy the balls of fire, mid-air. The Ice Elf was everywhere, ducking and weaving as she struck deadly blows with her knives. The Bramble Hawk dived and grasped a witch with its talons. The woman shrieked as the bird shot to the vaulted ceiling, and then dropped her. As she landed heavily, Savannah burnt her before she had time to rise.

Pela was already clawing at another witch's eyes. Kept busy blocking the fiery bolts of magic, Savannah saw Tamasin take a blow to the head and sprawl to the floor. Unable to help, she watched in horror as the witch lunged with a sword at the stranded Ice Elf. The blow never landed. In one swift movement, Valeria plucked a knife out of her boot and threw it. When the blade sank up to the hilt into the witch's left breast, she collapsed with a gasping cry.

Finally, only Agatha remained. Though Savannah had been able to destroy her missiles, she hadn't been able to breach the witch's defenses. She was a far more formidable opponent than the others and had erected some sort of shield around herself. As they circled her, prodding for an opening, Savannah kept chipping away at the barrier. She knew eventually she would bring it down.

Agatha knew it too for she screamed out her rage. Then she abruptly stopped her tirade, stood up straighter, and raised her hands. She began to change, growing bigger, her perfect skin thickening into scales, her face elongating until she completely lost her humanity. When the metamorphosis was complete, a demon stood in her place.

Revolted, Savannah recoiled. The thing was a monstrosity.

Warily, she watched it snatch the whip from the floor. Before any of them could step back, the pronged lash whistled through the air and wound around the Hawk's leg. Even as the demon pulled her down, Pela was changing. By the time she landed, Tamasin had thrown her a knife and Pela was cutting through the throng. Once free, she dropped into a squat to avoid the next lash which narrowly passed over her head. She drove the knife into the demon's belly. It roared in fury, swiping at her with her massive claws, but Pela had already rolled out of reach. When the demon went forward to strike again, blinding light erupted from Savannah's hand.

It hunkered back, eyeing her guardedly, ignoring the blood dripping from its knife wound. Savannah held its gaze, trying to come to terms with the fact that this monster was Agatha. But there was no doubt, for as she stared into its eyes, she could see the silver thorns in its dilated pupils.

Then she remembered something Leon had said, "They say she sucks the soul out of them," which had seemed odd at the time. The Wind Howler had been male—she had seen him full frontal. So why had Leon said *she*. And why had he been petrified of her? He was a guard, not a slave.

The awful truth hit. It wasn't the Wind Howler who visited the dungeons—it was Agatha in a demon form. The life essences of those poor people in the laboratories were keeping the witches alive and *she* was sucking them dry. Although she had sought black magic long ago to stop aging, Agatha had eventually turned into a demon herself. The Wind Howler had served his purpose years ago and was only coming into the canyon to eat the poor souls who had escaped or who were discarded.

Her disgust and horror must have been reflected in her face, for Agatha slunk back until she was jammed against the throne. Righteous anger began to build in Savannah.

Without turning, she called out, "Everyone get out of the room immediately."

At the sound of the retreating boots, she reached into the depths of her power, commanding it to come forth. She felt it stir and her body began to hum and glow until electricity bled from every cell.

The demon witch jumped to her feet. "No," she hissed.

Regarding her coldly, Savannah called out, "There will be no mercy. For your crimes, Agatha, I sentence you to death."

The demon's mouth twisted into a rictus of horror. "You can't kill me."

"I can and I will." With no hesitation, Savannah spread her hands and launched the power. Energy arched from her fingertips in a blinding flash of lightning. As the ensuing thunder clap reverberated violently through the room, the demon blew apart. Pieces of Agatha flew off the walls and ceiling, and the obsidian dais split into jagged cracks. The throne was the only thing left standing in the room.

Exhausted, Savannah fell to her knees and fought back tears.

Chapter Thirty-Eight

Savannah didn't know how long she'd knelt there, but when she looked up, Pela was standing in front of her.

Pela's face conveyed her pride. "You were spectacular."

Savanna flushed, inordinately pleased at the praise. "I couldn't have done it without you and Tamasin."

"It was an honor to fight by your side."

As they turned to go, Savannah took a last look at the devastation in the room. But when her eyes landed on the throne, she froze. A complicated pattern of glowing lines every color of the rainbow, shone from the back of the handsome red-oak chair. "My God, Pela," she exclaimed. "Look at the throne."

"That wasn't there earlier," Pela said in surprise.

Savannah felt a surge of excitement. "It has to be the Prophecy Chart. The spell that keeps the magical beings from leaving the Forgotten Realms for any length of time. I got that out of Agatha by pretending I served a wizard."

Pela frowned. "Very few have ever left the Forgotten Realms. Folks believe they will wither and die if they stay away."

"They will. That's the spell. It's also called The Curse."

Pela eyed her dubiously. "Then why aren't I affected? I thought it was rubbish."

"Or Malkia," murmured Savannah. She clicked her fingers. "Maybe it's because you both flew out. The spell is a barrier separating the Forgotten Realms from the rest of Rand, an invisible fence woven by the magicians and demons. You didn't hit that barrier and become infected, because you were high enough in the air."

"But Tamasin went in and out without any effect."

"It wouldn't effect half breeds," Savannah replied.

She gazed at the gleaming lines on the throne and mused, "Agatha was certainly cunning. What better place to keep an eye on something she didn't want found. That would explain why the throne was able to withstand the savage magic. It was protected with very strong black spells."

"But why are we seeing it now?"

Savannah chuckled. "Agatha outfoxed herself. She became a demon, but once a demon is destroyed, its spells no longer work."

"Then why hasn't the Chart been inactivated?" asked Pela.

"Because Agatha had nothing to do with the barrier spell to the Forgotten Realms. It was cast long before she was born. Her spell simply hid the chart." Savannah tugged Pela's sleeve. "C'mon. Let get it and get out of this ghastly place."

The chart was on stretched animal hide and proved relatively easy to remove. Pela rolled it up and tied it with a tassel on the floor, the only thing remaining of the canopy. "I'll take it home with me," she said.

Savannah followed her out through the broken doorway, the euphoria of finding the Prophecy Chart gone. When Pela had said *home*, her heart had given a leap, but she now had to face facts. Her stay at Falcon's Keep was at an end.

As they passed the War of Creation tapestry, Savannah gave it a wide berth. That bloody battle would remain etched in her memory for many years to come.

Tamasin eyed her with newfound respect when she approached. Though Savannah knew she was curious to know who had taken over her body, she didn't ask. Savannah resolved to tell them all soon, for they might know something about the old blind woman. There were many puzzles to solve, especially the identity of the mysterious father of Elsbeth's child, her ancestor as it turned out. She wondered what enemy had been such a danger to the unborn baby that she had to escape through the portal.

From what had transpired here, she doubted the Silverthorne witches had any agenda other than self-interest—the blind seer had been more interested in the Prophecy Chart than Agatha's coven.

Valeria reached out to take Savannah's arm. "Come. Let's walk out together."

The other two fell behind respectfully, letting the Queen have a private conversation.

"You had to invoke the Death Vale, Savannah."

"I hated doing it, Ma'am. It was so…so brutal."

"I understand how you feel," Valeria said in a tired voice. "It'll take me a long time to get over what I had to do in there. It took a lot out of me, physically and mentally. Doing something so enormous changes one." She eyed Savannah solicitously. "I feel for you as the Chosen One. You have a great burden to carry, for with such power comes great responsibility and often unwanted repercussions. The mental and moral strain will be difficult."

Savannah felt moved by Valeria's compassionate words. Few people would understand what it was like to take someone's life so violently.

"I'll have to train my mind to prevent it from overwhelming me. In my world, we have people called therapists who help manage stress."

"You are always welcome to discuss things with any of the Mistresses in Iona."

Savannah nodded gratefully. "Thank you. I'm sure Mistress Moira will be a sympathetic listener."

"You are ready to leave Falcon's Keep?"

"It's time," said Savannah, and pushed open the front door.

The courtyard hummed with activity. Soldiers were busily organizing the bondservants into groups, while others stood battle-ready in a cordon around the front of the building.

A hush fell as Valeria made her way over the wide marble porch to the top of the stairs. Savannah sensed the apprehension and fear in the air.

The Queen looked down at the crowd. "It is over, my friends," she called out. "The Silverthorne witches have been executed for their crimes against the people. All men and women who have been forced into bondage, are now free. Commander Pela's Elite Guards will take you out of this accursed place to Falcon's Keep as soon as she can organize the transfers. From there, we'll arrange to have you returned to your families. For those without anyone, you will be resettled in a town of your choice. But first, you must swear allegiance to the Crown."

Savannah had expected the servants to be happy but was nevertheless surprised to hear the jubilant cheers that erupted and how enthusiastically they bent their knees to the Queen.

Tamasin appeared at Savannah's side. "I'll take you home. You look exhausted."

"Thanks. I just want to get out of this place. I'll let Pela know before I leave that the people will have to be flown out. The room past the rats is full of lethal spells."

†

Falcon's Keep felt like paradise.

"I'll see you tomorrow, Tamasin. What time do you plan to head off?" Savannah asked as she climbed off Malkia's back.

"After lunch. Eric and Luna are giving me a tour of Kandelora in the morning."

"I'll see you in the mess before you go. Would you say hello to Sunflower for me?"

"Will do. I'd better get back to Valeria. Jocose is escorting her home shortly," replied Tamasin.

Savannah hurried across the common, calling greetings to the horses but not stopping to give her favorites a scratch. All she wanted to do was get home and wash away the stench of the black magic.

Freshly washed an hour later, she heard footsteps coming up the path and flung open the door. And then she was in Pela's arms, kissing her.

Savannah moaned—she needed this woman like she needed to breathe.

When they broke apart, Pela was panting just as hard as she was. She buried her face in Savannah's neck. "I want our first time to be just right. I've been waiting years for you, and I have to show you how much it means to me that you're here at last." She gave her a lingering kiss. "I'll have quick a wash."

Savannah was nervous as she watched her disappear into the bathroom. She didn't know why she was, for she had never been anxious with a new lover. But she hadn't been with someone as important to her as this woman. It was simultaneously daunting and exciting.

As soon as she reappeared, Pela had her hand in her hair, pulling her close. When their lips met, Savannah sank into her. Her nerves disappeared replaced by a flood of desire. Her bones went to liquid when Pela shimmered her fingers down her neck and began to undo the buttons of her shirt.

Impatiently, Savannah stripped naked and fell onto the bed. When Pela's mouth claimed hers again, Savannah pressed closer. As Pela crushed her hungrily to her, Savannah arched her hips, offering her body. And then she was drowning in her as Pela brought her slowly and thoroughly to her climax. When she peaked, power surged through the medallion in an explosion of light and she cried out exuberantly. Through the wave of exquisite pleasure, Pela climaxed with her, gasping out her name.

Savannah woke to find the bed beside her empty. She stretched languidly, glancing out the window to see it was nearly noon. Not surprising it was so late, considering how many times they had made love during the night. Pela was everything she'd ever want or hoped for in a lover. Strong, tender, passionate, and completely in tune with her needs. All former lovers faded into insignificance.

She realized now that with Heather she'd always held back a piece of herself. Savannah hadn't been able to completely share. She'd had her own life, her own course planned which hadn't included anyone else. There had always been something missing and she'd finally found it with Pela.

She crawled out of bed and dressed for lunch.

As she entered the mess hall, to her surprise, all the recruits in the room rose to their feet and thumped their chests to salute her. Savannah felt a wave of humility. That these fearless warriors were saluting her was inconceivable.

Pela appeared beside her, "Elite Guard Savannah. I would be honored if you would join my table for the meal."

Clapping broke out as she followed the Commander to the head table. She acknowledged them with a smile, though knew she was blushing. Tamasin was sitting at the table and bowed her head when Savannah took a seat.

"Do they know I'm the Chosen One?" she whispered to Pela.

"No. These warriors are aware now you control magic, but they foremost admire bravery. They saw you enter the Silverthorne witches' palace with the Queen and heard you defeated Agatha. And Xavia spread the story of your mercy visit into the dungeons to help those poor misshapen people. She thought that was the bravest thing she'd ever seen."

"Oh," said Savannah, for once lost for words. She turned to Tamasin to cover her embarrassment. "When do you fly out, Consort?"

"Straight after lunch. I have something to show you before I leave."

Savannah chuckled. "I hope it's pleasant. I've had enough surprises to last me for a while."

"You'll see," said Tamasin cryptically.

After giving Pela's leg a squeeze under the table, Savannah rose to follow Tamasin out of the mess hall. She gave a cry of delight when they reached the stables and she saw Sunflower prancing impatiently in the holding yard. With a whinny, the mare galloped over when she saw her open the gate.

Savannah threw her arms around the silky neck. "Hello, gorgeous."

Sunflower buried her velvety muzzle into her hair. *"I've missed you, Savannah."*

"Me too. I have something to ask you."

The mare's ears pricked. *"What is it?"*

"Would you consider coming with me as my special mount?"

"The Blue Fjord horses always carry the Chosen One. It will be my honor."

Savannah eyed her, surprised. "You know I wear the Circle of Sheda?"

Sunflower snickered. *"I heard that big oaf with the donkey ears talking."*

"He was a bit slow, wasn't he?" said Savannah with a laugh.

She gave Sunflower one last pat and turned to Tamasin. "Sunflower has agreed to be my mount."

"I'll put in a request to the office here. These horses are the property of Falcon's Keep."

"She is of the Blue Fjord bloodline. They don't belong to anyone," said Savannah sharply. "They choose to be here."

Tamasin looked at her curiously and said, "I was under no illusion that Malkia chose me and not the other way around. But you say the others choose to be here?"

"They serve the crown as you all do, but if they were maltreated or unhappy in any way, they would leave. They're magical folk," replied Savannah.

The old blind seer's voice broke into her thoughts.

You know, sweet girl, that Elsbeth was sent through the portal to protect her child, your ancestor. What you may not understand is why Hola didn't want you here. Your father was part magical. You have a unique new bloodline.

Savannah gave a soft laugh. *I worked that one out myself, Grandmother, and Floris confirmed it.*

A chuckle echoed on the wind. *Clever girl!*

Savannah smiled. It was quite clear now why she had been chosen to wear the medallion and been transported to Rand. This was what she was born to do, her destiny.

✝

End of Book 1

Book 2: The forgotten Realms

✝

I hope you enjoyed *Rand*. I'd appreciate if you left a review at the Amazon site.

Printed in Great Britain
by Amazon

82385390R00202